IN A PERFECT STATE

Joseph R. Garber

POCKET
BOOKS

LONDON · SYDNEY · NEW YORK · TOKYO · SINGAPORE · TORONTO

First published in Great Britain by Simon & Schuster UK Ltd, 1999
This edition first published by Pocket Books, 1999
An imprint of Simon & Schuster UK Ltd
A Viacom company

1 3 5 7 9 10 8 6 4 2

Simon & Schuster UK Ltd
Africa House
64-78 Kingsway
London WC2B 6AH

Simon & Schuster Australia
Sydney

A CIP catalogue record for this book is available from the British Library

ISBN 0-671-85467-4

Typeset by SX Composing DTP, Rayleigh, Essex
Printed and bound in Great Britain by
Caledonian International Book Manufacturing, Glasgow

IN A PERFECT STATE

For Tippi Hedren, cast herein as Olivia,
to whom more than a mere novel should be dedicated.

After obtaining a degree in philosophy, and making a tour of duty in the US Army, Joseph R. Garber has spent the balance of his career as a business person, initially with AT&T and later with the international management consulting firm of Booz, Allen & Hamilton. He is now a West Coast-based mergers and acquisitions specialist. He lives in California.

Each man flees fastest from himself.

Lucretius – *De Rerum Natura*

We read in books that in the old days gods and goddesses changed men into beasts and birds at will, and so did women. So it may be that that bear had been a knight hunting in the forests of Biscay. Perhaps he angered some god or goddess in his time and was changed into the shape of a bear and was working out his punishment . . .

Froissart – *Chronicles III*

I long ago come to the conclusion that all life is 6 to 5 against.

Damon Runyon – *A Nice Price*

Singapore

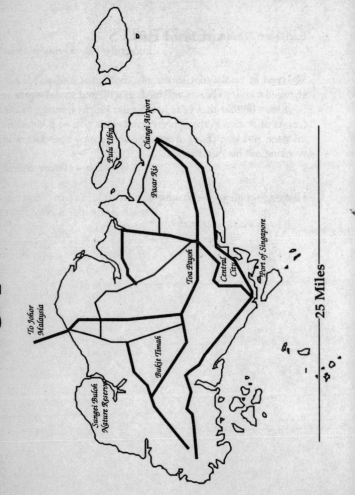

Sungei Buloh
Nature Reserve

To Johor
Malaysia

Bukit Timah

Toa Payoh

Central
City

Port of Singapore

Pasar Ris

Changi Airport

Pulu Ubin

25 Miles

CONTENTS

ONE: THE SENDING

Scratch a lover, and find a foe.

Dorothy Parker

SOCRATES: Few persons ever reflect, as I should imagine, that from the evil of other men something of evil is communicated to themselves.

Plato – *The Republic X*

1

San Francisco International Airport

On an October Sunday afternoon, Jack Taft, innocently unaware that he was marked for death, sat slumped in Singapore Airlines' first-class lounge. He'd never been in a first-class lounge before. Less lavish than he'd expected, its decor reminded him of his too-pricey New York dentist's reception room. Only with newer magazines.

Rumpled from six hours' air travel, JFK to San Francisco International, and mindful of a middle-aged midriff to which every calorie gravitated, he sipped a complimentary Diet Pepsi while trying to focus scratchy eyes on the thick document in his lap.

But not succeeding. Jack didn't travel well, and was already jet-lagged. Besides, the document in question was more than merely tedious.

The latest ITAR regulations. Straight from Washington. Flimsy paper, tiny type, one hundred and thirty-three pages of mind-numbing government jargon.

The bane of every exporter's existence, ITAR was a red-tape relic of the Cold War originally intended to keep the Evil Empire from getting its hands on American strategic technology. However, while the Soviet Union was long gone, ITAR lived on. Before his promotion, Jack hadn't had to worry about it. As LBTech's logistics director for America and Europe he dealt only with countries that could import whatever electronics they wanted. Now, however, he was the corporate Vice-President of Logistics and responsible for worldwide shipping. The International Trade in Armaments Regulations buck stopped on his desk.

The problem with ITAR was you never knew what the government's paper-shufflers had decided to blacklist this week. Or why. One day a component or subassembly would be perfectly legal. The next day selling it to certain countries carried a five hundred thousand-dollar fine. Among the goods ridiculously banned from export were scuba gear, upgrade kits for Radio Shack multiband scanners, and – for God's sake! – bows and arrows. Can't sell them to Saddam Hussein, oh no, the fate of the free world hangs in the balance.

What a joke. There was a thriving black market for the stuff ITAR banned – at higher prices of course because legitimate companies weren't allowed to compete. The illogicality of it made Jack grind his teeth. True, there were ways – theoretically legal – LBTech could get around the silly rules, and if the dumb dopey government didn't clean up its act . . .

He shook his head. *Uh uh*, he thought. End-running Federal regulations wasn't his style. Not conscientious, honest, and – this-above-all – *rational* Jack Taft. That he'd even think of skunking the law was a sure and certain sign that he was too tired to concentrate on his work. Blowing between his cheeks, he snapped open the latch of his beautiful new briefcase, dropping the ITAR binder inside. Then, not caring whether other waiting passengers noticed him doing something eccentric, he brushed the bag against his cheek. The leather was soft, warm, supple, and its almost liquid touch reminded him of Gabrielle, whose gift the gorgeously expensive thing had been.

Gabrielle . . . she was back in New York, had a flight of her own to catch, and Jack missed her so much it hurt. Being away from her for three whole weeks would be agony. Gone less than a day, already he was eager to be back at her side. Especially since that chest-thumping goon Simon was eyeing her like he still owned her. Broad-shouldered, blow-hard, cock-of-the-walk Simon Burton . . . Jack wondered what she saw in him in the first place.

But he supposed he knew the answer to *that* question.

Three weeks. He'd do it as soon as he got back. He'd take her in his arms, pull her close, kiss her deeply, and then . . . Well, he'd just blurt it out: I love you. Marry me.

There, that wasn't so hard, was it? Five words. Surely he could get them out, not choke up while doing so. He should have done it months ago. It was easy. Would be easy. No problem. He could do this, he knew he could.

Then an all-too-familiar inner voice whispered, *too good, son, too good for the likes of you*, and Jack began to feel his self-confidence ebb. *Only the brave deserve the fair . . .*

2
New York

– 1 –

That same afternoon, three time zones east, Gabrielle Dunn, dressed in a tobacco-coloured suit and wearing slightly sassy shoes, breezed through LaGuardia security. Unlike the weekdays, there were no crowds, no long lines, no irritating delays. She'd make her flight with time to spare.

She guessed Jack had an easy trip to the airport too – at seven in the morning Manhattan's streets were empty, and there were no traffic jams on the Van Wyck. His cab would have taken less than forty-five minutes to travel from her apartment to Kennedy Airport. Yes, Jack would have been on time for his flight even though, long after he was supposed to leave, they'd still been . . . well . . .

Now he was far away, going farther. It would be three weeks until he returned from his first ever trip to Asia – three weeks for her to think things through, and decide how she really felt about him.

Red hair bouncing on her shoulders, she smiled as she walked. Jack was so obviously . . . so nervously . . . steeling himself to propose. She could imagine how he'd do it – some tongue-tied nonsense about both of them no longer being teenagers, she thirty-seven, he forty-two, and they'd been going together for a year, and gee, Gabrielle . . .

He'd nearly done it Friday. She'd seen it in his eyes. At lunch – Morton's steakhouse off Fifth Avenue because Jack was a meat and potatoes kind of guy – she'd given him a promotion present: an extravagantly expensive black bridle-leather briefcase. All at once Jack had got a look in his eye. First, he muttered (typical Taft, typical self-effacing bullshit) that the briefcase was too good for him. Then, ever emotionally inarticulate, he'd swallowed hard and begun stammering about how much he cared for her. Had Simon Burton, her editor and make-no-mistake-about-it *former* flame, not swaggered up to the table interrupting him, Jack would have stuttered it out. She was sure of it, the same as she was sure she wasn't ready to deal with it.

But there was Simon, the resplendent object of every female eye in the room, and Jack, green with jealousy, never managed to blurt out his proposal.

Thank God.

Now, he was gone, and she was on her way to Boston for a breakfast meeting with the grand high moguls of Fidelity Investments. With Simon in tow. The lecherous pest insisted on joining her. She'd have to spend the whole trip fending him off. *Arrgh!*

Fidelity was the sort of story she could write in her sleep. She'd knock it out as soon as she got back. Then . . . then there was another story to start investigating. Jack had given her the lead. Only two words. He wouldn't give her any details. Boy scout that he was, he never gave her details. After all, she was a business journalist and he, too cautious about possible conflicts of interest, was a loyal corporate executive.

Conflicts of interest? Gabrielle turned the phrase over in her mind. Had Jack held back details because he feared a conflict? Did the tip he gave her imply he'd found something awry at his company? Was he hinting that he was going halfway around the world because he smelled a rat? As LBTech's newly elected vice president of logistics, he was visiting his company's distribution centres in Singapore, Malaysia, Thailand, Indonesia, the Philippines, and Taiwan. Some of those countries were pretty dicey. If there was something fishy going on, Jack could find himself in danger.

But no, that was silly. 'Danger' was the last word you associated with Jack. A good guy and a great lover, he was balanced, reasonable, and safe, dammit, safe! No thrills, no chills, no unpredictable excitement. And that, thought Gabrielle Dunn as she boarded her airplane, was why she needed three weeks to think about where the relationship was going – if, indeed, it was going anywhere.

Hearts are earned, not given, wrote William Butler Yeats, whom Gabrielle, being Irish, worshipped immoderately, thus asking herself: was Jack Tuft – annoyingly humble Jack – the one to love her *in that high old way*?

She didn't know, wasn't certain, had to think. She needed time.

– 2 –

Taft was gone and Denise knew he wouldn't be coming back. The people in Singapore would see to that. She didn't want to know how they went about it. It was like calling the exterminator. The guy in the coveralls shows up in the morning. You come back to your apartment in the evening. The mouse, or whatever was in the wall, isn't there any more. Maybe it's dead or maybe it's in a little cage being tortured in some laboratory. You'd rather not hear the details. All you care about is it's gone.

Like Taft.

On Sunday afternoon, no one else on the premises, Denise Donald sat in a cramped office she believed beneath her station in life. She pecked an e-mail message into her personal computer – Taft's flight number: Singapore Air 15; his time of arrival on the far side of the International Dateline: 1.55 a.m.; his hotel: Raffles.

The man to whom she addressed the message would be waiting. Or men who worked for him. It didn't matter which. The outcome would be the same.

Tilting her head left, tossing her golden-girl hair right, she permitted the slightest moué to form on lips that appeared to be the product of a plastic surgeon's art, but were, like everything else, entirely natural, utterly perfect. She was furious at her computer's creaking slowness. Had she, rather than that wimp Taft, won promotion to the title of Vice-President – Logistics of the world's largest electronics distributor, her first act would have been to toss out these antiquated 486s and replace them with the new Pentium-II PCs. But Jack, always a pokey plodder, had insisted that no one in the department needed faster computers. Best save the budget, keep the old machines for another year, stay with the tried and true. It was just so typical of the man; and why she'd kept fucking him for so long would always be a mystery.

The computer screen went blank. Stayed blank. She chewed her lip in frustration at its speed. Oh sure, it was true that LBTech's ordinary software ran fine on outdated computers. Spreadsheets, word processing, databases – all those things purred along. But Denise had special needs, needs that no one else had, and they moved like molasses on a vintage 1991 IBM PC. Which was, like so much else, all Taft's fault.

A digital chime sounded. The screen displayed: CONVERTING, CONVERTING, CONVERTING. FACTORING, FACTORING, FACTORING. ENCRYPTING, ENCRYPTING ...

It just took for ever. Before passing her words through the Diffie-Hellman encryption algorithm, the computer had to do a glacially slow look-up on what cryptologists called 'a one time pad' – a book used to scramble messages into indecipherable code. The 'pad' could be a novel or a cookbook or a travel guide – it didn't matter as long as you kept it secret because as long as you kept secret, no one could break the code.

2 Kings xii was Denise's 'pad', her secret cryptographic key. The computer selected her text for the day: 'If any of the men whom I have brought into your hands escape, he that letteth him go, his life shall be for the life of him.'

Denise smiled, although very faintly: *How appropriate*, she thought. To which, after a moment's reflection, she added, *Bye-bye, Jack*.

Ding-dong. Rentokil calling.

3
Singapore

Four on a New York Sunday afternoon is five o'clock Monday morning in Singapore: an hour upon which all good citizens are asleep in their beds.

Chan Gin was not a good citizen.

Bored and bone weary, he unlocked his apartment door, and shuffled numbly to the living-room window. Standing in silence eighteen storeys above Orchard Road, he studied the silent streets of his paradoxical island nation – a ruthlessly capitalistic country that swaddled and coddled its citizens from cradle to grave. The authorities boasted that Singapore was the world's most perfect state. Chan snorted at the thought. If Singapore was so perfect, then why did it have a place for a man like him?

Two deep-cut furrows formed between his eyes. Not for the first time he meditated that Singapore's smotheringly protective society was a republic of little white mice, comfy-safe in government-subsidized cages, docilely obedient to their masters' whims. But where there are mice, there are mousers. Chan Gin reckoned himself first among their ranks – a predator born, forged by nature for pursuit and for the kill.

Although not tonight.

He sighed, his spirit drained but for a faint sense – more an instinct than conscious knowledge – that somewhere down among the shadows plump tasty prey ran free. After a long hunt, he'd come home empty-handed. But patience is the hunter's primary virtue and Chan knew that on some other night the chase would begin again, and upon whatever hour it concluded, he, the hunter, would come home happily sated. On such nights as those he felt less weary, but, oddly, slept more soundly.

After some moments of drowsy reflection, Chan removed a toothpick from the inside of his sports coat, slipped it between his teeth, and walked to the bedroom. He flicked on the light, glancing at his answering machine. An LED display told him he had four messages. He'd listen to them in the morning, teacup in hand, while reading the e-mail his computer had accumulated during the past twenty-four hours.

Chan's bedroom, like his living room, was decorated with classic movie posters – all framed, all glassed, a few quite valuable. Three posters, the prizes of Chan's collection, bore autographs: Joan Crawford's on *A Woman's Face*; Spencer Tracy's on *San Francisco*; and best of all *Dead End*, signed by both Joel McCrea and Humphrey Bogart.

He opened the closet. A floor-to-ceiling mirror was fixed on the inner door. He studied himself, taking sleepy pleasure in what he saw. Tall, broad shouldered, black hair parted on the right and falling a finger's length over a wide forehead – a good-looking man with almost Occidental eyes, and a ladies' man beyond any doubt. *You handsome dog . . .*

He sloughed off his Armani sports coat, hanging it next to a tidy row of other, equally expensive, jackets. He draped a blue and green Sulka tie over a tie rack that contained two dozen more, all silk, all in perfect taste. He removed his Smith & Wesson Sigma from a nylon holster beneath his left shoulder – fifteen rounds in the clip, one in the chamber, sapphire-lensed Trijicon glow-in-the-dark nightsights, a gun designed to meet the demanding specifications of the American FBI. Its .40 calibre rounds were guaranteed to stop any target dead in its tracks; 'dead' being the operative word, and intended outcome.

Setting the Sigma on its shelf, he unholstered the Russian-made sawed-off Baikal IJ riot gun he carried underneath his right armpit. In a nation with the world's most stringent gun-control laws, the Baikal had been expensive to come by.

Leaving the closet, he sat on the edge of his oversized bed. The sheets smelled fresh – the cleaning service was under orders to change them every three days. He bent at the waist, rolling up his right pants leg. Beneath his sock, a twenty-two-ounce, poly-frame Glock Model 27 semi-automatic was tucked neatly in an ankle holster. Chan removed it, placing it on his nightstand. Then he folded back his left pants leg, and withdrew its twin from under his left sock. Both accepted nine-round magazines, and both were chambered for the same lethally heavy slugs as his Sigma.

Sometimes, but not tonight, he carried a bobbed-hammer, Ruger SP101 revolver clipped on his belt, just at the small of his back. Because semi-automatics can jam, Chan believed in having more than one backup. So too did he believe in firepower, preferring weapons that delivered a minimum of three hundred and fifty foot-pounds of energy, and thus capable of lifting an enemy into the air, and depositing him, down and dying, some several feet from where he started. After all, a practised marksman (which he most certainly was) firing a production pistol from a benchrest at a stationary target twenty-five metres distant will, at the very best, produce a shot group with a five- to eight-centimetre spread. Take the benchrest away, put the target and the shooter in motion – not uncommon in a running firefight – and the very concept of a shot group disappears. Bullets go everywhere, and even the most experienced gunman counts himself lucky if one in ten hits the mark.

The framed poster over Chan's bed advertised the 1970 film *Patton*. Beneath a jut-jawed photograph of its star, George C. Scott, appeared an excerpt from orders penned by the film's bellicose subject: 'There is only one tactical principle which is not subject to change. It is: use the means at hand to inflict the maximum amount of wounds, death, and destruction on the enemy in the minimum time.'

Chan drew more than mere inspiration from the words; they seemed to him a decree bearing the weight of religious law, a divine commandment, issued from on high, one of life's great revelatory truths. So far this profound yet simple principle had served Chan Gin well. After all, he was still alive and walking; the same could not be said of several other people he could name.

He stood, unfastened his belt, and let his trousers slide to the floor. In those Singaporean circles where such things were discussed, it was rumoured that he had a holster for a .25 Baby Browning automatic sewn into the crotch of his Jockey briefs. The rumour was false. Chan Gin favoured boxer shorts.

Practising a gesture learned through the viewing of countless Warner Brothers movies, Chan *bogarted* his toothpick into an ashtray. Then, switching off the light, he slid beneath cool sheets. An indicator light lit on his modem – incoming e-mail, a message about a man with an expensive new briefcase.

Chan was already asleep, dreaming of prey.

Two: Rogue Male

In an attack of automatism the patient becomes suddenly unconscious, but, since other mechanisms in the brain continue to function, he changes into an automaton. He may wander about, confused and aimless. Or he may continue to carry out whatever purpose his mind was in the act of handling on his automatic sensory-motor mechanism when the highest brain-mechanism went out of action . . . Thus, the automaton can walk through traffic as though he were aware of all that he hears and sees, and so continue on his way home. But he is aware of nothing and so makes no memory record. If a policeman were to accost him he might consider the poor fellow to be walking in his sleep.

Dr Wilder Penfield – *The Mystery of the Mind*,
Princeton 1975

ADEIMANTUS: Which appetites do you mean?
SOCRATES: I mean those which are awake when the reasoning and human ruling power is asleep; then the wild beast within us, gorged with meat or drink, starts up and having shaken off sleep goes forth to satisfy his desires; and there is no conceivable folly or crime . . . which at such a time, when he has parted company with all shame and sense, a man may not be ready to commit.

Plato – *The Republic IX*

1
Singapore

Taft was beyond jet lag. He had passed into it, through it, and out the other side. Now he inhabited a grey, cottony world of muffled sounds, fuzzy pastels, and watery light.

United Airlines Flight 988 takes about six hours to cover the distance separating New York and San Francisco. At SFO the arriving New York passenger must wait three hours before Singapore Air Flight 15 departs for its twelve-hour haul to Seoul. After another layover – two hours in a thankfully smoke-free airport – Singapore Air 15 continues on to Singapore, landing six hours after leaving Korea.

In total Jack had endured approximately twenty-nine hours of travel to reach a destination 9,530 miles and thirteen time zones from the island of Manhattan. His body, fatigued beyond mere exhaustion, had shut down its primary systems hours earlier. The only brain functions still operating were those seated in Jack's medulla oblongata – the old brain, the lizard brain, the alligator-IQed seat of the mind's most basic instincts: the three 'F's, flight, feed, and flee. As none of these imperatives (much less the very few other F-words to which alligators respond) suited Jack's current condition, he was, to all intents and purposes, a human zombie.

The International Dateline being what it is, Jack's plane touched down at Singapore's Changi Airport at two o'clock Tuesday morning, *two days* after his departure from JFK. Jack peered through the airplane's window. The airport's tropical landscape was brightly lit, lush and gloriously green. But Jack didn't see it. Not really. To his eyes, it was mostly a monochrome haze.

One of the flight attendants opened the first-class cabin's closet to retrieve Jack's seersucker sports coat. She was a heartbreakingly beautiful woman, an amber-skinned Malay in her early twenties.

Her full lips wore a gorgeous shy smile; her large eyes sparkled with warmth; her shoulder-length hair was richly brown, almost black; and her waist was so slender as to astonish, especially given the delightful geometry of a body fetchingly displayed in a two-piece, tightly tailored, floral batik *sarong kebaya*. Her name was Zaitun, and she not merely brought Jack his jacket, but helped him put it on. As she hovered over him, long silken hair brushed his face, the aphrodisiacal aroma of expensive perfume filled his nostrils, and the gentle warmth of nubile youth caressed his skin. She sweetly asked if there was anything else she could do for him, anything at all. Jack reluctantly rotated his head, staring at but not seeing the splendid creature who had been, for the past eight hours or so, his more-than-willing slave.

He grunted something anthropoidally incomprehensible.

Many, many hours earlier, the comfortably upholstered pleasures of first-class travel had struck Jack as the very best perk to arise from his elevation to the exalted rank of Vice-President LBTech, Inc. Farewell, he smirked, to squalling infants on every side; goodbye three bucks for a can of tepid domestic beer; *adios* harried stewardesses, filthy lavatories, no-leg-room seating; and so long to the sweaty, sneezing, far-too-talkative fat guys who invariably were wedged into the seat next to him.

Jack Taft was now an officer of a multi-billion-dollar company. No more back-of-the-plane for him!

– Dad, I got you and Mom opera tickets for your anniversary. *Faust*. Sills, Triegle, Rudel conducting. Right up front in the orchestra.

– Too fancy for the likes of us. The balcony's where we belong. Take them back. Get a refund.

He'd winced at the memory, one of many, and tried to put it out of his mind . . . tried for once in his life to enjoy the fruits of success without feeling guilty.

Zaitun almost made it easy. She was so perfect a specimen of Singapore Airline's legendary stewardesses that he'd actually gulped when he saw her. And blushed when, at dinner time, she knelt beside him to serve his appetizer with all the irresistible deference that only unliberated Asian women display. *O master*, said the demure expression on her delectable face, *please accept a humble offering from this lowly and unworthy creature*. And Jack felt . . .

. . . Jack felt guilty. Exquisitely prepared spicy satay, sweet rolled chicken, and chocolate-peppermint ice-cream cake were ashes in his mouth. He wished he was flying economy. That was where the likes of him belonged.

Zaitun Binte Samsudin – intelligent and not entirely as shy as she seemed – knew the odds of finding an unattached man in the first-class cabin were nearly zero. By the time they reached that status in life where they flew first class, American males were encumbered with wives, ex-wives, and child-support payments. Nonetheless, she could not help but notice that the haggard and hollow-eyed Mr Taft wore no ring. Moreover, he was (at least before the jet lag had set in) a most charming gentleman – polite, modest, and witty. And, she had to acknowledge, kind of cute. One might almost say cuddly, like a slightly over-stuffed teddybear. He looked like the sort of man who . . . well . . . was a big believer in hugs.

Thinking such thoughts, and wondering whether the exhausted American was genuinely unattached, she pressed a lacquered fingernail against her lower lip. Most men would have melted at the gesture. Mr Taft didn't even notice. He stumbled by, clutching his briefcase as if it was the most important thing in the world, and headed out the jetway. 'Goodbye, Mr Taft,' she trilled. 'Hope to see you again on Singapore Airlines.'

To which, unable to stop herself, she silently added: *Or, perhaps, elsewhere*.

Zaitun pursed her lips. Certainly not. She was a good Muslim girl – or at least good enough to regret it when she wasn't. Besides, *that* sort of behaviour was strictly against her employer's policies.

Nonetheless, she knew that if she really wanted to escape the suffocating confines of her protective little nation, there was only one way to do it. It would take a marriageable foreigner to set her free. And while the sacred Koran forbade Muslim women to wed unbelievers, the Prophet in his wisdom had opined that both Jews and Christians *were* believers, and hence, technically speaking, Muslim in their faith.

Zaitun watched Mr Taft depart up the jetway. Rather embarrassed by the thought, it came to her that a girl could do worse.

Later, during the interrogation, she would furiously deny having any interest in the man, any at all. But by then, of course, it was too late.

– 2 –

Zaitun was making one last sweep of the now-empty first-class cabin. Everything seemed in order. No one had left behind his briefcase or his jacket or his . . .

There was something wedged between the armrest and the cushion of the seat recently vacated by the interestingly unwed Mr Taft. Something grey. It had been pushed in deeply; only one nearly invisible corner of it showed.

She forced the seat into its full reclining position. Careful not to break a nail, Zaitun slid her fingers beneath the cushion and tickled the object up. 'Oh,' she murmured, 'poor Mr Taft.'

What she had found was a slate-grey Psion Series 5, a pocket-sized computer that almost certainly contained Mr Taft's personal phone directory, his daily agenda, and a sizeable number of critical spreadsheets and word-processing documents.

Again Zaitun pressed a lovely finger to the lovely lip. The correct and proper thing to do was to hand this device over to Singapore Airlines' Lost and Found Department. They would arrange for it to be returned to Mr Taft's New York home.

However, from what Zaitun had seen during her five years ministering to those who travelled via Singapore Air, American businessmen were lost without their computers. Perhaps, she thought, it would be best if she returned the Psion to Mr Taft herself. If only she knew where he was staying . . .

But of course that was easy enough to find out. Psions were popular with executive travellers. Zaitun had seen them in the first-class cabin often. She knew how they worked.

Mr Taft's Psion opened like a wallet. The top half was the screen, the bottom half was the keyboard. She tapped the 'on' key. Then she pressed the 'agenda' function. A picture appeared on the screen: a pocket diary displaying today's date. And typed into the diary, just at 2 a.m., were the words: 'Arrive Singapore. Hotel: Raffles. 1 Beach Road. TN: 337-1886. Guaranteed late arrival. Confirmation number 3248-183.'

Boh meng tui, no problem. She could stop at Raffles on her way home to Toa Payoh township. It wouldn't be inconvenient at all. Then, from the lobby she would call Mr Taft, the rather cute Mr Taft, and . . .

She blushed. Well, she couldn't do that. Such would be much too bold for a well-raised Muslim girl. But she could drop Mr Taft's Psion off at the front desk. And she could leave word that she was the one who'd found it.

And, now that she thought of it – just in case he wanted to call and thank her – she could even leave her phone number.

At this late hour Changi Airport was empty but for the passengers debarking Flight 15. Jack stumbled away from customs, out the exit, and into the balmy tropical night. A row of taxis waited near the kerb.

He slung his luggage into the open truck of a pale blue Toyota Crowne cab. Clutching his new briefcase against his chest, he negotiated his uncertain way into the back seat. The driver, a turbaned Sikh, turned and asked, 'Where to, sir?'

'Hotel.'

The driver looked at Jack. Jack looked at the driver. Some moments of poignant silence ensued. Then the driver asked, 'Long flight, sir?'

Jack's chin moved up and down, travelling a distance measured in millimetres.

'What is the name of your hotel, sir?'

Jack thought about it. Some few cells in his cerebral cortex grudgingly stirred, presenting him with an answer. 'Raffles,' he murmured.

'We'll be there in twenty minutes, sir.' The taxi pulled away from the kerb.

The battleship-grey Mitsubishi Lancer GLX was a nondescript vehicle with tinted windows and a licence plate bearing a 'QX' prefix. Its driver waited until Jack's Toyota taxi had passed, then swung on to the road five car-lengths behind. As the driver accelerated, the occupant of the passenger seat lifted a matte-black Motorola SPYCIRA-model radio to his ear, and depressed the 'transmit' button.

Taking a toothpick out of his mouth, Chan Gin asked: 'CPS, do you copy?'

'We copy. What's your status?'

'Departing Changi Airport now. Subject is in a Tibs-operated taxicab, licence two-Y-A-four-nine-zero. Headed west on the East Coast Parkway.'

'I'll order the team into position.'

'How many men?'

'Four. They'll be ready in thirty minutes.'

'Tell 'em to take their time. This one will be a piece of cake. Chan over and out.'

– 3 –

During his air-conditioned ride from the airport, Jack – or rather Jack's alligator brain – eyed the passing landscape sleepily, and with no curiosity. Such sights as might have caused him, a New Yorker born and bred, to gape went unremarked upon. For example, the first few miles of the highway (unbeknown to visitors, a cunningly disguised emergency landing strip for Singapore's armed-to-the-teeth air force) were flanked with sparkling clean public housing projects. The fact that in these projects no windows were broken, no trash littered the ground, and no graffiti was spray-painted on the walls would, under normal circumstances, have elicited from Jack a reaction of astonishment – and, perhaps, a reluctant recognition that the threat of ten strokes across the buttocks (administered via a rattan cane wielded by a martial arts expert) made would-be street artists think twice.

He had been looking forward to this, his first business trip since becoming LBTech's vice-president of logistics, and his first visit to the Lion City of the Orient. He'd studied his guidebooks avidly: a tiny island Utopia with peculiar laws – mammoth fines for pigeon feeding, gum chewing, and forgetting to flush the toilet. A charismatic leader named Lee Kuan Yew who once micromanaged everything from the recruiting of airline stewardesses to the national defence. A multicultural population of three million, mostly of Chinese, Malay, and Indian extraction. Prosperous beyond reckoning, forecast to be richer per capita than America in a year or two. Renowned for its comfort, cleanliness, and efficiency (New Yorker that he was, he'd never before heard those adjectives applied to the word 'city'). Friendly, law-abiding citizens (another new concept, and one to be viewed sceptically). No dirt, no litter, and no tipping (*sounds like science fiction to me*).

However, to Jack's sleep-starved eyes central Singapore's skyscraping architecture looked less exotic than downtown San Francisco. It was only another business centre, more modern than most, but otherwise no different from Houston or Atlanta or Phoenix or any of the other commercial hubs to which he, like millions of other businessmen, routinely travelled. *The mysterious Orient*, Jack reflected, *this is not*.

The only thing that actually caught his attention was his first glimpse of the Merlion, Singapore's peculiarly grotesque national emblem: an enormous alabaster white statue of an ungainly hybrid, half lion, half fish. Jack didn't like the way it looked, found it oddly disturbing, a beast possessed of conflicting souls, the inhabitant of two mutually exclusive environments, adapted to neither, and forever destined to be at war with itself. He thought that it might stand as an apt metaphor for the country it represented, a nation perpetually unsure as to whether it was a Western democracy or an Oriental patriarchy.

Raffles' lobby was the nonpareil and archetype of British colonial splendour – Carrara marble floors, fluted snow-white Victorian columns, a three storey-high central atrium all lined with polished teak; slowly spinning ceiling fans beneath which Kipling, Conrad, and Maugham had sipped rum punches; oil paintings of prosperous Imperial gentry; potted palms, of course; a softly chuffing Smith & Sons grandfather clock imported in the days when ships were still propelled by sails; Persian rugs the size of handball courts; and every sparkling inch of the place scrubbed and brushed and polished and buffed until it shone from within.

Exhausted though he was, Jack remained alert enough to recognize that a few nights in this place were going to do major damage to his American Express card.

'Welcome to Raffles, Mr Taft. I'll have the bellman show you to your room.' The clerk, having registered Jack and passed him his key, was glancing at his computer screen. 'Oh, and you have a message. You'll find it on the desk in your suite.'

Jack grunted. He had barely managed to complete the oddly difficult act of inserting his wallet into his right hip pocket. It had taken three tries. Now, out of the corner of his eye, he noticed someone bending over by his side, taking his luggage, and . . .

. . . suddenly he was not himself, he was a stranger, was the sort of ball-fisted bully he hated most.

His hand shot out, snatching the briefcase – Gabrielle's gift – from the hands of a startled Chinese bellman in a white linen jacket. And in a low voice, angry and carnivorous, an alligator growled: 'This is *mine*!'

The bellman took an alarmed step back. 'Yes, sir. Of course, sir.'

Jack wrapped his arms around the briefcase, holding it as he would the woman who gave it to him. 'Er . . . I mean, I'll carry this. I mean, if you don't mind.'

'Whatever you say, sir.' The bellman, scared out of his wits by the expression that had crossed the new guest's face, looked at the desk clerk for guidance. The clerk silently mouthed two words: 'Jet lag.' The bellman nodded. 'Follow me, sir. We'll have you in your suite in just a minute.'

Jack, shocked at his own behaviour, blushed and obeyed.

As the new guest walked away, the desk clerk lifted his telephone and hurriedly dialled room service. 'Suite two-oh-one has just checked in. Send up something to help him unwind – a nice brandy, I think – compliments of the management.'

Returning the phone to its cradle, the clerk glanced up. Five men were entering the lobby. Their leader was Chinese – tall, broad shouldered, and good looking in a thuggish sort of way. He dressed well too, looked fine in tropical slacks, an open-collared white cotton shirt, and an expensive, creamy sports coat. His face seemed familiar. The clerk thought he might be a film star or a politician or . . .

Taking off a two hundred and fifty-dollar pair of Oakley sunglasses, the tall Chinese man reached inside his shirt pocket, withdrawing a toothpick. Grinning a predator's grin, he slid it between his teeth. That's when the clerk recognized him. Chan Gin. His photo had been on the front page of the tabloid *New Paper* only a week earlier – right next to the photos of the dead men.

The clerk snatched up the telephone and dialled another number – hotel security. There was no ring; the line was dead. The security phone was the first thing Chan Gin had gone for.

Now he was going for the second.

– 4 –

'Will there be anything else, sir?' the bellman asked.

'Wake up call,' Jack mumbled, surrounded by luxury he was too exhausted to appreciate.

'What time, sir?'

'Nine-thirty.' The bellman had put his luggage on a rack, given him a quick tour of his suite, flicked on the radio, and all the while had kept his distance. Jack, tired as he was, noticed that.

'Very good, sir. I'll tell the switchboard.'

'Uh, thanks.' Jack fumbled a two-dollar bill out of his wallet, numbly noting that it was Singapore currency – a fact that meant he had cashed a traveller's cheque. He wondered where. In the airport? In the hotel? Who knew? Who cared?

The bellman declined the tip. Jack, somewhat ashamed of himself, said, 'Please. I was . . . down in the lobby . . . you were just trying to help and I—'

'No apologies necessary, sir. Enjoy your stay at Raffles.' He left, shutting the door gently behind him.

Jack – no more than half his brain cells awake and painfully functioning – stared stupidly around his quarters. Three rooms: fifty or sixty feet from the entrance to the enormous bath; a parlour and dining room in the front; a bedroom larger than Gabrielle's entire apartment; carpets and furnishings that looked to be genuine antiques; fresh flowers everywhere; and, most important of all, an exceptionally comfy-looking bed.

Nice. Pricey too – well beyond any amount that he could legitimately expect to turn in on an expense report. He'd planned to stay in the Holiday Inn, *good enough for you, son*, but Gabrielle insisted he try Raffles. He was a vice-president now, she argued, entitled to pamper himself and live – if only for a few days – like a white rajah.

He'd let her talk him into it. He'd let her talk him into anything. He loved her too much not to. His conscience nagged him anyway.

An aroma tickled the nerve cells in his nostrils. Warm, friendly, savoury. Something that made him salivate. Something that his tortured and exhausted system yearned for beyond all other desires. Something so wonderful that the anticipation of it was almost erotic.

Oh, dear God, brandy!

Jack lifted the crystal snifter from the desk, tilted its rim towards his lips, inhaled deeply. The odour gave him the sort of rush (he imagined) a junkie feels when he pops a vein. He let an amber teaspoon's worth slide over his tongue.

His whole body shook with pleasure. He felt his knees weaken, and his groin stir, and suddenly he was thinking of Gabrielle on white sheets, stripes of autumn sun through the Venetian blinds; her hair in sweet disarray, skin aglow, lids half lowered over emerald eyes, and . . .

Christ! Jack thought with a start. *What do these people put in their booze?*

The answer had little to do with the brandy, except that it served to stimulate certain lethargic nerve endings, thereby bringing into grudging consciousness some few higher cortical functions. To the medulla oblongata's three F-word imperatives, a fourth could now be added.

Jack trudged to the parlour, stared half-awake out the window at neatly manicured gardens. No thoughts came. After a few moments, he shuffled back to the bedroom. The desk was there. And a letter.

It was typed on the personal stationery of Rajiv Sethanar, general manager of LBTech's Singapore operations. As Jack read it, he could almost hear Rajiv's musical voice:

```
Dear Jack:

Welcome to Singapore, and warm congratulations on your
much-deserved promotion. I am so very pleased to have you
as our new leader and look forward keenly to working with
you. Well done, Jack!

I was most surprised to receive your secretary's fax this
morning  announcing  your  imminent  arrival  and  cannot
imagine  the  reasons  why  your  visit  calls  for  such
secrecy. I trust you will inform me when we meet in the
morning.

Until then, congratulations and best wishes from your
friend and colleague,

Rajiv Sethanar
General Manager
LBTech Singapore, PTE

P.S. Please find enclosed in this envelope a soporific. It
is common for travellers from America to suffer sleep
disorders after so long a trip. A sleeping capsule will
relax you in preparation for the rigours of the morning.
```

Failing to notice that Rajiv had added a few words on the note's reverse, Jack dropped it back on the desk. *How nice*, he thought.

Rajiv was a good guy, one of Jack's few allies in Southeast Asia. Most of LBTech's other Pacific Rim managers were downright hostile to their new boss; not unexpectedly – after all, they'd been handpicked by Denise Donald, loyal serfs in her personal fiefdom.

Which, starting tomorrow morning, he planned to dismantle.

A new broom sweeps clean. He grinned. *You guys down here are in for a few surprises. One of them is that I'm going to light a fire beneath your lazy feet. The other is that I'm not the pushover Denise says I am.*

Thus boasting to himself, Jack brought the brandy snifter to his mouth. *Odd,* he wondered, *it's empty. And where's that pill Rajiv sent me?*

All the while, consciousness was ebbing away, blessed sleep tiptoeing closer.

Aw, nuts, I took it . . . Jack hated drugs, and used them only when he had to. *Cripes! With a slug of high-voltage booze, no less!* Now he had no choice but to go to bed.

But first things first. Ever cautious, he wanted to make sure his wallet and his passport were safely hidden from view. Even though he was staying in the best hotel in the most thoroughly policed city in the world, he didn't want those two items out in plain sight. He'd heard too many stories from international travellers more seasoned than he about the horrors to which an American businessman can be subjected if his passport, wallet, cash, and credit cards are pilfered.

He patted his hip pocket. The wallet was there. What about the passport? Gone. *Drat!* Pants pockets? *No.* Jacket pocket? *No. Uh oh. Now where the . . .*

He remembered.

It was in his briefcase, the glowing bridle-leather bag that Gabrielle had given him as a promotion present. He loved the briefcase, loved the way she had surprised him with it, loved the look in her eye as she'd lifted it from a shopping bag, loved the note she'd taped to its handle: 'So you won't forget me while you're in Singapore . . . or anywhere else.'

Not that he could ever forget her. Nor, unfortunately, could he forget how macho, swaggering Simon Burton drooled at her. But

Simon, the jerk, didn't have a chance. He was history, and she'd chosen the better man. No better evidence of that than her love gift, this wonderful, wonderful briefcase. And suddenly the briefcase, sitting on his lap in the airplane, hugged to his chest in the taxi, snatched from the hands of a hapless bellboy, *was* Gabrielle. Holding it brought him closer to her, and he could lie down now and wrap his arms around it and dream that instead he held . . .

Jesus! His eyelids snapped open. *I'm in bad shape. Gotta get to bed. Gotta do it now!*

– 5 –

The sleeping pill that Rajiv had enclosed with his letter, and which Jack had unthinkingly swallowed, was a two-milligram tablet of Rohypnol. As an afterthought, Rajiv had scribbled an unnoticed warning on the back of his note, cautioning Jack (as Rajiv himself had been cautioned by his personal doctor) not to take the drug with alcohol.

For very good reason:

Singapore Department of Public Health Physicians' and Dispensing Pharmacists' Reference Manual © 1994
(page 237)

ROHYPNOL (generic name: flunitrazepam): manufactured by Hoffman-LaRoche, Rohypnol is a high-efficacy member of the benzodiazepine family of tranquillizers (e.g. Valium, Xanax and kindred medications).

1. *Classification*: Class II regulated substance. Strict controls apply. Penalties for misadministration include imprisonment, fines, and the cane. (see Appendix F, xii)
2. *Administration*: oral
3. *Dosage*: 1 milligram; 2 milligrams in exceptional cases
4. *Diagnostic indicators*: sleep disorders not resolvable with milder soporifics
5. *Potency*: approximately 10x the sedative strength of Valium

6. *Anticipated effects*: after a period of 30 minutes (+/- 15 minutes) following ingestion, deep sleep for up to twelve hours, with eight hours being the norm.

7. *After-effects*: mild lethargy for up to four hours in a small percentage of cases

8. *Contra-indications*: under no circumstances to be prescribed for patients suffering from alcohol-related disorders or being treated with any other tranquillizer, soporific, antidepressant, or mood-altering medication. Under no circumstances to be prescribed for patients with a history of narcotic abuse or dependency.

9. *Hazards and warnings*:
   a. Dispensing for export purposes is strictly prohibited by Singaporean Law.
   b. In an indeterminate number of cases Rohypnol causes short-term memory loss and acutely erratic behaviour before engendering sleep.
   c. Singaporean Public Code 387-78 requires that patients must be advised both orally and in writing that Rohypnol is not to be consumed with alcohol. A considerable body of research indicates severe behavioural changes result.

RELEVANT CITATIONS: United States National Institute on Drug Abuse report 'Epidemiologic Trends in Drug Abuse, Advance report, Community Epidemiology Work Group, June 1995'; Terrance W. Woodworth, Deputy Director, United States Drug Enforcement Administration, Congressional Testimony of July 16, 1996; Partnership for a Drug-Free America, 'Report of Rohypnol, 1998'.

TESTIMONY AND REPORT ABSTRACTS: *'Rohypnol has a synergistic effect when used in conjunction with alcohol. This combination produces disinhibition and amnesia. Common effects include blackouts, disorientation, disinhibition, and persistent senses both of fearlessness and aggressiveness . . .*

'When taken with liquor, Rohypnol eradicates self-control, rendering subjects insensate although they appear alert. In medical terminology, those under its influence are deemed to suffer from "automatism" – a state similar to sleepwalking. Reason and reflection absent, an "automaton's" powers of observation are disabled; judgement is not merely impaired, but rather is wholly incapacitated;

subjects act as robots programmed to perform some few primitive
survival functions, and are governed only by elemental instinct . . .'

Those under the combined influence of Rohypnol and alcohol are
not responsible for their actions. They are, in point of fact,
dangerous.

– 6 –

But for the handful of money-be-damned suites (each a demi-
palace) arrayed around its inner atrium, Raffles is a great
meandering maze of breezeways with guest rooms on one side,
lush gardens on the other. After stationing a backup team near the
elevator, Chan Gin, followed by his remaining two men, jogged
past doorways bearing brass plaque tributes to former occupants
(Charlie Chaplin, Ava Gardner, André Malraux), and down what
seemed to be miles of gleaming teak-floored walkways.

At this hour, the city of Singapore, never boisterous, was silent.
Even had it spoken, it would not have been heard; not inside
Raffles where thick walls, broad-leafed Livistonia palms and
woven frangipani shrouded all sound except for the click of
purposeful footsteps on burnished wood. In this hotel enclave it
was still the 1920s; not America's roaring decade, but rather the
gilded age of genteel travel, a time of decorous journeys via
leisurely Cunard liners, not cloud-shattering 747s; an era of no
CNN and precious few newspapers, when the gentry congregated
at hotels whose turbaned doormen called women 'memsahib,' and
did so with solemn courtesy.

Chan loosened the Sigma in his shoulder holster. Behind him, his
two subordinates drew their pistols, both holding them two-
handed in practised combat grips. Chan generally used only one
hand. It gave the target a sporting chance, and made things more
interesting. Although, now that he thought about it, there'd be
nothing interesting tonight. The prey would be travel-worn and
off-guard. It would be over fast. No fun at all.

He paused, edged around a corner, looked cautiously down an
empty breezeway. Singapore was a damned convenient place for

someone in his line of work. Everything was automated, monitored, and with few exceptions – Chan being one of them – controlled. If you wanted to find somebody, all you had to do was tap into one of the government databases. Houses, apartments, automobiles, hotel reservations – in a society that kept an eye on everything, you pretty much knew where anybody could be found.

Taft, for instance. His room was just ahead. Suite 201, at the furthest end of the building. An out-of-the-way part of the hotel. And particularly quiet. But not for long.

– 7 –

Jack dropped his wallet next to his passport, and snapped his briefcase shut. Even though Singapore was, by all reports, the most crime-free city in the world, the briefcase would spend the night on the floor, right next to his bed. *Better safe than sorry*, thought Jack, always a cautious man. As he turned towards the bed and blessed sleep, he noticed the door to his suite. He couldn't quite remember whether he'd locked it.

Probably not. The bellman had left, and the brandy beckoned, and . . . *hmmm . . . nope, pretty sure the darned thing is still open . . .*

Jack twisted the door handle, and pulled. As expected, the door swung wide. Less expected were the three hard-faced men standing in the breezeway. One of them had his fist raised – some sort of card between thumb and forefinger – and was preparing to knock on the door. The other two held stubby blue steel objects in their hands – things with barrels and butts and muzzles and triggers. Jack – a little drunk, more than a little drugged, and not quite understanding what was going on – said the wrong thing. He said, 'Hi, I'm Jack Taft. Can I help you?'

Then he was face down on the carpet. He had only the vaguest recollection of how he got there . . . someone spinning him around, an order being barked, his arm wrenched behind his back, and quick-march the length of the suite's sitting room, then . . . what? . . . he suspected he'd hit the floor rather hard. Had someone kicked his feet out from under him? He wasn't entirely sure. There had, however, been some pain. No doubt about that, none at all.

Whoever had done this to him was probably the guy now pinioning him prone while unsuccessfully trying to fasten something around his wrists.

With dazed disinterest, Jack watched a chromed and shiny object tumble clink-clank over his shoulder, landing beside his nose. The man straddling Jack spat a Chinese word – a curse, Jack suspected.

His eyes focused on the fallen object. *Oh*, he thought dully, *I know what that is.*

Handcuffs.

Handcuffs?

The man reached out to retrieve them. Another man – a deeper voice and further away – spoke. Jack sensed satisfaction in his words. 'This has to be the item.'

Jack, in a state of borderline unconsciousness and not really curious about these odd proceedings, twisted his neck, woozily trying to see what was going on.

A broad-shouldered Chinese man in a cream-coloured jacket (he was the one who had been about to tap on the door) was holding Jack's beautiful new briefcase in one hand and a pocket-knife in the other. He was using the knife to pick at the latches, and already had scratched the brass. Jack didn't like that. Didn't like the way the guy looked either. A big beefy hunk, a swashbuckling lady-killer booming in a belligerent braggart's voice like Simon Burton's . . .

A second voice, this one harsh and gravelly, vocal cords too friendly with nicotine: 'Shit! Chan Gin!'

The voice's owner stood directly outside the door. He was short and stocky in a flashy suit, and he seemed to be holding a very large gun in his hand.

Jack, in the thrall of a soporific he could not name, floated outside himself, a disinterested observer looking through a gauzy curtain as dreamy deeds were done that he, in his blissful trance, could not entirely comprehend. A man moved metal in the air. Something sparked like a welder's torch on steel. Jack's ears rang, a noise too loud and too near. A ballet of sorts: this dancer leaping left, another bending down, a third pirouetting with arms flung out, a fourth reeling Scottish in a Highland fling. Some shouted words, Chinese mostly, but also sulphurous English curses. A dozen lightning flashes all in a row, strobe-light bright and accompanied by earsplitting thunder and an acrid smoky smell. A heavy weight slumped limp on Jack's back; a dead man's last sigh whispered in his ear.

Jack watched indifferently as a face materialized beside his own, cheek flat on the carpet, eyes closed, chin washed with scarlet. It was very bright, a narcotic hue, red as a blood-red poppy, and Jack thought it very beautiful. He did not dream colours; black and whites and greys, but colours never. *How odd*, he thought, *that now I should dream in colour*. But of course it was the pill, the pill he'd taken; strong stuff, and now he dreamed eye-catching tints and that was very nice.

Less nice the noise, the hateful sharp noise, and the shouting all around. But it seemed more distant now, disappearing in hazy clouds, and he could barely, could barely, could barely hear it any more . . .

– 8 –

Chan was a little disappointed. Taft was on the floor, and had been even easier to take than he'd expected. As predicted, it had been no fun.

Then a short bulky guy materialized at the door, exclaiming, 'Shit! Chan Gin!' And Chan, thinking *who the fuck are you?* was rolling left, reaching beneath his armpit.

The short guy made a big mistake. He stopped to take count: Chan, two of Chan's underlings, Taft on the floor. *Never*, Chan thought, *never inventory your targets*.

Second mistake, he shot the man nearest him first. That man wasn't Chan. By then Chan had dropped his knife, had the welcome bulk of a fine FBI-model Smith & Wesson in his hand, was already squeezing the trigger because that's what you did in these situations, and sooner or later the muzzle would be pointed in the right direction, and to hell with it.

It's easy to get rattled when bullets are headed your way. Shit, it's the goddamn natural thing to do. The fuckhead at the door flinched and tried to jump out of the line of fire. Mistake number three, asshole. What you're supposed to do, the only sane and rational thing to do, is to shoot back as fast as you can and pray to your gods that you're quicker than the man who's emptying his pistol at your face.

Or guts, as the case may be.

At about the fifth shot, Chan's barrel lined up with his opponent's midriff. A .40 calibre slug, one thousand and twenty feet per second, exploded into the cocksucker's stomach. It hurled him back against the wall, arms cruciform, his pistol spiralling in the air. Chan kept firing. Another to the belly. Lift the sights. Two in the chest, both square in the sternum, down a notch to the groin, then up again because it's time for a head shot.

Some men are hard to kill. Shoot them once, shoot them twice, and they keep coming at you. They're strong enough to take a few bullets, and when they're supposed to be dead, they're still alive and meaner than before. It's a bad experience having someone down at your feet, someone you're sure you've wasted, then you turn your back and hear behind you the click of a cocking hammer. Chan had seen it happen. He never wanted to see it again.

He pumped the trigger. Pinioned by gunfire, the dead man danced like a puppet, falling only when Chan's magazine was spent, and Chan could shoot no more.

Now Chan had one of his own men down, a kid by the name of Liu, and another standing frozen with dumb shock on his face. Hal Leung was that one's name, and Chan knew he'd have to comfort him. But first things first. Top priority was always – *always* and under every circumstance – getting a new load in your piece and never taking your eyes off the late deceased, who may not be so deceased after all. Jacking the empty from his Sigma's butt, Chan snatched a fresh clip from his pocket. That's when he remembered that there was one exception to the rule that you reloaded before you did anything else.

Too late.

Jack Taft, non-confrontational master of corporate compromise, sinks through clouds of slumber. The waking world disappears in a narcotic haze. He hears faint noises – a curse, a voice cold with hate, hissing: 'He's got the drop on us,' the clink of pistols falling on expensive carpet, the slam of a door; but these come, no doubt, from a television playing in some other room and have nothing to do with him.

A shout, far louder than the others, almost penetrates his consciousness. The words, however, do not make sense. 'Police Superintendent Chan Gin!' Nope, never heard of him. 'You're under arrest!' Preposterous. 'Stop in the name of the law!'

Jack, comfy and oblivious, goes back to sleep.

– 9 –

In a peaceable country where fewer than fifty thousand largely non-violent felonies are committed each year, most of Singapore's impeccably trained and wholly incorruptible law-enforcement officers spend their time on mundane matters: littering, petty theft, white-collar crime, domestic troubles, and, given the population's seemingly insatiable appetite for the vice, gambling.

But not Chan Gin; Chan being, in the Chinese style, his last name, and Gin his first.

Chan's superiors had recognized him as a special talent from the day, twenty-seven years earlier, he reported for induction. The special talent they saw in him was this: he was the kind of cop destined from birth to bring to justice only one sort of criminal – the worst sort.

There's not much violent crime in Singapore; Police Superintendent Chan Gin had the market to himself.

It had been different when he first donned the uniform. Secret societies, Tong wars, small-time rabble-rousers with big-time guns, race riots that left hundreds dead and wounded – those were the legacy of Singapore's earliest days of independence. But no more, not for a long time now, and Chan missed old times past. With no adversaries worthy of his mettle, he felt useless, drained, bored clean through. Life lacked its necessary thrills: the euphoria of smiling into the face of death, the God-like exhilaration of standing astride a fallen foe – stronger than strong, omnipotent, alive! Chan knew no wine so intoxicating as the adrenaline rush that came just as a firefight was about to begin . . .

. . . As it was about to, any second now.

That scumbag took my gun! He was furious beyond rage's ordinary boundaries, and hungry to kill. It didn't show. The expression on his face was cool, relaxed and confident. Nonetheless his senses tingled and the old hormones were potent in his veins. There was an officer down. The corpse of a hatchetman – a Thai or Cambodian by his looks, and no doubt Taft's contact man in Singapore – sprawled on the floor. An American thug brandishing stolen police weaponry was on the loose.

Prey.

Chan tugged both his backup pistols free of their ankle holsters.

Corporal Leung licked his lips. His face was white, and he wiped a sweaty palm against his trousers. Chan forced himself to grin; the smile was meant to lift Leung's spirits; his own needed no encouragement. 'Looks like I'm going to have to take the fucker down the hard way.' Then he slipped a toothpick between his lips.

Moments earlier the American hoodlum had disappeared through the door. 'Sir,' Leung whispered, 'what if he's waiting for us on the other side?'

Chang answered by putting four hollow-point slugs through the door. He waited for return fire. There was none. It was as he thought: the sonofabitch had run. Now he, Chan, would run after him, catch him, and what happened after that would make amends for an escape that was, *fuck me!* a humiliating loss of face. He should have been more careful. The anonymous e-mail alerting the police of Taft's arrival had warned them that the thug was as hard a hardcase as had ever been born. Chan cursed himself for turning his back on the damned dangerous gangster.

It was going to be intense now, exactly the way Chan liked it. Taft, lethally armed, was somewhere out in the hall. If he was as dangerous as Chan guessed, he wouldn't have used the past few seconds to flee for the exit. Instead, he'd go just far enough to find cover – an alcove, or behind a whitewashed pillar, or one of those deceptively flimsy-looking rattan table and chair sets with which Raffles lined its walkways. That's where he'd be waiting, mostly out of sight, stolen police pistols braced in his fists, sights aligned and steady and pointed at the place where, very shortly now, Chan Gin needed to be.

Chan loved this, the final tick of the clock before the shooting started. It was better than sex. He could see the pulse throbbing visibly in his wrists, blood pressure raging high enough to kill.

He whispered a prayer. Though devoutly Methodist, he directed his plea to Chinese deities; they were a grittier crew, did their business at street level, and they seemed appropriate given the circumstances. However, God and gods notwithstanding, Chan's most ardent faith was reserved for the Federal Arms Corporation's PD-model bullets: twelve inches minimum penetration and a wound channel the size of the Carlsbad Caverns. It took only one hit, only one . . .

He forced a single deep breath. He was the good guy, invulnerable, nobody can kill the good guy.

Quite the contrary.

He thrust his pistols – one in his right hand, the other in his left – straight out, elbows locked, and drop-rolled into the corridor. His chest slid on varnished teak flooring. He twisted his hips, turning over one, two, three times. He was prone, a low target, weapons braced and primed. And there his enemy was, not fifteen metres away, in clear and plain sight, and Chan squinted and aimed and began to squeeze both triggers and the terrified shriek of a middle-aged Indian cleaning woman echoed through the night.

Oh shit! He jerked his sights away from the target. It wasn't Taft. It was some pudgy lady in baggy slacks and a loose white dhoti, and she was pushing a utilities cart all stacked with towels and soap and mops and buckets, and she was running as fast as her stubby legs could carry her, and she and her cart filled the hotel breezeway, and she was, *goddammit!*, running towards him.

He started to shout at her, order her out of the way. A pistol cracked, flat and lethal. Plaster and teak splinters exploded above the running woman. She shrieked again. Dust and ceiling fragments burst over her head. Her legs pumped, tears filled her eyes, a white froth of fear bubbled from her lips. Another shot. Another scream. Another rain of debris.

Taft, damn him, it was that fucker Taft! He was in the shadows at the far end of the breezeway, his body blocked by the woman and her cart, and he was shooting over her head to keep her running, keep her pushing that cart hard and fast towards . . .

Chan tumbled back into Taft's room. Keening like a wounded cow, the cleaning woman raced past. Chan reached out, snatched her by the arm, sent her spinning into the room. '*Ayeee-EEEEE!*' she shrieked. 'Shut up!' snapped Chan. She whimpered. 'Just shut up, and stay put!' The woman dashed to the rear of Taft's suite, and cowered out of sight.

Chan leapt back through the door. Taft was far away now, a dark blur at the end of the walkway. In a moment, he'd be around the corner and out of view. Chan started running.

In the hotel room the American hoodlum had looked too plump to move that fast. Now, somehow, he was faster than Chan. By the time Chan reached the branching walkway that Taft had taken, his prey was even farther away, sprinting up a short flight of stairs leading to the elevator lobby.

Grinning fierce hatred, Chan ran after him. There were two cops, good cops, stationed on the ground floor, just by the elevator. When Taft stepped out of the elevator, he'd be dead meat and . . .

Shit! Taft, damn him, jogged straight past the elevators, didn't so much as glance at them, spun left, and was once more out of sight.

Bad news.

The fugitive was now on the second storey of the hotel's central atrium. That's where the six thousand-dollars-a-night luxury suites were, and Taft might shoot his way into one looking for a VIP hostage. Or, worse, he could simply keep running. Hallways at the far side of the atrium led to a rat's maze of corridors, walkways, stairs, and, worst of all, emergency exits. If the sonofabitch made it out of the atrium, then he'd make it out of the hotel.

Superintendent Chan Gin had no intention of letting that

happen.

He bounded up the staircase three steps at a time, crashed through the double doors leading to the atrium, and spotting Taft, a silhouette behind distant potted palms, snapped off four fast shots at a target he could barely see.

Come on, you prick, stand still. Step into the light. Let me get one good look at you. Just one.

Taft whirled around. He straddled his legs, bent at the knees, whipped two pistols straight out at eye level, and – icy calm in every movement – shot back.

Chan's twin Glock 27s carried nine-round magazines. He'd put four bullets through the door. Fourteen were left: fewer than fourteen, ten; Chan had already fired another four. Taft had stolen his Smith & Wesson Sigma, Leung's Model-36 S&W .38 calibre, and the long-barrel the hatchetman had wielded. Twenty-eight bullets in total. Chan was outgunned, and that only made him madder.

Smaller target, he thought. *I've got to . . .*

He dived into the air, straight as a board, body level, parallel to the floor. He jerked his trigger fingers, left–right left–right, laying down a wall of fire in front of him. In the far distance, at the shadowed edge of the atrium, Taft replied in kind. Craters detonated in the walls. A fog of plaster shrapnel and dust clouded the air. Two great ugly gouges appeared in Raffles' Persian carpetry, directly below where Chan flew. A priceless antique opium couch – venerable walnut and carved marble – collapsed, its leg made many splinters by a stray bullet. As it collapsed, a porcelain vase decorated with a blue and red butterfly motif crashed to the floor, strewing yellow roses and puddled water in its wake. Another vase, one with a cracked celadon glaze, burst into jade pebbles; it had overflowed with chrysanthemums, now a snowstorm of sunshine petals fluttering among the carnage. A foolishly pyjamaed hotel guest opened his door to see what all the uproar was. He blanched, and disappeared. Left of Chan's grimacing face, a mirror shattered into a hailstorm of diamond shards, a flight of microscopic silver bees, and they stung Chan's cheeks as he kept pulling, pulling, pulling the triggers.

He came down sledding on his belly. He heard the fabric of his sports coat rip – two thousand dollars' worth of fine Cerruti linen rendered into rags.

Luck was not with him . . . Only one of his shots even came close to his target, destroying a hanging plant near the man's head.

Luck was with him . . . None of Taft's bullets had touched him. They had blasted holes in the wall, ceiling, and floor, and destroyed any number of tasteful and doubtlessly expensive furnishings. But not a single shot had so much as grazed Chan's skin. The bastard had emptied two pistols, and missed him clean.

Now Chan's guns were empty. And Taft, still distant and scarcely visible, had dropped his own empty weapons, fleeing around a corner.

Shoot at me, will you? Well, asshole, you only get one chance to do that, and, buddy boy, you blew it!

Ripping off his ruined coat, Chan rolled on his side. Then he was up with a sawed-off Baikal shotgun in his arms, and a bad expression on his face. The shotgun's barrel was only eleven inches long. Its muzzle had been flattened slightly, the better to spread shot in a wide and murderous arc. The shot in question was goose gauge, ball bearing-sized spheres of lead that would, at distance, knock over a running target. Close-in, they'd vaporize a man's midriff, pulping his guts, and cutting him untidily in two.

The Baikal was semi-automatic. No shoulder stock – Chan's gunsmith had replaced it with a high-impact polymer pistol grip.

Five shells in the magazine. None in the chamber.

Chan pumped the action. *One in the chamber.*

His face was flushed, his breath coming in great huge gulps, and rage was a furnace in his heart. That motherfucker Taft had tried to kill him. Now the only thing he wanted to do was kill him back, and to do that, he had to *move, move, move!*

He heard the tinkling of an elevator bell. *Dammit!* He began to run. The main elevators were behind him; Taft must have been looking for a service elevator all along. Chan had brought only two backup men with him, Toy and Wong; both were watching the passenger elevators in the main lobby. If Taft made it into the service elevator, he'd have a clear escape route. Chan ran harder, sprinting as fast as he could. The end of the corridor was just up ahead, a left–right T-junction. Taft had turned right. The sonof-abitch couldn't be far.

Chan listened for the *whoosh* of an arriving elevator, the sigh of automatically opening doors. Not yet, it was not yet, and there was still time. His jaw was tight with anger, his body taut, and the corner around which Taft had disappeared only paces away, and the man had three guns, had dropped two, kept one, and was waiting right there, right ahead, ready to shoot and kill and laugh as he made his escape, leaving Chan dead behind him.

Or so the American shitheel doubtless thought.

But Taft didn't understand *kiatsu*, the Singaporean ethic. Winning's not the most important thing: winning's the only thing. Every merchant, every executive, every corporate worker bee, and sure as hell every public servant held no value so dear. Chan most of all. He'd been *kiatsu* for twenty-seven years; he wasn't turning loser now.

No matter how good Taft was – pretty damned good so far – this punk, this American thug, was only second best. Chan believed that with all his heart and flung his right arm out before him, wrist angling the sawed-off Baikal around the corner, and pulled the trigger before his body hurled itself into his enemy's sights. The shotgun kicked like a mule, snapping Chan's wrist hard and sharp, and Chan ignored the pain. The lights went dark, shattered by his wild shot. He was down on one knee, sliding on polished teak, torso turned and both hands wrapped around his weapon as he fired again. In half-lit dimness pieces of skin flenched away from Taft's chest, red confetti fluttering with crumbs of a pale sports coat shredded to ribbons. A third shot took the bastard in the knee, punching his legs out from under him; and as he tumbled forward crimson streamers curled through the air. Chan fired again, this time straight into Taft's stomach, a distance of barely three metres, and the shot ripped through the falling hoodlum's midriff, pocking brass elevator doors behind. In younger days Chan took an almost sexual joy at such sights as this; truly, he'd be shocked and amused to find his manhood stiffening at the sight of the dying foe.

. . . Although Taft was not dying, but dead. The stench of his guts, ripped open to the light of day, was enough to tell Chan that he'd killed his man, and need not shoot again. But, oh what the hell, there was one more shotgun shell left, and taking the prick's head off with it would not be ungratifying. Chan pushed himself to his feet. He cocked a toe beneath the dead man's shoulder, thrust, and rolled Taft's body over. Pointing the Baikal's muzzle straight at the corpse's face, be began to tighten the trigger.

The face was Eastern, a mahogany-skinned Filipino. Not Taft. Taft was elsewhere, had fled left around the corner after leaving his hotel room. Chan had turned right. And this man, the *wrong fucking man*, was only another hatchetman, backup to the Thai Chan had aerated back in Taft's suite. Transfigured with fury, swearing as he'd never sworn before, Chan jerked the trigger, but took surprisingly little pleasure in the result.

Sleep is safety only if dreams do not disturb.

Jack is two minutes and forty seconds into a most disturbing dream.

He sleeps soundly as a rule, although nightmares are known to come. Because he is an ordinary, conventional man, his infrequent nighttime dreads are the common thing; psychiatric clichés, the prosaic fears of someone who leads an unexceptional life and whose sleeping mind is insufficiently imaginative to evoke genuine terror. Jack's tritely recurring nightmares are these: finding himself naked in a public place, visiting the dentist because a tooth is falling out, slipping and falling from a great height, and being betrayed by the woman he loves.

But now Jack, narcotized with exhaustion, drug, and drink, dreams a different nightmare. A thing of solid shadows stalks his sleep. It hungers, atavistic appetites unrestrained. It moves like smoke, silent and flowing and seemingly random, yet there is a terrible precision in its movements, which are purposeful and impelled by icy cunning. This creature of his nightmare is possessed of goals, objectives, ends. So, too, is it armed with the wherewithal to achieve them. It cannot be said to have emotion – it is a beast without passion – yet there are dark urges driving it forward, a purpose that is all consuming, and which cannot be resisted.

Jack Taft, tangled in subconscious nets and dreaming that he has bad dreams, is unable to scream himself awake. He can only watch the nightmare unfold, and pray for morning . . .

– 10 –

From Raffles' driveway of arctic-white gravel, three broad steps lead to a wide veranda, enormous glass doors, and, beneath a canopied portico, a spotless red carpet intended to assure deep-pocketed guests that, yes, they have well and truly arrived.

Zaitun Binte Samsudin – Zaitun daughter of Samsudin – slid a long, denim-clad leg through her taxicab's left rear door. She had shed her *sarong kebaya* flight attendant's uniform at the airport, changing into snug Levi's, comfortable canvas walking shoes, and a loose man's cotton shirt which, although oversized, emphasized rather than diminished her allure. 'Please wait,' she said over her shoulder. 'I'll just be a second.'

Watching the fetching roll of her flanks as she paced towards Raffles' main entrance, the cab driver whispered to himself that he'd wait for her for ever.

Zaitun barely took a half-dozen steps before spotting Mr Taft. As she saw him, her heart gave an unexpected skip. On the plane she'd thought she'd sensed something in him – a hint of sadness, a touch of vulnerability – that no woman finds entirely unappealing. Now, to her surprise, she found herself rather glad to see him again.

He was striding briskly out of the hotel, right hand in his jacket pocket, and a purposeful look on his face. Zaitun was pleased; he seemed to her much more alert than he had been when he'd disembarked from the plane. No doubt he had recovered quickly from jet lag. 'Mr Taft.' She raised a hand – fine long fingers, amber skin set off beautifully by the white of her shirt.

Coming down the stairs with a handsomely athletic bound, he looked her in the face, saying something both odd and unexpected. He whispered hoarsely, 'Friend.' His voice sounded peculiar to Zaitun's ears. What he did next was even more peculiar: still keeping his right hand in his pocket, he put his left arm around her waist. He pulled her – with a certain urgency, she thought – against his side, and walked her quickly to the waiting cab. Before Zaitun knew it, she was back in the taxi, and Mr Taft was sitting next to her.

The cab driver glowered. Such a beautiful young woman, much too young for the middle-aged American who, obvious to the driver's eyes, was her lover. He knew where to go – the woman had already given him her final destination, one of the thirty-year-old apartment buildings in Toa Payoh not far from the McRitchie Reservoir Park. Gritting his teeth with sexual envy, he tapped the 'en route' key on his dashboard computer. The computer reactivated its fare meter, sending a satellite-radio message to the taxi company's dispatch and tracking centre. The driver stamped on the accelerator.

Gunning on to Beach Road, cornering left at Seah Street, the taxi's rear wheels squealed. So did Zaitun, as the cab's momentum threw her against Mr Taft. She'd been sitting in a half-turn to the right. Suddenly she found herself flung against him, one arm around his neck, her chest pressing with embarrassing intimacy on his. She blushed furiously. He must think she was a terribly forward girl.

Unable to stop herself, she giggled at the thought. Mr Taft had swept her into her cab, and she hadn't had a moment to think about it. All she really knew was that giggles were likely to be taken the wrong way, and she had to stop it, stop right now.

'Excuse me,' she said, pushing herself away from the American. He made no reply. That was most odd. He sat there like a stone statue. It was as if he hadn't even noticed her wholly accidental embrace. And because Zaitun was used to being noticed (especially when an embrace was involved), she found herself a little annoyed. Not that she wanted Mr Taft to take advantage of the situation. But still . . .

The taxi swerved into another tight left, and onto North Bridge Road. The blaring horn of a cut-off late-night bus shrieked. Rush hour was four hours away; traffic was light. The taxi driver had the road almost to himself. He pressed his foot down hard, the acceleration forcing Zaitun back into her seat.

The street, no different from any business thoroughfare in the world, was flanked by high-rise office towers. Their architecture too was the same as business district architecture the world over. Were it not for the fact that some – surprisingly few – of the buildings' signage was in both English and Chinese, Zaitun might have been speeding through downtown Atlanta, Dallas, or Denver. All that was different was that her taxi drove on the left side of the street, not the right, and that one façade was too luridly pink to be acceptable anywhere in America. Except, perhaps, in Dallas.

More confused than alarmed by Mr Taft's behaviour, Zaitun reached into her handbag. The American's pocket computer was right on top. She'd rubber-banded an envelope around it. Inside was a note explaining where she'd found the Psion. Rather courteously, she thought, she'd concluded the note by inviting Mr Taft to call her at home if he had any questions about Singapore, or if there were any problems with his computer. She had, she added, taken the liberty of typing her phone number and address into his Psion's phone directory.

Now she was going to tell him to stop this cab. Give him the Psion and ask him to get out. To be sure, she'd ask him with deference, deference being what she, a Muslim, had been schooled in. But ask she would. Insist, really. Mr Taft seemed to have formed a horribly wrong impression of her, completely misunderstanding why she'd come to his hotel. *Jia lat* – very troublesome, although, of course, it was her fault. She was an Oriental woman, and men's mistakes were of necessity her fault – as it was her responsibility, not his, to remedy those mistakes before things became even more *jia lat*.

'Mr Taft . . .?'

He rotated his head left. There was something eerie and mechanical about the way he moved. Zaitun thought he looked like a robot, one of those simulacrums that populate theme parks the world over, an automaton that, despite the lifelike texture of its exterior, carried nothing inside but motors, rods, and gears.

'Yes.' A lifeless and artificial voice, the almost reptilian metallic hiss of machinery at work. Zaitun felt slightly, just slightly, uneasy.

'This is yours.' She held out the miniature grey computer and her note.

'It is,' Mr Taft said tonelessly. He took the Psion, and slid it into his jacket pocket. Then he rotated his head forward, not so much as thanking her.

Cold, frightening, his demeanour made her throat catch. She knew she should order the driver to pull over. The words wouldn't come out.

Something was chirping on the taxi's dashboard. Zaitun recognized the sound. By law, Singapore's taxis were equipped with velocity sensors. Should a cab exceed, even by a kilometre per hour, safe speed limits, an alarm would sound alerting the driver to decelerate or run the risk of penalties that were by any measure draconian. For this reason, Singapore cabbies were the most cautious in the world.

However, Zaitun's driver was not driving cautiously, not at all: the beeping alarm was deafening. Zaitun bent forward: 'Driver, please slow down. I want to . . .' Taft, arm still around her waist, pulled her back. 'Faster,' he grunted. Zaitun looked at him. His jaw was set, his face neutral, and his eyes half hooded, frighteningly like a lizard's. He seemed different, not at all the kindly, cuddly man on the airplane. What was he doing holding her like this? How dare he commandeer the cab that was supposed to be taking her to her tiny apartment?

Men instruct women in all things – so she was taught from birth. The role of the female is silent obedience. Or so the zealots of her faith would have it, the Koran to the contrary notwithstanding. Raised as a conservative, but reckoning herself moderate, Zaitun felt her colour begin to rise.

'Mr Taft . . .?'

At Coleman Street the cab veered across two lanes of traffic, screamed through a changing light, and screeched right. Moments later, it turned left, again heading south, now on Hill Street.

'Mr Taft, this is wrong!'

'Faster.' His eyes were empty. He was looking at her, but not hearing a word she said. A thought came to her, a thought that should have come – would have come – earlier had she not been raised so strictly in the customs of her faith: perhaps she had good cause to fear this icy, mechanical foreigner.

The cab shot across the Coleman Bridge, and on to New Bridge Street. It was headed straight towards the heart of Chinatown, the busiest of Singapore's neighbourhoods. Even at three-thirty in the morning, people were on the street – some few night hawks on the prowl, cruising a predator's circle to and from the alleyway leading to their city's sole X-rated block; others scurrying workers, hurrying back and forth as they unloaded trucks bearing food and merchandise for the morning's hectic buying and selling.

Zaitun craned forward, peeking over the driver's shoulder. What she saw registered on the cab's speedometer put her heart in her mouth. She tried to shout; could only whisper, 'Stop this cab!' The driver, eyes not on the road but rather on the message displayed by a small LED display on his dashboard, ignored her.

Two Chinese workmen, long poles straddling their shoulders, heavy cardboard boxes roped and dangling at waist level, leapt aside. One screamed an unintelligible curse. The other slipped and rolled in the taxi's wake.

'Faster!' Mr Taft was positively growling. Zaitun tired to pull herself free of his grip. He tightened his arm, tugging her closer.

The driver, concentrating on the words scrolling across his dashboard screen, ran a red light at the corner of Hong Kong Street. Zaitun let out an involuntary shriek. Then she glanced at Mr Taft's face. He was showing his teeth, and that made things worse.

As the taxi roared past Hong Lin Park, its left bumper clipped the edge of a fortunately empty wheelchair being pushed by an orderly from the Thong Chai Medical Centre. Now traffic was thicker. The cab weaved its way in and out, rocketing among slower-moving vehicles, sometimes making three lanes of a road intended for two. Zaitun felt faint.

Then she noticed the LED screen of the taxi's on-board dispatch computer. The same terse words ticked across the screen over and over again: CAR 782 REDIRECT TO CPS PEARL HILL TERRACE . . . CAR 782 REDIRECT TO CPS . . .

'CPS? What's that mean?' Mr Taft's hoarse voice made Zaitun jump. She'd been asking herself the same question. The cab was headed south on New Bridge Road. The north lanes of the same avenue were called Eu Tong Sen Street. In this neighbourhood, Eu Tong Sen was flanked by the Great Southern Hotel and the People's Park office complex. Pearl Hill Terrace was right behind . . . oh yes . . . now she remembered. Utterly surprised, she blurted out the words, 'Central Police Station. That's where they're telling us to go.'

The driver flicked on his indicator, and began to slow.

Zaitun felt Mr Taft take his right hand out of his pocket.

Five minutes, ten seconds, and the nightmare has worsened.

Sweating, sleeping Jack is wrestling with himself, trying to claw his way back to wakefulness and to sanity. It is hopeless. He is paralysed, unable to move, powerless in the possession of a dream that has travelled far beyond the bounds of nightmare ordinary or extraordinary. In a procession of visions illuminated by shallow light, he sees things stir as if beneath the surface of a sewer, and is terrified to know that this sewer is his subconscious mind. These things – long repressed – are rising, hungry to feast on what heretofore has been denied them.

All that is wanted by the beasts, all necessary devices and desires, are ready to hand. A nubile woman, a ready weapon, satisfactory enemies, and the dark of night to cover it all.

– 11 –

'Got him!' The woman's voice snapped loud and clear over Chan Gin's handheld police radio.

'Tell me,' Chan ordered, lips tight and teeth clenched at the totality – the sheer magnitude – of this fuck-up.

'CityNet! No, SkyTrack! I mean . . .' The woman on the radio was an non-commissioned officer in the Singapore Police Force's communications centre, one of the seven on duty during the graveyard shift. She'd never walked a beat, never driven a patrol, and never confronted an armed and dangerous criminal. Now, from the remote safety of her computerized workstation, cozy in a blue-carpeted cubicle, she was helping the legendary Superintendent Chan Gin track down a gun-toting American hoodlum. It sounded to Chan like she was ready to wet herself.

'Calm down,' he snapped, voice hoarse with humiliation. Pacing like a caged tiger, back and forth in Raffles' bullet-scarred second-storey atrium, he snarled, 'Just tell me where the bastard is.'

'There's only been one pick-up at Raffles in the past hour, sir!' The words tumbled out of the woman's mouth. 'The cab company is on one of the satellite-tracking and dispatch systems! Full AVL – Automatic Vehicle Location! I've got their map display patched into my screen! It's overlaid on the TrafficScan system! This is great, Superintendent! I can see exactly where he is!'

Of course you can, you dumb bint, Chan thought. *That's the fucking point of all the millions of dollars the government spends on this computer shit. They want to see everything.*

'Are you sure it's him?'

Before she could answer, a second voice broke into the transmission. 'Sergeant Toy here, Superintendent. I'm with the doorman out front of the hotel. He says a man resembling the suspect took a taxi only minutes ago.'

Chan reached the end of the hall. He wished there was something to punch near by. There wasn't.

Details, he thought. *It's not one-on-one any more; it's teamwork, police procedures by the numbers, and details, details, details.* He spun on his heel. 'What taxi company?'

Chan heard Sergeant Toy prompting the doorman, who apparently didn't quite remember. 'Tibs? Comfort? CityCab? Star . . .? It was Star, sir. He's pretty sure.'

Chan glanced to his left. A shattered mirror, rococo gilt framed, lay in shards on the floor. The damned thing was an antique, priceless, maybe irreplaceable. And that was not the worst of the carnage. Chan swore beneath his breath. It was a disaster. And he had no one to blame but himself. He snarled into the radio, 'Did the doorman get the number?'

'No, sir.'

Chan hissed in frustration. 'You there, in the computer room, what's your name anyway?'

'Susan Lim, sir. Constable Lim, sir.'

One of the computer kids, Chan thought. He pursed his lips. He didn't much care for desk cops, but this time he needed one. 'OK, Lim, did you hear what the sergeant said?'

'Oh yes, sir. And I'm definitely tracking a Star fleet taxi. Car number seven-eight-two.'

Toy's voice came over the radio. 'The doorman's not sure, sir. Maybe Taft's cab was seven-eight-two, maybe not.'

'Maybe's good enough. Where is car seven-eight-two, Constable Lim?' Idly Chan counted the bullet holes in Raffles' doubtlessly expensive flooring and fixtures. Plaster from cratered walls crunched beneath his feet. This section of the hotel was going to need a lot of renovation before it was reopened to guests: a very costly, very visible public relations disaster for the Singaporean Government. Who hated Chan Gin to begin with. Who had been waiting a long time for him to screw up so badly that they could . . .

'New Bridge Road South, sir! The computer says he's exceeding the speed limit!'

'Ticket him later,' Chan snarled. 'Where on New Bridge?'

'Just north of the feeder into Kampong Bahru Road!'

Chan knew the neighbourhood. 'Get central dispatch, Lim. I want every cruiser in the central city on this! Stop him before he hits the expressway.'

'No need, sir.' Constable Susan Lim, snugly seated in a windowless room with *café au lait* walls and blue carpet, sounded far too smug. 'I sent a satellite message direct to the cab, sir. It's almost right by CPS, so I told the driver to –'

Lim's voice fell off. Chan felt his jaw tighten. Constable Computer Whiz had decided to show some initiative. That was unfortunate. It was *always* unfortunate when desk cops stuck their noses into real police work. Chan tried to keep his voice calm. 'What's going on, Constable?'

She sounded puzzled. 'The cab's turned round right in the middle of the Temple Street block. It's . . . stopped . . . it's . . .'

Chan fought to keep his voice level. That damned woman didn't have enough sense to order a roadblock. Instead she'd done something that, unless Chan missed his bet, was a calamity in the making. 'What? Come on, Constable, what's going on?'

'Oh dear,' whispered Constable Susan Lim.

Chan's patience was at an end. 'Goddamm it! Speak to me, Lim!'

'Sir . . .' she stuttered. 'Uh . . . it's . . . sir, he's disappeared.'

Chan asked very slowly, 'What do you mean "disappeared"?'

'He's off the screen. The cab is gone, sir.' She swallowed. 'It isn't on the computer map display any more!'

Seven minutes, twenty-nine seconds since Jack fell asleep.

He's almost awakened, is just below the surface of the sleep. Noise and tumult have raised him there. Flat and sharp, the horrible percussion of a pistol shot in an enclosed space. A clangour of tortured metal, crumpling in strident collision with stone. Screams. A fearful woman, the hiss of steam, boiling water from an exploded radiator, a shrill pedal-point to her cries. He thinks he should try to wake himself up. But a voice, there on the brink of consciousness, cautions him that slumber is the better choice. In wakefulness he will find awareness, and find memory. Best not to, yet. Best let things take their course. Recognition of what's been done will come, but let it not come too soon. Besides, Jack, it's all a dream; only a dream . . .

2
New York

– 1 –

No matter how large or small, all corporations consider it their duty to bring into the life of every worker some weekly ritual of tedium.

Such events invariably occur in conference rooms.

Conference rooms are the oubliettes of American office life;

sensory-deprivation chambers designed to isolate their inhabitants from the outside world and, therefore, render them immune to the unnecessary distractions of reality. They are windowless, lit by aseptic fluorescent light, and tiled with sound-absorbing floors and ceilings – accoutrements which police-state interrogators and middle management employ to much the same ends. Invariably furnished with a long table and chairs that do not lean back at relaxing angles, conference rooms are laid out with an obligatory whiteboard at one end, and a much desired exit at the other. Somewhere off to the side there will be a credenza of inexpensive make containing magic markers, pointers, spare bulbs for the slide projector, and other meeting supplies. Atop the credenza will rest a stack of styrofoam cups, chemical sweeteners, powdered cream substitutes, and a pot or two of institutionally odious coffee. There also may be a single telephone, a device at which the room's yawning inhabitants – three hours into a two-hour meeting – look wistfully, hoping that the thing will ring, that the call will be for them, and that the message will be that they are needed elsewhere.

No such luck.

The weekly ritual through which Gabrielle was obliged to suffer was unique to journalism. Called 'the story meeting', its ostensible objective was to allow editors and reporters to air ideas for future stories. Its equal, although unstated, purpose was to provide a forum for innuendo, backbiting, and character assassination.

Gabrielle hated office politics. She was a reporter. She researched and wrote stories. It was what she was good at, and all that she wanted to do. She'd reached the highest rung on her ladder of ambitions. Any further promotion would (*God forbid!*) propel her into the ranks of management, make her an editor rather than a writer, force her to supervise *other* people's reporting – a fate worse than death.

Loathing political games, and having a fine sense of what she should or should not be investigating, Gabrielle resented story meetings as a waste of time. She sat bemused, doodling on a note pad, and daydreaming.

Daydreaming again. About Jack Taft. About how he was both sexy and affectionate. Cuddly and erotic. Warmly romantic and downright dirty . . . a lethal package to be sure.

This guy, she thought, *is not the right guy, right? So then why has this guy turned into a problem?*

She'd never meant to get involved with him. He'd just been this man she'd once interviewed for a story. Something about intermodal freight. Boring story. Boring guy. But then what did you expect from a logistics director? Especially one who actually *boasted* that his was the dullest job in America.

But he knew his stuff; had it cold, every tepid fact and tedious figure in the wearisome world of international shipping. And so, the next time her editors assigned her a story about the transportation industry, she'd called him. He'd been more than helpful. Some weeks later, she'd phoned him again, this time for no particular reason.

And then again.

And so forth.

She started buying him lunch, and wouldn't you know he kept trying to pick up the tab. For a while she'd do it every month or two. Then every week or two. Pretty soon she started thinking of him as a friend. Only journalists don't have friends; they just have sources.

But suddenly there was Taft, and he was her friend, and pretty soon he was a damn sight more than that.

She asked herself, so what is it with this guy? Why was she spending time with him when she could be spending time with . . . well, the kinds of men she normally spent time with?

She was a prominent journalist with a prestigious magazine. The executive suite was her milieu; the magnates who dwelled on the top floor her customary companions. She travelled in high-testosterone, big-money circles, way up high on the corporate ladder where the power lay. And power, they say, is the most potent aphrodisiac.

God knows, she'd had offers. The heady deal-driven days of the 1980s were gone, and it was no longer fashionable for corporate czars to be seen with vacant-eyed mannequins clinging to their arms. But a successful, accomplished woman? Ah, that was another matter entirely. Such women were much in demand. Gabrielle could have had her choice of any number of wealthy, influential older men. And she'd been tempted. Picking the right protector could do wonders for any business reporter's career.

Instead, she'd picked Taft.

She still didn't know why.

Maybe because he was a bit of a puzzle. Journalists find puzzles hard to resist, and Taft was downright bewildering.

Turned out – once she got to know him – he wasn't entirely the dull drone he pretended. Far from it. He was smart, exceptionally smart, one of the smartest guys she'd ever met. Gabrielle interviewed *Fortune* 500 CEOs and *Forbes* 400 billionaires every day. She knew smart when she saw it. Taft was right up there in the major leagues. He had the same swift perspicacity and creative intellect as the best and brightest. But he was a logistics director, a corporate hack, a man who boasted of being the dullest of dullards and the most plodding of plodders.

Interesting.

He also claimed he was a risk-averse compromiser. Which was bullshit. She knew her way around office life, and she knew the jobs he tackled – which he always described in the most understated way – were politically explosive problems no ordinary middle manager would dare take on. But Taft did so. Then, low-key and self-deprecating, he made it sound like he'd really done nothing, and that all the credit belonged to somebody else. It was as if he wanted to hide his accomplishments from everybody, maybe even hide them from himself.

More interesting still.

And he was fun to talk to, too – but only if the subject was something other than the life and works of John Gregory Taft. Ask him about books, music, theatre, cats, whatever, and he was witty and provocative. Ask him a personal question and he clammed up, changed the topic, disappeared to the washroom, remembered a phone call he had to make, ducked the subject, dodged the bullet; and it drove her nuts.

A mystery man, an enigma, a goddamned puzzle, and he really got under her skin. Why did such a clever man pretend he was nothing but a wuss? Why didn't he strut his stuff rather than hide it? Why was he always the last to claim credit, the first to accept blame, and never so much as argue the merits of his case?

Investigative reporters love mysteries.

Which might just be the reason why she *thought* she'd fallen for Taft.

Yeah, she groused, *yeah. I've solved the puzzle. I know why he's the way he is. And, dammit, now I love . . . er . . . like him more than ever. Or do I? I mean, do I really? Am I fooling myself here? I mean, is this guy ever going to get his act together? I can't live with a guy with zero self-esteem, can I? I mean . . .*

The story conference droned on. Gabrielle, silently posing questions she could not answer, ignored it.

– 2 –

'Gabrielle?'

She was lost in thought: *You know, I could still dump him. It's not like he hasn't been dumped before. I mean Taft's got practice and—*

'Ms Dunn, if you please.'

Gabrielle looked up. She blinked. She blushed. At the head of the conference table Jonathan Harley Sutton – founder, publisher, and editor-in-chief of *EPS Magazine* – was frowning at her; the expression on his face was, of course, Jack Taft's fault, not hers.

'Oh? My turn?'

'Indeed.' Sutton's voice was frosty, and his jaw was set. Unlike others in the conference room, he treated story meetings as serious business. 'Having heard, and dispatched to the netherworld, proposals to publish pap about Canada Our Friend To The North, The Future Of Eastern European Currency, and The Prospects For Tax Exempt Funds In Latin America, I now look to you to recommend at least one story idea that will not cause our readers to expire from ennui!'

Consulting a notepad that contained no notes, Gabrielle said two words. The words were precisely the same ones Jack had spoken a few days earlier: 'Customs scams.'

Sutton peered over his half-frame reading glasses. 'Tax avoidance? Pray tell, what light can we shed that those villians at *Forbes, Fortune,* and *Business Week* haven't?'

The most annoying voice Gabrielle knew – faux-British and toadying – chimed in, 'Just so. I couldn't agree with Jonathan more. Tawdry little frauds make tedious reading.'

Gabrielle glared. *Sonofabitch!* She'd made sure that Simon Burton knew in advance what she was working on – and that he approved it. *The rotten rat bastard!*

But then what did she expect of someone as inhumanly loathsome as Simon. Looking – but for his odiously tiny teeth – like the very model of masculine Anglo-Saxon gentility, Simon was the editorial bane of her existence. He'd also been, to her undying chagrin, her lover.

'At. Least. Have. The. Courtesy. To. Hear. Me. Out.' She bit her words one by one.

Sutton leaned forward. 'Go ahead, Gabrielle.'

'But I suppose the least we can do is let you say your piece.'

Gabrielle gritted her teeth. He'd been making her life hell for a month, hacking her work to ribbons, belittling her story concepts, keeping all the plump assignments out of her reach. Now it was payback time.

'Tawdry little frauds, is that what you think, Simon? Well, my sources in the Treasury Department tell me customs evasion costs this country a hundred and fifty billion dollars in lost taxes every year, so I think "tawdry little frauds" understates things, don't you?'

Simon looked elsewhere. Jonathan leaned forward. 'What's your angle, Gabrielle? What spin do you see on it?'

'It's a double play. One, we whack Congress for not funding enforcement.' Jonathan Harley Sutton smiled. He loved denouncing Congress, even when a Republican majority was in power. 'Two, we name big names. It's not just the taxpayer who's getting hurt. There's one swindle going on that's ripping off the likes of Johnson & Johnson, Procter & Gamble, Quaker Oats, Duracell, and half the electronics guys in Silicon Valley.'

'And that is . . .?'

'Export diversion. The big multinationals price products differently in foreign countries – they do it to adjust for local law, taxes, distribution costs, competition, whatever. Something that may cost a hundred bucks in the US is maybe priced at eighty overseas. So you get these crooks who buy stuff at a big discount in this country claiming it's for export. Only it's not. It's sold here, black market and below market.'

'Hard to catch?'

'You bet. And one more thing – the best thing – Uncle Sam pays hefty incentives to exporters. So these guys, these crooks, not only rip off the largest companies in the country, but they also get Federal subsidies for doing it.'

'You're kidding!'

'I've got the name of one swindler who's collecting a quarter of a million dollars a month.' Folding her arms, Gabrielle leaned smugly back in her chair.

Jonathan Harley Sutton scribbled a note on his pad. 'I want you to run with this story.'

To which Simon fawned, 'That's exactly what I was going to say myself, Jonathan. The story's a perfect fit for Gaby. After all, she does enjoy a certain degree of *intimacy* with the shipping industry.'

– 3 –

'Simon, dammit, you said you'd support me on that story.' Gabrielle, her nose inches from Simon Burton's, was standing outside her small cluttered office.

'Oh, sorry.' Simon held up his hands at chest level in a gesture of mock surrender. 'I'd forgotten completely. Honour bright, it had slipped my mind.'

Like hell it had.

She'd been twenty-four, University of Colorado, MA Journalism, *Cum Laude*, and on her first job. She wrote stories for a holding company that owned a gaggle of trade magazines – one week she'd be covering the steel industry, the next pulp and paper, the week after that medical supplies. She was struggling to make ends meet on a twenty-two thousand-dollar salary, struggling harder to master her craft, struggling most of all to find a better job. Back in those days, the mid-1980s, Australia's Rupert Murdoch and Britain's Robert Maxwell were on acquisition binges, buying every American media company they could lay their hands on. Maxwell's organization – later bankrupt and disgraced, its flim-flam artist owner dead under suspicious circumstances – had bought her company. One of the contingent Maxwell had assigned to oversee the new acquisition was a gorgeously handsome Anglophile Australian named Simon Burton.

He'd dazzled her. Ten years her senior, square of jaw, buffed of body, faultlessly attired in the best Savile Row had to offer, and glibly eloquent (*oh, that well-practised Oxbridge accent!*), he was the strutting embodiment of masculine charm. And he knew it.

He'd stood courteously when she'd first entered his office. He'd held her chair when she sat down beside his desk. He'd handed her a handkerchief when he'd told her she was fired. Minutes later, he'd placed a call to a friend at one of the other Maxwell magazine companies, recommending that she be given a job interview. Then he took her out to the most expensive lunch she'd ever eaten.

When, two years later, she announced her intention to move out of his apartment, he'd placed another phone call. She was fired the same day.

A decade later, Simon showed up at *EPS*. Deputy managing editor, her new boss. And there he was again with his perfect upper-crust polish, his elegantly impeccable taste, his virile good looks, his lazy Michael Caine bedroom eyes . . . and his implacable appetite for getting exactly what he wanted. He was ever so single-minded, was Simon, and ever so persistent. *It's certain fine women eat a crazy salad with their meat,* thank you, William Butler Yeats, and damned if he hadn't seduced her again!

Only because she'd had too much wine at lunch.

Only because she'd been feeling pissy about Taft that week.

Only once.

Well, technically speaking, it was more than once.

But even once was one time too many.

Now it was over, five weeks over, and she hated the very memory of it. Even more, she hated Simon's refusal to let her forget. And his enthusiasm for an encore.

'Confession time, Gabrielle. Please do hear me out. It does not come easily to me, but I am here to apologise. I have misbehaved these past weeks, and I regret it. Do forgive me. Do let's be friends again.'

Gabrielle wrinkled her nose. 'You're forgiven. Just please don't—'

Needless to say, he did. 'It's a pity we couldn't make it work. My fault really. I know that now. No blame accrues to you, none at all. But let me say I do believe we had something special.' He smiled, showing his tiny baby teeth. The sight of them made Gabrielle shudder. 'The rare sort of thing one doesn't experience very often, which one remembers with a certain *tristesse* . . .'

'Like a yeast infection.' Gabrielle almost bit her tongue. The man was her boss. She should be making an effort to get along with him.

'Beg pardon?'

'Nothing.'

'You must admit, we are rather well suited to one another, don't you think?'

She was ready to say something that could cost her her job. Instead she said, 'Simon, I'd rather not talk about this.'

'Ah me,' he sighed. 'See here, Gabrielle, of late our working relationship hasn't been all it could be. There's a, shall we say, hint of acrimony between us. I accept my share of the blame, truly I do. But not all of the blame can be said, in honesty, to be mine.'

'Simon . . .' Her voice was rising.

'Let me finish, if you will. Past *contretemps* notwithstanding, and for old times' sake, I'll be the first to raise the white flag of truce. A peace offering, if you will. As it turns out, I've tickets for *Don Giovanni*. Sam Ramey is singing the title role. Have you seen him in the part? No? He makes the most of it, I assure you. Astonishingly good. Well, why don't you join me? We can have dinner at . . . oh, let me see, you were always fond of Thai food, weren't you?'

Gabrielle looked daggers at him. 'I have other plans.'

'My dear, I haven't even told you which evening.'

'All of them. I'm involved with someone else, Simon. And you know it.'

Burton touched a finger to his right earlobe. He made a small moué of distaste. 'Indeed. Chap's a glorified shipping clerk in the wholesale trade.'

Gabrielle's voice was rising higher. 'Simon . . .'

'In any event, your little shipping clerk should not be an impediment to two old friends passing a pleasant evening together. And since he *is* abroad for a while—'

'No, Simon. The answer is no. Capital "N", small "o".'

Burton smiled. Charmingly, of course. 'Ah well, so be it. But I did have to try, didn't I?'

Gabrielle mentally proposed – and swiftly rejected – a number of tart retorts. Instead she merely shook her head.

Simon glanced at his watch. 'Dear me! I must move on. But one last thing: this story of yours, this import–export fiddle; Jonathan seems quite taken with it. I think we should make it a featured article, perhaps a cover story, don't you? Four pages, or perhaps five to allow the lads in the art department ample room for illustration. That means you'll need to turn in five hundred, possibly five-fifty lines. How long do you think it will take you to report it?'

'Three weeks. Three and a half.'

'Then a week for me to edit it, another few days for the fact checkers and for Jonathan's review. Fine, let's say we run it in the November thirtieth issue.'

Gabrielle winced. 'That's awfully tight. A lot of the story is on the west coast – Seattle, Oakland, Long Beach. I'll have to work on it full time.'

'Just so. Drop everything else. Top priority and all of that. Get your inquiring mind out west soonest, leave tomorrow, and conduct the obligatory interviews. After all, since you were so *persuasive* in explaining to Jonathan why you were right and why I was wrong, tardiness would be bad form.' He spun on his heel, smiled 'Ta-ta,' over his shoulder, and walked away.

Swearing softly beneath her breath, Gabrielle stormed into her office, slamming the door behind. As she slumped into her chair, she noticed that no red 'Message Waiting' light blinked on her telephone. *No message from Jack*, she wondered. *That isn't like him. He always calls me when he's on the road. Gee, I hope he's doing OK.*

But of course he would be. Taft was always OK – no high, no lows, just even-keeled reliable, and unadventurous Jack. Which was, she knew, the *real* problem.

– 4 –

In a darkened boardroom, Olivia Thatcher checked her wrist-watch. LBTech's directors' meeting was behind schedule. Olivia, who loathed unpunctuality, would be late for drinks with Gabrielle.

Even more irksome, the person currently presenting a depart-mental summary to the Board of Directors was Denise Donald. At the last board meeting, three months earlier, Denise had been one of the two candidates the Board had considered promoting to Vice President of Logistics. Young Jack Taft, Gabrielle's beau (Olivia being of a generation that referred to a lady's lover in elliptical terms) had won the promotion by a vote of eight to one. Accordingly, *he* should have been today's speaker, not she.

'. . .where less-than-truckload carriers will save us five cents a ton.' Denise paused a perfect pause, the few well-timed seconds it took an executive audience to realize the speaker was preparing to conclude her remarks. Pressing a button on her remote control she concluded: 'Last slide. Recommendations. Net–net, LTL carriers can reduce our operating expenses by seven-tenths of a per cent . . .'

Even though young Jack was quite mysteriously (in Olivia's estimation) out of town, inviting one of his underlings to review departmental operations with the Board was a breach of protocol. Olivia wondered why Joel Greenberg, LBTech's CEO, had done it. Perhaps it was because he had backed Denise for the logistics vice-presidency. However, the other directors – showing uncommon independence for once in their lives – had voted for Jack. Now Joel was perversely putting Denise in the spotlight again.

'. . . coupled with an additional point-three inventory turns and stretching our payables by another eight to ten days, thus yielding an overall increase in cash flow of . . .'

It was tedious stuff, no different from all the other minutiae around which business life revolves. Nonetheless, Olivia acknowledged that Denise, unlike Jack, had a talent for making it seem interesting. The choice between Jack and Denise had not been easy. Denise was forceful, articulate, resolute. Jack was analytically brilliant and absolute master of his field. But both also had their weaknesses – Jack annoyingly acquiescent, and too compromising; Denise shallow and inaccurate. Which should it be: the good manager or the good mind? The Board decided on the intellect. Joel bridled at the choice.

'. . . yes, that's correct, Mr Ackerman. But I don't think it changes the conclusion in a meaningful way. However, we'll rerun our numbers tomorrow and get back to you. Are there any other questions? No? Well, thank you.'

Dear me, Olivia thought, *how very smoothly done that was. First 'I' don't think the mistake is significant. Then 'we' shall check 'our' math. Quite clever, and now Charlie and most everyone in this room will think it's one of Denise's minions who made the error.*

Denise, impeccably attired and attracting every eye in the room, strode out the door. The lights came up. Olivia took another peek at her watch. Charlie Ackerman, Secretary of the Board and master of its agenda, cleared his throat: 'Well, that seems to be the last item for the day. So if there's no further business, I'll ask for a resolution to adjourn until—'

'Actually there is further business.' Joel Greenberg, Chairman and Chief Executive Officer, rose. Olivia arched a disapproving eyebrow. Was Joel up to his old tricks again – springing last-minute surprises on the Board?

Charlie – a dithering idiot in Olivia's unspoken estimation – grovelled, 'Yes, Joel.'

Joel stood. Olivia watched him with distaste. An even six feet tall, lean and tanned and perfectly fit, he was handsome in the way snakes are handsome. And as cunning.

'The Board should be aware that shortly before we convened this meeting my office received a cash tender offer for LBTech and all its subsidiaries. The offer is a solicited offer – that is, after due negotiations, I invited it.'

Olivia inhaled sharply. It had only been six months since Joel had staged a palace coup, driving the company's founder, L. B. Tischman – Joel's own father-in-law – into retirement. Now, much sooner than she'd expected, Joel was moving on to the rest of his programme. Of that she was certain. Joel Greenberg planned to steal the company whole.

'A group of foreign trading companies has proposed an asset purchase priced at a thirty-five per cent premium over our present stock price. My secretary is making copies of the proposal – a rather lengthy document – and they should be available for the Board's review shortly. I feel obliged to say that I consider this offer generous. I believe it demands our serious consideration. Further, it is my—'

Her warm blue eyes suddenly glacial, Olivia interrupted him. 'What's *your* piece of the action, Joel? I think we should know that right now.'

Everyone at the table – four outside directors, three insiders, and Joel – turned towards her. Slender, with silver-shot ash-blond hair, more beautiful in her sixties than most women in their thirties, Olivia commanded attention under all circumstances, none more than when her blood was up.

'I was just about to disclose that, Olivia. Between my equity holdings and options, my personal profit will be . . . would be in the order of eight million dollars. Further, the buyers have offered me a five-year contract with a low-end value of another five million.'

'Upside?' shot Olivia.

'Difficult to estimate.'

'Try.'

'Forty million or more.' Joel frowned as somebody in the room whistled.

'I believe you should leave the meeting now, Joel. The Board will be better off discussing this matter in your absence.'

Charlie Ackerman had known Olivia for thirty years. He didn't even think about asking for a vote on the question.

3
Singapore

– 1 –

'Meat wagon's here,' Chan said.

Police Corporal Harold Leung gave his boss a perplexed look.

Cryptic at best, sometimes incomprehensible, Chan Gin did not speak like other Singaporean policemen. He had his own bizarre lingo, the peculiar patois of Hollywood cop thrillers. Most officers referred to suspects as 'the accused'. Chan called them 'perps'. Standard practice was to classify criminals by section numbers of the civic code. But not Superintendent Chan. In his bizarre dialect, a plain vanilla '354' – an offender against public modesty – became a 'weenie wagger'. If Chan had used Chinese slang – say, *ah cit* for informer – it wouldn't have been so bad. But no, an *ah cit* was in Chan-ese a 'snitch', 'stoolie', 'squealer', or whatever other uninterpretable neologism Sylvester Stallone had mumbled in the latest noisy movie to hit town. Chang's jargonized commands often left Harold Leung scratching his head.

'Ah . . . what kind of wagon was that, sir?'

'Meat wagon, Hal. The bag 'em and tag 'em team. They're right on time.'

Understanding only the part about being on time, Leung checked his wristwatch.

It was 3.56 a.m. Twenty-eight minutes since he, Chan and the now-dead Constable Liu had burst into the hotel room. Twenty-one minutes since the felon's taxi disappeared from the satellite-tracking system. Nineteen minutes since a dozen patrol cars had converged at the intersection of New Bridge Road and Temple Street. Eighteen minutes since they'd reported finding a crashed taxi, an unconscious driver, and no John Gregory Taft.

Taft had put a bullet into the cab's dashboard satellite transponder. The driver lost control. The American gangster fled into the night.

Now there was a sweep going on. Half the cops in Singapore were on the pavement; street by street, alley by alley, doorway by doorway – down in the Chinatown rabbit warren where Taft had made his getaway.

They wouldn't find him. Taft was a cop's worst nightmare: an iceman – fish-white skin, corpse-cold eyes, impassive and unblinking as, stolen guns in hand, he had backed out of his hotel room. The scary thug wasn't even breathing hard. Taft was special, a stone killer: rock hard, glacially intelligent, lethally emotionless. The only man on the force capable of dealing with a monster like that was Chan Gin. Who, thank God, was in charge.

Most definitely in charge. Hal Leung was only six months out of the academy – a draftee working off his two years' obligatory national service. Rookie that he was, he was more than merely honoured to have been assigned to the legendary superintendent's elite squad. No doubt his marksmanship rating had something to do with it – that and the fact he was a Chinese Christian, one of the privileged 14 per cent of Singapore's population who held 80 per cent of the important jobs.

Regardless of why he won the assignment, Leung found working with Chan a revelation. He was even braver than the newspapers claimed, and – truly a surprise given the superintendent's shoot-first reputation – a relentless investigator.

As soon as Taft disappeared from the cab, Chan had clicked his radio on, coolly ordering an army of officers into action. The case wasn't a simple arrest any more. Now it was a formal investigation – an *exhaustive* investigation, Chan Gin style. A half-dozen officers were downstairs grilling everyone who had encountered Taft: the bellman, the nightclerk, the doorman, and a kid from room service who'd delivered a snifter of brandy to his suite. Another team was on its way to Changi Airport, their mission to question the immigration and customs officers who'd cleared Taft; it did not matter that those officers might have exchanged only a half-dozen words with the man – at this point in the investigation everything was important. Two other members of Chang's squad were at Singapore Air's headquarters on Robinson Street; their job was to get the names and addresses of the crew from Taft's plane – pilots, stewardesses, ground crew, the whole lot, any one of whom might have noticed something that could break the case.

Meanwhile every available street cop – the 'Land Forces', to use the official lingo – was sweeping Chinatown, knocking on doors, rousing honest citizens from their sleep, asking whether anything unusual had happened – an odd sound in the night; something inexplicable in an alley; were you awakened by a noise, a movement, the sound of voices, a flash of light, by anything at all; did you happen to glance out the window; did you worry that someone had broken into your house . . .?

Take names, take addresses, take phone numbers, take notes . . . Here's my business card. If you remember something later, call us immediately. Yes, sir; yes, madam; every little bit of information helps. Sorry for the disturbance. Oh yes, one last thing: if anyone from the Western press happens to stop by, you'll slam the door in their face, won't you? Of course you will. You understand Policy-with-a-capital-P, and, after all, this *is* Singapore.

Police procedure – Chan's mastery of it rivalled his marksmanship. Being smart, he said, was important. Being thorough was better. The one place you forgot to look usually turned out to be the only place you should have looked.

In six months Leung had learned much from Chan Gin. Most of all he learned that the man the public worshipped as *Chenghaung* was the best cop he'd ever met.

– 2 –

His subordinates called him Chan. His mother called him Gin. The media, which Chan manipulated like a puppetmaster, called him by whatever nickname they'd plucked from the latest high-body-count action film. 'Dirty Harry', 'Terminator' ('T2' for short), he'd been called them all. While Chan welcomed the press's adulation – without it, the bureaucrats would have shut him down long ago

– the nicknames were another matter. The only one he'd liked was 'Tequila', a reference to the hero of the most popular Hong Kongese cop movie of the Nineties. Chan admired the fictional Tequila, and conscientiously modelled his style on the character's well-dressed, flippant, and wholly lethal screen persona.

But that had been years ago. These days the media no longer called Chan 'Tequila'. Now he was *Chenghaung*, in the Chinese pantheon the *genius loci* of cities, and high sheriff of hell. In other words, devil cop.

The Oriental concept of 'devil' had little to do with fallen angels or Lucifer Morningstar, but rather denoted a supernatural entity specializing in the administration of well-deserved retribution. Chinese devils were indefatigable instruments of vengeance, relentless in their pursuit of wrong-doers – and uncommonly violent in their rendering of justice.

Devil Cop. It worked.

Inside Taft's hotel room the medical examiner did his messy job. Five ambulancemen hovered near by, stretchers ready, black body-bags wide and waiting. Chan loitered impatiently until they were done. Only then could he examine Taft's belongings.

Pacing tiger steps, he prowled Raffles' darkened breezeways. Rounding a corner, he found three hotel employees – two Chinese, one Indian – talking in hushed tones to a foreigner with a notepad. As Chan approached, their jaws snapped shut. No surprise. Singaporeans simply didn't speak to foreign journalists, or if they did, they made sure they weren't overheard. Indeed, prudent citizens – Chan among them – never talked about official matters except in whispers, and then always glancing over their shoulders to make sure no one was eavesdropping. The government was everywhere, and bad things happened to those who were indiscreet.

The blabbermouths fled. Mulling over the slender facts of the case, Chan walked on. An anonymous tip, an e-mail message routed through one of those Internet services that protects the secrecy of the sender: *a hardcase with a briefcase is coming in on Sing Air 15.* But the bosses say don't bust the punk at the airport; tourists are worth six billion dollars a year to the economy, and we don't want them forming a bad impression of our perfect little country. Be so kind, Superintendent, as to arrest him at the hotel. Easy job, nothing to it, the guy will be woozy with jet lag. Taking him down will be a cakewalk.

Bad mistake. A Thai and a Filipino, Taft's local contacts, are waiting for the bastard. The Thai recognizes Chan – it's hard not to, given his media coverage in Singapore and neighbouring nations. Then bang-bang, and the world's thug population decreases by one. But Taft gets the drop on the good guys, scoops up their guns, and runs for it. Seconds later Chan walks into a firefight. The shooter, Taft's height and wearing a pale blue sports coat, is far enough away that Chan figures he *is* Taft. So Chan goes after him. Bang-bang, again. The thug count goes down another click, and this is not so bad a thing.

The Filipino – Chan thought hardest about him. *Pinoy* hoods were all cock and no balls – brave as lions if they were behind you but gutless pussies face-to-face and man-to-man. They weren't the sort to go looking for trouble outside their native land.

But this one had. Together with a crazy fucking Thai, Chan thought. Trigger-happy lunatics, that crowd – 80 per cent of Singapore's violent crimes were committed by visiting Thailanders.

A Thai and a *Pinoy*, two goddamned foreigners, imported muscle in a country which did not tolerate imported muscle. The last bunch of outsiders to make the mistake, the *fatal* mistake, of trying to encroach on Singapore had been a contingent of American Mafiosi from the Verasano mob. That was almost a decade ago. One night on his island's wild northeast coast, Chang had left their remains for the crocodiles.

Word gets out. Foreign mobsters kept away from Singapore.

So what, then, were two immigrant thugs doing in *his* city?

No answers. He'd have to think about that puzzle later. What he had to think about now was the exceptionally unpleasant fact that tens if not hundreds of thousands of dollars' worth of antiques had been shot to shreds in a landmark hotel. Not covering it up. It isn't like the guests won't notice. More bad news: one dead cop, stolen police firearms, a ruthless felon loose on the streets; and Chan Gin himself, self-made media darling and always front-page news, brought low in an exceptionally high-profile way.

It was a disaster. Chan was a living contradiction to the image –
a kinder, gentler Singapore – the powers-that-be tried to impress
on the outside world. They'd wanted to put him out of business for
a while. Now they had the excuse they needed. Unless Taft was
brought to justice quickly, Chan's career was at an end.

Equally important – no, truth to tell, *more* important – the man
had disgraced Chan, made him lose face in front of the press, the
public, and his very own handpicked team. There was only one
way for Taft to make amends for that particular sin: get very dead
very fast.

Which could be arranged.

But first he had to track the fucker down.

Where would Taft go? Who would he look to for help?

Chan thought about it. *Yeah, who? Southeast Asia's underworld
is a protected market. Our local warlords don't like outsiders
poaching on their territory. Interlopers like Taft – unless they're
doing business with one of the natives – get floated out on the
morning tide. So Taft's no fool bound to have a go-between, an
authorized and licensed franchisee in Singapore. And I bet I know
who.*

Poh Kay Siong. The last of his kind in Singapore. The nation's
sole surviving *Tsung li*, its only real kingpin. Poh was the one hood
big enough to deal with a man like Taft. And, coincidentally, the
only gangster with the balls to import two foreign gunmen.
Carrying guns in Singapore was a hanging offence. The nation
took firearms so seriously that even brandishing a *toy* pistol got
you five years in Changi Prison.

So it had to be Poh. The rest of Singapore's penny-ante mobsters
were too timid to let hired hands pack heat. No question about it,
the two dead scumbags were Poh's emissaries to Taft.

Good news, in a way. Chan had been after Poh's head for a long,
long time. So far the cunning bastard had eluded him. He'd always
had an alibi. Or the evidence was flawed. Or witnesses disappeared. Or the prosecutor dropped the case for no good reason
at all.

For as many years as Chan had been a cop, and for more years than that, Poh Kay Siong beat the rap.

But maybe not this time. Taft was a major bad guy. Major bad guys left Singapore off their itinerary unless something big was going on. And big meant Poh. Chan almost smiled at the thought. Taking Taft down would save his ass. Taking down Poh would be the capstone of his career.

Suddenly unable to help himself, Chan laughed out loud. *Hell! If I bust Poh and bag Taft they'll have to pin a medal on me. Goddamn, wouldn't that piss the big boys off!*

– 3 –

No more than fifteen kilometres east and north of where a baffled Harold Leung listened to his superior's booming laughter, the *Jade Lady* rocked gently at her berth on Singapore's Pasir Ris coast. She was seventy-two feet long, a twelve million-dollar Bertram yacht powered by twin Detroit Diesel two thousand-horsepower engines, and equipped with every luxury money could buy.

Poh Kay Siong could buy whatever he desired, although – the sorrow of his life – certain things were not for sale.

He was lean, narrow shouldered, graceful, and few who met him guessed his years – seventy-three now, although he looked no more than sixty. He bore age well; the only hints of its price were some few lines etched into his cheeks, and a certain weariness that sometimes dulled his otherwise lively eyes.

As was the case at this sleepless hour.

Poh stood upon *Jade Lady*'s bridge, sipping oolong from an antique cup and listening attentively to a quite illicit police radio receiver. He was dressed, as ever, in a tastefully subdued black silk suit, an impeccably tailored Sea Island cotton shirt, glowing John Lobb loafers, and a quietly understated tie, cinnabar in colour with a lampblack dragon motif. The tie was cut of four hundred-year-old Thai silk, seventy-five dollars a square yard. A recent widow had given Poh a bolt of the cloth, although not willingly, in part payment of her late husband's unfortunate gambling debts. There remained a sizable balance due. The woman had a five-year-old son; Poh was confident she'd find the money somehow.

The money was not important; the principle was.

The same could be said of his present embarrassment. The income provided by the American woman, annoyingly assertive as Western women felt obliged to be, was less significant than the relationships her ingenious scheme made possible. The first to ally itself with Poh was the Mong Tai Army, depressingly vulgar but a *sine qua non* of doing business in Laos, Cambodia, and Myanmar. Now the Green Gang, China's secret sempiternal rulers, the Reds notwithstanding, had opened negotiations. Why, even the Sanoh Society, most progressive of Japan's Yakuza, had dispatched a tattooed diplomat for elliptical exploratory discussions.

All jeopardized by the oafish inefficiency of underlings.

Poh pressed his lips together. As *Tsung li* of the Seventy-Eight Dragons, the last, really, of Singapore's once great *chiu chow* brotherhoods, he could ill afford this faux pas. Too much was at stake. Balance and order had to be restored.

But how? Things were, when all was said and done, an utter botch. A Singaporean policeman had been killed in the line of duty, the first in so many years. The government would seek costly vengeance for that blunder. Add to this the dangerous and unpredictable Superintendent Chan Gin, the annoying matter of Mr Taft's briefcase, the most distressing escape of Taft himself, and one had the makings of a difficult situation.

Solutions to such problems were easier in the old days. Then – the British departed, Singapore floundering between independence and subjugation to Malaysia – the *chiu chow* brotherhoods, prosperous Triads and Tongs, settled business affairs with forthright directness. A hatchet to the neck, a torso deposited beneath a rival's window, a small and unimportant race riot fomented in a poor neighbourhood – these once most efficacious methods were now sadly unworkable in a society with no qualms, no qualms whatsoever, about eradicating those who employed them.

Other stratagems were required.

Poh had already ordered the manufacturing of evidence to implicate Taiwan's Ah Kong syndicate in the shooting at the hotel. The Green Gang, the Ah Kong's fiercest rival, would appreciate the gesture, and the resulting confusion at police headquarters would purchase some time.

That, Poh reflected, *leaves Taft. And the strident Miss Donald, she who seems to trust me so little as to do something nasty to Mr Taft's briefcase. Had she not meddled in this matter, Mr Taft would have been dispatched, the authorities would think it a simple hotel robbery, and all would be well. Instead her rash action – not the first of her irritating miscalculations – has attracted Chan Gin's never welcome attention to what should have been a simple business affair.*

Ah me, Chan Gin. Again, Chan Gin. All these years, Chan Gin. What shall I do about him? He is immune to the commands of my few remaining allies in the upper world. Dispatching him, or any officer of the law, is quite out of the question. Yet too much is at stake to allow him to interfere. As he will do unless action is taken. So immoderate is his hatred of my brotherhood that he will never relent. Nor has he ever been a man who could be suborned.

That which cannot be bent must therefore be broken. But how? No easy solution presents itself. Here is a predicament, a dilemma, and a danger.

Sipping tea, staring into the night, Poh sought solace in ancient wisdom. And as he searched his memory, an old saying came to him. *Lu yao zhi ma li, ri jiu jian ren xin* – distance tests a horse's strength as time reveals a man's heart. There was truth in the proverb, great insight, and perhaps a key to the present puzzle. For, unless Poh misunderstood his greatest enemy, the heart of Chan Gin had never been revealed.

Reveal the heart of Superintendent Chan, he thought. *Quite so. Here is the solution to many difficulties.*

Better to let an unbending man destroy himself than to do it yourself.

And more gratifying.

THREE: THE COURTESY OF DEATH

All men dream, but unequally. Those that dream at night in the dusty recesses of their minds awake the next day to find that their dreams were just vanity. But those who dream during the day with their eyes wide open are dangerous men; they act out their dreams to make them reality.

T.E. Lawrence – *The Seven Pillars of Wisdom*

SOCRATES: . . . there is a further stage of the evil in which a man is not only a life-long litigant, passing all his days in the courts, either as plaintiff or defendant, but is actually led by his bad taste to pride himself on his litigiousness . . . he not knowing that so to order his life as to be able to do without a napping judge is a far higher and nobler sort of thing.

Plato – *The Republic III*

1
Singapore

Though he told no one, not even Gabrielle, he would have preferred to be called John, not Jack. However – a small lie, an insignificant disguise – he pretended to like his nickname, urged everyone to use it.

Jack, not John, was a more ordinary sort of name, and to his ears it made him seem more down-to-earth, really just one of the guys.

He wasn't. Never had been. He was different, and learned early that those differences were best kept hidden.

At the age of eight, report card in hand, he walked proudly into his Astoria, Queens, home. His father, a chemist with Brooklyn Gas, sat expressionless on the living-room sofa, studying the latest copy of *Chemical and Engineering News*. Jack presented him the report card together with a note from the principal. The report card contained nothing but 'A's. The note recommended that Jack be advanced a grade. Jack's father frowned. 'You're no better than anybody else; quit trying to be a show-off.' Then he went back to his magazine.

At the age of twelve, Jack's father taught him how to play chess. The two would play a single game every Saturday evening. It was the only real time they spent together, and they spent it in silence. At the age of fifteen, Jack won his first game. He won again on the following Saturday. His father never played chess with him again.

He was allowed to apply only to City College of New York, CCNY, denied permission to seek admittance to those more prestigious schools his teachers recommended. After class, he commuted to New Jersey, worked as an apprentice longshoreman, earning his tuition, his books, and his living expenses. From these wages, his father extracted a sum agreed by both giver and taker to be fair reimbursement for lodging and food. His grades were never discussed.

At age twenty-one, he graduated. His mother came to the ceremony; his father did not. By then Jack had accepted the first job offered him. Thereafter, he never considered changing companies.

At the age of thirty-eight, while walking east on Seventy-eighth Street, he found himself threatened by two knife-wielding muggers. He put up his hands, politely told the pair in which pocket they might find his wallet, and averted his eyes as they removed it. The better to avoid trouble, he did not report the incident to the police.

At the age of forty-two, after some twelve hours of drug-induced sleep, John call-me-Jack Taft remembered what he had done the night before. He thought he'd gone mad.

At first he didn't know where he was.

He was sweating, as he always did when bad dreams came; was drenched with perspiration because this time it seemed no nightmare, but the real and undoubted thing.

He was with Gabrielle in her tiny West Side apartment. I'm not worthy of you, he said, at last confessing to his greatest fear. She – clear green eyes that he adored – gave him a fixed and level look, answering, *That's true; you're not*. He could only nod because he'd known it all along. Then, pointing a finger as she often did when stating the self-obvious, she continued, *I need more than a man like you can give me. That's why I've decided to become the mistress of the chairman of the city's wealthiest investment banking house. He's powerful and he's rich and he's all the things you'll never be. He's promised to introduce me to the people I want to write stories on – presidents and prime ministers and the chief executives of every large corporation in the world. All you can do is introduce me to shipping managers. And because he's involved in so many companies, he only has to make one phone call to any of the magazine's important advertisers, and they'll put pressure on Simon, and I'll never see a story of mine killed again.*

You could never do anything like that for me, Jack, you could never carry me up to the top of the social ladder either. You could never give me much of anything.

You're right. All I could do is give you love, and love is never enough . . .

He snapped awake, sick with misery because he knew, because she'd told him, that she'd been propositioned by such a man, and been offered all those things; and he, Jack, was afraid he could detect in her voice a hint, just the faintest note, that perhaps she wondered whether being with a man who wielded such power and influence wouldn't be very nice indeed . . .

Bad dreams. It had been a night of phantasm and nightmare. He couldn't remember any but the most recent, although he knew they'd all been horrible. The only way to get them out of his system was to shake his eyes open, get out of bed, forget the fears, and commit himself – yes, *commit!* – to being the sort of resolute and successful man whom Gabrielle deserved.

He'd do that. No more compromises and no more going along to get along. He'd start today. This very morning. As soon as he got to the office.

He was going to the office today, wasn't he?

No, that didn't seem right. There was something else he should be doing, some other place to which he was supposed to go.

Not quite ready to open his eyes, he puzzled over a question that suddenly and inexplicably had popped into his mind: hadn't he already travelled there?

The mattress upon which he was lying felt different, softer than the one in his Seventy-eighth Street apartment. His head rested on a foam rubber pillow; but he hated foam rubber, bought big over-stuffed goose-down things to which, unfortunately, Gabrielle was slightly allergic. Then, too, an air-conditioner was humming near by. That didn't make sense. It was October, cool in New York, no need to turn the temperature down.

He opened his eyes.

Utter mystification – he recognized nothing.

Of course, such had happened before. It is the not uncommon although always unnerving by-product of too much business travel: two weeks on the road, a different hotel every night, long hours coupled with treks across multiple time zones; never enough sleep, always too much drink – inevitably those who overdo the regime waken confused and not entirely remembering where they are.

This was different.

Jack rubbed his gritty eyes. No question, he was *not* in a hotel. Hotels don't use frilly chenille bedspreads. Nor seat plush teddy-bears on the nightstand.

Then, too, there was the question of the furnishings, dimly seen by curtained light, unquestionably feminine. A small vanity table covered with lacy cloth. More of the same atop a tiny dresser. A rattan lounger nearly invisible beneath flowered pillows. Even the lamp on the bedstand looked like something a woman rather than a man would buy.

No question, Jack was in a woman's apartment. In bed to be precise. And neither the apartment nor the bed was Gabrielle's.

Bad news. All the evidence suggested that he had gotten himself into some sort of . . . well, situation.

But what situation? And with whom?

He shook his head, trying to clear its sleep-clogged confusion. Where was he? How had he ended up there? Who owned (or at least occupied) these surroundings, smelling sweetly of unfamiliar perfume?

Jack was utterly baffled. He had not the faintest memory of the night before – it had to have happened at night, didn't it?

'Oh God,' he prayed with whispered anguish. If Gabrielle found out about this, he was a dead man. *What to do?* he thought, promptly answering himself: *Get out of here fast!* He paused, reflecting that while making a surreptitious escape from the bed of an accidental lover was far from gentlemanly, it prudently sidestepped the possibility of further . . . well, situations.

Jack swung his legs on to the floor. To his surprise, he still had his pants on. Likewise shoes, shirt, and seersucker jacket.

A hopeful expression flitted across his face. *Maybe*, he reflected, *there hadn't been a situation after all. Maybe he had been in an accident, or had drunk too much. Maybe someone from the office had steered him to the nearest bed. Or maybe . . .*

The phone on the nightstand rang. Reflexively, Jack picked it up. He tried to say, 'Hello', but his tongue was thick, his mouth horribly dry, and his throat so scratchy that he might have had laryngitis. All that came out was a squeaky croak.

A boasting macho voice – a voice like Simon Burton's – boomed, 'Miss Samsudin? This is Police Superintendent Chan Gin, CID.'

Jack bleated a high-pitched, 'Uh?'

'We've been trying to reach you all day. We have some questions we need to ask you. The need is urgent. I'm at the Tampines police post, and can be at your flat in . . . oh, traffic's light at this time of the day, it won't take long.'

Jack's blood froze. Images – not yet memories – flashed before his open eyes: murky pictures, dim and doubtful, indistinct shadows faded like old photos left too long in the sun. He did not know what they were. Yet for all their ambiguity, he knew they were more terrible than he could imagine, grey ghosts of bad dreams somehow trespassing on waking hours.

'I'm sorry for the inconvenience, Miss Samsudin. I'll try to take as little of your time as possible. While you're waiting for me, I'd like you to think about one of the passengers on last night's flight from San Francisco, a man named Taft.' As Chan spoke his name, Jack heard the policeman's tone turn hard and hollow, and now the memories of how he'd first heard it flooded back. 'John Gregory Taft.' Chan bit each syllable hard, lurking fury in his voice. 'Anything you might remember about him could be useful. I'll see you shortly.'

Chan hung up. Jack sat on the edge of the bed, the phone trembling in his hand. Only that single hand moved. Every muscle in his body was numb, frozen immobile in the grip of horror at his memories.

It had all happened. He'd done it. God knows how, but it had been him, and it had been no nightmare. Those men . . . the guns . . . the shooting . . . the dead man falling on his back . . . the pistol right under his nose . . .

Oh Christ! They'd been cops! No badges, no uniforms, plainclothesmen! He'd stood up. They'd turned to face him, paled, and let their weapons tumble to the floor. They thought he'd got the drop on them. But he hadn't. True, he'd picked up that pistol, the dead man's, had it in his hand, but he wasn't pointing it at them.

Was he?

Then – *Jesus, Jesus, Jesus!* – he'd snatched more guns from where they'd fallen.

And strolled out the door. Ambled around a corner. Jogged down a breezeway and . . .

His blood was up and he felt strong. Belly a furnace hot with hunger. Stalking animal. Predator. Mad, quite mad. And loving every minute of it.

Had that been him? Jack Taft, werewolf by night? No, no, no! He kept no animal inside him, or if he did it was chained, muzzled, locked behind bars. Nor did he ever let anger rise. Temper always subdued, he swallowed insult, smiled at affront, sympathized with the other person's point of view; spoke softly and sought logical compromise. He was good old non-confrontational Jack, and he never lost control. So, no, absolutely not, whatever beast prowled the halls of Raffles Hotel was not, could not, could never be, him. He wasn't the sort of man to . . .

Do what? What is it that I did? I didn't go back. I ran; no, walked, and put one gun in my pocket and tossed the others into the bushes. Then . . . then . . . there was something with a taxicab . . . there was someone else too . . . who? . . . He couldn't quite remember . . . didn't want to remember. But it couldn't have been worse . . . or could it? . . . no, no, no nothing could have been worse than the deranged exhilaration that had gripped him.

How could he have flouted police authority, stolen weapons, felt so gleefully violent? That wasn't him, wasn't quiet, analytical Jack.

But God help him, it was!

And why? Not why had he gone temporarily insane. But rather why had three policemen come crashing into his hotel room with guns in hand as if he was some sort of crazed desperado? He'd broken no law, or at least none that he knew of. How the hell many laws could he have broken in the space of a twenty-minute cab ride from the airport? It was nuts to think he'd broken any laws. But, if he hadn't, then why, why, why had they . . .

It was his briefcase. They were interested in his briefcase. Were they looking for something? What? Contraband? Did they think he was smuggling in illicit currency or pornographic videos or narcotics or communist propaganda or . . . *oh hell* . . . chewing gum? Right, same as pigeon feeding, chewing gum was a harshly punished crime in Singapore. Jack sometimes chewed sugar-free spearmint on long flights, but, law-abiding citizen that he was, this trip he'd left it at home. Besides, smuggling prohibited candy wasn't exactly the sort of offence that got a SWAT team's adrenaline pumping. *Hey, Fred, we got a Juicy Fruit incident over on Fifty-Third Street, break out the riot guns, get the dogs, and . . .*

He brought himself up short. *This isn't helping.* He had to think about the briefcase. But there was nothing to think about. He carried the usual things in it, nothing special at all, merely the ordinary paperwork generated by the ordinary bureaucracies of ordinary corporations the world over. There was nothing in the bag that would interest the police, nothing incriminating, nothing that broke the law.

Or at least what he knew about the law . . .

I'm in another country, a stranger in a strange land, a foreigner who doesn't know much about local law and custom. But the country is Singapore, for God's sake, the safest and most orderly society on the planet. It isn't someplace where the authorities shoot you just for the fun of it – Bosnia or Lebanon or East Los Angeles or someplace like that. And it sure as hell isn't some marginalized third world tyranny run by a flaky Führer wannabe. Christ, it's free market central, Reaganomics without the deficit, Clintonomics without the taxes. No tariffs, minimum bureaucracy, great work-force, the World Economic Council rates Singapore the best place in the world to do business, which is all I'm trying to do here only I can't because all of a sudden I'm a wanted man! Me! Jesus wept! I'm a wanted man!

Preposterous! He wasn't a lawbreaker! There had to be another explanation for last night's . . . mistake. Yeah, mistake. That's what it was. A misunderstanding. The cops thought he was some-one else, a visiting Mafioso or Colombian drug lord or some who-knows-what-kind-of psychopathic hoodlum, wanted dead or alive and shoot to kill. These things happen. You read about them in the newspaper. A DEA team crashes into some little old lady's apartment because they've got the wrong address. An accountant from Westchester gets picked up off the street because he's wearing the same colour shirt as a guy who just stuck up a liquor store. Then you get red-faced officials stuttering excuses to the *Live at Five* Action News Team, and the mayor writes a letter of apology, and a year or two later the courts give the little old lady or the accountant a couple of hundred grand, and that's that.

It was a mistake. The cops had come after the wrong guy. The whole thing was a screw-up. Once they knew about it, it would be heh, heh, heh, and sorry, sir.

Except that he'd stolen their guns, and turned fugitive from justice!

Oh my God!

Jack Taft, phone still clutched in his hand, still shuddering with fright, whispered an understatement: 'I think I'm in a little trouble here.'

He had to get out of here, wherever the hell 'here' was.

There was only one sane thing to do: find the American Embassy. He was an American citizen. The embassy would help him sort this mess out. The icy paralysis of terror was ebbing away now. He was able to move now. And to think.

And to recognize that he'd been sitting like a stunned rabbit for God only knows how long while an angry-sounding cop was headed his way.

He dropped the telephone back in its cradle, and stood. A needle of pain shot through his groin – his bladder was agonizingly full. He could barely walk, hadn't urinated for more than half a day. Police or no police, his first priority was finding a bathroom.

Jack hobbled to a door, pulling it open on a minuscule living room. Afternoon sunlight poured through an uncurtained window. He caught glimpse of a tiny sofa barely big enough for two, a coffee table, bookcase, and two stereo speakers. The toilet wasn't in that direction. He turned. There was another door at the opposite side of the bedroom. Jack pressed his legs together, scurrying urgently towards it.

He jerked the door open, felt for a light switch, and flicked it on.

It was the bathroom all right; but for a tiny, curtained bathtub it was no bigger than an airplane toilet, and it was what he needed. *Thank God!*

Jack lifted the lid with one hand, unzipping his fly with the other. Then he let himself go. As the stream of urine geysered into the toilet, a voice said, 'Mmmpffff!'

Jack jerked. He almost spun on his heels. Modesty and the immediacy of long-delayed relief stopped him. Instead, he finished, shook himself, and refastened his fly.

'*Mmmpffff!*'

The voice was coming from the bathtub, coming from behind the curtain. He reached out a hand, squeezing a fold in the bath curtain between two fingers. Then, vary warily, he lifted a corner.

There was a woman in the tub.

Dressed in tight blue jeans and a man's dress shirt that had come all bunched up around the amber skin of her belly – Jack thought she was one of the most bewitching creatures he had ever seen. Or rather she would be had it not been for the expression on her face, a mixture of naked fear and bitter fury. *No wonder she's angry*, he thought, *the poor girl's bound and gagged with her wrists tied to a faucet. Now how could that . . .*

Jack stumbled back. All at once he remembered the rest of the previous night, and what had happened *after* he'd fled from his hotel.

He felt it again: the vertigo of approaching insanity, the panicked fugue that paralyses – it was so overpowering that he wanted to crawl beneath the blankets, hide in the dark, pretend if he closed his eyes it would all go away.

It was not going to go away.

– 2 –

'Look, I'm sorry. I swear to God, you don't know how sorry I am.' Jack was begging. 'Now would you please, please, please not scream.'

'*MMMPPPFFFF!*'

He was bent over, extending his hand towards the white adhesive tape crisscrossing her lips, and the balled-up hosiery stuffed into her mouth. She flinched, and jerked her head to the side.

Which was what he would do, he supposed, if he was in her position. After all, he'd kidnapped the poor girl at gunpoint. And that wasn't the half of it . . .

In a cab barrelling towards police headquarters, he – crazy like a dog gone bad – pulled a pistol from his pocket to frighten an already frightened cabby. And the stupid thing went off. He didn't know how. Suddenly *Bang!* there was a big hole in the dashboard, and God help him he had smiled! The taxi veered into a mid-street spin, jolting over a kerb and slewing through the window of something called The Christian Conscience Bookstore. Cheaply printed books scattered on to the sidewalk; a ceiling fan crashed through the windshield; the driver's gashed forehead bounced against a now-warped steering wheel. And, with steam boiling out of its shattered radiator, the cab slammed to a stop. Smiling fiercely, he burrowed the barrel of the stolen revolver into *whatsername? Zaitun, that's right,* Zaitun's side, forced her out of the cab, and told her goddammit she'd better take him to her apartment, take him right now. Forcing her to run by his side, he sprinted through a maze of darkened streets, each block an obstacle course of narrow sidewalks, trees and bushes sprouting from the very walls of ancient buildings, sleeping parrots chained to perches, pedal-powered rickshaws parked by gates and grills, chairs and tables in front of tiny *al fresco* food stalls, cardboard boxes piled high in front of stores, trash cans waiting for early morning garbage trucks, and all the while Zaitun weeping and panting out of breath, and he, no longer Jack Taft but rather somebody else, cool and calm and not even winded. Arches, Jack saw arches, pleasing geometry endless in a line. Up a step, down a step, another arch. They were low, too, and his head brushed awnings already lowered for the day's cooking of paper-thin pork wafers, peddling of shoes and shirts and tourist bric-a-brac. At the top of one block the last few food-hawker stalls had just shut down; at the bottom, an industrious merchant, up before his competitors, was arranging his wares – cheap Indian safari jackets and trays of costume jewellery. Jack's passing tipped a case of counterfeit Rolex watches to the ground. The merchant cursed. Jack was gone.

It didn't look Chinese, this Chinatown; no pagodas, no curved roofs of green-glazed tile; it was only a nondescript zone of narrow streets lined by two- and three-storey buildings, pastel louvred windows on the upper levels, plain-jane shopfronts below. It might have been the borders of New Orleans' French Quarter, some older town in Baja, California, La Paz perhaps, but the Exotic East, no, it was too ordinary for that. And Jack kept running hard, pulling a woman nearly breathless with hysteria.

Then a subway entrance: **MRT** in bold letters, 'Mass Rapid Transit' and a red circular logo beneath it; escalators down from the street into a brightly lit, granite-floored tunnel. A sign: 'National Holiday, Extended Hours'. He paused there, thinking hard. White middle-aged New Yorkers don't willingly brave the subway late at night. Daring the trains during the wolf hours of early morning is an undertaking of uncertain hazard, dicing with destiny and tempting fate. For who is up and about in New York City at 4 a.m., and upon what dubious errands do they go? But there was a sound of sirens in the distance; Zaitun seemed utterly cowed, and he wasn't cautious Jack but rather an outlaw, Mad Dog Taft, armed and dangerous, and he knew no fear. With gun hand in pocket, he descended. All was clean; blindingly white-tiled walls, no litter on the floor, no sticky patches of chewing gum either. It was air-conditioned here, cooler than the streets above, and the only sound that could be heard was the whisper of well-lubricated escalators. No bad-eyed crazies lurked in shadows. No hunted-looking night owls cowered near tollbooths, the better to find safe harbour. Menace seemed wholly absent, and Jack, his New York-bred senses quivering, felt doubly suspicious of that. Zaitun pumped a few coins into a machine. Two tickets popped out. She led him through computerized turnstiles, down on to the platform for the northbound line. A train hissed into the station. Burnished steel doors sighed open. Clutching his pocketed pistol tightly, Jack hustled his prisoner aboard. A handful of passengers sat demurely in moulded plastic seats. Most read newspapers or magazines; one young couple talked in earnest whispers; a brown-skinned Muslim matron in scarlet scarf, gold bangles everywhere, stood erect in an ankle-length dress, holding more casually than any female New York subway rider a handbag the size of a picnic basket. At the end of the car, a pretty Chinese woman chatted on a cellular phone while simultaneously checking the readout on her digital beeper – was she a call girl with insomniac clients? Jack couldn't even guess.

No one so much as looked at him. He felt no apprehension, and recognized this was an unusual sensation for a New Yorker riding the subways at night. The train sped north. It was a remarkably quiet ride; no shriek of tortured metal, no jolting or flickering light. And the cars were cool and spotless, without so much as a scrap of paper on the floor or a blotch of graffiti on the walls. There were, however, signs: ads, mostly for push-up bras, but also maps in many languages, cautions about the size of the fines levied on those who smoked, ate, drank, or misbehaved on trains, and a very large warning to admirers of the Orient's most malodorous delicacy: 'No Durian Fruit Allowed On MRT'. Having become a man he did not know, Jack was disquieted by a world he did not understand. There were no transit police gingerly patrolling the trains, vigilantly watchful, hands resting on sidearms, ready for the worst. There seemed to be no need for them. At the sixth station, Toa Payoh, Zaitun led him off the train, through a tunnel tiled in sunflower yellow, and on to an escalator. Then he was on the streets, in a neighbourhood of wide avenues, towering trees, ten-storey apartment buildings surrounded by small parks and tidy playgrounds. All brightly lit; all too dark and dangerous to Jack's suspicious way of thinking. But somewhere, not far away, he could hear the low rumble of late night traffic on an expressway, and the streetlights showed no danger, and he forced Zaitun to run and run until they reached her building, the ground floor given over to shops shuttered with flimsy metal grilles, up above all windows black, and all silent inside and out. The girl's apartment was on the fourth floor. He was fading then, sinking into irresistible sleep.

Still, he knew what had to be done, and so he did it. Wolf-happy and smiling.

Now he was awake again, looking at his handiwork, and wishing that he could find the words to explain to this lovely young woman that it had all been a hellish mistake.

She probably wouldn't buy it. He had to try anyway. 'Look,' he said, 'I know you're, uh, scared, and probably, well, upset—'

'MMMPPPFFFF!'

Wrong thing to say. Try again. 'Aw, Jesus, I don't know what to say. I . . . er . . . this is not like you think. I mean . . . I really wasn't quite myself last night. Uh, look, I'm sorry, I'm really, really sorry, and I know you won't understand, but . . .'

No, she would not understand. He could see that in her face. She felt nothing but hatred, pure and unrefined. 'OK . . . I mean, OK. All I want to do is take the gag off. Right? That's all. Honest. I only want to ask you a question or two. I'm in a lot of trouble, and I just need a little help. Swear to God. This . . . this . . . what I did last night, tying you up and all of that . . . Jesus! . . . it's . . . there were these men after me. They almost got me. They wanted to . . .'

The tiniest glint of an unformed question flickered in Zaitun's eyes. Jack knew he had to take advantage of it, and knew he had to lie. 'I don't know who they were. They broke into my room. I managed to get one of their guns.' He felt into his pocket, and pulled out a revolver with chequered wooden grips. 'This one.'

Beneath her gag, Zaitun squealed. Jack held the weapon by the barrel, between two fingers, and quickly dropped it in the sink. 'I'm not the kind of guy who carries a gun. Look at me, for heaven's sake. Do I look like some sort of a hoodlum or something?'

Her eyes, now curious, told him that he did not. He attempted a humble smile. 'I don't know who they were or what they wanted, but I got lucky and got away. Then I did what anybody in his right mind would do – I ran for my life.' Jack wiped a calculated hand over his forehead. 'That's when I saw you outside the hotel. Those guys were right behind me. There wasn't any time to explain. And I was afraid they would follow the cab. That's why I made you bring me here after . . . Oh Christ! When that gun went off in the cab . . . I've never been so scared in my life . . .'

He saw that the moment had come. 'All I want to do is get to the American Embassy. I'll be safe there. But I don't know where it is. Heck, I don't even know where *this* is. So let me take the gag off, and tell me how to get to the embassy, and I'm out of here. I swear to God, that's all I want.'

She was on the borderline, almost ready. 'Think about it. If I'd wanted to hurt you, I would have done it last night. Or I'd be doing it now. But I'm not that kind of jerk. Really, I'm just an ordinary guy in a lot of trouble, and I don't know why.'

Zaitun half nodded, stopped, and then nodded earnestly. Jack reached down and began to peel away the tape. 'I hope this doesn't hurt.' Obviously it did.

He pulled the sticky stuff off, then removed the gag from her mouth – a sopping, well-chewed blue stocking. 'Thirsty?' he asked. 'Let me get you some water.' He filled a glass from the tap, and brought it to her lips. She drank deep and appreciatively. When she was done, Jack said, 'OK, where are we, and how do I get to the embassy?'

She licked her lips. 'You'll let me go? Untie me and let me go?'

'No! I mean, yes. I mean, you won't call the police, will you?' The police! Oh hell! The one on the phone would be here any minute. 'As soon as I get to the embassy, I'll tell them where you are. Honest, I promise. They'll send the cops here to set you loose.'

She thought about it. 'I don't trust you.'

Jack pressed the palm of his hand against his eyes. The doorbell was going to ring. He knew it. It would be whatshisname Chan Gin, and by now he'd have his big black pistol back. 'OK, OK, OK.' He touched the bonds holding her to the faucet – it was a narrow leather belt, soaking wet from a dripping shower head, and too tightly tied to be unknotted. 'I'll have to cut this. I need a knife. Or scissors or something.'

'In the kitchen.'

Jack dashed through the bedroom and into the living room. There was a door at its end, right by the window. That had to be it. It was – a minuscule kitchenette, smaller than the impossible

ten- by five-foot kitchen in Gabrielle's apartment: three cramped
cabinets above a Lilliputian butcher-block counter, a pygmy range
with two electric heating coils, a tiny stainless-steel sink, the kind
of pocket-sized refrigerator he was used to seeing in hotel mini-
bars. There was linoleum tile on the floor, and a blank windowless
wall at the far end.

He threw open a cabinet: cleaning supplies – soap powder,
laundry bleach, ammonia, fabric softener, sponges and rags.
Another cabinet: dishes, cups, glasses. Third and last cabinet:
foodstuff, mostly the usual brands and packages seen everywhere
in the world, and reminding him that he was famished. He opened
a drawer: tableware, knives included, but none of them sharp
enough to saw through wet rawhide. Where the blazes was a
carving knife? Ah ha! Underneath the sink! He opened a pair of
varnished but otherwise plain wooden doors, and there they were,
Zaitun's spatulas and scissors and kitchen knives. She even had a
serrated bread knife. That was the one that looked like it would do
the job. Jack seized it, stood, and left the kitchen. As he did he
caught a glimpse out the living-room window. A white-topped,
midnight-blue Range-Rover Defender was parked by the kerb. It's
door bore Singapore's official seal – a lion and tiger holding a
shield of five stars above a crescent moon; there were blue, red, and
white emergency lights across the top; a police car and no doubt
about it. A man had just climbed out, was walking briskly towards
the building. Jack already knew who he was.

He felt his forehead bead with sweat. He choked, heart in
mouth, fear bubbling in his stomach. He was too late. There was
no way out. None. Even if he had time to run, he didn't know
where to go. It was hopeless. He was alone in a foreign country,
believed guilty of a crime he couldn't imagine, pursued by a cop
who sounded like he hated Jack's guts and looked like the sort of
swaggering bully who never listened to reason. What would that
cop do if he got his hands on Jack? What would any cop do?

*The accused, known to be in possession of a stolen weapon,
reached into his pocket, sir . . . While resisting arrest, sir . . . While
attempting to escape, sir . . . While assaulting a police officer, sir
. . . Down a flight of stairs, sir . . . Out the window, sir . . .*

The police thought Jack was an American gangster or worse. There wouldn't be any questions. The medics would bag what was left, and Chan Gin would get a pat on the back.

Even if Chan didn't kill him, Jack was certain the man whose gun he'd stolen would . . . what? . . . gleefully beat him to a bloody pulp. Break bones. Put him in a hospital. Cripple him for life.

He was trapped, no escape, pain or death or both coming up the elevator. It was all over, and he was . . . he was . . .

. . . Who?

Just an ordinary guy. Nothing exceptional. A plain vanilla American businessman. Sedentary and a little overweight, possessed of no skills that could help him in this kind of situation, none at all.

But if that was all he was, then how had he been cunning enough – or crazed enough – to escape from a police squad the previous night? Who was the man who had gleefully seized the guns, merrily fled through hotel halls, hijacked a taxi, and looked like he was enjoying every minute of it?

Was that Jack Taft? No! Inside of every fat man, there's a thin man trying to get out. Inside of every timid man . . . No, no, no, and no again! Violence was no part of his make-up. Exhaustion, jet lag, the pill Rajiv had sent him, those explained his behaviour. A momentary aberration, happenstance, bodily chemistry out of balance, people black out, don't they? Something snaps and they do things they'd never done before and will never do again.

Who?

Who am I? Plain old Jack, that's who. I'm the quiet one, the low-key keep-your-head-down one. Analytical. Rational. I'm the guy who thinks his way through problems, not the one who bulls ahead, all guns blazing, ready-fire-aim. I'm a corporate bureaucrat, not a high-rolling bet-your-company entrepreneur. You don't go into Jack Taft's office to get flashy creative insight, you go in to get practical problem-solving.

Problem-solving. Right. This is a problem. That means there is a solution.

Calm, he told himself. *Keep calm. Don't panic. You can do this. The trick is not thinking about it. The trick is that there is no trick. You just let your mind go, forget about your passions and fears, and you think about the problem and the alternatives, think about what's natural, what a reasonable man would do . . .*

Something clicked.

He glanced narrowly at the kitchenette. He'd lived a bachelor's life. He knew about kitchens, about their contents, and about the stupid mistakes that a single man, unschooled in domestic arts, could make.

Maybe . . . yeah . . . maybe . . .

He ran back to the bathroom. Smiling a false smile, he said cheerfully, 'Here, I got it.' Regretting the look of happy trust in her eyes, he slipped the bread knife's blade beneath the belt binding Zaitun's wrists to the bathtub faucet. 'OK, how do I get to the embassy?'

'It's easy,' she answered. 'Turn left when you leave the building, then walk straight to the MRT station. Take the train six stops south. Get off at the C2 station; that's City Hall. Walk right one block, then left one block. Your embassy is on Hill Street at the corner of Loke Yew. It shouldn't take you more than fifteen minutes to . . .' She saw the balled-up blue stocking in Jack's left hand. 'No! You promised you'd untie—'

'I lied,' he whispered, and felt the sleepy purr of last night's inner animal dreaming in its slumber.

– 3 –

No leads. Nothing. Taft was the invisible man.

Chan had tossed the punk's luggage – would you believe: off-the-rack suits, wash 'n' wear shirts, off-brand ties, discount-store underwear, and – Jesus wept! – in his toiletries bag a little sewing kit bearing the words 'Compliments of Ramada Inn'. Every item the guy carried – always excepting his briefcase – positively goddamned screamed that he was a dull, ordinary businessman.

It was the best disguise Chan had ever seen.

And the least evidence.

The only thing they had, the one fragile thread that might lead to Taft, was what the doorman had belatedly got around to telling them: a woman had climbed out of Taft's cab, greeting him with a hug at the hotel steps. A *jute Ah Lian*, the doorman said – a young woman, a pretty woman.

Taft had a lady friend in Singapore.

It wasn't too much to go on, but it was better than nothing.

Now a whole bunch of cops – plenty of volunteers for the job – were making the rounds of Singapore's pickup joints. Who's got a Western steady? Who boasts of an American boyfriend? Who went trotting off for a rendezvous in the wee hours of the morning?

Maybe one of those cops would get lucky. Maybe some girl or some bartender spotted something. Maybe.

Meanwhile, Chan had a massive investigation to run. And to do. No believer in leading from behind, he was out in the field, same as everybody else. Walk and talk – that's the heart of a successful investigation, that and covering every detail, large and small, and making sure nobody missed a thing.

He'd shoehorned eight interviews – none of them worth a shit – into the day so far. Now it was number nine. One of the first-class cabin stewardesses from Sing Air 15, Miss Zaitun Samsudin, a real babe from the picture in her personnel file.

Idly, Chan wondered why she lived in Toa Payoh, an old and unfashionable neighbourhood, and how she'd managed to get a private apartment. The Housing Development Board controlled 80 per cent of Singapore's residential property; it didn't permit single people, not even single parents (who, according to the prudish government, were most definitely *not* 'family units'), to occupy apartments by themselves. So . . . Chan nodded to himself . . . so Miss Samsudin no doubt had family living in Toa Payoh; and no doubt had worked some sort of fiddle with a relative so that she could have a flat to herself.

Smart girl, he thought, smiling at himself because he knew he had a weakness for the bright ones. Good looks and a good mind – that was the real reason why he decided to interview her himself. She probably wouldn't have any information, would know nothing about the passenger in seat 2B. But rank has its privileges, and so Superintendent Chan Gin steered his police blue Range-Rover towards Toa Payoh.

*

Driving Toa Payoh's broad avenues, Chan did not see a tidy little community of middle-class government flats. He saw another place, thirty-plus years gone, the bad heritage of British colonial policy – divide and conquer, ghettoize the races, don't let the dusky-hued heathens cooperate with one another.

Like most of Singapore, Toa Payoh had been a rickshaw slum; a muddy warren of alleyways, tin-roofed shacks, scabby dogs, open sewers, vacant-eyed junkies, swaggering pushers, cheap thugs and cheaper whores. How old had he been? Early teens. What had he been doing here? Didn't remember. But he remembered the man with the Molotov cocktail, he'd never forget that. Nor would he forget the screams of an Indian family in flames, and the exaltation of a swirling mob, and a boy younger than he was hacking at the legs of a fallen Malay Muslim, the meat cleaver drawing a rainbow arc of blood with each wet fall. There were four hundred casualties that night – Malay against Indian, Indian against Chinese, Chinese against Westerner – and the new government of this tiny nation, independent only a year, had called it a race riot, although in truth the powder train had been ignited by warring Tong societies, and suddenly a row of stern men in blue had materialized at the head of the street. They carried wicker shields and weighted batons, and they marched lockstep, relentless, grim, and they were not Chinese or Malay or Indian or Western, but rather they were . . .

. . . something new under the sun . . .

. . . a nation unheard of, a people unknown . . .

. . . Singaporeans!

A fierce Sikh sergeant with a bullhorn roared orders to clear the streets. *State of emergency declared. Civil rights suspended. Officers advance. Jail and flogging for anyone who resists.*

The gutters ran ankle deep in blood. Truly. It flowed over Chan's shoes, clotted on his socks. But death and butchery were driven from the streets, the riot quelled before it spread; and next morning, young Chan Gin came out from his refuge, the home of a friend, and knew his life's vocation.

The law is harsh. Lawlessness is harsher.

Now he'd been a cop for twenty-seven years. He was proud of

it, and had no plans to quit. But unless he brought that Taft bastard down, brought him down hard, he'd never celebrate his twenty-eighth anniversary.

Why? Simple. A proverb heard everywhere in the Orient has it that the nail that stands above its fellows is always hammered down. And in his docile nation, Chan Gin stood tallest, a nail that cried out for hammering, a man who dated back to times and techniques Singapore's masters wanted to see forgotten. Sure, they'd loved him in the old days, oh yeah, and praised his ruthless efficiency. But that was long ago. Now Singapore was a different place, and Chan the last of his embarrassing kind. They would have forced him into retirement if they could; but Chan played the game as well as them, often better. As long as the public loved him, the big boys couldn't touch him.

'I don't think of my job as law enforcement,' he said, showing his teeth to the television cameras. 'I think of my job as garbage disposal.'

They lapped it up. The press and the people. Chan was the one thing nobody in Singapore could be: an honest-to-God badass. They adored him because they were mice, and he was the cat, and the cat is what all mice want to be.

After all, men need heroes. From William Hart to John Wayne, from Clint Eastwood to Arnold Schwarzenegger, the world over they dote on the tough guy, the good guy, the hero.

Chan Gin.

Hero worship was all that kept the government from crushing him like a bug. As long as he never blew a case, never gave the assholes at the top an excuse to shut him down, the media would keep him safe.

Only now he *had* blown it. Big time. Right out in the open where it couldn't be covered up. And the powers-that-be were licking their chops.

Two days maximum. He figured that was all the time he had. If he couldn't get Taft – better yet, Taft's remains – on the nightly news, then *wham!* the hammer falls, and the nail named Chan gets driven out of sight. Permanently.

Two days.

Either Taft or Chan was going to pay for last night's highly visible fuck-up.

Easy choice.

– 4 –

Chan flipped open his notebook, double-checking a scribbled page: 'Zaitun Binte Samsudin, Lorong 4, bldg 468, Apt 4J, Toa Payoh, no SPF rcrd.' He hit the elevator button.

An ugly industrial-style door groaned open. Chan grimaced. These older apartment buildings, the first government-subsidized housing built after independence, weren't his cup of tea, even if they had been personally designed by Lee Kuan Yew, Singapore's omnipotent Prime Minister emeritus.

There was no mirror in the elevator. Working from instinct and long practice, Chan Gin ruffled his hair so that his forelock fell boyishly across his brow, then tugged the hem of his tropical blue blazer so that it draped squarely across his shoulders, hanging loosely enough to conceal the holstered artillery beneath.

The elevator clanged to a stop on the fourth floor. Chan chose a smile from his large repertoire; it was a toss up between the Mel Gibson not-quite-a-smirk or Harrison Ford's self-deprecating grin. He instinctively picked the Gibson look; Miss Samsudin was young and single, and Ford appealed, he believed, to married matrons.

Apartment 4J was at the very end of the breezeway, a corner apartment and a good location. Chan rehearsed his script: an apology for the inconvenience, then: Where have you been since you debarked your flight? Oh, you slept through my phone calls? I'm sorry; I hope I didn't wake you up. Yes, I am *that* Chan Gin, but, ha, ha, the television people really exaggerate about my adventures, no really, and the newspapers do too. Anyway, as I mentioned on the phone, I want to ask you about one of your passengers: John Gregory Taft, pudgy American, seat 2B on the aisle. Did you happen to talk to him during the trip – did he say anything beyond the usual ordering a drink and choosing a meal or asking for an extra pillow? *And don't*, he sternly ordered himself, *don't under* any *circumstances, no matter what she says, let your face show what you think about that lousy prick; and the fucker took my guns and made a fool of me in front of all of Singapore and the truth of the matter is that the newspapers don't exaggerate at all* . . .

4H 4I 4J. There it was. There was no bell, there never was in these older buildings. Chan shot his cuffs, then knocked briskly on the door.

It swung open.

The apartment was dark, the windows curtained, Taft's face shadowed and hard to see. His gun, however, was visible enough. Chan went rigid, jaws clenched, fists balled, ready to kill, no remorse. The night before, after the fiasco in the hotel, he'd come to hate Taft as bad he hated any gangster he'd ever wasted. That a criminal – *a goddamned motherfucking scumbag hood!* – so easily escaped him was more than merely humiliating to a man not known for taking humiliation well. Now, caught off guard again, Chan's hatred turned to murderous rage, and all he wanted, his sole yearning and passion, was to get his hands around the shitheel's neck and . . .

'In,' Taft hissed. 'Hands up. Kick the door closed behind you.' Chan coldly obeyed. Taft took two quick steps backward, keeping a safe distance. It was what Chan himself would do in the same situation.

Professional, he thought grimly. *This punk is very, very professional.*

The two stood still, looking at one another. Some seconds passed. Chan finally broke the silence with a bitter monosyllable. 'Well?'

Taft's answer was low, nearly inaudible. 'Well, I could kill you. You know that, don't you?'

Chan wasn't going to let his emotions show. Not to this asshole. Not to any asshole. Instead he'd show some class, taunt the bastard, prove who was the better man. 'That's what I'd do under the circumstances.'

'I could have killed you last night.'

The man is a stone killer, best thing to do is wound his pride.

'Could-a, should-a, would-a.'

'But I don't shoot people.'

'Really? Well, I do. All the time.' *Heh! The sonofabitch didn't like that answer.*

Taft hissed through his teeth. Then he muttered, 'I was afraid you'd say something like that. Look, Mr Gin – or can I call you Chan?'

'Gin's my first name. So yes, you should call me Chan. Although most people on your side of the law call me "sir". Sometimes it comes out "thir" because they don't have any teeth left, but at least they make the effort.' Chan smiled. He was on a roll here, starting to get the upper hand.

Taft seemed to think about Chan's answer. 'We're not going to be friends, are we?'

'Doubtful.'

'That's a shame. I could use a friend right now.'

'Shacking up with a hot little stewardess isn't enough for you, eh?' Chan heard bitterness creep into his voice. *Get a grip on yourself, man.*

Taft seemed confused. 'Her? Aw, you don't think . . .' He licked his lips. 'Nuts, she's a . . . I don't know . . . victim. I sort of kidnapped her, I guess. She's tied up in the toilet.'

'Kinky,' Chan leered.

'Screw you, pal.' Taft's voice had become angry and low. 'The woman, whatshername in the bathroom, is *your* problem. *My* problem is this: I don't know what the hell is going on.'

Chan tilted his head. He raised his right eyebrow, and gave Taft the full benefit of his most practised stare of sceptical incredulity. 'What is going on is that I'm the law and you're the lawbreaker. That means I get to arrest you, and you get to go to jail. That's how these things work in Singapore. I imagine they work much the same in America. Or am I misinformed?'

Taft snorted. 'Yeah, maybe you are. But that's not what I meant. What I meant was *why* do you want to arrest me?'

'Oh no!' Chan shook his head and forced merriment into his voice. 'Oh please. Don't tell me you're going to try *that* one! "Oh, Officer, I'm only an innocent bystander and I can't imagine why you're putting the cuffs on me and this all must be some sort of dreadful misunderstanding!" Come on, Taft, you can do better than that.'

'As a matter of fact, I can't.'

'Fucking pathetic!' Chan spat the words. 'Save your act for the courthouse. They've heard it there too.'

'Jesus, won't you even listen to me?'

Chan said nothing. Instead he coldly studied the fugitive gangster, pondering what his next move would be, and wondering what kind of lame bullshit lies were on the scumbag's twisted little mind.

What was on Jack's mind was no longer the surrender he'd toyed with offering. Instead his mind was on the aftermath of a ten-year-old boy's confrontation with what all ten-year-olds must confront: a strutting schoolyard bully.

- Never pick a fight.
- He started it, Dad.
- Look the other way.
- My back was turned.
- You've got to go along to get along.
- How?
- Offer to help him. Promise him you'll do his homework. Now go wash your face. You're filthy.

And so, on his second encounter with his tormentor, Jack had offered to do the lout's arithmetic for him. Sometime later Jack limped home with a blackened eye, a cut lip, and a permanent understanding of the psychology of bullies. No finer example of which existed, he believed, than the Oriental Simon Burton clone glowering at him.

OK, Jack thought, *it looks like we're going to have to go with plan 'B'.*

Static crackled. A miniature Motorola radio clipped to the back of Chan's belt chirped twice as it came alive. 'Corporal Leung here.

Superintendent Chan, do you copy?'

Taft glared at Chan. Chan smiled back.

'Superintendent Chan? This is Corporal Leung. Please answer.'

Taft hissed, 'Take your coat off. I want to see what you've got under it. Do it slowly. Left sleeve first. Let it slide off the right shoulder to the floor.' Chan obeyed. As the jacket slipped to the floor, Taft added, 'Use your left hand to answer the radio. Don't even think about touching that gun.'

'I have no desire to die.' Gripping the radio, Chan flipped the transmit switch, and lifted it to shoulder height, the mouthpiece well away from his lips. 'Chan here. What's up, Hal?'

'Sir, I just got word from the hospital. That cab driver is finally conscious. He's still woozy but he says that girl – the one Taft met at the hotel – he says he picked her up outside the Singapore Air flightcrew exit at Changi. He says she was carrying a Sing Air stewardess's bag. And the driver thinks she gave him a Toa Payoh address. If you're headed out to the Samsudin girl's apartment, you'd better have backup.'

Taft shook his head. Chan pushed the transmit button again. 'I can handle it.'

'Don't try it alone, sir. I'm on the Pan Island Expressway just past the Turf Club. I can be at the girl's apartment in five minutes, ten at the most. Wait for me.'

The radio went silent. Chan grinned, and turned up the heat. 'Hal Leung's a very cautious officer. In America, you'd call him a "belt and suspenders" guy. Unless I miss my bet, he'll invite a couple of patrol cars to meet him here. If you surrender now, you can avoid all of the unpleasantness that involves. You know, tear gas, riot guns . . .'

Taft shook his head. He wore a hangdog frown. 'I wanted to talk to you, Mr Chan—'

'It's not Mr Chan, it's Superintendent Chan. Or sir. Take your pick.'

'Whatever. Now I can't, not with your buddy on the way. So do me a favour, slip that holster off – and do it slowly – then go through the door over there, into the kitchen.' Taft indicated the direction with the pistol.

'Going to steal my gun again?'

'No!' Taft raised his voice, then immediately lowered it to a whisper. 'No. I don't want your lousy gun. I hate guns. Heck, you can have this one back. I'll leave it behind when I go.'

Chan lifted an eyebrow at the improbability of Taft's words. Then, following the bastard's orders because he had no choice, he sloughed off his shoulder holster – only one; the sawed-off Baikal was too unwieldy to take on interviews. Praying that Taft would get just a foot or two closer, he backed into the kitchen. Taft, cool professional that he was, kept several paces distant.

'OK, Mister-Superintendent-Chan-sir, go to the end of the kitchen and stand with your face to the wall.'

Chan stepped around a bucket at the kitchen entrance, doing as bidden. He sniffed. There was an unpleasantly heavy aroma of ammonia in the air. 'Going to kill me now?' He was ready for it, but he didn't think it would happen. At least not like this. *But then*, he reflected, *people never do think it will happen like this*.

'Nope. Just make you cry. Bullies hate to cry, right?'

What the fuck is that crack supposed to mean? thought Chan, hearing a noise behind him, the gurgle of an up-ended bottle and the splash of liquid being poured into liquid.

The kitchen door slammed closed. Outside, something heavy thudded across the carpet. Chan was already bending, reaching for the backup guns holstered on his ankles. When the fumes hit him, he reeled, almost tumbling over.

Overpowering in the confines of the tiny kitchen, the stench seared his throat, made his lungs burn like fire and his eyes brim with tears. He gasped for air. That was a mistake; it made things worse. He ripped his shirt-tails out of his pants, jerked the shirt open. Buttons popped. Chan, blind eyes squeezed closed, could hear them ping off the walls and floor. He covered his face, groping for the door.

The fumes – thick choking gas – were worse near the bucket. *The bucket?* Chan asked himself. *What did the rotten prick put in the bucket? This is tear gas, CS or something like it. Sonofabitch, where did the sonofabitch get his hands on . . .*

Then he knew. He'd done it himself. Years ago when he was

starting out. His first apartment. Way the hell out in Pasar Ris. He was a sloppy housekeeper. One evening he was having a girl over and noticed the bathtub. It was filthy. Girls usually went to the toilet first, and a nasty-looking bathroom was the sort of thing that made them have second thoughts. The girl in question was going to show up in a half-hour. He grabbed a scrubbing pad. That helped, but the grime still showed. He hastily buffed the tub down with ammonia. Not much improvement. So – bright idea! – he decided to use scouring powder, and better still to mix the stuff with the ammonia. That was bound to do the job.

The job it did was to create a cloud of homemade tear gas, chloramine, as poisonous as hell. He couldn't go back into the bathroom for hours. The girl refused so much as to set foot in the apartment.

Ammonia and calcium hypochlorite scouring powder. That bastard had gassed him blind with cleaning supplies.

Chan shoved his shoulder against the kitchen door. Blocked of course. Taft, ever professional, had braced it closed with something. Living-room furniture more likely than not. Chan threw himself against the door, hard as he could.

Bad mistake. Knocked the wind out of himself. Made him inhale. More gas in the lungs. He could scream with the pain, but that would only kill him faster.

The door had moved a few inches. Chan held his breath, hurled himself at it. And again. And one more time. He stumbled through it, into the living room. He lashed out with his foot, kicking the door closed behind him. Forcing himself to open his eyes – *goddamn it that hurts* – he groped his way towards watery light, towards the window.

Neither looking for nor caring about the window latch, Chan Gin rammed his head through the glass, and swallowed deep cooling gulps of nourishing air.

He was still there, still too blind to see, when two cars screamed up in front of the building, and the gunfire began. 'Get him!' blind Chan roared. 'Kill the sonofabitch!'

– 5 –

Two years earlier – back when they'd been lovers not rivals – he running LBTech's Western logistics, she in charge of the East, Denise Donald had told Jack that Westerners working in Singapore measure walking distances in shirts not blocks. *How far is it to the bank, Mary? Oh, that's about a two-shirter, Fred.*

Now Jack understood what she meant. The temperature was above ninety, the humidity about the same. Heavy clouds billowed across a sky hot with blue. The air was smothering, pregnant with the promise of imminent rain. The night before, Jack hadn't noticed the clamminess; it was cooler after dark, and his jet-lagged system seemed not to care. Now awake and rested, he suspected that even a short trot to the subway station would leave him soaked in sweat.

He was perspiring already. Fear as much as heat was responsible.

Turning left, the direction which Zaitun said the subway was to be found, he began walking briskly. *Make it quick, but don't run. Someone will notice if you run.*

And there were plenty of 'someones' on the street – young mothers pushing strollers, old ladies laden with grocery bags, idling teenagers; a tiny brown Tamil man, bald and seemingly ageless, sitting on a kerbside bench sewing the sleeve of his embroidered dhoti. As Jack passed, most stared at him with open curiosity. *I wonder what I look like? Clothes rumpled and filthy. Haven't shaved since God knows when. When the cops ask the neighbours if they saw anyone suspicious leave that girl's building . . .*

Apartments lined the broad avenue – each building, like Zaitun's, cream coloured and decorated with a slightly institutional-looking blue motif. All were spotless, surrounded by well-manicured grounds, and numbered in big black figures painted on yellow backgrounds. Their ground floors were given over to stores – clothing, jewellery, a hairdresser, a pharmacy – open-air markets, and little clusters of bustling restaurants.

Public housing, Jack thought as he paced down a street shaded by trees he could not name. Those were words that made New Yorkers reach for the roach spray. But this neighbourhood looked to Jack no worse than his own. Indeed, now that he thought of it, it looked quite a bit better.

He passed the Convent of the Holy Infant Jesus Primary School. Cute kids in navy-blue uniforms frolicked in front of it. No one seemed to be guarding them, vigilant against the kind of people who push dope in playgrounds, peddle discount firearms, offer to 'Drive you home, Daddy sent me, I'm an adult and you can trust me.' There were bicycles and motor-scooters parked everywhere. The owners simply left them, leaned them against railings, didn't bother to chain them to anything. Nobody would steal them. Nobody would bother your kids. It was Singapore, the safest place in the world, the one city where nobody except dissidents had anything to worry about.

Unless you were an unsavoury Westerner in filthy clothing hurrying towards the MRT.

A Chinese woman with an umbrella, enviable protection against a brutal sun, passed Jack, eyeing him nervously.

Cripes, do I look that bad? Yeah, probably.

Now he was leaving the public housing complex, a Philips Electronics factory on his side of the street, a construction site on the other. 'Bougainvillea Chalets', the sign in front of the site read, 'More Luxury Town Houses From Hwa Development Company, PTE'. The construction itself was walled off, hidden from view by a chainlink fence and eight-foot-high sheets of ugly white plastic. But its gates were open.

Workers trundled wheelbarrows in and out; just outside the fence two men sat on the rear gate of a Toyota pick-up, smoking and chatting and waiting for their supervisor to arrive. A handful of other men stood haggling with a young Indian pushcart hawker over the prices of his wares: cans of chilled leechee nut and sugar-cane juice, soy milk soda, and American soft drinks. Were it not for the foliage – greener than green, exotic Asian trees and bushes and flowers that Jack had never seen before – the neighbourhood might resemble those middle-class precincts of Astoria in which he'd grown up: venerable but not rundown apartment buildings, pockets of new construction, an ethnic hodgepodge chattering on the sidewalks (albeit a different and friendlier-seeming one than any seen in New York), and a slow traffic of passenger cars and commercial vans on quiet streets.

No, not entirely slow traffic.

Two automobiles were coming his way faster than seemed safe. Black and gleaming, smoked windows, boxy chrome grill-work, four-door sedans – expensive 700-series BMWs, and to Jack's eyes they didn't look like they belonged in this part of town.

They barrelled towards him. On the other side of the road, a Malay construction worker in khakis and a cheap cotton shirt put his hands on his hips, and shook his head at their reckless velocity. One car hit a puddle; a roostertail of muddy water plumed behind it. Two Indian boys tossing a ball on the sidewalk looked up worriedly, and scuttled to the safety of the lawn.

Jack, walking as fast as he could, guessed both cars were doing fifty in a twenty-five-mile-an-hour zone.

The sedans sped by. Jittery and becoming more so, Jack glanced over his shoulder as they passed. Behind him, not far from Zaitun's building, the front BMW braked hard, slewed left, spun in a moonshiner's turn. Tyres screamed, a cloud of blue smoke spewing from tortured rubber. The car behind it swerved to avoid its partner, bumping over a kerb and on to the grass. As the two vehicles jolted to a stop, men boiled out of their doors, four from each automobile. At a distance of forty yards, Jack could see them clearly – dark suits, white shirts, bright ties, and each and every one of them fumbling for something holstered beneath his jacket.

Jack did not think. There was no time to think. There was only time to . . .

He was three-quarters of the way across the street when the first shot came. The slug – hastily fired by a trigger-happy gunman more anxious to empty his revolver than draw a bead on his target – ricocheted off the pavement. A moment later a volley of bullets pockmarked the Hwa Development Company's protective wall, punching holes in its sign and filling the air with a fine rain of plastic shrapnel. Those shots were better aimed. Jack heard them cut the air inches from his head and torso.

He was running low, half crouched, weaving through a crowd of shouting labourers, Hwa Development workmen on their afternoon tea break. More gunfire, sounding nothing at all like the guns Jack heard in the movies, Arnold and Sly and Bruce wielding oversized hand-cannons that thundered big bass drum booms. No, the noise was more horrible than Hollywood imitations, less loud but more lethal, the flat percussion of packed cordite soon followed by an angry whine of hurled metal, and the shattering of objects vaporized by jacketed rounds. These were killing sounds, nor could Jack doubt for even a second their intended effects.

Another sound, this one pulpy like ripe fruit dropped from a height. Someone to Jack's front howled in shock – the Indian hawker, the white of his dhoti suddenly red, spilled Burgundy on damask, a bloom of tattered red showing beneath a hole far too small, or so it seemed, for the shrieks that accompanied it. The soda-pop peddler sprawled to the sidewalk. His legs drummed with appalling speed, then went slack, and his cries fell to a gurgle and became silence.

Jack's stomach churned.

Most of the other men around him were flat, crawling for cover, huddled whimpering behind tipped-over wheelbarrows, or face down with their hands over their heads. Only two, no three, of Hwa Development's employees were still on their feet. Any second now Jack would be alone, the last man standing.

In the distance a voice roared with rage, and Jack knew the voice, and Jack understood the words: 'Get him! Kill the sonofabitch!'

There was nowhere to hide. He was captured in the afternoon sunlight, framed against chainlink and plastic, all the other targets cowering around him, the nearest street corner ten long yards away. No hope of reaching it; he was dead unless he did the one, the only logical, the only rational, the only *intelligent* thing.

'I surrender!' Hands high. Palms open. Shouting at the top of his lungs. Dropping to his knees. Arms still above his head. 'Don't shoot! I give up!'

The gunmen paused. Pistols wavered, aimpoints out of plumb. Jack held his breath. One dark suit snapped a question to another dark suit. That dark suit shook his head and fired too high. Jack somersaulted, scrambled hands and knees, hurled himself towards the corner, rolling in an oily puddle, scuttling low, one prone body among dozens of terrified workers lying face down beneath a hailstorm of bullets. A second fusillade followed, but Jack was already out of sight and running.

– Dad, I want to go out for the track team. The coach says I can make it.

   – Don't waste your time. You don't have what it takes.

He pumped his legs faster than he could remember doing, not ever, not even as a boy had he run like this. The street intersected another. Jack threw himself right, raced another block, and turned left. He was soaked with perspiration. His breath was short, and a needle stitch of pain seared his right side. There was an alley, and Jack sprinted into it. He heard the sound of sirens in the distance. He ran harder. His face was hot, fevered like the flu. His feet slapped puddles, water which wasn't cooling splashed his pants legs. He tripped over a strip of lumber left lying before an open door, stumbled to his hands and knees, bounced bruisingly against the pavement. He wanted to rest there, crouched and gasping and dripping with sweat. He forced himself up, tottering back into motion, racing with a swiftness that he did not know he had.

A second alleyway branched off to his left. It was narrow, cluttered with trash cans and a small green dumpster. No pavement, only mud, best not to go that way or he'd leave footprints. He lurched by, one leg in front of another, hands balled into fists, elbows jutting back and forth, forcing himself to run, run, run.

Across an empty street, around a corner, and around another. People looked up, saw him running, a mud-splashed man with torn trousers. Some seemed concerned. One man started to move towards him, then thought better of it.

Uphill now. Jack worked his elbows, felt like retching, made himself keep moving, wanted to lie down and die. It was a narrow winding street, no traffic in sight. Gasping, he sped past a high wall topped with concertina wire and a sign that said: 'Toa Payoh Girl's Home – Ministry of Community Development'. Leave it to

Singapore's prissy politicians to call the ministry responsible for juvenile jails 'Community Development'.

Downhill now. Out of Toa Payoh. High-rises far behind him. On one side of the street stood rows of expensive-looking three-storey town houses, no doubt more Hwa Development company luxury chalets; the other side was thick with almost impenetrable foliage. It looked like raw jungle to Jack.

The sound of sirens rose and fell, but it was farther away, well behind him. Nor could gunshots be heard. Those had stopped, although their terror had not.

Further downhill, the steep slope adding to his speed, making his running easier, though not easy enough. There was some sort of major intersection ahead. Jack ran and ran, and then he was there, and there he stopped.

His eyes seemed unable to focus. Small explosions of yellow and red made it difficult to make out the scene. He was dripping, his clothes soaked through and through as if he'd taken a shower and forgotten to undress. Gasping and ready to collapse with exhaustion, he felt about to faint.

Jack closed his eyes, pressing his forefingers against them. His chest felt as if someone was crushing it in a vice. He tried to cough the pain out, but that only brought on a wave of nausea. He wasn't in good shape, hadn't been for twenty years. *Much more of this*, he thought, *will kill me*.

He forced his eyes open, shook his head to clear it, and tried to study his alternatives. To the left the nature of the street changed. There were more apartment buildings that way, more women and children and elderly folks in baggy clothing.

Had he run in a circle? Was he back at the place he'd begun?

He wasn't certain. He'd turned too many corners, changed direction too often, did not know whether he might be suicidally headed straight into the sights of those gunmen.

He looked to the right. It was a riot of green, a place thick with trees and bushes, and it seemed enormous.

He could make out a sign: 'McRitchie Reservoir and Nature Preserve'. Perfect. A park of some sort. A quick dash across the intersection, and he'd be in it. Another few minutes of running and he'd be so far out of sight they'd never find him. In a park there would be places of concealment, lonely places where he could hide, rest, regain his breath, and, most important of all, try to figure out what, *what the hell*, was happening to him.

He forced himself to move. *One foot after another, you can do it, Jack.*

It wasn't getting easier. It wasn't getting less painful. The heat and humidity were as deadly as the men who had tried to shoot him. His strength was almost gone. He was less running than staggering. But still, he was going forward, now pounding on soft grasses.

Wet. His hair was wet, his face, his shirt; it was rain, cooling rain, and it helped a lot.

What did not help was this: just as his last ounce of strength spent itself, it came to him that eight men – nine counting Chan – had recently demonstrated that they wanted him dead so bad that they thought nothing of pouring gunfire into a crowd of unarmed civilians. No compunction, no remorse, nothing but *Get him! Kill the sonofabitch!*

Were those other men cops like Chan? Did the nation of Singapore hate him enough to kill their own in the hope of killing him? *Jesus H. Christ! What do they think I've done?*

– 6 –

Jade Lady coasted soft swells as she rounded the south coast of Pulu Ubin Island. In his cabin, a treasure house of antiquities, Poh Kay Siong listened to Peng Xiu-wen's haunting rhapsody on the terracotta warriors of Xian. Music of distant dreams – all history's sadness made symphony – it soothed Poh's mind, brought serenity to his soul, drove away his unseemly exasperation at what had just been reported to him.

Another blunder. An innocent civilian fallen in harm's way, a hapless street seller of soft drinks shot down by the workers sent to dispatch the increasingly irksome Mr Taft. Singapore's implacable authorities would exact a blood price for this impropriety. Most regrettable.

But necessary.

Such restitution was in the proper order of things. All life is give and take. Buyers and sellers, borrowers and lenders, are but two sides of a single coin. There is no dishonour in the payment of honest debts, for the settlement of equitable obligations is an unfair world's sole unfailing justice. Such he'd learned long ago.

When, in those days of violence and sweet anarchy, Lee Kuan Yew ascended to govern Singapore (no velvet glove cloaking *that* iron hand), Poh made the sacrifices survival demanded. The new prime minister had been his playground rival, a boy of equal age, equal abilities, different inclinations. Most of Poh's profession dismissed Lee's vows to bring order at any cost. Poh did not. He took his old foe seriously, respecting him as a worthy enemy should.

Other warlords went to the barricades, allying themselves with insurgents like Red Feng Chuang Pi. Anyone of Lee's camp who dared run for office awoke to the sound of dynamite. To contribute to Lee's People's Action Party was to mark yourself for death. The Tongs, the Triads, the *chiu chow* brotherhoods swore they would prevail.

Poh Kay Siong, slipping into shadows, made a different pledge – that he would endure.

When the last bomb exploded, when the last rioter was clubbed unconscious, when the last hatchetman fell victim to Lee's merciless crusade, Poh Kay Siong smiled on the ruination of former colleagues, and on their graves.

True, survival had not been inexpensive. Not bribery – harsh Lee Kuan Yew punished purchasable officials harshly – but rather the procurement of certain documents carried a steep price. Here a photograph, there a letter, elsewhere a transcript of banking records.

A brown-stained Communist Party membership card of 1940s vintage cost Poh ten thousand dollars, but saved him a hundred times that in grief. The sworn testimony of a Bugis Street effeminate kept Poh's most useful underlings from prison. A wife's indiscretions persuaded a humiliated attorney to remove papers from an evidence folder intended for use against Poh himself.

That men sin is no revelation. Nor that they strive to keep their sins secret.

But many years, and years beyond years, had passed. A bureaucrat behind a prosecutor's desk is a useful slave. A doddering pensioner beneath a palm tree is not, for he is old past shame.

At first only Chan Gin, not yet the demonic incarnation of *Chenghaung* that he now preened himself, had been Poh's sole, easily eluded adversary. A dog whose leash is held by servants may growl and lunge, but cannot bite.

Leashes stretch. Aging servants slacken their grip. Other dogs congregate in hunting packs.

Then what is to be done? A simple answer. In numbers lies safety. One may fail, but many prevail. For this reason Poh wove a web of alliances, bonding his fragile Singapore brotherhood with less precarious associations in alien lands. Alas, the profession being as it was, the web was a delicate thing of slender threads. Stronger hands were needed if it, and the Singapore *chiu chow*, were to survive.

Delight of delights, an obstreperous American woman offered him ropes of cabled iron. A gift from the gods, Miss Donald's machinations promised not merely income, but the wherewithal to secure the loyal support of East Asia's strongest warlords.

Once the things the woman promised were in place, Poh's position would be unshakable. More important, the brotherhood and all it represented would triumph. No force, Chan Gin least of all, could threaten it for, when all was working as it should, the brotherhood would be protected by powers greater than the police, greater indeed than Singapore itself.

That which had eked out a tenuous existence only through Poh's cunning would live for ever, his monument, the legacy of Poh Kay Siong, greatest practitioner of his art.

If Mr Taft was put out of the way.

If Superintendent Chan was brought to heel.

Sitting at a desk once owned by no less than Sir Stamford Raffles, Poh spoke softly over his shoulder. 'Summon Mr Teng and Mr Lin.'

A uniformed servant replied, 'Yes, sir.'

Chan had foolishly misread what this business was about. If he continued to operate on a misguided theory, then his bull-headed ignorance could be put to propitious use. Indeed, with any luck at all, not only would the superintendent resolve the vexation Mr Taft represented, but would annihilate himself in the process.

Here was a felicitous thought: *Let each man be the weapon that destroys the other.*

Poh studied the pattern of falling raindrops on the sea. There was an omen here. Each drop might be a man, each ripple the circle of that man's acquaintances. See how they overlap. Once intercepts another, they extend, they link, and, though no man can fathom how, they weave a web bridging the wide, wide sea from one shore to another. All things touch, or touch things that touch the goal you most desire.

A scratchy nicotine voice, Sam Lin's, spoke behind him. 'We're here, boss.'

Poh did not turn. Soft and reflective, as if speaking to himself, he said, 'Our gambling customers – how many tens of thousands do they number – I wonder what one of them might do to have his debts forgiven? I wonder even more how eagerly, the gambling fever being a hot disease, they would work on our behalf should a sizable credit at the tables be offered to anyone, to the first one, whom the god of luck blesses with a fortunate gift?'

'A gift, boss?'

Smiling, Poh turned. 'The gift of useful information. The gift that allows me to bring two foes face to face. Have the workers spread the word: Poh Kay Siong is of a lenient frame of mind, and he who gives him the gift he desires will be the richer for it.'

2
New York

– 1 –

Tito was a big muscular tom, mostly black, but for a distinguished white bib and matching spats. His fur was short, although his whiskers were enormous. Gabrielle adored him.

A few weeks earlier a maroon fibreboard pet kennel with a handwritten note taped to the handle had materialized outside her apartment door. The note was from one of Gabrielle's friends, a woman who lived uptown. She had to leave New York in a hurry (no explanation given); she would be gone for a while (no duration given); please take care of Tito (no thanks given).

Gabrielle had damn near called the humane society on the spot. But – love at first sight – Tito loped out of his box and into her heart.

She ruffled the fur behind his ears. 'Gonna miss me while I'm out west, babe?' The cat nodded, or so it seemed. It was almost spooky. Yeats had opined that cats were supernatural, nearest kin to the moon; Gabrielle was coming to believe it – the damned animal seemed to understand every word she said. 'OK, bye now. Be good.'

Purr.

Shrugging on a Walking Man origami jacket, she went to the window and peered down three storeys to the corner of Broadway and Seventieth Street. It looked like rain. Most people had topcoats on. Gabrielle usually wore slacks, a blouse, and a blazer to the office. Today, however, she was scheduled to catch United's 6.30 p.m. flight to San Francisco, rent a car, and drive across the Bay so that, next morning, she could begin a round of interviews on the Oakland docks. A full day's work followed by a long trip called for comfortable clothes – a loose gabardine skirt, a slightly sloppy grey cable-knit sweater, penny loafers, and, of course, a comfortable jacket.

And now, given the weather, a Burberry trench coat with a rolled-up Knirps umbrella in the pocket.

Blowing a kiss to Tito, Gabrielle picked up her purse, briefcase, and garment bag, and stepped through the door.

When she moved out of the bullpens, got her very own office, Gabrielle had sworn that she would never allow her workspace to degenerate into the sort of pigsty typically inhabited by journalists. Uh uh, no way. She'd have pretty art prints on the walls, a blooming plant or two on the windowsill, a neatly organized desk, tidy file cabinets, and a floor that you could actually see.

Fat chance.

She was as bad as everybody else in the business. Her desktop was invisible beneath scribbled notes, outdated galleys, yellowed clippings, and analysts' reports. The floor, if anything, was worse. A path, flanked by heaps of documents and dusty file folders, wormed its way from her door to her chair. Some carpet was visible, but, having last been vacuumed during the Reagan years, its colour was uncertain.

Dropping briefcase and handbag on top of a tottering heap of corporate annual reports, Gabrielle headed for the coffee room. She entered cursing. Two coffee-makers, two pots each, all four pots empty. In the male-dominated world of journalism, nobody had the courtesy to start a fresh pot.

The coffee grounds were in a cabinet over a stained vinyl counter. She seized three foil-wrapped bags and a single paper filter. She put the filter in the coffee-maker basket, and heaped all three bags into it. Then she filled a pot with water, decanted it into the machine, and promptly snatched two styrofoam cups from the cabinet. Triple XXX-rated coffee gurgled as Gabrielle placed one cup beneath the spout, filled it, then slipped the other cup into place. Once both cups were brimming she slipped the coffee pot into place, pulling a jar of Taster's Choice instant coffee out of the cabinet, shovelling two heaped teaspoons into each cup, stirring, and, at long last, sipping her first, necessary, coffee of the day.

A fireball of caffeine lit up her system. 'Ah,' she shivered, awake at last.

As she did every morning, Gabrielle ignored the blinking e-mail indicator on her computer and red message light on her phone. Instead, coffee cup in hand, she unfolded her copies of the *Wall Street Journal* and the *New York Times*. As usual, she started with the *Times*, ignoring the front section. First things first, and the first thing was the business section. There wasn't much of interest: a struggling toy company suddenly had a hot set of play figures; Christmas was going to be good to those guys. Another clutch of investment bankers had been indicted; so what else is new? Airbus won a contract that Boeing wanted, the yen was up against the dollar, everybody was nervous about the discount rate, and tech stocks were on a roller coaster.

Yawn.

The important thing was that nobody had scooped her. Journalistic misery, that. You spend weeks researching and studying and analysing and figuring out your angle, then you pitch it, and the editors love it, and everyone is all hot and bothered and you know you've got a cover story, and *wham*! some jerk from a daily runs a story of his own.

Then you're screwed. No way a fortnightly business magazine can publish a feature on something that the *Times* or *Journal* has just written up. By the time your readers saw it, it would be old news, and done to death.

Gabrielle's current terror was that somebody would latch on to her idea – well, Jack's idea – about import–export swindles. Bang, bang, you're dead, and worse, you have to take whatever assignment that rat Simon dishes out to you.

Ugh. Simon. If he were a little shorter or Tito was a little taller . . .

She flipped the *Times* business section in the approximate direction of the trash can, then scanned the front page. It was a dull day, and there was nothing of interest. No, not totally true. A story down below the fold, lower left, caught her eye:

**American Businessman
Sought in Singapore**

Interesting, she thought. Jack might have something exciting to talk about when he got home. Gabrielle started to read. She blinked in confusion. The story didn't make sense. There was something wrong here. She stopped, took a deep swallow of coffee, and began rereading the story from the top.

This time she finished it. She read it again. And one more time. She still couldn't believe her eyes.

– 2 –

But for poverty-row brokerages, most Wall Street firms employ armies of securities analysts. Their job: evaluating companies, estimating earnings, and recommending stocks. A good analyst takes home a seven-figure salary. A bad analyst takes home plenty of postage stamps, the better to circulate his résumé. Good or bad, no analyst wants to be scooped by a riffraff reporter from the business press.

For this reason, analysts – otherwise happy to chat with journalists (who, by putting their names in print, add to their short-lived credibility) – do not welcome members of the working press to those private 'show and tell' conferences at which corporate chief executives, armed only with thirty-five-millimetre slides, cower behind podiums while formally presenting their companies' financial performance to an audience overflowing with sceptical Wall Street hitmen.

The conference in question, held in the Waldorf-Astoria's grand ballroom, was one of the year's most important. The guards wouldn't let Gabrielle through the door.

In the end, she persuaded a latecomer to find and summon Olivia Thatcher. Some minutes later, Olivia, dressed in an expensively simple forest-green dress – no jewellery but for a plain gold wedding band and a single strand of perfect pearls – materialized, whispered something sufficiently fearful as to make the chief of security blanch, linked arms with Gabrielle, and marched majestically back into the ballroom.

Eyes turned. Olivia Thatcher had that effect.

The two women, close friends despite the difference in their ages, walked down the centre aisle, turned left, and disappeared through a curtain. Small sighs were heard to emanate from a mostly male audience. Wall Street being the place it is, the sighs had more to do with Olivia's wealth than with her beauty.

Behind the stage, Olivia's husband, Scott Claymore Thatcher III, worried an unlit cigar while glowering at a large 'No Smoking' sign. He welcomed Gabrielle with a growl: 'A fine cigar is a pleasure and a consolation, the finest perquisite of capitalist success. But its comforts are refused me. I blame your Puritan generation for this.'

Olivia placed her palm on her spouse's forehead, as if feeling for a fever. 'Ignore him. He's got stage fright.'

Thatcher brushed her away. 'Of course I have stage fright. Quite shortly now I'll be out there being mauled by savage beasts. Earnings per share of the company it is my otherwise joyful duty to govern were four cents under forecast this quarter. I refer to the analysts' forecasts, not mine. But no matter, they'll hold me accountable, and feed me to the lions. Nero Caesar never sent Christians into the arena with fiercer glee than a disappointed securities analyst. I tell you, Gabrielle—'

'Shh!' Olivia hissed, 'I think that's your cue.'

On the other side of the curtain, the day's master of ceremonies, a vulpine senior vice-president from Lee, Bach & Wachutt was sneering into a microphone, 'Our next speaker is the celebrated Chairman and CEO of PegaSys. A few months back I invited him to come wolf-hunting with me in Canada. He declined. Today, I'm sure he wishes he'd taken the opportunity, as I expect the wolves in *this* room will be howling for his blood. Gentlemen and ladies, Scott Thatcher.'

The audience tittered appreciatively. Thatcher squared his shoulders, ran his fingers through his snow-white mane, and strode out. Olivia peeked through the curtain to watch him begin. Gabrielle reluctantly joined her.

'The hunt was an invitation which I was obliged to decline. It is

my firm conviction that a gentleman should never shoot anything
he doesn't plan to eat.' Thatcher grinned a slow grin. 'Always
excepting lawyers.'

Gauging the laughter with the eye of a practised raconteur, he
moved his hand from left to right, drawing an invisible bead on an
invisible target. Then, glancing at the ceiling as if in search of
angelic inspiration, he smiled sweetly, and in a most reasonable
tone of voice, continued: 'You know, I have often hypothesized
that the whole of civilization might be greatly advanced, the lot of
humankind bettered, and the general moral tone of the species
uplifted were the law schools to make gelding a precondition to
graduation, thus removing from the breeding pool the genetic basis
for at least five of the seven deadly sins . . .'

Gabrielle rested her hand on Olivia's arm. 'Livy, I hate to ask
this, but can we go somewhere and talk. It's important.'

Olivia nodded. 'Of course. He's got them under control now. He
always does.'

The two women wove their way through a cluster of nervously
pacing chief executives, each anxiously awaiting his fifteen minutes
on stage. They found a door, and through it a small conference
room with a table and a half-dozen gilded chairs. Gabrielle held a
chair for the older woman, then sat next to her.

'Livy, have you seen this morning's papers? No? Look at this.'
Gabrielle pulled a clipping from her handbag, setting it on the
table.

Olivia read. Her eyes bulged. 'This can't be right! Not your Jack
Taft! Good heavens, it must be someone else!'

'There's only one Taft at LBTech, Livy.'

Iron entered Olivia's voice as she hissed. '*This* is preposterous!'
She stabbed the newspaper clipping with her finger. 'Your young
man is as annoyingly honest as my Scott. I certainly hope you want
me to do something about this, because I intend to!'

'That's why I'm here, Livy.'

Olivia smiled fiercely, and the colour in her cheeks was natural,
not out of a pot. 'Good. I *am* a woman of resources, you know. We
will have this *nonsense* cleaned up in two shakes of a cat's tail. I
think I shall begin with the State Department. Longer ago than I

care to admit, the Under-secretary was my beau, or at least wanted to be—'

'Livy, there's more to this . . . something else, I mean.'

'I beg your pardon?'

Gabrielle swallowed. She was having trouble getting the words out. 'There's something we have to find out. Something I have to find out. It's the briefcase . . . it was a present, Livy, a present, and I gave it to Jack right before he left . . .' Gabrielle fumbled open her handbag, snatching for a handkerchief, and hating herself for needing one.

Olivia spoke a husky contralto, a voice that might have been mistaken as belonging to a smoker, a drinker, someone who lived hard. But Olivia did not smoke nor drank nor, least of all, lived hard; she simply talked the way all the women in her family did and thought that women who sounded otherwise were girlishly squeaky. 'Tell me about it, dear. All about it. As it turns out I have more than one reason to be concerned about Jack, and about LBTech. Anything you tell me could be of rather more importance than you imagine.'

As Gabrielle stuttered out her story, Olivia fingered the *New York Times* clipping. Then, annoyed beyond words, she wadded it into a ball and hurled it towards a trash can.

– 3 –

American Businessman Sought in Singapore

SINGAPORE, October 12 – An American businessman is being sought by Singaporean authorities after a gun battle in the prestigious Raffles Hotel that resulted in the death of a police officer.

According to police spokesman Tan Chua, New York executive John Gregory Taft is being sought in connection with the case. In a press conference held today at Singapore's Central Police Station, spokesman Tan said that Taft, 42-year-old vice-president of New York-based electronics distributor, LBTech, Inc., is accused of smuggling contraband morphine into the country.

Taft, who arrived in Singapore last night after flying from New York via San Francisco, is reported to have overcome police sent to arrest him in his hotel suite. During the affray, an as yet unidentified gunman fired several shots, killing Constable S. Liu and delaying police while Taft made his escape.

Raffles Hotel management reports no guests were injured during the gun fight. Hotel property damages are estimated at US $250,000.

Subsequent to his escape, Taft hijacked a taxicab. Although details are unclear, the taxi's driver, 32-year-old Mohammed Abdul Kadir Othman, is currently hospitalized in Singapore's Tan Tock Seng Hospital.

Police have called for a nation-wide search for the fugitive American, while national emigration and security forces have been advised that he is considered armed and dangerous. The Singapore Taxi Drivers' Association has posted a $5,000 (Singaporean) reward for information leading to his capture.

Official sources claim that 0.2 kilograms (approximately four-tenths of a pound) of morphine were found sewn into the lining of Taft's briefcase. Possession of more than 30 grams (about an ounce) of morphine is, under Singapore law, a capital crime punishable by hanging.

Representatives of Mr Taft's employers, LBTech, Inc., were unavailable for comment. US officials pledged cooperation in the investigation.

– 4 –

At first, Gabrielle had sat in her office dazed, turning the *Times* story and its implications over and over in her mind. She asked herself if it was possible that she'd bought a briefcase with drugs sewn into its lining, some smuggler's booty gone astray?

It was not.

The preceding weekend she'd shopped long and hard for Jack's present, visited five stores, examined and rejected more than a dozen bags. Before unlimbering her MasterCard, she'd scrutinized every inch of the thing. The one she picked was perfect, not a flaw, not a scratch, and certainly no evidence that the stitching had been tampered with. No suspicious bulges either. It was in pristine condition when she bought it, still in pristine condition when she picked it up after having Jack's initials embossed. And in pristine shape it had remained, safely cached in a shopping bag beneath her desk.

There was only one time anyone could have put something into it: right after she'd given it to Jack at lunch on Friday. There was only one place someone could have got to the bag: at LBTech. Jack had gone straight back to the office on Friday. At six-thirty Friday evening, he'd left, and, briefcase in hand, met her on the street outside his building. From then to his departure for the airport, he'd spent every minute, *every minute*, in her company.

But for Friday afternoon, no one could have touched the briefcase. Whoever had done it was someone at LBTech. There was no other time, no other place, no other opportunity.

Olivia Thatcher tapped a fingernail on the tabletop. She pretended that the gesture was a thoughtful one; in truth it bespoke irritation. Sometimes Gabrielle reminded her of herself at a younger age – a *much* younger age. Olivia reckoned that at the age of eighteen she had been wiser than Gabrielle was at nearly twice those years. It was a shame, really.

And so sadly typical of the current generation, the misguided lambs. To a man and to a woman, they wanted perfection, thought they could get it, turned their noses up at anything less. Give me the perfect body, they said, the perfect child, the perfect peace of mind, the perfect mate.

Ha!

As her husband Scott perpetually assured her, the perfect is the enemy of the good. Those were words she'd taken to her heart. If she hadn't, her marriage wouldn't have lasted as long, or as happily, as it had.

Much as long, she imagined, and much as happily, as a marriage between Gabrielle and her young man would last. Oh, to be sure, Jack had his flaws – not enough starch in him for one thing. But she knew promising material when she saw it. And Jack was surely that. All he needed, no different from Scott Claymore Thatcher III, was a strong-willed woman to round him out.

However, that was by the by. Poor Jack was in trouble and Olivia could not help wondering what LBTech had to do with it. After all, if Gabrielle was to be believed there was no conceivable way drugs could have been put in her beau's briefcase except by someone at the company's Fifty-Seventh Street headquarters office.

But who? And why? And, perhaps most interesting, did it have something to do with Joel Greenberg's scheme to sell the company? Possible, but improbable. Contrary to the impression one might form from reading too many paperback novels, ninety-nine out of every hundred business people (always excepting the investment bankers) were too overworked and too unimaginative to carry so much as an ounce of larceny in their hearts. Drugs and attempted murder – for that was what this nastiness surely was about – would scare the pants off any executive Olivia knew.

But still . . . it appeared that someone at LBTech was up to no good. Finding out who and why could prove more useful than Gabrielle knew.

There were very few ways to stop an acquisition after it was proposed. Boards of directors generally had a fiduciary duty to accept a well-priced offer. Joel's loathsome plan to liquidate LBTech would succeed unless the buyer withdrew its offer; as it very well might if there was evidence of wrongdoing at the company.

Scare the pants off them, Olivia thought. *Quite so. No one will touch a company tainted with management misdeed or culpable executive negligence. If Joel or one of his minions has dirtied his hands with drugs and attempted to frame poor innocent Jack, then there must be something wicked going on. Find out what, and the group offering to buy LBTech will run away as fast as their little feet will carry them.*

Olivia allowed herself a smile of satisfaction. *Save Jack, stop Joel; dear me, it's killing two birds with one stone.*

But first things first. And it would seem the very *first* order of business was to stop Gabrielle's almost hysterical jabbering.

'. . . oh, Livy, he's so smart, even though he tries not to show it, and I can't see how he'd let someone do this to him except that he's such a pushover, and he's never gotten over what his father did to him, and you wouldn't believe it but the first time Jack introduced me to his parents, you know what his dad said? He said, "Gabrielle is much too pretty for someone like you." And Jack can barely talk about it, but every time he brought a problem to the old man, the guy blew him off. Then there's Jack's mother. She had problems when he was born, couldn't have any more children, and kept him tied to her apron strings, and Jack can't handle himself, Livy, he really can't, and he doesn't have any self-confidence, he's no hero, he's not even a survivor, and, Livy, they'll kill him, I know it, they'll kill him and he won't even fight back!'

She paused to take a breath. Olivia seized the opportunity to stop the tumble of words pouring from Gabrielle's mouth. 'A protective mother and a distant father. I'm surprised Jack turned out as well as he has. One would expect a bundle of neuroses.'

'He has them too.'

Olivia knew the look in Gabrielle's eye. It was the one that told a woman that another woman was prepared to make certain intimate revelations about her beau. *That* simply would have to wait for another time. 'I'll disagree with you about Jack, pet. I've seen him in action. He is resourceful and he *always* gets his way. Although how he goes about it can be quite offputting. It's his style, you know – hesitant, apologetic, compromising. But he gets the job done quite decisively.'

Gabrielle sniffed, on the verge of tears.

Olivia had no intention of letting that happen. 'You are confident the briefcase had not been tampered with before you bought it?'

'Yes.'

'You are equally confident that Jack couldn't have been tricked somehow, the briefcase switched at the airport, or perhaps some confused-looking traveller asking Jack to help him get a gift through customs?'

'No way. The drugs were sewn into the bag; the newspaper says that. Besides, Jack is so paranoid about airplanes that when the flight attendant tells everyone to read the safety information card in the pocket in front of them, he does.'

Olivia snorted. Clearly, Jack Taft had to be married off to a capable woman, and the sooner the better. 'That's by the by. For the moment, I think I should agree with you – the deed probably was done by someone at LBTech. That's fortunate in a way, because there are so few people there.'

'Huh? It's a seven or eight billion-dollar—'

'My dear, it *is* a distributor. It buys from manufacturers and sells to far-flung customers. The real work's done at warehouses and shipping centres all around the world. Besides, except for a few accountants, Jack's logistic department, and the headquarters staff, Joel has quietly moved everyone off to states with lower tax rates. I doubt if there are more than forty or fifty people left in New York these days.'

'Oh. I didn't know. Jack doesn't really talk . . . well . . . about work . . . but . . .' Gabrielle darted a look left and right. 'Livy, there's another thing. Something I haven't told you.'

Her voice was a whisper. 'Jack said something a few weeks ago. It was about LBTech. Or it might have been. That's why I came to you this morning, I mean because you're a board member and all, and . . . and . . . Livy, I have to ask you, is there something going on at LBTech?'

Suddenly wary, Olivia pursed her lips. Few corporate affairs are more sensitive than an acquisition offer. Premature announcement could cause LBTech's stock price to veer out of control, and – if the deal later fell through – result in all manner of litigation. Because the purchase contract was far trickier than Joel let on, the Board had asked the buyers for a letter of clarification. Until it was received, the whole business was a matter of utmost secrecy. 'What makes you ask that, dear?'

'He gave me a tip, a lead for a story.'

'Did he now?'

'He said I should look into export swindles.'

Olivia breathed a sigh of relief. *The cat's not out of the bag yet,* she thought. 'At LBTech?'

'Not specifically. All he said was that it would make a good article.'

'What kind of swindle, pet? There are so many.' *Although it would only take one to put paid to Joel's little plot.*

'He didn't give me any details. He never does.'

Of course he wouldn't. Young Jack is too discreet to blab to a reporter, even if he is in love with her. 'You think Jack's found something amiss at LBTech?'

'I bet. And I bet that's why somebody planted drugs on him. They know Jack's on their trail, and want to get him out of the way.'

Mine enemies have been delivered into my hands. 'Well, this is most certainly worth looking into. As we shall. You and I together. And I believe I know precisely where to begin.'

'Where?'

Export fraud. A distinct possibility given the size of LBTech's international business. And if so . . . why then, if we can find the same evidence Jack has found, we'll know who's done this to him. 'Why, at LBTech, pet, in their offices, in their files.'

'They won't let me look at their files, Livy. I'm a reporter.'

Management wrongdoing, executive negligence – export fraud certainly fits that bill! 'And I am a director of the company. Who has a better right to – is the proper word here burglarize? No, I should imagine not – *scrutinize* the Logistics Department's records?'

– 5 –

As soon as Gabrielle returned from the Waldorf-Astoria, she swung into action, doing what Livy had ordered her to do – and what she was best at: nuts and bolts investigative journalism.

Step one: tell the library to fire up a no-holds-barred database search. You got the librarians started early because siphoning the right information out of the right computers took time. First place they'd look would be the Securities and Exchange Commission's EDGAR database, downloading LBTech's financial reports. Next up, Lexis and Nexis, big mothership repositories of online information, the first full of legal data, the second chockablock with newspaper and magazine articles. Either could provide an important lead. Meanwhile, other librarians would be accessing TRW and Equifax to extract credit files that might depict a peculiar pattern of payments. Then they'd move on to the general US and foreign information services – PR Newswire, Standard and Poors, Hoover's, Thomas' Register, Dun & Bradstreet, Moody's, Disclosure On-Line, Teikoku, Reuters, Morningstar, the Financial Times, and more than a dozen others. Gabrielle wanted it all, and she wanted her magazine's virtuoso researchers fetching it, studying it, and looking for those little red flags, known to experts, that warn you when something isn't quite right in someone's executive suite.

Step two: call your sources. In the final analysis, a journalist is only as good as her sources. She had plenty of people she could call – although, apart from Olivia, none of them was an insider at LBTech.

Step three: call everybody else. She'd begin with LBTech's competitors, because there is very little a corporate officer likes more than badmouthing his rivals – off the record, of course. After that she'd get LBTech's lobbyists on the line. Nobody sells his clients out faster than a lobbyist – especially if the sale earns him a favour from a magazine as influential as *EPS*. Then she'd start phoning up the Wall Street types. Interviews with those guys were trickier, with the trick in question being to make them believe that you, poor little innocent that you were, thought they were the most powerful, knowledgeable men on earth. Once you did that, most of them tried to prove that, well, yes, my dear, they were precisely as omniscient as you pretended to think they were. Finally – all other avenues exhausted – she'd try to wheedle information out of other journalists. Sure, they were *supposed* to be competitors, but there were times when they'd help you out, the same as there were times when you helped them.

Step four: run down to the library, see what they'd found out, jot down the names and phone numbers associated with whatever looked promising, run back to your office, and start working the phones again.

No corporation, least of all a publicly traded one, can keep the truth hidden from a good reporter. Not if that reporter knows what she's looking for and has the time to find it.

But Gabrielle didn't know. And time was short.

Lunchtime, and she had no appetite. She stood, stretched, and walked to the window. The sky had lowered, clouds the colour of city snow. South, past Thirty-Fourth Street, a veil of rain rippled in the wind, a storm curtain dropping on New York, autumn rain beading on window glass; no rivulets or drips, only rolling beads the hue of dirty quartz.

Street sounds were muted; she only heard the drum of rain, the hiss of wind. Sickly light, fog and storm – Thomas Hardy weather, sky and clouds foreshadowing a turning plotline, the approach of destiny, the fate the author has contrived for his puppets. It came to her that she feared this weather, and wished to flee.

She searched for more pleasant thoughts – something warm against encroaching winter. Then Taft was there, their first time together, a sunny September afternoon, a late lunch at the Boat House in Central Park urgently abandoned during the salad course, a taxi that seemed too slow; she tumbling whoopsadaisy on to her bed, blankets balled up at the bottom of the mattress, and she was carried away, Jack bearing her on a quickening current over warm cascades, sweeping her at last over a wonderful waterfall down down down to paradise's most peaceful lagoon . . .

Yeats had written of *the quivering of half-closed eyelids, the rags of cloud or lace*, and it was perfect.

Some little time later Jack whispered, 'You were faking, right?'

Typical. It was just typical Jack, and the memory made her smile.

Sometimes she suspected he'd committed to memory one of those damned dumb New Age sex manuals written by feminist psychologists who want men to give, never to take, and fear nothing more than the smell of a slightly dangerous male. Jack, who didn't seem to understand that self-restraint was less exciting than its opposite, left her feeling awash with bliss but never satisfied that he himself had taken all she could give.

Which only made her try harder.

Jack, dear sweet Jack, needed her. She knew that, guessed she'd known for a long time now. And, dammit, it was nice being needed. It made her feel . . .

Maybe she was in love with the big lug after all.

– 6 –

Standing at her own office window, Denise Donald looked out at the same rain as Gabrielle. Her features were composed, skin smooth, eyes bright – the warmly pleasant look she taught herself to wear at all times.

Inside, she was boiling.

Taft was still at large. Poh Kay Siong had let him get away. The stupid little Chinaman should have had his men waiting at the airport, ready to whisk Jack out of sight and do what had to be done. But no, they'd let him make it to the hotel, and Jack, unbelievably, escaped. Now the police were involved. If they caught him, if he started yapping, there'd be hell to pay.

Denise silently cursed a curse that would make a sailor blanch.

She wondered if she should have handled it differently. She could have. Just a snap of her fingers, and he would have come crawling back. That redheaded reporter slut wouldn't have a chance if she, younger and more beautiful by far, had invited Jack back to her bed. And what the hell did he see in that tramp anyway? The first time she'd spotted them together, she couldn't believe her eyes. That hair! Those clothes! Unbelievable!

Would Taft dump the little frump if she wanted him to? In a second!

However, seducing Mr Missionary Position again wasn't the answer. Jack was too nosy, and too damned smart. He'd eventually find out what she was up to. Then, boy scout that he was, not even Denise's well-practised skills would be enough to stop him from blowing the whistle.

Besides, the wimpy little fuck had been promoted into *her* job. Hers! She was the one who should be Vice President of Logistics, not him! That alone was reason enough to get him . . . get him . . . taken care of.

Best let Poh and his bug exterminators fumigate the man out of her life. And this time the little Chink had better get it right.

Time was running out. Joel's friends had launched their acquisition offer weeks ahead of schedule. Pretty soon now, auditors would be crawling all over the books. That's what they did when a deal was going down – due diligence, examining everything, and there were records Denise would much rather no one ever laid eyes on.

Those records – too much paper, too many computer files – spelled trouble. She really didn't need them. Poh had duplicates in Singapore. It had been a mistake for her to keep them. She did that from time to time – small errors, tiny oversights, nothing serious (although it got on the nerves of anal retentives like Taft). And besides, she always went back and fixed things later.

Which was what she should do now. Better safe than sorry, and thank you for that advice, Jack, you jerk!

Denise touched a fingertip to her lips. Had anyone seen her face, they would have thought it the tender expression of a woman thinking fondly of her lover.

She wasn't. What she was thinking about was the mail room. That's where LBTech kept the heavy-duty office equipment. Photocopiers. Fax machines. Document shredders. Things like that.

3

Singapore

– 1 –

Sitting astride a beautiful roan with a white blaze, Gabrielle was gorgeous in her riding habit. Just out of earshot, a paunchy little man thirty years her senior sat on a thoroughbred of his own, covetously eyeing his paramour with a purchaser's pride. She looked down at Jack, tapping her crop against a coal-black boot. 'When we're in Ireland, she said, we stay here at his stud farm. He has another one in Normandy. It's even bigger. Do you know how nice it is to have servants, Jack? No, of course you don't. I just adore having a chauffeur meet me at the airport, and a man to walk the dogs, and a maid to lay out my clothes. Did you know he's giving me an apartment in The Carlyle – well, it will be in his name, but that doesn't matter. Six rooms, Jack, it's six whole rooms. No, of course. It isn't only the material things; there's more to it than that. Oh, Jack! How can you say that? I don't write positive stories about those people just because they're his clients. It isn't like that at all. He really loves me, he does, and he's not using me, and I'm not using him. No, Jack, he won't leave his wife. I don't mind. It would be such a scandal for a man in his position, and you know how the Church is about divorce. Marriage isn't important anyway. What we have will last for ever, regardless of what you think. It's love, Jack, I'm sure of it. Even if it wasn't, you could never give me all that he does, and you could never be a man who can make things happen with a single word, or one whom people respect. Or if they don't respect, they fear. You don't have it in you. You're not strong enough, you don't have the self-confidence. Oh, do you have to go now? Wait, before you leave, we'd love you to join us for dinner tonight. The *Taoiseach*, the Prime Minister, is coming. We always dine with the most powerful people wherever we go. No? Don't want to come? I'm not surprised. You've never been comfortable around the people who count, have you? Well, I'm glad you stopped by so we could have this little talk. It was nice to see you again, Jack, honestly. Maybe we can do it again sometime.'

Then she spurred her horse, trotting off to join the lover whom she'd kept impatiently waiting – no longer a rich old roué, but rather Simon Burton, arrogant and self-assured. Jack was pierced to the heart by the greedy gloat on his face and the hateful hunger in his eyes, and Gabrielle was waving her fingers bye-bye, bye-bye . . .

Jack snapped awake, nauseous, trembling, and asking himself what sick subconscious demons haunted him that were so foul as to caricature Gabrielle with much cruelty. That he could dream so vile a dream filled him with self-contempt. Even to suspect she could be false to all the goodness in her was loathsome beyond words. Nothing is more horrible than doubting the one you adore. When distrust is set free to gnaw the soul, the first thing it devours – and with relish – is love.

He did not suspect her. He could not. Yes, he was possessive. Yes, he hated knowing that she'd had other lovers. But that, and all of that, was only natural for a man deeply and genuinely and *trustingly* . . . dammit! . . . *trustingly* in love.

The dream and the hateful questions it raised about her love had nothing – *nothing*! – to do with her. It only had to do with him – with his misgivings about himself and his fear that while she was capital 'T' The Woman for him, he might not quite be capital 'T' The Man for her.

– Too good for you, son, too good for the likes of you.

He ground his teeth in misery, wallowed in doubt, and despised himself for dreaming a dream that left him nauseous with self-disgust.

At long last pulling himself together, Jack opened his eyes, and was again puzzled at where he found himself.

In the open air. Lying on the ground. A slackening pewter rain falling. He looked morosely at the leaden sky as the memory of how he'd ended up there came surging back.

Drenched and exhausted, he had fallen beneath a hellconia

plant. All energy spent, he'd lain there unable to move. At first, dehydrated but not entirely recognizing his condition, he'd gorged himself on tepid rainwater streaming off a leaf the size of a beach blanket. Thirty horses on airplanes, nothing to drink except a slug of brandy the night before, a punishing run, tropical heat that had sweated every drop of fluid out of his body – he was lucky not to be in a coma from heat stroke.

The rain helped. Warm though it was, it cooled his skin. And he drank and drank until his stomach bloated.

The rain concealed him too, a tropical cloudburst inundating the island, reducing visibility to nearly zero. At the height of the storm – wind-whipped bushes, snapping branches, the distant crack of thunder – a police patrol, six officers uniformed beneath blue-black rain slickers, swept into the park. They'd come close to where Jack, out of breath and incapable of fleeing, hid. But they'd missed him. Instead they'd flushed some other prey, a man who wore a seersucker sports jacket that, in the gloom, made him seem Jack's twin. The man, guilty of something or feeling so, had run. The police gave chase. A few minutes after they left a bratty-looking teenage girl had tip-toed past Jack, straightening her muddy skirts as she crept from the park.

And Jack went unconscious where he lay.

Now he was awake again. The day was drawing to an end, equatorial nightfall coming with visible speed.

He didn't know what to do.

Wiping a wet hand across a sopping face, he supposed he probably should be teetering at panic's edge, borderline fugue, terrified and ready to fall apart.

Instead he was calm, cool, rational. Policemen were trying to gun him down in the streets. He was running for his life. He hadn't a clue as to what was going on. It was as if he'd wandered into one of those lunatic Hong Kong action movies. Really, he thought, he ought to be gibbering with terror.

Tempting, very tempting. Let yourself go, curl up in a ball, shiver and sob: Help! Save me, save me, save me!

That was what Gabrielle – or rather the Gabrielle of his night-mares – would expect.

But he wouldn't. Not now, not under any circumstances. He might be a compromiser, but he was no coward. Oh, sure, he always tried to negotiate, tried not to ruffle the other guy's feathers. But he didn't do that out of timidity. He did it because it got the job done. No muss, no fuss; being the nice guy worked.

Probably wouldn't work with that Chan Gin jerk, though. Uh uh. I don't think he's the kind you reason with.

He'd met the type before, the Simon Burtons of the world. Chest-thumpers given to primate posturing, and a 'my way or the highway' attitude towards anyone who crossed their path. They didn't bother him. Nor was he afraid of them. Far from it. The reason he stepped aside, letting them bull through and have what they wanted, was that arguing with bullies accomplished nothing. The only way to accomplish something was to put your head down and get on with the job.

Which was precisely what he intended to do. Right now. Immediately.

What he was *not* going to do was lose his head. Sure, he'd been scared; was scared, but he would not let fear overwhelm him. Nor any other emotion. That simply wasn't the sort of thing he did.

The sort of thing he did – his solution to every problem – was thinking. And now was as good a time as any to get started.

Where to begin? he asked himself. Then answered grimly, *In hell. In your basic worst-case scenario oh-my-God-they're-all-out-to-get-me paranoid nightmare. I'm on my own in a foreign country. No money, no credit cards, no passport, no nothing. Some cop wants me – Get him! Kill the sonofabitch! – dead. No friends and no place to run.*

Definitely no place to run. That stewardess, Zaitun – once the cops took the gag off, her first words would be, 'He's trying to get to the American Embassy.'

They'll have the place surrounded. Snipers on every roof and that Chan Gin guy with machine-guns in both hands. If I get within a mile of the embassy, I'm hamburger.

And I'll never know why.

Obviously, the authorities thought he'd committed some crime. What crime, he couldn't say. All that he could say was that the cops thought they had evidence, and damningly persuasive evidence at that. But how could that be? There was no evidence, and dammit, it didn't make sense and there was nothing he could think of, nothing that might explain it . . .

– What's this on your report card?

– Philosophy 203, Dad. Introduction to Logic. They teach you how to think.

– That's a lesson you'll never learn.

He took a deep breath, letting himself sink into the cooling embrace of reason, logic, dispassionate analysis, the only truly trustworthy things in life, and the words, those brilliantly lucid words, came back: *Entia non sunt multiplicanda.*

Occam's Razor. Loosely translated: simplest solutions are best.

Jack concentrated. *Simplify, simplify. Take it one step at a time. Start with a hypothesis. If it seems to work, keep going. If not, start over. OK, hypothesis: there was something in my bag. Why? Because that's the first thing that goon Chan went for. Is this a viable hypothesis? Yeah, sure. So what was in that bag?*

Nothing but boring reports and dopey Federal regulations. Nothing but some file folders containing financial printouts on all of LBTech's Southeast Asian operations.

And, of course, his new logistics plan for Southeast Asia.

The plan? Could that be it . . .?

The plan was dynamite, and that was certain. Implemented on a *fait accompli* basis, it would give LBTech a commanding lead in what increasingly was the centre of global electronics manufacturing. But the plan was also a closely guarded secret. You just didn't let word about that sort of scheme leak out. The stakes were too high.

But if it had . . .?

If it had, would any of LBTech's rivals feel so threatened by the coup that they'd try to kill the man behind it? Nonsense. Utter drivel. The stuff of Michael Crichton novels and made-for-TV movies – all businessmen are evil swine and they're greedy and they kick their dogs too . . .

If somehow or another the competition had found out what he was up to, what they'd be doing was scrambling to catch up. There'd be no point in trying to eliminate the architect of LBTech's strategy. The strategy was already there. It was going to get implemented one way or the other. The death of a recently promoted corporate vice president wouldn't change things at all.

Then what about LBTech's employees? The new plan was going to shake things up. Did someone resent what he was about to do so badly that they'd . . .?

No, no one in Asia knew what he was about to do. No one in LBTech but Joel Greenberg knew. The plan was the best-kept secret in the company. Likewise the fact that Jack was flying down to execute the new plan office by office, country by country, starting in Singapore. Hell, no-one in LBTech except for Joel knew that! It was the best kept secret in the company.

Nope, it wasn't the plan. Couldn't be. There was nothing in the plan that would interest the cops. It was something else. But what, dammit?

The financial reports? Detailed computer printouts on the results of every one of LBTech's Asian operations? Jack shook his head. He doubted that was what the police were looking for. The Logistics Department's numbers were clean but for a single minuscule anomaly – something he'd meant to study on the airplane but had been too jetlagged to make the effort. Anyway, it was probably only a data-entry error, small potatoes, and besides, the money wasn't big enough to trigger a police investigation.

He chewed his lip in frustration. Trying to figure out what had been in the bag was a blind alley. Best start over, reason it through again. *First premise: I put nothing in my bag that could interest the police. Second premise: there was something in my bag that interested the police. Conclusion: somebody put that something in my bag.*

Jack nodded. It made sense. It was logical. It worked. And therefore: *Hypothesis: somebody put something in my bag to get me arrested. Corollary: whoever did must hate me bad enough to want me in jail for a long, long time.*

Again the logic – so pure, so perfect, so clear – worked. He had an enemy; the enemy had framed him; now who could that enemy be? Easy answer. Jack, cautiously affable man that he was, had only one.

She'd been twenty-eight. Undergrad in economics, Columbia MBA, four years with a big blue-chip consulting firm named McKinley-Allan, recently recruited into the Marketing Department. He sometimes saw her in the hall, thought she was the most improbably perfect woman he'd ever seen, never so much as exchanged a word with her. Too beautiful, too blonde, too good looking for him.

A year or so later there was a shake-up in marketing. The vice-president who ran the department went through a nasty divorce and self-destructed on booze. Things were a shambles. Jack, who avoided office gossip, never heard the full story. What he did know was that an outsider, a tough-as-nails woman executive, had been headhunted away from LBTech's biggest competitor to clean up the mess. Shortly afterwards, the improbably perfect young woman was sitting in his office. 'Hi, I'm Denise Donald. We haven't met, but I've noticed you in the halls.' Oh? 'I've always really been fascinated by logistics.' Is that so? 'There's a big reorg going on in marketing.' I've heard. 'I think the time is right for me to get some operations experience.' Good career move. 'They say there's an opening in your group.' Well, yes. 'I know I have a lot to learn about shipping, but I'm sure you could teach me.' Uh, there's another candidate. 'Look at the clock, I've got to get back to my desk. But could I buy you a drink after work so we can talk more about this.' Gulp, sure.

And he *had* taught her the job, every tedious detail of it, all the tricks of the trade from building elaborate linear programming modules to cutting bargain-basement deals with freight consolidators. He taught her about small packages and boxcar-sized container loads; he taught her about ships and trains and trucks and planes and transmodal carriers; he taught her which ports had fast customs procedures and which slow; in short, he taught her everything there is to know about moving high-tech electronic components around the world efficiently. He taught, and taught, and every step of the way held her hand and corrected her mistakes and made her a rising corporate star. Then he sat down and taught her more.

But then she taught him some things too. Oh yeah, oh definitely.

And afterwards, he'd wondered if he'd ever trust another woman again.

Yup, he thought, *Denise hates my guts, and that's for sure. She's wanted my head stuffed on her wall ever since we broke up. Then when I got promoted into the job she wanted . . .*

But there was an empirical fault to his analysis, a fatal flaw of fact: Denise didn't know he was travelling to the Orient. He'd made sure she didn't learn about the trip until after he'd left, and, ideally, until after he'd begun dismantling the little empire she'd built for herself in Asia. More to the point, even if she had somehow found out, there was no way she could have planted something in his briefcase. Why? Because she hadn't been in the office until late in the afternoon – the one and only afternoon – that the briefcase was someplace where she could tamper with it.

Jack pursed his lips. The key to the puzzle was that nobody had known he was going to Singapore. But only someone who knew about the trip could have framed him. A dilemma. A paradox.

Logicians abhor paradoxes.

Not Denise. Somebody else. But there isn't anybody else is there? It had to be someone who knew about his trip. Who the hell knew? Nobody knew. Or rather, almost nobody . . .

Only one other person: Joel Greenberg, LBTech's chairman and CEO. Not even Jack's secretary, Josephine, knew his destination. At Joel's insistence, Jack had made his own travel arrangements, kept everything hush-hush, confidential, for your eyes only, and we'll make the announcement when we release next quarter's earnings report.

Could Joel be behind this? Of course not. A corporate chief exec has an arsenal of bloodless techniques for getting rid of people he doesn't like; no need to resort to violence, none at all. True, Joel didn't seem to care for Jack very much. But like or dislike, the man had no reason to kill him.

No, not Joel. Not Denise either. But, goddammit, there's no one else who knew I was going to Singapore. No one. No one . . .

. . . Uh . . . no one but . . .

All the poisons he'd flushed from his system flooded back.

. . . Gabrielle

– 2 –

Chan was back on the streets. All that hi-tech bullshit – computers and DNA analysers and surveillance gear and whatever other whizbang toys the department had wasted this year's budget on – was no substitute for real police work. Real police work was what you did on the pavement, not behind a desk.

Go grab a punk in a bar, twist his arm up behind his back like this, quick-march him into an alley, bounce him up against a wall until he understands the sincerity of your interest, then tell him to start singing. *Gong simi*, dickface, what's going down? Hey, how about Poh Kay Siong and this Taft guy? How much dope and how many bucks are in the deal? And while you're at it, where's Poh hiding him? Come on, asshole, make it easy on yourself.

It usually worked. Solved cases fast. But not this time. This time it was: *uh uh, man, I dunno nuttin 'bout nuttin'. This Taft dude's bad karma, lah? Like people have fuckin' died. That's way too heavy for me. No, man, no – I mean why would Poh buy Yankee dope? It ain't like his sources in Cambodia and Laos have dried up or somethin'. Jesus shit! Don't hit me like that, man! Come on, I'd tell you if I knew! Only thing I hear is Poh wants information just as bad as you. Says he'll pay big time, no pissy kei gao reward, real money. That's all I know. Honest. Please! Not again!*

And Chan moved on to a different bar, a different punk, and the same story over and over again.

Whatever Poh was up to was buried deep. The bastard had covered his tracks so well that nobody on the street knew what he was doing. Or was too scared to say. And if they were more scared of Poh than they were of Chan, not only was Poh's scheme deep, but it was also very, very big.

Or . . . Or maybe the street trash really didn't know shit. Maybe

Taft was an interloper, a lone wolf come to Singapore to do business on his own. No, that didn't make sense. In the brightly lit hotel room, Chan had seen Taft's eyes – flat and dead, the icy stare of a machine programmed to kill. Men like that, men at the top of the profession, only did work for hire; and the only people who could afford their *per diem* rates were warlords like Poh.

So why was Poh polling the punk population for information on Taft? Easy answer: the shootout broke their connection, and they'd lost touch. Taft had gone to ground with his *chioh bu* bimbo. Poh was still trying to find him so the two of them could get back on track with their business.

Chan had to catch him first. The American gangster had humiliated him twice – first at the hotel, then in the girl's apartment. There would not, could not, be a third time. All there could be, was the saving of face. Taft was going to die, and that was that.

Maybe the Samsudin babe would talk. She was his best shot. Knowing that he himself was lousy at interrogating pretty girls, he'd left her in the hands of an officer who was infinitely less susceptible to a pretty face. If that cop couldn't break her down, no one could.

But if she didn't spill her guts . . . *Some*where there had to be *some*one who knew *some*thing. Walk and talk was the only way to find out who.

He was out in the Indian neighbourhood now, just past the shopping mall that was Singapore's largest market for pirated software. Despite the fact that the Land Forces busted 'em once a month, the Indian minority seemed unable to resist that particular scam. But apart from that, they generally kept their noses clean. The most you expected out of them was domestic violence, and even that not very often. Nonetheless, there were a few hardcases around, same as in any community. And usually, Chan thought, they could be found sipping exceptionally sour beer in the basement poolhall of the tenement towards which he was walking.

He eyed the building's façade. Somewhere up there one or two well-disguised video cameras were concealed. Maybe. Then again maybe not. That was the beauty of the Singaporean system. It wasn't that you were always watched; it was that you *might* be.

And, therefore, the course of prudence was to act as if you were. Threats can be more intimidating than deeds, and putting armed police on every street corner was too damned expensive anyway.

Would one of the island's several thousand cameras spot Taft? Probably not. From what little Chan knew of the surveillance system, most of the invisible eyes were in the high-rent neighbourhoods and heavy retail traffic areas. Taft was too smart to leave the shadows. If he was caught on video, it would be pure blind luck, and nothing but.

The odds were against it. The only thing the odds favoured was street work.

Readying himself to collar and quiz another punk, Chan reflected his job would be easier if the goddamned pussy bureaucrats hadn't ordered him – how many years ago? – to stop breaking bones. That was a real pain in the ass. Break a few bones and punks talked faster than you'd believe.

He squared his shoulders. Fuck it. Maybe he'd crunch some fingers anyway. It wasn't like the scumbags didn't deserve it.

Smiling like a wolf, Chan Gin pushed through the door. *Heeere's Johnny!*

– 3 –

It was a neighbourhood open-air market. And it was mobbed.

As Jack, across the road and concealed in the darkness of the park, studied the scene, his stomach growled.

The pavement, bricked and freshly washed with rain, was lined with bins and crates and tables overflowing with *food, glorious food!* A tiny man, his head no higher than Jack's chest, slung an enormous sack of rice to his shoulder. The phrase '50KG' was stencilled on the bag – one hundred and ten pounds. The man looked to weigh barely more than that, but his load didn't make him so much as bow. Hefting the sack, he lumbered past awning-covered booths. A Chinese woman – red bandana, indigo *samfoo* workdress – lean and smiling and with cheekbones that would put a *Vogue* model to shame – called out to him. He laughed. She plucked a pomelo fruit from a mound in front of her, tossing it to him. He caught it with one hand, put it in his mouth, and bit. Jack salivated at the sight.

Up the street, coming from the opposite direction, a tawny pedlar pulled a wooden wheelbarrow overflowing with spiky, grapefruit-sized objects. Buyers clustered around him, money changing hands at a rapid rate. A boy – the Indian's son perhaps – stood to the side wielding what looked to be a miniature meat cleaver, cutting each piece of fruit neatly in two. Jack could smell it from where he stood – rank, an odour of something as sweet as it was rotten. Though he'd never smelled it before, he guessed the fruits were durian, delicacies treasured in the Orient but looked upon askance by those who had not acquired a taste, or a tolerance, for the pungent things.

Jack swallowed hard. Foul though they might smell, he'd happily eat one now.

Further away, past the produce stalls there was a small restaurant centre beneath a Housing Development Board apartment building. Ten tiny kitchens shared a common restaurant area and three dozen common tables. Signs above each kitchen touted certified Halal Muslim, Syrian, Vegetarian, Seafood, Cantonese, Tandoori, spicy Thai cuisine. Another booth sold beer, soft drinks, and potato chips. One place specialized in – *sounds great to me!* – deep-fried carrot cake. Another exhibited its menu on a six-foot-tall board:

Steak dinner $5
Lamb chop dinner $4
Spicy spring chicken dinner $7
Bacon, sausage, egg omelet $4

Oh God, God, God, I want a steak!

Underneath striped awnings charcoal glowed and mouth-watering smoke drifted. Someone not far away was grilling king-sized prawns in a sauce of butter and wine. Elsewhere steam arose bearing the redolent fragrances of plum and pork dumplings plucked hot from boiling water, glazed with sweet mustard, nested on beds of rice and kale. Three competing satay shops stood side by side, their proprietors proffering skewers of meat and vegetables to every passerby. Jack heard them auction their price down for prospective customers – two dollars, one-fifty for the finest satay in Singapore, tastier than bird's nest soup and only a quarter the cost, you can't resist.

No, he could not resist.

No wallet, no money, no plastic, no passport. He was going to steal his dinner, and to hell with it.

Edging out of the darkness, warily preparing to cross the street and join the crowd, Jack tried to look as innocent as possible. He pushed his hands into his pockets, glanced left and right, framed an insincere smile, and . . .

He felt something in his right pocket. Paper and metal. What was that . . .? Of course! It was, *how marvellous!*, cash – the tip he'd tried to force on an unwilling bellboy at Raffles, and the coins the taxi driver had given him in change after transporting him from the airport to the hotel.

Jack Taft, famished miser, fished his new-found wealth from his trousers and greedily tallied up the extent of his riches. A single bill, the word 'Singapore' printed across its top in four languages, an etching of an antique boat on one side; on the other an image of twelve frolicking citizens – representatives from each of Singapore's minorities, all in national garb – smiling and lifting their hands and cheering a New Year's ritual lion dance. And across the bottom it said: '*TWO DOLLARS*'.

He was rich.

– Earn a little money and you think you're Rockefeller.

– Dad, I've been promoted. I'm an executive.

– The higher the monkey climbs, the more he shows his butt.

There was more than just a two-dollar bill. The coins tallied up to another eight dollars and twenty-five cents. Ten dollars and twenty-five cents in total, a bit more than seven dollars in US currency, and more than enough to eat very, very well.

Syrian food, Jack could smell it, and he narrowed his eyes searching out the stalls. Early in his career, he'd once visited the Middle East. Ever since, he'd loved the Arabic peoples, their courtesy, and their cuisine.

Especially the cuisine. God, he *adored* their cuisine!

Maghrib, dusk prayer, was over now. Evening meals were being prepared – shami bread, stuffed vine leaves, lamb shwarma in a tahini sauce of cream and spices. Desserts too: hot om ali, bakhlava, date and nut pies, and he was going to die unless he got his hands on something to eat.

He was halfway across the street. A child, a little girl, clutching her mother's sari, turned and saw him. Her eyes opened wide, and she tugged hard at yellow-dyed cotton. The woman glanced over her shoulder. Her eyes, a second earlier wide and warm, narrowed into slits. She pulled her daughter close to her side, hissing a word of warning to her neighbours.

People looked at Jack, and went silent. One hawker reached beneath his booth to retrieve a carving knife. A tall turbaned Sikh took a step forward, hand on hips, a threatening expression on his face.

Jack backpedalled, slinking into the shadows from which he'd come. Sixty hours or thereabouts without a shave. Sopping wet from the rain. Torn slacks stained with mud. Jacket like a dirty rag. *Jesus Christ, I must look like some sort of New York street crazy! The kind of guy, you see him on the sidewalk, you hold your breath, walk a little faster, hope that your number hasn't come up and tomorrow you're not a five-paragraph story on page three: 'Exec Killed By Homeless Man: Promising Career Cut Short On Lexington Avenue: Bellevue Officials Defend Discharging Dangerous Patient: Mayor Pledges Full Investigation . . .'*

He edged back into the park, into the darkness where creatures like him could not, and should not, be seen.

No question, he thought, *I'm a high-profile case. Passport photo on the front of the tabloids. Same picture* Live at Five. *Wanted man, armed and dangerous; mad dog, shoot on sight. Half the people in that market are probably dialling 911 right now.*

Or rather 999, the Singaporean equivalent. There were advertisements for the police emergency number everywhere.

He vaulted a low park wall, jolting on to soft, muddy soil, spinning right, away from the lights and bustle of the street market, and beginning to jog. His muscles were sore, the tendons in his knees shaky. He was too out of shape, had run too hard fleeing Chan Gin and those men who'd tried to kill him. Now he could move no faster than a trot. Even that was painful.

He kept close to the park border, streetlights every thirty yards or so marking out his path. He slipped once, landing on his back, another layer of mud on clothes ruined beyond redemption. An instant later he was back on his feet, forcing himself to move.

For a moment back there, for the merest second, he'd tottered on the brink of fear, almost lost his grip. A sweat having little to do with tropical heat had beaded on his lip. His heart spiked as terrified flight presented itself as a most desirable course of action.

But no, he'd not run in terror, although run he would. In control, mastering himself, keeping emotion at bay, and thinking, thinking, thinking ahead.

Priorities, he thought. *I've got to set priorities. First, a safe place to hide. Second, food. No, make food the priority number one. If I don't eat something, I'm going to fall over. Third, get help, call somebody, call Gabrielle or the embassy or . . .*

Gabrielle . . . He loved her. He didn't doubt her. Not for a moment. He never could doubt her. She loved him as much as he loved her, and anyone else who might have . . . might have . . . *tempted* her was irrelevant, and he didn't care, and he didn't want to know . . .

He shook his head in exasperation. *When am I going to get over this? Jesus, it's becoming an obsession. Come on, Taft, pull yourself together and get this crap out of your head! You've got more important things to worry about.*

Jack nodded to himself. He did have more important worries. And one of them was what Gabrielle would do when she heard about how much trouble he was in. Would she know by now? Sure. He was big news, and his face was splashed all over the newspapers. Which meant she'd be in action. That was a comforting thought. Crack investigative reporter that she was, she'd be burrowing into things, doing her damnedest to find out what was in his briefcase, and who put it there.

She gave me that briefcase, she did, she was the only one who touched it, and . . .

He pushed the thought away.

She was a reporter, a business journalist, someone who knew how to find the facts. And the first place she'd look was LBTech, which was, Jack guessed, the right place to start.

Where in LBTech? What would she look for? *Uh oh . . .* The first thing Gabrielle would do was think about the story leads he'd given her. From time to time he dropped tips that she turned into articles. But he never gave her hints that had anything to do with LBTech. He was too loyal to tattle on his own employer. Instead, always discreet, he just dropped a word or two that pointed at a hot topic, an issue, a problem, something that was on every distributor's and shipper's mind. Industry gossip – that was all he *ever* gave her, even though, sceptical reporter that she was, she often thought otherwise.

Red herrings. She'll think something I heard about another company is going on at LBTech, and start chasing red herrings. To which he involuntarily added, *But at least that will keep her too busy for that conceited jerk Simon Burton to . . .*

Pushing aside such inappropriately jealous thoughts, Jack wondered where he could find a telephone. *I have to call her. Call her now. Get her to talk to the authorities. Have her find somebody to help me. Tell her to look in the* right *places at LBTech.*

The food stands were far behind him. The buildings lining the side of the street opposite the park were nondescript shopfronts, all dark but one. Before that one building's doorway stood a phone kiosk.

Sighing with relief, Jack hobbled out of the park.

A few seconds later, he was cursing. The damned phone didn't accept coins – prepaid cards only. And he had no card, hated the things, had been burned more than once by the scamsters who peddled them. He spun on his heel in frustration.

Before his eyes, a single light glowed behind a plate-glass window emblazoned – Gothic letters, gold-leaf paint – with the words 'Quint & Claggart, Attorneys-at-Law'.

– 4 –

The citizens of Singapore and the United States hold in common a naive belief that the imperatives of justice are absolute. Being British, Messrs Quint and Claggart, attorneys-at-law, knew otherwise, thus concurring with a lenient judge that, why yes, m'lord, it was indeed quite the opportune moment for them to emigrate to some sunny, distant land.

The two lawyers, upon necessarily hasty consultation, selected Singapore as their destination. They reasoned that the climate was not inclement, the culture a comforting relic of Britain's colonial era, the liquor supplies inexpensive, and the island itself, while unpleasantly illiberal in carnal matters, only a short airplane flight from the recreational opportunities afforded by Bangkok's boy-child brothels.

Once settled in Singapore, they swiftly established a lucrative legal practice serving the discreet needs of remittance men and exiles like themselves.

One well-lubricated evening, Quint had toasted Claggart, 'The good die young.' To which Claggart, clinking Quint's glass, had responded in wretched Latin: '*Ad vitae aeternum.*'

Now, darkness fallen, and the hour for the evening's libation at hand, Quint sat alone in his office, putting the final touches on a letter to a small but growing circle of foreign friends. The letter announced that a second interactive CD-ROM containing enticing scenes of Singaporean culture could be purchased, £100 no credit cards accepted, remit to Account 50–7685, Banco Rodriguez, Grand Cayman Island, et cetera, et cetera.

As a sideline to Quint's and Claggart's legal practice, the first CD-ROM had proved a remarkably lucrative proposition. Quint purchased them for twenty-five dollars Singaporean currency, or about twelve pounds sterling, and sold them via mail order for six times that sum. Given the enthusiasm with which his customers back in Great Britain had ordered the product, Quint suspected he'd grotesquely underpriced the thing.

Created as a student project by the apple-cheeked moppets of Temasek Polytechnic school, the CD in question was entitled

'Youth Crime', a delightfully sincere and well-intentioned multi-media program intended to educate Singaporean children about the lamentable consequences of juvenile delinquency.

What consequences? Why, caning of course!

The students' interactive software contained the only footage available *anywhere* of an actual, genuine, accept-no-substitutes Singaporean flogging. Administered at Changi Prison, the film showed a nearly naked prisoner stretched out with buttocks to the ready; then *WHACK!* the furious arrival of Singapore's notorious rattan cane, a scream of horrified agony, and the swift appearance of the most deliciously bleeding wound. To the side of the writhing victim stood a licensed physician ready to administer emergency cardiac aid should – as sometimes happened during these most thoroughly Oriental tortures – the prisoner's heart stop. Ah, but the scene was positively medieval, worthy of the Inquisition, unrivalled in brutality and more than merely graphic in its portrayal of a brine-soaked inch-thick whipping rod inflicting unimaginable anguish. *Perfect*, thought Quint the first time he saw the video, *utterly perfect*. To connoisseurs, the disk brought a most satisfying shiver of lubricious delight. There being a sizable number of aficionados among Quint and Claggart's kindred spirits, the disk was an instant best-seller, and . . .

The bell rang over the front door. *Bloody hell!* Quint thought. *I forgot to lock the thing.* He looked up in irritation. There was some man limping clump, clump, clump through the unlit waiting area and straight for his office. Well, this simply wouldn't do, wouldn't do at all. Client or no, whoever he was, he could do his business with Quint & Claggart during working hours, or not at all.

Quint began to rise. The intruder, instantly recognizable, entered his chambers. Quint promptly sat back down.

'Excuse me,' the man began.

'Out,' hissed Quint. 'Out, I say.'

'I need a lawyer.'

Quint set his jaw. 'No doubt about that, sir. I wish you Godspeed and good fortune in finding one. And now, if you'll be so kind as to close the door as you depart . . .'

The man, what was his name, ah yes, Taft, had the temerity to take a seat. 'Please, just give me a minute. You're a lawyer, and I'm in some sort of trouble—'

'You've a talent for understatement!'

'But I don't know what it is that I'm supposed to have done. If you're not a criminal lawyer, maybe you could refer me to one.'

Quint leaned forward, began to offer a helpful word, then snickered. He'd almost been fooled, and mightily appreciated the talent it took to bamboozle a man whose career had been devoted to bamboozlement. 'Well done, sir! Damned well done! For a moment, you had me going. That look of boyish perplexity on your face, the querulous vibrato in your voice, the disingenuous innocence in your eyes. Do keep it up, I urge you. It may do you some small good when you stand before the Bar.'

Taft pursed his lips, furrowed his brow, looked so guilelessly simple. 'Look, Mr Claggart—'

'Quint. And *not* at your service.'

'Mr Quint. Look, if nothing else, let me make a phone call. Heck, I'll call collect. To someone in the States, I mean, and—'

'Phone? From my office? Our government being what it is, your call not only could be traced, but most likely would be. No, sir, I think not. No one who lives in Singapore is so foolish as to allow a criminal, even one so gifted at play-acting—'

'Mr Quint, this isn't an act. I honest to God do not, repeat *do not*, know what I'm supposed to have done. Not only that, I'm an American, a foreigner, I mean, and I don't know anything about this country or its legal system or anything else except that I'm in big trouble and I don't know why. So please, Mr Quint, I need a lawyer's help . . .'

Quint bent over and retrieved the day's newspapers from his wastebasket – the sober and staid *Straits Times*, and the *New Paper*, which was anything but. He flung them across his desk. 'Have it your way, sir. Scan the headlines, and then, to quote the Bard, "At once, good night: Stand not upon the order of your going, but go at once".'

With fingers as filthy as a street urchin's, the wretched fugitive picked up the the *New Paper*. He blinked several times, and his face blanched. It was, all in all, the most convincing performance Quint had ever seen.

While Taft sat dithering through the newspapers, Quint had pondered the affair. It could well be, he allowed, that this man actually *was* as innocent a lamb as he seemed. If so, defending him could prove to be an interesting proposition – even though, this being Singapore, Taft, guiltless or not, was destined for the gallows.

For the briefest moment, he thought about taking him on as a client. But no, that wouldn't do. The legal practice of Quint & Claggart, Attorneys-at-Law, did not need the scrutiny a high-profile narcotics case would bring. Then too there was the all-important question of the fees.

Quint leaned forward. 'Finished now, Mr Taft? Read it all? Seen what is to be seen? Good. Then if you would be so kind as to vacate my chambers . . .'

Taft let the newspapers slip to the floor. He fluttered his fingers, looking altogether like a lost waif. *How touching*, Quint thought. *A few pounds lighter and many years younger, my lad, and you might win my heart.* 'Ah, Mr Quint, this . . .' He gestured at the fallen papers. '. . . Jesus. I mean, this is . . . this is nuts. Look, I really do need a lawyer, don't I?'

Quint allowed himself an avuncular chortle. 'In your circumstances, it is the done thing. But tell me, precisely how do you propose to recompense one for his services, hmmm?'

Taft nodded. Fees were very clearly an issue he understood. 'I don't think there'll be any problem there, Mr Quint. I'm a reasonably well-to-do man.'

'Oh are you now? And how much might you have in your bank account, Mr Taft? Just an estimate, if you please.'

'CMA, CDs, checking, securities and bonds . . . All told, I guess I'm worth at least two hundred thousand dollars.'

'Incorrect!' Quint boomed, knitting his fingers across his belly.

'I beg your pardon.'

'Your net worth, sir, is zero. You have no cash management account, no certificates of deposit, no checking account, no stocks, and no bonds. Narcotics offences . . . spare me your denials for the moment . . . allow *your* government to sequester your assets. The very moment a warrant for your arrest was issued in this country, little red lights started flashing in yours. Blink – freeze his bank account. Blink – cancel his credit cards. Blink – seize his safety deposit box. Such is the law in your fine country, Mr Taft; such is the law in this one. And so I say to you, sir, that you've not the least hope of paying my fees. Nor those of any other attorney of my, *harumph!*, stature. Under the very best of circumstances, you will be assigned some state-appointed counsel of dubious abilities who will urge you to throw yourself on the mercy of the court, the more swiftly to end your suffering and the more rapidly that he may submit his invoice to the authorities.'

'I've got friends. They can pay for a lawyer. And they can post bail too.'

Quint guffawed. 'Bail! Oh dear me! Unless you count among your blood kin that computer chap, Mr Billy Gates, I most sincerely doubt if you'll raise the ready cash needed for bail in *this* country.'

Taft shook his filthy locks, incomprehension wreathing him like a glum miasma. 'How much bail do you think they'll ask for?'

Quint felt a glow of pleasure. Explaining Singaporean law to Taft was rather amusing. Torturing the vulnerable usually was. 'I cannot even begin to guess. Understand, sir, our government views drug smuggling as a most serious offence – much more so than, oh, say, cigarette smuggling. Therefore, let your perspective be shaped by the fact that rather recently a cigarette smuggler's bail was set at the not unimpressive sum of four hundred and thirty-three million dollars. Singaporean currency, of course. In American dollars it would be about three hundred and seventy-five million.' He paused. Heretofore he'd believed that saying someone went white with shock was a mere literary device. But it wasn't, no not at all; no better evidence of that than Taft's chalky face.

'Three hundred and seventy-five million dollars? For cigarette smuggling? Oh Jesus, I don't believe it.'

'*Do* believe it, sir. The case was this past January. Now perhaps you've the faintest glimmer of how the justice system works in these parts.'

'*But . . . Goddammit . . . I . . . Am . . . Not . . . Guilty!*' Taft's bleached aspect had been replaced by a ruddier hue. Quint was pleased. It seemed the man had some spunk in him after all. 'There is no jury in the whole world that would—'

'A moot point. Singapore has long since dispensed with the unnecessary impedimenta afforded by the jury system. Our criminal proceedings are adjudicated by but a single judge, or sometimes two. Thus our trials are a less costly, swifter, and more predictable sort of proceeding.' *Ah*, Quint thought, *what colour will he turn next – the baleful blue of cardiac arrest perhaps?* 'And so quite briskly it shall come to pass that you, sir, miserable specimen of wrongdoing that you are, will stand in the dock before a fuller-wigged, black-robed judge of our just and reputable courts, and receive your preordained sentence – "Unrespited, unpitied, unrepriev'd", if I might quote a poet doubtless unfamiliar to you.'

Quint threw his head back, braying at the ceiling. It was for this reason that he did not see the colour of Jack's skin change again, this time to a darker shade.

'The words they speak are in keeping with honoured Imperial tradition now elsewhere abandoned. I can recite them from memory, for, after all, our courts pronounce them two or three times every month. The judge leans down and casts his coldest look upon the hapless felon. With a handkerchief of midnight black upon his head, he intones, "And so, John Gregory Taft, I order that you be taken from this court to a place of imprisonment, and there . . ."'

Quint fished his own handkerchief from his breast pocket, and mopped it across his cheeks, failing to notice that Taft had come to his feet, and was in the process of balling his fists.

'". . . and there, upon the date and time specified, to be removed from your cell and carried to the place of execution, where you shall be hanged from the neck until you are . . ."'

Taft was leaning across the desk. Quint saw him too late. For reasons that he would later be unable to explain, he did nothing but finish the sentence he had begun. Finish it he did, although Jack put the punctuation mark on its conclusion.

'". . . until you are dead, dead, dead!"'

Whereupon John Gregory Taft threw his first punch since passing the age of puberty.

– 5 –

Accidentally touch an open wire. Feel the lightning.

Sudden shock, a strobe pulse so swift you don't understand it. You jerk your fingers from the current before you understand what's happening. Comprehension comes later. The body has moved, the brain has been left behind.

That's what it was like. One second he was sitting aghast at the lawyer's sneering diatribe. The next, Quint was face down and still.

Jack had been prepared for fear, and ready to fight it off.

He wasn't prepared for rage.

Pure and very red, it had boiled up, come from nowhere, overwhelming in its urgency, and he, mild logical Jack, had driven his fist straight into the smirking sonofabitch's fat face.

Now his knee was cocked, his foot raised, his shoetoe aimed at an unconscious man's groin.

Sharp, deep, and stinging to the bone, his knuckles hurt. This was the first thing he noticed.

Then he noticed the rest.

His right leg was quivering, ready to lash out. Very slowly, very carefully, he lowered his foot to the floor, shifting his weight on to it as if to hold it in place.

He brought a hand to his cheek. His skin was feverishly hot. And his heart was jackhammering. Breath coming in fast little pants. A muscle twitching under his left eye.

I don't believe it. I do not believe I did that.

The evidence of his eyes assured him otherwise.

This was bad. This was the worst. This was everything that Jack Taft was not. He didn't have this in him, never had, or if he did he'd driven it out, expelled it, vomited it from his system like a tainted meal. He did not lose his temper. He did not explode. He did not lash out.

Anger was counterproductive. It solved no problems, only made things worse. There was always a better way to handle things, there was never anything that couldn't be settled by a rational discussion. If you had a temper, if you felt it rise, you stuffed it back in its cage, shut the bars, locked the lock, turned out the lights, and never, never let it show, because it did no damn good, and there was no problem so extreme that you and the other guy couldn't work it out.

Anger is no answer, violence is no solution.

Damn, but smacking that jerk in the face felt so good!

Ten minutes later, Quint was still on the floor. Jack had tried to call Gabrielle twice – once in the office and once at home. There was no answer, and he, remembering Quint's paranoid insinuation that every phone in Singapore was tapped, decided not to leave a message on her voice-mail system.

Now, breathing regularly and trying to ignore the implications of what he'd just done, he studied a detailed streetmap he'd found while rifling the lawyer's credenza.

Quint kept a stack of business cards in a clear plastic box on his desk. Jack noted the office address, and drew his finger across the map. *Ah ha! I am here. Off Upper Thompson Road. OK, finding where I am was easy enough. Next question: how do I find a way out of this lousy country?*

The map showed him a fearfully small island – a half-dozen major freeways spanning a landmass twenty-five miles long at its widest point. No exit but for a single causeway across the Straits of Johor and up into Malaysia.

Malaysia? Jack asked himself. He turned the idea over in his mind. It made sense. If he could get to a foreign country, and Malaysia was the nearest one, he'd be that much further from danger. Quint's wallet – *Did I really take his wallet? Aw man, what's wrong with me? I ought to put it back but . . .* – contained more than a hundred dollars, plenty of money to buy a train ticket to Kuala Lumpur, Malaysia's capital.

It's easy. It's logical. All I have to do is make it to the first train station across the border. The map was sufficiently detailed to illustrate the exact location of the Johor station, tantalizingly close to the causeway's terminus.

Then a train to Kuala Lumpur – 'KL', as everyone who worked in Southeast Asia called it – a few hours north on the railway. There'd be an American Embassy in KL. Besides, LBTech had a branch in the city. You couldn't be in the electronics business and not have an operation there.

Yeah, get to KL, get to the embassy or LBTech. Get to someplace where Chan Gin is not.

Once away from Singapore and beyond Chan's reach, he'd be able to find a sympathetic ear. *No sympathetic ears in Singapore. Uh uh. Only henchmen of a boss who orders them to 'Kill the sonofabitch!'*

Besides, according to that fatuous ass Quint, Singapore was a country in which criminal cases were not tried before a jury, but rather were decided by the opinion of a solitary judge. *Uh uh, no way. I'm not throwing myself on the mercy of some government flunky, beholden to the powers-that-be.*

He had to find an American official who, unlike anyone in Singapore, would listen to him. Once he did that, he might not be out of trouble, but at least he would be out of Singaporean reach. American Embassies were American soil, or so he'd always been told. That meant that the laws of the United States held sway. No gun-toting cops could come barging through the doors to carry him off. They'd have to extradite him. And that would mean American law and an American investigation.

Which would in turn demonstrate that he was innocent. Sort of. Innocent at least of drug smuggling. As for his other . . . er . . . technically speaking, they were crimes . . . but really they were only self-defence . . . *resisting arrest, kidnapping a flight attendant, assault and battery on Peter Quint . . .*

Best to think of these problems later. Solutions would present themselves. When he put his mind to the job they always did.

Right now the job at hand was getting out of Singapore.

All I have to do is get across that bloody causeway. Which will be guarded by cops. Who will be checking passports which I do not have.

Nope, he was *not* going to cross the causeway. He'd be a fool to try.

There had to be another route off the island. Jack studied the map, looking for it. The gears of his mind engaged. All his energy, all the mental power he could muster was concentrated on this one, this single problem. The world went away. Jack was no longer crouched over a desk, tattered and filthy, every man his enemy. He was somewhere else, all alone, all at peace in the privacy of perfect concentration.

Ideas drifted by. Most he let float on. Some few he fingered, turning them over, then allowing them to pass. *Island. Water. Boat. I could steal a boat. No, I've never sailed a boat. Besides, there's probably some sort of coast guard or harbour patrol cruising the island.* He continued to think. Other concepts presented themselves. For some few minutes the best of them appeared to be Singapore's port – the nine hundred-acre expanse of docks, loading derricks, and space for cargo containers on the south shore of the island. Jack was a logistic man. Cargo, ships, and shipping were his life's blood. Better still, as a college student he had been a dockworker, knew loading procedures, equipment, and all the rest like the back of his hand. If he could get to the port – get past what was touted as the tightest security system in any port in the world – then he might be able to stow away on an outbound freighter. *Might, but not could.* Singapore ran a zero-theft harbour, the only one in the world that could make the boast. Jack had studied the Port Authority's documentation thoroughly before drafting his new logistics plan. He knew how secure Singapore's docks were – cameras, bright lights, plenty of guards, fences that were high and well patrolled . . .

. . . *still* . . .

He squinted at the map. There was freeway along Singapore's south coast. To the east it was called the East Coast Parkway; to the west the Ayer Rajah Expressway. There was a short section that ran right next to the Port of Singapore's boundary. And if the map was accurate, just where the fence line began . . .

No. To reach that spot he would have to travel through the heart of the central city. It was too dangerous. He needed a safer escape route.

All at once he saw it.

He pulled a ruler from Quint's desk, measured the distance, compared it to the scale on the map. The causeway wasn't very long, about a kilometre in length. *How long is a kilometre?* About a half-mile, he thought, maybe a little further. He wasn't quite sure, he always had trouble keeping the metric system straight. Not that it mattered. The distance was definitely under a mile.

And definitely over water.

Which could be swum.

Once or twice a week – *more often once than twice, you liar* – Jack swam twenty-five laps at his athletic club's pool. The boasting, fitter men who worked out in the club sometimes bragged of how many miles they swam each evening. They said . . . Jack had trouble remembering . . . they said something like seventy laps were a mile. If so, then Jack's own workout was about a third of a mile in length.

Could he swim further than that?

Sure.

Twice the distance?

Yeah.

Three times?

Uhh . . .

– 6 –

Even though the *Jade Lady*'s bridge was comfortably air-conditioned, the clerk was damp with perspiration. He sweated in fear of the consequences if it was discovered what he'd done. He sweated in fear at what would happen if he'd done anything else.

Singapore, stalwartly committed to extirpating corruption, paid its officials salaries that made most nations' bureaucrats sick with envy. Nonetheless, the wages enjoyed by a less-than-exalted clerk to a deputy under-secretary were insufficient to cover certain expenses. Gambling expenses, to be precise – obligations past due, accruing mountainous interest, and owed to an organization whose bill collectors employed battery acid as a motivational tool.

The average Singaporean squanders six thousand dollars a year on gambling. The clerk was neither an average man nor a lucky one.

Poh Kay Siong steepled his fingers beneath his chin, and listened to the clerk's tale. Every few minutes, in response to a particularly telling point, he removed an IOU from the folder on his lap, and tore it in two. There were many IOUs. The clerk kept talking.

The Deputy Under-secretary was duty officer that evening. His superiors were off partying a group of Korean shipping executives through Singapore's hottest nightspots, and in particular Studebaker's (native habitat of the so-called Sarong Party Girl, the most industriously predatory species of golddigger in the word). There was no one else in the department to answer the phone if it rang.

As it did. It was the red phone, the phone connected to the highest office in the land. Signalling his clerk to pick up an extension line and take notes, the Deputy Under-secretary answered on the first ring.

And winced at what he heard.

An aide to the Senior Minister growled that his superior was not a happy man. His superior wanted the drug-smuggling American's head on a platter. Likewise the head of Chan Gin.

Poh Kay Siong tore up an IOU. How gratifying that the old man had taken a personal interest in this affair. While others might dither and debate, Senior Minister Lee Kuan Yew was possessed of an attribute to which few Singaporeans could lay claim: lightning-fast decisiveness. The old man had always been that way. As had his childhood rival, Poh Kay Siong. *Two lives lived in parallel,* Poh thought. *I might have been him. He might have been me. There is not much difference between us, not much at all . . .*

Lee had not been Singapore's first prime minister, a fact that rankled, but he'd been its second, and he'd resolved to make the experience last. After he and his People's Action Party swept to power in 1959, they had never relinquished it. Oh, certainly, Lee had quote-retired-unquote as Prime Minister in 1990. But that was a joke. Upon resigning, Lee had appointed himself Senior Minister, a title connoting power approximately equal to God Almighty's; he'd been pulling the strings ever since.

No one complained. The people loved the cunning old tyrant. How could they not? Singapore's per capita wealth was greater than Britain's, and quite soon now its citizens would be the richest in the world – thank Lee Kuan Yew for that, and no one else.

Lee was the last of his kind, the sole surviving member of a species disappeared from the earth. He had been born too late, was more properly a member of that generation that brought Roosevelt, Churchill, Stalin, de Gaulle, and Hitler to history's centre stage – charismatic, autocratic, visionary, deadly when aroused. A Cambridge-trained lawyer and the finest orator of his time, Lee had single-handedly taken Singapore from a muddy colonial backwater torn by ethnic strife and savaged by gang warfare to one of the most prosperous, safe, and smugly conceited nations in the world.

There was nothing miraculous about what he had done in creating his perfect little state. It was merely *laissez-faire* capitalism practised in its purest form, governed by a dictator more benevolent than most.

Though no less ruthless, reflected Poh.

As every pragmatist knows, none more pragmatic than Lee Kuan Yew, you can't make an omelette without breaking eggs. During those early elections, few of Singapore's best and brightest dared stand for office. The Tongs, the Triads, the communists wreaked bloody vengeance on those who challenged their power in the streets. Lee Kuan Yew's solution: go calling on the Tongs, the Triads, and the communists before they call on you. Taking a leaf from Lenin's book of wisdom, Lee deemed that those who could not be persuaded should be bought; those who could not be bought should be intimidated; those who could not be intimidated . . .

States of emergency were declared; civil rights were rescinded; uncooperative newspapers were abolished; paramilitary police marched lockstep down the streets.

In short, eggs were broken. The omelette turned out fine.

The clerk to the Deputy Under-secretary wiped his brow. Poh, momentarily distracted by his old man's memories, felt slightly annoyed with himself. 'Be so kind,' he said, 'to repeat what you just said. I wish to understand it better.' Then, more in apology than because it was earned, he tore up another IOU.

The clerk obliged. The Senior Minister's aide was in a towering rage, as, no doubt, was the Senior Minister himself. He'd fulminated: bad enough that the courts will be obliged to hang an American smuggler, thereby precipitating more corrosive editorials in the American newspapers and more carping from their politicians – they who love decrying Singapore, they with a crime rate ten times ours, they with a national debt of five thousand dollars for every citizen, sneering at us whose debt is six dollars per person. Can you imagine, Lee's aide shouted, a country whose leader has spent every moment in office pursued by scandal having the temerity to call Singaporean elections corrupt, merely because every voter is required to attach his identification number to his ballot? Can you believe they accuse our country's most respected figure of nepotism because he appointed his quite talented son Deputy Prime Minister . . .

Poh smiled faintly. He was reminded that, behind closed doors, every Singaporean called the son in question 'the minister in charge of doing what Daddy wants' – a fact which none dared to bring to the attention of his father, who was, after all, Lee Kuan Yew. Relishing his amusement, Poh deigned to destroy another IOU.

. . . And all these noisy nuisances do is cause foreign executives to hesitate before doing business in a country carefully designed to be the best place to do business in the world. What is more distasteful is that Chan Gin is involved in this affair. Chan believes that because he once did Singapore a service, Singapore owes him service in return. Folly and arrogance! Society owes nothing to any individual; on the contrary, it is the individual who owes all to society. Chan was but a minor piece in a game this nation won many years past. The game is over; the pieces should have long since been swept from the board. That they still can be seen is an embarrassment. Singapore is not Haiti. Singapore does not station gun-toting *tonton macoutes* on every corner. Singapore does not rule by terror or by force but by informed consent . . .

Of those who are informed as to what happens to non-consenters, thought Poh, tearing one of the clerk's debts in two, and letting the shreds float softly to the floor.

. . . But the world press and the world business community will not see that. No, all they will see is armed warfare in the streets of Singapore, Chan Gin a strutting bravado out of a romantic novel.

No more of this, Lee Kuan Yew's aide had hissed. No more. The American gangster is to be taken immediately. There will be no violence accompanying his arrest. None. If there is, then the Senior Minister will personally intervene.

Personally intervene . . . the Deputy Under-secretary had swallowed hard at the words.

Two more scraps of paper dropped from Poh's fingertips. He whispered a question.

The clerk answered, yes, the aide had given detailed instructions. The clerk had taken them down word-for-word. Then, once his superior had made the requisite phone calls, he had, as ordered, burned his notes, each and every one of them . . .

Poh Kay Siong arched a disappointed eyebrow.

. . . but not before making surreptitious photocopies.

Poh lifted the folder containing the clerk's IOUs between two fingers, and extended it forward. The clerk reached into his jacket pocket and withdrew an envelope.

Both men were satisfied with their bargain.

After the clerk departed, Poh allowed himself a permissible self-indulgence, a minor vice, a single glass of port – Fonseca, '37, a priceless pre-war vintage.

Pre-war . . .

He was a teenager when the Japanese came. Then the world was turned upside down, its one unalterable truth overthrown, the eternal British Empire disgraced in battle, eternal no more. Jaw slack with amazement, Poh watched an Asian army – mark you, *Asian!* – march shamefaced English troops off to what was to become one of the world's most notorious prison camps.

Lee Kuan Yew watched with him.

It had all begun then, modern Singapore's history, every jot and tittle of it. As the English disappeared from sight, the teenaged Lee saw his path shining before him: independence from a defeated Britain, a backwater colony set free to pursue its destiny among the nations.

Poh too saw his path, although it did not shine, and soon was running errands for a junior *Kempeitai* officer. There was profit in it then, profit in it later, profit down all these years from a Japanese secret policeman grown old as he.

And as wise.

The river of wisdom, he thought, now flows in a single flood; all a boatman need do is steer its predestined course. Mighty Lee Kuan Yew has come to recognize that Superintendent Chan has outlived his usefulness to the state. Singapore has no further need of his skills. Indeed, it has come to be an embarrassment that men such as Chan and techniques such as he employed were ever sanctioned by our peaceful and enlightened government. He reminds Lee of that which he would prefer forgotten.

And so, and now, Chan is within a single step of overreaching his bounds. One more act of the violence he will not forswear, one more deed that might make foreign businessmen have qualms about this nation, and the superintendent will find himself across the line drawn by no less than Lee Kuan Yew.

The hour open which Chan killed Taft would toll the superintendent's day of reckoning. All Poh need do was advance the clock.

FOUR: RED ANGER

The weaker a force, indeed, the greater the importance to it of surprise, whether it is taking the offensive or standing on the defensive. It is indeed the only way by which inferiority in strength can be compensated . . . The commander who wishes to impose his will on the enemy – which is, after all, the object of all military operations – will seek also to *deceive* him; to implant in the adversary's mind an erroneous image will not only help to conceal his true capabilities and intentions but will lead that adversary to act in such a way as to make his own task easier.

Michael Howard – *Strategic Deception in the Second World War*

SOCRATES: Did you never observe the narrow intelligence flashing from the keen eye of a clever rogue – how eager he is, how clearly his paltry soul sees the way to his end; he is the reverse of blind, but his keen eyesight is forced into the service of evil, and he is mischievous in proportion to his cleverness?

Plato – *The Republic VII*

1
Singapore

– 1 –

Quint's map told Jack that the most promising place to swim from was called Sungei Buloh. Labelled as a wildlife preserve, and thus likely to be empty at night, it was out in the middle of nowhere; a single road in, a single road out, and surrounded by uninhabitable wetlands.

Perfect.

Equally perfect, the keys in Quint's pocket fitted the door of a Honda Civic parked right outside his office. Armed with his stolen map, and hungrily devouring the single, scrumptious orange he'd found in a mini-refrigerator otherwise cluttered with gin bottles, it had taken Jack an hour of exceedingly cautious backstreet driving to reach the preserve . . . driving well beneath the speed limit . . . and keeping a wary eye on the rearview mirror every mile of the way.

Sungei Buloh was not well marked. Jack missed the turn-off twice before finding the access road. A mile later he arrived at an entrance conspicuous only because of a sign stating that the park closed at five-thirty. But no gate barred the way. No gate was needed. Jack was in Singapore. If the authorities said a place was closed after five-thirty then no one would even think of entering at five-thirty-one.

He looked for a place to hide his stolen Honda. There was a deep ditch across the road. The car's bumper collapsed with a sigh as it thudded to the bottom, and its badly twisted hood popped open.

From what he had read in his studies of the country, Singapore's government relentlessly encouraged its citizens to use public transportation. Highway-clogging, pollution-spewing private vehicles were frowned upon, and, therefore, automobiles were monumentally expensive. To own a Honda costing fourteen thousand dollars in the United States, Quint had bid sixty thousand dollars for a government 'Certificate of Entitlement' – the right to operate the car for ten years. Add the fact that Singapore imposed import duties of 140 per cent on automobiles, and Jack had wrecked a car costing as much (in the US at least) as a luxury Mercedez-Benz.

He found the thought strangely gratifying.

Silent and watchful against the possibility of park rangers on patrol, Jack spent more than an hour lurking out of sight near the visitors' centre. No one was to be seen; the pitch-black preserve as empty as he'd hoped it would be.

Then, increasingly thirsty, he'd burgled the cafeteria. The door was fragile and the lock weak. It had taken only a kick to smash it open. Jack had gulped down two cans of diet Pepsi before it struck him that although he was in mid-felony, his conscience wasn't bothering him.

Something had changed – no puzzling over the problem, no logical calculations; just lift the foot, kick the door, and steal to your heart's content.

Maybe his system was out of kilter – the after-effects of an extra-strength dose of hormones which rarely, if ever, had pumped through his veins. Whatever the reason, Jack was not uneasy with choosing force over reason, and suspected that, given the opportunity, he might do so again.

Thirst quenched, he trotted out of the visitors' centre and on to a short wooden bridge spanning an estuary. Once on the bridge he could look north, up the tidal flow, across the Straits of Johor, and into Malaysia.

It seemed further away than he had expected. More than a mile. Maybe even two miles. But, of course, he was far down an inlet. Once he reached the coastline, he'd be closer.

He hoped.

Meanwhile, there was the question of how well (and how frequently) the straits were patrolled. If the Singaporeans had a sizable fleet of police boats out on the water, he wouldn't risk a swim. But if there were only a few, one or two an hour, then, under the cover of darkness, he could elude them. Boats were big noisy things. A swimming man could float still as a drifting log, ambiguous in black water.

Time passed. He used his wristwatch to clock the appearance and disappearance of running lights on the water. As he did so – one hour in the dark, then two, then three – he let his mind run free. No concentration, no if-then-therefore logic. Just let it go. Float above your thoughts. Don't study and don't observe. Look the other way while puzzle pieces drift through your consciousness, finding their own pattern.

Somebody planted drugs in my briefcase. There are only two candidates: Joel, because he's the only one who knew I was going to Singapore. Denise, because she's the only one with a motive.

Motive, motive . . . what is it the cops ask themselves? Method, motive, and opportunity.

Jack closed his eyes. He forced himself back . . . higher . . . way up above the details of the conundrum.

Never focus on the details. Details are distractions. If you look at the details, you'll never see the whole.

Method. Motive. Opportunity.

Drugs. Hatred. Question mark.

How the blazes did she get her hands on that briefcase?

– 2 –

Chan Gin disapproved.

The new interrogation rooms were furnished with comfortable chairs, attractive coffee tables, museum prints on the walls, and even an ashtray permitting illicit behaviour in a country where indoor smoking was mostly banned. Those weren't the accoutrements you wanted in an interrogation room. A good interrogation room, a real one, should look like something out of *Detective Story*, 1951, Kirk Douglas and William Bendix with Wyler directing. A single straightback wooden chair, dingy white walls, one glaring light bulb dangling from the ceiling above the suspect's head; now that was a *real* interrogation room.

Chan believed you had to give the criminal classes what they expected. And what they expected were a couple of sweat-stained cops, ties loose, jackets off, shoulder holsters visible, maybe an ominous length of rubber hose discreetly on display. Those were the props crooks wanted to see, not this . . . this . . . goddamned American whatshername Martha Stewart crap!

Insult to injury, you had to have a medic check the suspect over before entering and after leaving the interrogation room. That particular procedure made confessions a wee bit harder to obtain than they were in the old days. New rules, new practices, new policies – Chan chafed under the burden of Western-style criminal-coddling.

Coddling didn't work – no better evidence than the fact that the Samsudin girl was, even at this late hour, still proclaiming her innocence.

They'd been going at her since six in the afternoon, damned near eight hours ago. And all they'd got out of her was the same old same old. Innocent stewardess returning a pocket computer to one of the passengers, *eeek!* he's got a gun, then he held me down and tied me up, and I spent all day in the bathtub and had to pee so bad . . .

Fuck!

Chan, standing in the darkness and glaring through a two-way mirror, was beginning to believe her. Bad news. If she really was just an innocent victim, then Chan's one and only lead on the elusive Mr Taft evaporated into thin air. After almost twenty-four hours of full-scale investigation, the woman was the only thing he had. Without her, Taft might as well not exist.

In the final analysis, every police force the world over is organized into three principal sections. While their names may differ from country to country, their functions are the same: operations, administration, and support services. Chan Gin was an operations man, wouldn't have it any other way. But he knew how to use the other bureaux; it was one of the many things he did well. And relentlessly.

As in the present case.

The support services crowd had been working overtime. Records, data processing, communications, the laboratory, intelligence – no time off, and double teams in the computer room. Hal Leung was coordinating things, but Chan was calling the shots. Especially where computer boys were involved.

Every database, he'd ordered, every database they could get at. There were thousands. And with the help of the American authorities, Singapore searched them all.

It was a dry hole. Zero, zip, nil, thirty metres of computer printouts told Chan nothing.

Taft's record was spotless, utterly so, not a derogatory word, not even a hint. The crafty bastard had concocted an immaculate history, the perfect cover story, an alibi to beat all alibis – the tale of a boring American businessman, so dull and ordinary that no one would ever suspect him of being a major drug dealer.

Could that be true? Is he only what he appears to be – innocent? For the tick of a clock Chan thought someone behind him had whispered the words in his ear. But no, it was just a thought. A really stupid fucking thought.

The truth was that Taft wore the perfect disguise. The truth was the cocksucker was perfect in almost every fucking regard. The truth was he was so damned perfect that Chan was almost scared of him.

That was what the truth was – one more good reason why the sonofabitch had to die.

Behind two-way glass Chan flipped a toothpick into his mouth and listened to the Samsudin girl again proclaim her innocence. The officer doing the questioning was Inspector Seri Najib Tan Sri Muhyiddin Tun Ponniah, a Malay name, of course, and as long as most. He was short and wiry, with pockmarked skin. He also was the best 'bad cop' interrogator on the force.

Muhyiddin, speaking gutter Malay laced with Chinese slang, tore into her. 'OK, *hua ping*, you claim—'

The woman's face blushed scarlet. 'Don't you dare call me that!' *Hua ping* translated as 'flower vase', but meant something far less complimentary. 'I'm a good Muslim woman!'

'Oh yeah, then how come you're single? I mean, face it, at your age—'

'I'm only twenty-three.'

'Like I said . . .'

Zaitun shook an angry finger in Muhyiddin's face. 'Muslim men! Do you know why you can't find decent wives . . .?'

Off duty, Muhyiddin's speech was rich with *budi bahasta*, the genteel graciousness of Malay formality. But in the interrogation room, it was rude, hostile, and calculated to demean. 'Sure I do. It's 'cause the government lets broads go to the university. Education makes 'em argumentative. Guy comes home after a hard day at work and gets bitched at because wifey thinks a college degree makes a woman as good as her man. Hell, read the *New Paper*, there's a story every month, interviews with poor slobs driven nuts by pushy wives with too much schooling.'

'A husband should be proud of his wife—'

'You say you're a good Muslim, huh? Well, babe, let me tell you, a good Muslim woman is married at eighteen! At the age of twenty-three, a good Muslim woman is in the kitchen feeding her first couple of sons! Most of all, a good Muslim woman doesn't spend her off-duty hours playing hide the salami with scumbag international dope dealers! Hey, doll, just between you and me, if you get off on being tied up in the toilet, I can arrange something for the two of us, and put down that ashtray or I'll have your butt up on an assault charge . . .'

Innocent, Chan thought glumly. *The girl has nothing to do with it.*

A door opened behind him. 'Superintendent Chan?'

'Yeah, Hal. I'm here. Come in.'

Leung walked to Chan's side, stood with him looking through the mirror. He spoke softly: 'Pretty woman.'

Chan merely nodded.

'Are we getting anywhere with her?'

'Hell no,' Chan sighed. 'She's exactly what she looks like – a nice wholesome girl who was in the wrong place at the wrong time. She doesn't know anything about where Taft is, where he's going, or what he's going to do next. Shit, Hal, I think we're screwed.'

Both men stood in silence. However, Chan thought, Leung's silence was somehow different from his. The young corporal was looking at his shoes, running a forefinger across his lower lip. 'Er . . . sir, on the subject of being screwed, sir . . .' Leung took a cautionary step backward.

Chan gave him a bleak look. 'More good news?'

Leung took a second step away. He wasn't able to meet Chan's eyes. A bad sign, Chan thought, guessing he wasn't going to like what he was about to hear.

'The business out in Toa Payoh this afternoon, the shootout in front of the girl's apartment?'

'Yeah.'

'It wasn't Taft.'

Chan felt the colour of his cheeks change. His voice edged up a notch. 'What do you mean it wasn't Taft?'

'The Land Forces questioned everyone, sir. All the witnesses. Most of them twice. They tell the same story. Taft wasn't the shooter. What was going on was that somebody – a bunch of somebodies – was firing at him, and . . .'

Chan folded his arms, looked at the ceiling, and swore.

'. . . we've got bullet casings all over the place out there .38s, .357 magnums, 9mm Uzi shells, some .45s, you name it, somebody was carrying it. And the problem is, all the brass was on the street near the Samsudin girl's apartment. None of it was down where Taft was, down where that poor pushcart hawker got killed.'

'You're saying what, Hal?'

'The way we've pieced it together, Taft is walking down the street when two cars screech up. These hatchetmen jump out, and start shooting at everything that moves. Then Taft runs for it, and the gunmen see they've hit a civilian, and they jump back in their cars, and they're out of sight about thirty seconds before me and the rest of the guys arrive.'

'And you and the rest of the guys see a body on the sidewalk and assume Taft has gone postal . . .' Chan paused at the perplexed expression on Leung's face. '. . . That's a "thirty-two", Hal, man amuck.' He bit down hard. His toothpick snapped in two. He spat it into his hand. 'I made the same mistake. I couldn't see what was going on. I thought the gunfire was you greasing – shooting, Hal – Taft. Later when you told me that somebody had been shooting up the civilians before you got there, I figured it was Taft trying to clear his way through a crowd or something—'

'Couldn't have been. He didn't have a gun.'

'The hell you say! He had *your* gun!'

'No, sir. When we searched the woman's apartment, Constable Singh found my gun. It was stuffed beneath a sofa cushion.'

Chan spun on the ball of his foot. He needed something to hit. There wasn't anything in sight. 'He left the gun? You're telling me that Taft left the gun? Come on, Hal, what kind of a gangster dumps a perfectly good gun? Damn it to hell! Why wasn't I told this earlier?'

'The Land Forces were checking serial numbers, sir. And I guess some of the witnesses on the street ran away after the shooting. Our guys didn't get around to finishing their interviews until a little while ago.'

'Shit! Let me get this straight. We've got a serious bad guy in town. He's a stone killer and he's got a gun. He knows you and half the force are on the way to his hideout. So what does he do? He trots out the front door, politely leaving his one and only firearm behind, sashays down the street, stumbles into a firefight, and just fucking strolls away from it! Is this your story, Hal? Come on, tell me, I'd really like to know.'

'Uh . . . well, sir, according to the witnesses, sir, that's sort of pretty much the way it was . . .' The corporal's voice fell to apprehensive silence.

Chan glowered. He folded his arms, unfolded them, and balled his fists by his side. The thing that separates ordinary cops from outstanding ones is intuition. And Chan's intuition was telling him that he was missing something important. He started to speak, then stopped himself. He didn't know what to say.

'Sir?'

Chan pressed his fingers hard against his eyes. He was exhausted, unable to digest the facts. Hell, he was having trouble keeping his eyes open. Unless he got some rest, he was going to start making mistakes, bad ones – or maybe he already had. 'Screw this. Look, I don't know about you, but I've had two hours' sleep in the past twenty-three. I'm dead on my feet. I say it's Oscar Echo time. Let's catch some Zs, and get back on this thing in the morning.'

Leung understood 'Oscar Echo' – 'OE' being patrol-car letters for 'we're going on break'. But the part about 'catching some Zs' was pure Chan-ese, movie talk, and Leung didn't have a clue as to what it meant. Nonetheless, he nodded. 'Sounds good to me, sir. I've got a metre and a half of documents stacked on my desk, and every time I try to look at it my eyes cross.'

'By the way, has the lab sent over its report on Taft's dope?'

'Yes, sir. It's there somewhere. Along with everything else except the fingerprint analysis. It's late. Computer problem or something.'

Chan blew a frustrated sigh. It looked like he needed to spend some desk time helping Hal get caught up on the paperwork. He hated the idea, but there was no alternative. 'Okay, I'll pitch in with the documents. Let's get started at, oh, does eight-thirty sound OK to you? Good, I'll see you then. You head on home. I'm going into the interrogation room, kick bad cop Muhyiddin out of there, play good cop for a bit, then offer to escort our guest, Miss Samsudin, back to her lawful place of residence. Or wherever.'

Both men turned back to the two-way mirror. Detective Muhyiddin, who was approximately as devout a Muslim as the Lubavitcher Rabbi, was heckling the Singapore Air girl for – Islamic heresy! – her membership of Singapore's Social Development Unit, the world's only government-subsidized dating club. Muhyiddin was sneering that any decent Muslim woman would let her parents, and no one else, arrange her *pak-tor* – dates – and, more important, chaperone her every step of the way.

Leung muttered something. Chan couldn't quite hear him. 'Speak up, Hal.'

'Nothing, sir.'

'There's no such thing as "nothing". Tell me what you said.'

Hal dropped his voice nearly to a whisper. 'I said, maybe I could play good cop this time.'

Chan looked at him out of the corner of his eye. 'What's your rank, Hal?'

'Corporal, sir.'

'What's my rank?'

'Superintendent, sir.'

'When the suspect looks like Tia Carrere only better, who gets to play good cop?'

'The superintendent, sir.'

'You learn fast for a rookie, Hal.' Chan slapped Leung on the shoulder, then pushed him towards the door.

– 3 –

By two in the morning, Jack was sure that the straits were not heavily patrolled. Being Jack Taft, and therefore being a cautious man, he waited another hour to be sure.

A shed of some sort stood at the far end of the bridge. Hung on its wall, covered by glass, was a map of the park. Jack peered at it, trying to pick out the best trail to the shoreline.

Too dark. Need a flashlight.

He didn't have one. If there'd been one in Quint's office, he'd forgotten to look for it.

Quint's car. Everyone carries a flashlight in the car.

He walked across the bridge – *Don't run, don't jog, just walk at a normal pace, you need all your strength for the swim* – through the parking lot, and out to the gully where he'd concealed Quint's now damaged Honda.

There was a flashlight in the glove compartment. He switched it on. The batteries were fresh, the beam was bright. Jack breathed a sigh of relief.

Leaving the Honda behind, he scrambled out of the ditch. And straight into the lights of an oncoming car. The driver braked, cruising by Jack slowly, and studying his face. But he didn't stop. *That's odd*, Jack thought. He would have guessed in this country, if nowhere else, a driver who spotted a tattered-looking man clambering up beside the road would pull over to see if there had been an accident, and someone needed help.

But not this particular driver. He kept going. Even accelerated as he left.

Jack wondered if the man had recognized him. He didn't think it likely – not by carlight in the dead of night. Besides, Jack had thrown away his seersucker jacket, was now wearing Quint's baggy blue blazer. Unshaven, hair mussed, different clothes – no, the driver hadn't known who he was. The man had simply been curious. And, quite like Jack himself, too cautious to offer assistance to a scruffy-looking stranger in the dead of night.

With flashlight in hand, Jack studied the park map. It was a nice map, clear and simple, precisely the sort he liked. The route to Sungei Buloh's shoreline looked easy enough: left down a long looping trail, left again and on to a boardwalk, branch right where the boardwalk forked, take another fork left to the next cross trail, then turn right. That should do it. The Singapore Park Services Department had been courteous enough to label each leg of the trail not only with its distance, but with its walking time. *Should take less than an hour to get out to land's end*, he thought.

Another sign caught his eye: DO NOT DISTURB WILDLIFE. He wondered what kind – *probably birds and stuff*. Shrugging, he turned left and started down the trail. Before five minutes had passed, he was having second thoughts.

Things were dark, too disturbingly dark for the tastes of a New Yorker born to city lights. Worse, things were *not* too quiet. Rustling noises came from the reeds and rushes flanking the trail. Something heavy, and therefore large, splashed in shallow waters. Night birds cawed and chittered. A creature that was most definitely not a bird grunted in the undergrowth. As Jack edged past its lurking place, it moved. He could hear soggy mud sucking beneath its feet *or paws or maybe claws* . . . Jack inched on. Concealed by swamp growth, the animal, whatever it was, seemed to be keeping pace with him, carefully metering its steps so that it was just a few yards from where Jack walked.

He quickened his steps. Picking up its pace, the animal stepped on a branch, breaking it with a heart-stopping crack.

Spinning his flash towards the sound, he saw only a tangle of undergrowth and the trunks of coconut palms soaring above bushes . . .

. . . And in the far distance, the reflection of his light off waters that should have been still, but weren't. They rippled, although not at random. A line glittered across the pond, the wake of some creature that swam on the surface and was sufficiently large to churn wavelets as it passed.

For Christ's sake, what am I doing in this jungle? Hell, I was never even a boy scout . . .

He swallowed hard, kept walking. Kept the flashlight lit too, moving it back and forth across the trail, searching for a rock, a branch, a stick, anything he could use for a weapon.

The animal grunted again, a low deathly groan, a noise that sounded more suitable to a graveyard. Jack's skin crawled. He almost broke into a run.

No, he ordered himself, *they're more scared of you than you are of them.* Or so said such nature books as he'd read. And because the naturalists who wrote those books survived long enough to see their words in print, it seemed logical to believe them. It also seemed logical to jump up in the air, come down as hard as he could, and make a loud 'Unnnngh!' sound.

The animal in the reeds grunted in fear at Jack's cry, then fled.

Some minutes later, however, the snake did not.

– 4 –

Chan would drop the Samsudin girl at her flat. *Outside* her flat. He read her mood, and knew that he had to handle her gently if he ever wanted to see her again.

He was pretty sure he did.

She was young and a real looker and the walking embodiment of the *true* reason Western executives liked doing business in Singapore. Which was fine, but no big deal – you couldn't throw a stick on Orchard Road without hitting a dozen like her.

Only they weren't like her, not really. From what he'd seen in the interrogation room, she was whip-smart, nail-tough, able to give as good as she could take. You didn't get much of that in Singapore; all you got was the deference little white mice pay their masters. But she was no mouse. He liked that. He might even respect her, if that's what you did with women, which he didn't. Although in her case he might make an exception. She was his style, had iron in her, and yeah, he definitely wanted to put some moves on her. But not tonight.

Tonight Miss Zaitun Binte Samsudin was not disposed to welcome any of the well-practised ploys that Chan might assay. Better politely leave her to at the kerb, press his business card into her hand, and tell her to get some rest. Then he'd extend one more apology for her trouble, and tell her he'd stop by sometime within the next day or two to make sure she was OK.

Given enough time, she'd calm down, get over her outrage, be honoured to receive a visit from Singapore's best-known police-man – handsome, heroic, mediagenic Chan Gin, the cop who always got his man, and who, by tomorrow evening if not sooner, surely would have killed that bastard Taft.

He glanced at her. She was staring straight out of the window of his Range-Rover, jaw set, mouth downturned, eyes sullen. Chan wondered what she was thinking. *Nothing nice about Taft, no doubt about that.*

Zaitun's thoughts, had Chan been able to read them, were quite different from what he guessed: *Bismallah al-Rahman a-Rahim* ... In the name of Allah, the merciful, the compassionate ...

The rest of the words, comforting to the faithful, would not come. What came instead were the stinging insults to which Detective Muhyiddin had subjected her – jibes heard too often by independent Muslim women, heard more frequently with each passing year.

The Prophet Mohammed, peace be upon his name, had said of the sexes, 'Men and women are equal as two teeth on a comb ... He who honours women is honourable; he who insults them is lowly and mean.' Men like Muhyiddin ignored these words. They looked not to the Koran for guidance, but rather to the *hadiths* and the *Shariah* – laws contrived by self-serving caliphs after the Prophet's passing. 'A girl should be like water, unresisting. It takes on the shape of the container into which it is poured but has no shape of its own.' So quoted one bearded zealot, hectoring her as she left the mosque. And when Zaitun, well studied in her faith, snapped that the Prophet had never penned such a statement, the fanatic screamed her heretic, roaring that she and her kind should suffer death by stoning. Zaitun had furiously challenged him to identify which verse in the Koran called for the execution of *any* transgressor but for highway robbers. The man spat and swore and named her whore. Livid at insults to her person and her faith, Zaitun quoted the Koran one last time before storming away: 'There is no compulsion in Islam.'

Once, not long ago, radicals among the ranks of believers were rare. Now there were too many. Richly funded by the oil-producing states of the Persian Gulf, they hid beneath the cloak of putative charity: 'The Muslim Brotherhood', the MB for short. For Islamic women, modern but no less devout for their modernity, those two letters, MB, had the same connotation as the initials KKK possessed for Black Americans.

The Prophet had not enjoined that women hide their hair with the *hijab*, much less don the preposterous *abaya* full-body cloak. But with each passing day, ever more MB extremists commanded that they do so, threatened violence if they did not. Now the worst reactionaries called for complete *purdah* – women forever concealed behind locked doors – adding to this outrage a horrible insistence on the religious necessity of compulsory infibulation, or 'female circumcision' as it was called by prissy Westerners unable to confront the horror of clitoral removal.

Zaitun, torn between the strength of her faith and the sacrileges committed in its name, fretted for her future. She hoped someday to be wed, prayed that she would have children. But could she marry a man who might become infected by the MB's fevered delirium? Would she be able to retain her self-esteem if browbeaten into donning a *chador* . . . if ordered not to leave the house without a *mahram*, a male chaperone . . . if commanded, as the MB had been by Sheikh Bin Baz, holiest of the reactionary holy men, to believe that the earth was flat and that the sun and stars revolved around it? Such had happened to other Muslim brides. She knew too many, and knew their sorrow, rage, and impotence. So too did she know of more than a single suicide caused by a born-again fundamentalist exercising his right to polygamy by taking a new and younger wife.

Among her circle of friends it had become axiomatic that if you wished to wed and raise your children in your faith, then you had to look beyond the ranks of Islamic men. Best find a tolerant Westerner. Not one of those who believed Islam was synonymous with terrorism, but rather an intelligent and educated man who knew the faith to be the opposite of those things, and who would respect your devotion to it.

She felt herself to be nearing a crossroads, an exile's lonely freedom on one side, the threat of soul-destroying slavery on the other. She loved her faith, but loved freedom more; choosing between them would be the most painful decision she would ever confront.

And so Zaitun sat next to Chan, a troubled woman, wounded and unable to find the peace she sought in prayer.

Chan wondered whether he should say something to her, try to engage her in conversation. He thought better of it. She looked like she wanted to be left alone.

Which was fine with Chan. It would take another five minutes or so to reach her apartment. He could use the time to think.

There was something wrong about the Taft business, but he wasn't sure what.

Okay, Taft is leaving this girl's apartment. Theoretically, no one knows he's there except the girl and me. Neither of us is in any position to talk. Then a bunch of scumbags shows up and starts a firefight. This is not good. This is New York City stuff, and people do not do this shit in my *town.*

Reaching into his jacket pocket, he fingered a toothpick. He shot a look at the woman, decided she'd find his habit distasteful, and put his hand back on the wheel.

No question, the gunmen were Poh Kay Siong's boys. Nobody packs heat in this country except the police and Poh's punks. And even that crowd doesn't pull their pieces very often. They know the rules. Only now, all of a sudden, it's Gunfight at the OK Corral.

Why? Taft's here on a dope deal, and Poh's the only guy big enough to buy the stash he's smuggling, so why . . .?

Had Taft double-crossed Poh? That was a possibility. But there was another alternative, and Chan found the thought of it exceedingly disagreeable. Taft might not have come to Singapore to sell drugs to Poh; he might have come as scout for a competing organization.

Has he been hired as front man by one of the thousand goddamned gangs that operate all around Southeast Asia? Shit! I've got to get some information here!

The radiophone on the Range-Rover's dashboard beeped. Chan snatched up the handset. 'Chan here.'

'Corporal Leung, sir. I'm at the station and—'

'You're supposed to be in bed, Hal.'

'Yes, sir. But something started bugging me. I couldn't figure out how anybody knew Taft was at Miss Samsudin's apartment.' *Good man*, Chan thought, *I've got myself a damned good man here*. Leung continued, 'So I called a couple of *ah cits*. Second informer I spoke to said the question isn't who's trying to kill Taft, the question is who isn't.'

'Huh?'

'Then he tells me the word is someone's spotted Taft—'

'We've had a hundred phone calls on suspicious strangers—'

'Hear me out, sir. The *ah cit* says they're positive they know where he is. *Lim chu kang*, way the hell out the boondocks, in the Sungei Buloh Wildlife Preserve. And now they're on the way to get him.'

'"They?" Who the hell are these "they", Hal?'

Leung told him. Clenching his teeth, Chan glanced at Zaitun, checked that she was wearing her safety belt, then did something with the steering wheel that made her scream.

– 5 –

Singapore operates less as a nation than a tightly managed corporation. It provides employment, benefits, and security. In return, it requires work, loyalty, and adherence to a code of behaviour that, in the final analysis, is little different from that imposed on the employees of General Motors – albeit, Singaporeans are under their bosses' watchful eye twenty-four hours a day rather than the conventional eight. As in America, those who toe the corporate party line are rewarded, while those who quibble with company policy enjoy little in the way of career progression. Only the most flagrant offenders are actually terminated. Where a less enlightened tyranny – mainland China's, for example – punishes dissidents with labour camps and firing squads, Singapore merely demotes them. Much as a *Fortune* 500 company finding itself saddled with an ineffective executive nudges the underachiever into a job in which he can do no harm ('Charlie, we want you to run the United Way campaign this year'), so too will Singapore move those who get under the ruling powers' feet out of sight and most distinctly out of mind. Indeed, the country's most prominent dissident woke one morning to find himself bankrupt, unemployed, and assigned new quarters dead centre in Singapore's most popular theme park, there to spend the rest of his days as a little-visited attraction in his nation's version of Disneyland.

Please don't feed the socialist.

By the same token, in a corporate environment, every worker knows his or her place. Such holds true in Singapore. In this regard, the criminal classes occupy the bottom rungs of Singaporean society. Unlike other Asian nations where organized crime is often formally represented in the government, or, in some cases, *is* the government, Singapore does not like crooks; both police and ordinary citizens view them with utter loathing.

For this reason, Chan Gin, lifetime employee of Singapore Inc., reacted to the spectacle just inside Sungei Buloh's tiny, gravelled parking lot much as an American businessman would if, unexpectedly, he entered his company's board room to find a hostile takeover under way.

Chan whispered out of the side of his mouth, 'Stay put, keep your head down, and be quiet.' Zaitun, who had been anything but quiet, promptly obeyed.

Chan swung out of his Range-Rover. The propane-powered

vehicle was a muscular brute normally issued only to park rangers. Chan liked it well enough. But he would have liked a Hum-Vee more. The Singapore Police Force wouldn't authorize him one. Unhappily, Poh Kay Siong didn't suffer the same budget limitations. His gang had two of them, big beasts in desert brown.

The other vehicles in the lot – a brace of black Beamers, a single Mercedes stretch limo, and Poh Kay Siong's trademark midnight-blue Cadillac Coup de Ville, the only one of its kind in Singapore – did not interest Chan. But the fact that the Seventy-Eight Dragons *chiu chow* brotherhood had Hummers and he did not annoyed him greatly.

As he paced across the parking lot, the Cadillac's rear door swung open. Poh Kay Siong, expensively dressed in an under-taker's black, slid out. Although weariness was etched on his face, Poh held himself erect, stood tall like the figure of authority he imagined himself to be.

He wasn't the figure of authority here. That role was already cast, Chan Gin starring.

'Superintendent Chan,' Poh murmured. 'We've been expecting you.'

Chan ignored him, walked by, pretended the gangster wasn't even there. He strode to the nearest BMW, hurling the door open. 'Out,' he ordered. Five men clambered from the car. Second BMW: four men. The limousine: six more. Plus four in each of the Hummers. Twenty-four in total, counting Poh. It was not, Chan thought, a criminal gang, it was a goddamned army.

He folded his arms, and leaned back against one of the BMWs. Wishing he smoked so that he could strike a match on the car's expensive exterior, he rested his buttocks against a fender. Then, taking a toothpick from inside his jacket and placing it between his lips, he stared silently at what appeared to be a gathering of Southeast Asia's top hatchetmen.

No one spoke. Chan waited. There were, after all, rules. More in the Orient than elsewhere, but the same the world over, those who operate on opposite sides of the law achieve a certain level of understanding. Unwritten codes of behaviour are agreed on, although never out loud, and the protocols under which necessary business can be conducted are carefully defined. Chief among these protocols is that outlaws explain their behaviour to policemen, not vice versa.

Poh nodded, politely acknowledging the order of things. 'As I said, Superintendent, we've been expecting you.'

'Importation of multiband scanners or other equipment capable of monitoring police or defence radio transmissions is punishable by up to thirty-six months' confinement, a two hundred thousand-dollar fine, and ten strokes of the cane.'

Poh spread his hands. 'But of course we would never smuggle such equipment across our nation's borders. We expected you because your presence seemed merely logical. Call it intuition if you will. Just as it is our intuition that you did not summon backup, preferring to treat this affair as a private rather than public matter.'

Chan answered with a cold stare. It was dark out here on the northwest coast, the city far away. The only light came from the headlights of six automobiles. A softening wind whispered among swaying casuarina trees. Somewhere in the reeds, an egret squawked annoyance at having been awakened.

He knew this part of the island well. When he was young, back before the economic boom, and suddenly it was derricks and cranes and bulldozers everywhere, he'd come here to fish, to swim, to play with his friends, Malay boys who lived in *kampung perkampungans* on the coast flats. Those villages were gone now: no more picturesque stilt houses, no more graceful *palari* boats moored near by; all replaced with government housing, sanitary, clean, and sterile. Chan was old enough to know how things had been when his country was still listed as 'third world' by the banks. He missed the purity of those times.

'I believe', Poh was saying, 'you know most of the gentlemen here.'

Poh was playing a new role: senior diplomat. Chan could live with the charade – but only barely.

'Well enough to know they aren't gentlemen. Let's see, we've got the Ah Kong syndicate, the Siew Sam Hong, the Ghee Hin, the Sio Kun Tong – part of the "Eighteen" group aren't you? – and my,

my, my the Mong Tai Army well off its turf, and you boys better
be on an airplane tomorrow morning. I tell you, Poh, it looks like
the only branch of the family missing is the Underwear Gang.'

Poh flinched. 'Please. We are professionals here. Those, the ones
of whom you speak . . .' he flicked his fingers, as if brushing a smut
of dust off his sports jacket, . . . are mere thugs.'

'How do I tell the difference? And, hey, Poh, the guy on the side
there – the one in the *really* crappy suit – him and his *ah kua* buddy
I don't recognize.'

The man to whom Chan was pointing sneered, *'Ko-pao, jih ta
tsu-tsu!'* Then the muzzle of Chan's Smith & Wesson was burrowed into his groin. No one quite saw how it got there. One
second, or so it seemed, the sour-faced Chinese man was spitting
his sulphurous curse, the next he was standing still, sweating hard.

Chan, unable to resist quoting one of his favourite movies,
growled, 'You talkin' to me?'

The man started to mumble an apology for insulting Chan's
ancestors. Chan thumbed back the automatic's hammer. 'I said,
are you talkin' to *me*?' The man apologized more profusely.

Poh, now peacemaker, stepped to Chan's side. 'Forgive him,
Superintendent, he's from the mainland.'

'That explains his lousy taste in clothes. Now tell me about his
filthy mouth.'

'Please, Superintendent. He's with the Green Gang, and does not
understand—'

'The *what?*' Chan roared. 'I thought the Reds put those punks
up against the wall fifty years ago.'

'Communism is young. We are old.' Poh Kay Siong turned his
palms open – a gesture seeming to offer Chan a gift that was both
small and of inestimable value. 'In our world astonishingly little
changes, Superintendent, hardly anything at all.'

Chan grimaced. Philosophical hoods were a species he could live
without. Nonetheless, he eased his pistol's hammer down. Then,
having his audience's attention, and intending to make use of it, he
spun the gun around his finger, once, twice, three times before
whipping it back into his shoulder holster. It was a cheap and
flashy trick, but then these were cheap and flashy hoods. He

smiled, showing as many teeth as possible. No one smiled back.

'Okay, Poh, let's hear it. What brings our fair city's number one warlord and his pet pit bulls out to the middle of a mangrove swamp in the middle of the night?'

Poh nodded politely. 'There is a mosquito who has been annoying you. His name, if memory serves, is John Gregory Taft. We . . .' Poh swept his hand in a half-circle, pointing at his colleagues, '. . . hearing that he entered this area at about three this morning, thought to do some small civic service by detaining him.'

Chan despised Poh's elliptical vocabulary and falsely genteel façade almost as much as he despised the man himself. 'Detaining? As in at the bottom of the straits?'

'Come now, Superintendent, if you apprehend him, he most certainly will be hanged. Should we apprehend him, is it not reasonable that a similar outcome, although swifter and less costly to the state, be arranged?'

'I'm not getting this, Poh. Why would you, of all people, want a drug smuggler dead?'

'But surely you know, Superintendent, that no one here traffics in narcotics.'

'Of course not,' Chan agreed sarcastically. 'Same as I know none of you are carrying illicit firearms.' Bad as he wanted to put the cuffs on Poh, the rules were the rules. Both cop and crook had to abide by this *very* temporary truce.

Allowing himself the faintest of nods, Poh smiled, speaking well-rehearsed lines with calculated sadness. 'Superintendent, the answer is a simple thing. Our people are *our* people. Mr Taft is not. One does not welcome fresh competition in my industry. Best to quash it quickly. In this way, Mr Taft's masters, whomever they may be, will understand that the Singaporean free market philosophy is not all embracing. Our system of quite well-organized illegality, Superintendent, is much better than the anarchy of *condottiere* Mr Taft represents – better for us, better for you, better for the public at large. Let me add to that thought the fact that we, all of us whom you necessarily view as opponents, hold you in great esteem . . .' The expression on Chan's face made

Poh stumble. '. . . No, it is true. Not one of us who earns his livelihood on this island nation would think of showing you the least scintilla of disrespect. Such simply is not done. The etiquette of our relationship is otherwise. The behaviour of this foreigner Taft reflects badly on us. People will think that we are associated with him, and responsible for his unseemly conduct. Worse, those who live outside our borders will form a misimpression of what is and is not permissible in our territory. And so—'

Chan lowered his voice to a growl, 'And so you figured that I wasn't up to the job.'

'Superintendent, we hardly—'

'*That's* why you tried to take him out in the hotel room, *that's* why you went after him in Toa Payoh, and *that's* why you're out here now. Right? Yeah, right. You figured any guy tough enough to get by me twice might, just might, get by me three times. You figured, Chan Gin's getting old, he's lost it, let's give the poor bastard a hand so he doesn't hurt himself.'

'You overstate—'

'What I state is this. "What we have here is a failure to communicate." Great line, great movie. Newman should have got the Academy Award. Nobody here seemed to have seen it. 'Poh, I clean up my own messes. Understand?'

Poh smiled widely. Chan would kill Taft, and never think that the American was other than a foreign drug dealer trying to muscle in on Poh's territory. Then, Taft dead in yet another deed of public violence, the Senior Minister's personal retribution would fall on Chan's head. It was perfect, precisely what Poh had wanted, a gratifyingly complete solution to all his problems. 'But of course, Superintendent.'

'Fine.' Chan peered into the darkness beyond the parking lot – swamplands, mangrove islands, the distant hiss of the straits. 'Taft's somewhere in there, you say? In the middle of Sungei Buloh?'

'There is very little question.'

Chan paced to his Range-Rover, and lifted the back hatch. Inside there was a long, gunmetal case. He opened it to reveal a boxy weapon that looked less like a rifle than a bazooka – his pride and joy: an electric-blue Sugg-50. The titanium-breached Sugg was chambered for an enormous six and three-quarter-inch-long .50 calibre, leaded-steel 650-grain Browning machine-gun cartridge. A Red Army-surplus laser rangefinder and Leupold tactical police model 16X scope were mounted on the barrel – three thousand dollars of hi-tech optics, and worth every penny of it.

Chan cradled the Sugg in his arms, all twenty-two pounds of it. It felt good. No one else in Singapore owned such a gun, no one wanted to, no one even asked to test fire Chan's. The brute had a recoil that could dent forged steel; when you shot it, it was like hurling a twelve-pound weight against your shoulder at a speed of sixteen and a half feet per second. Ouch. Ditto ouch, only more so, for whoever was on the receiving end of a slug – fired with muzzle energy of twelve thousand foot-pounds – that was capable of knocking over a cape buffalo at a distance of one mile.

If – no, when – Chan got Taft in his sights, the Sugg would put a Honda-sized hole where his midriff used to be.

Chan looked over his shoulder. 'You people, clear out.'

Poh shook his head. 'If you don't mind, Superintendent, we would like to wait for your return.'

Chan coughed a laugh. It wasn't a real laugh. 'You want to stick around in case he takes me down? Okay, fine, waste your time if you want to. But let me tell you, the next time you see me, I'm going to have Taft. And the next time you see Taft, he's going to be dead.'

'I am more delighted to hear that than you can possibly imagine.'

What's the smug bastard grinning about? Chan asked himself. Unable to answer his own question, he started to turn, remembered one last piece of business, and faced Poh again. 'Oh yeah, another thing. This afternoon, somebody killed an innocent by-stander out in Toa Payoh. Shooter used a .357 mag. Long barrel, according to ballistics, maybe a Colt Python.' Chan unclipped a pair of handcuffs from his belt, tossing them at Poh's feet. When I get back from dealing with Taft, I want to find whatever cocksucker *ah kua* who owns a gun like that chained to my front bumper. You got that, Poh?'

'Consider it done, Superintendent.'

The man from mainland China, the one in the cheap suit, started to back away. Chan didn't stay to watch, and the sounds of the struggle didn't last very long.

– 6 –

Quite mistakenly – although he would not know it until later – Chan believed he knew what Poh was up to. It seemed obvious that Taft's two escapes had made Chan lose face with the underworld. Poh Kay Siong and his fellow crimelords were questioning his effectiveness, wondering whether he was over the hill, dreaming hungrily about how much they could get away with if he was. If such was the case, then he, Chan, had no choice but to stalk the deadly John Gregory Taft through a pitch-black swamp. No choice at all.

Poh had set him a test. Pass it, and Poh would back off. Fail, and . . . well, if he failed, what happened after that wouldn't matter very much, would it?

He was fifty metres down the main trail now, past the visitors' centre and across the footbridge spanning the Sungei Buloh Estuary. The parking lot was far behind him. Some few stray light beams, the headlamps of a Hum-Vee, made it out this far. Shadowed by trees, reflected weakly off swamp water, they barely marked out the trail. The path branched north and south here, and both branches led into impenetrable darkness.

Chan had no flashlight. It would have been foolish, perhaps suicidal, to carry one. All a flashlight would do was give Taft a target.

He paused at the fork, calling from memory a mental map of the place. The preserve spanned two hundred or so acres. There were, he remembered, only a few routes through it. Sungei Buloh was not as popular as Singapore's other nature reserves – it was too remote, and, in the final analysis, *too* natural. It was a long way from the manicured comforts that pampered little Singaporean mice liked.

It was a pity, Chan thought, that people didn't come out here more often. Wild and free, it was a reminder of the way things used to be.

The trails – Chan could remember them now. They wove a skein of three looping paths, each loop tangential to the others. The question was: which trail had Taft taken?

The answer was obvious.

At this hour, there was no more deserted place on the island of Singapore than Sungei Buloh. Not even the cigarette smugglers, crossing the Straits of Johor to run unlicensed Marlboros down from Malaysia, would bring their boats here. Sungei Buloh's shoreline was too far from the roads. Besides, while you had to be a little nuts to risk two-to-ten on a smuggling rap, you had to be downright loony to chance an encounter with one of Sungei Buloh's coastal crocodiles.

Crocs . . . He pursed his lips . . . *One more good argument against the protection of endangered species.*

On land, a hungry estuarine crocodile can move at ten kilometres – six miles – per hour; humans can run faster, and are advised to do so. As a child, Chan had seen one brute that was as long as a pick-up truck, twin rows of spiky scales all the way down its too-plump length, stubby legs with four horribly finger-like claws, and many, many teeth. Meat hooks, really, and they smiled over the sides of a mouth big enough to take a grown adult, much less a young Chinese boy, in a single satisfying gulp. Chan hated them, hated the way they lay all brown and barky like a sunken log, deceptive in shallow water, patiently waiting for the prey to take one, only one, step too close. There was no animal Chan feared more.

Except maybe snakes.

As a tropical island, Singapore had a surfeit of those. The venomous kind. Black or grey or sometimes speckled, but always camouflaged and invisible although they were right in your path. King cobras, yeah, there were definitely kings out in Sungei Buloh. When he was ten years old his best friend's uncle had had a run-in with one. The man had lasted longer than most: fifteen minutes. And he'd screamed like a soul damned in deepest hell for fourteen of them.

Then too, you got black spitting cobras. Bad karma, those. Most snakes are timid; they'll usually slither off into the weeds at the approach of a man. Not a spitter. The suckers come right at you, just looking for a fight. *Very bad karma.* Plus Sungei Buloh was renowned, at least among herpetologists, for its population of reticulated pythons, the world's longest snake, nine-point-six metres, thirty-one feet of reptile, and if it decided to coil its muscular links around your torso, buddy, you got pulped.

Fuck me! Chan thought. *What the hell am I doing this for? I should be the one waiting in the parking lot. Poh and his crowd should be the ones out here. Any luck at all – a cobra or two, a clutch of crocs – and my organized-crime problems are a long time solved . . .*

Something black, cougar-sized, clawed, slid out of the underbrush.

Jesus!

Chan's heart jumped as he saw it. His breath was gone. Lungs frozen, he was incapable of inhaling. The animal was no more than two metres from his feet, obsidian fur beneath a coal-black sky; two cat eyes shining, a mouth open, teeth on display.

He was cradling the Sugg in his arms. It was useless. Poh Kay Siong was right. Devil Cop had lost it. Lost it bad. Idiot that he was, he hadn't chambered a round in the thing.

His face was wet, salt sweat burning his eyes, the thud of his heart violent enough to make his shirt jump. Drop the Sugg? Go for the Smith & Wesson beneath his armpit?

Not with this animal at his feet. One false move, any movement at all, and the beast would . . .

Would what?

Would fall over in shock. *Shit!* Chan knew what the thing was – a lousy Malaysian binturong that had somehow wandered across the straits. *Goddamned animal!* All it was was an ordinary civet cat's bigger cousin. Sure, it looked like a panther – at least in the dark – but it had the personality of a house tabby. The reason why the miserable thing was standing in the middle of the trail, frozen as if coiled for a spring, was that it was more scared of Chan Gin than he was of it.

He kicked his foot out, hissing, 'Scat!' The terrified binturong scuttled into the undergrowth. Chan swallowed hard, mopped his brow, stood gulping air and waiting for his heart rate to slow.

In time it did. By then Chan had fished a railroad spike-sized Browning slug from his jacket pocket, jerked open the Sugg's breech, slapped the bullet into its chamber, and slammed the bolt home.

Locked and loaded.

And now for that dickhead Taft.

– 7 –

Chan looked to his right, north up the estuary. A hundred metres away it debouched into the Straits of Johor. In the distance, not far, two kilometres more or less, the lights of Malaysia twinkled in the darkness.

Malaysia was the answer. It had to be what had brought Taft out to this maze of sloughs and swamps.

Taft, being the thorough professional that he was, would have mapped out a fallback plan before he bought his ticket to Singapore. He'd have studied the lay of the land, charting an escape route in case things went wrong.

And here it was: the most remote part of the island, only a short ride in a fast boat to the mainland and to safety. The American drug runner would have a contact man over in Johor. One phone call, and the rendezvous would be set – meet me in the darkest hour of the night, meet me where the police coast guard cruisers never come, meet me in Sungei Buloh.

There was a speedboat out in the straits now, Chan was sure of it. Or if there wasn't, there would be soon. He checked his wristwatch. Three-thirty-eight. With luck, he thought, Taft would have set the pick-up time at a nice round number. Four a.m. Yeah, that sounded right. It fitted Poh Kay Siong's timetable: if Poh's people had seen Taft come into the park at three, then a four o'clock pick-up made sense. It wouldn't be at three-thirty because that didn't leave Taft quite enough time to get out to the one, the only, logical place for a speedboat to meet him.

Chan knew where that place was.

Taft's boatman needed a landmark, something he could steer for. But on an uninhabited coast of mangrove swamps, landmarks were few and far between.

There was only one.

Sungei Buloh was a birdwatcher's paradise. More than one hundred and seventy species migrated through the place, some of them extraordinarily rare. Birdwatchers are an aggressive, intelligent, and outspoken breed – the very opposite of the milquetoasts the media portray them as. They'd mounted a massive campaign for the protection of Sungei Buloh as a wildfowl preserve, and the government, oddly liberal on environmental matters, had bent over backwards to pacify them. The result: two dozen beautifully appointed observation blinds were scattered through the park.

And one observation tower.

It was built as a post from which birding fanatics could *ooh* and *ahh* as white-bellied sea eagles and fierce brahminy kites circled and swooped and slaughtered their prey.

The tower. That's where Taft had to be headed. It stood out against the shoreline, was easily seen from the straits, couldn't be missed. Taft's boatman would steer for it, a straight shot down the Kechil inlet. And a straight shot back out to freedom.

If you looked at a map of Sungei Buloh, as Taft no doubt had, you'd figure that the tower was a long way from where Chan was now standing. And you'd be right.

And you'd be wrong.

Chan knew Sungei Buloh as his prey did not. Taft would stick to the map, following the sandy trails and planked walkways that compassed the circumference of the park. Those trails were great sweeping loops, the north one circling a muddy pond where bitterns and painted snipe stalked the reeds, the south one rounding a shallow lake perfect for four different species of egret. It was about five kilometres to the tower either way.

What Taft didn't know, couldn't know, was that those two bodies of water were separated by a narrow levee roughly three hundred metres long. It wasn't marked on the maps, or anywhere else. Access was forbidden to all but the park rangers. And it would let Chan run halfway across Sungei Buloh in one-tenth of the time it would take a man walking the long, arcing trails.

With any luck at all he could reach the tower before Taft's boat showed up.

Locked and loaded, of course.

The park's largest birdwatching blind – bigger than the Samsudin woman's entire flat – was a few steps to Chan's left. The shortcut through the centre of the nature preserve began right behind it.

He held his massive blue rifle port arms, the same way he'd learned twenty-seven years earlier as a young draftee: centre of the barrel in his left hand, butt cradled in his right, the weapon's length tilted across his chest, and the sergeant bawling, 'Pointing at ten o'clock soldiers! The muzzle points at ten hundred hours!'

He started forward, fast but not too fast, not all pistons firing because that would be too noisy and too tiring. Instead he jogged, a nice steady pace, ten kilometres – crocodile speed – per hour. His leather-soled loafers whispered on gravel. Unconsciously, without even noticing what he was doing, his lungs began pumping to a military rhythm, pulsing quicktime, the old beat-beat-beat of an army on the jog. In the silence of his mind he heard a drill sergeant, his name long forgotten, calling out the repetitive chants: 'Left face! Forward march! Quicktime march! Left. Left. Left–right– left.'

American drill. American formations. American weapons. They all came in the same package. In those days ('National Serviceman Chan reporting for duty, sir!') the US was a big baffled animal wallowing in a small, lethal quagmire called Vietnam. There were Americans all over Southeast Asia, and a fair number of them were assigned to train quote-allies-unquote. Big guys in green fatigues, unfiltered Pall Malls forever in their mouths, heavy black Colts on their hips, and a slow rolling gait like John Wayne's in *Rio Bravo*. As you ran, the drill sergeants shouted, just like their American trainers had taught them, 'Left. Left. Left–right–left.' And you, and every other draftee in your unit, shouted the same thing back. 'Left! Left! Left–right–left!'

Carrying at port arms a rifle nearly five times heavier than the wood-stocked M-14 with which he trained, Chan jogged. The weight was good. The rhythm was right. The pulse of air in his lungs and the slightly faster beating of his heart were precisely what they should be. You needed that – more oxygen in the blood, a higher heart rate, extra hormones trickling, not flooding, into your system. It made the killing easy. Take it too hard, and you'd turn hyper. Then your hands shake and you jerk the trigger and you miss. Go too slow, and you think about it too much. Your nerve endings tingle. Your sweat runs faster. Funniest thing of all, you wind up breathing harder than if you ran.

The trick is the pace. The pace is the trick. It's a form of meditation, repetitive physical and mental mantras that centre peace in the soul, alertness in the mind, and perfect control in the body. Zen archery, yogic meditation, military drill – they all seek the same objective, all produce the same psychic result.

Left. Left. Left–right–left.

At one with himself, Chan jogged past salt marshes. Life stirred at his passing – night birds chattering territorial claims and amorous intentions, frogs no longer than a man's thumb booming croaks worthy of a carnivore; and all around estuarine waters, now rising with the tide, whispering among mangrove roots, and clapping tiny wavelets on the shores of mud flats.

He was a forty-minute drive from the downtown financial centre of Southeast Asia. He was a million kilometres from nowhere in a world the way it was before man was born.

Left. Left. Left–right–left.

He was at his peak now, perfectly relaxed and perfectly ready. Up ahead the dark weediness of the shortcut brightened into lighter sand. Twenty precisely paced strides took Chan there, on to the main trail, and, if the gods smiled, close and getting closer to his prey. A right turn, another kilometre and a half, and he'd be at the tower. Ten minutes, no, eight, of silent running; then slow to a walk, pick your steps carefully, make no sound, hope that Taft is sufficiently overconfident that he's climbed the tower, and is standing upright signalling into the night with a flashlight (even a match or lighter will do), a perfect target, well and truly silhouetted against the sky, the reflection of . . .

'JEEEEEE-SUSSSSSS!'

Chan stood still as stone. The screech came from his left, down a walkway leading into the densest part of Sungei Buloh's mangrove swamps. The voice unquestionably belonged to Taft.

'OH GOD! GET THE HELL AWAY FROM ME!'

Chan's face broke into a smile of grim satisfaction. It appeared that Mr Taft had just come face-to-face with some of Sungei Buloh's nightlife.

– 8 –

The snake was the last straw. *Enough is enough*, Jack screamed, although silently.

He'd been walking carefully, keeping to the sandy trail, making sure he was always on the proper route by periodically using his – or rather Peter Quint's – flashlight.

And this *thing* slithered into its beam. Slithered endlessly. Ten awful yards, thirty revolting feet, of pale, scaly, repulsive snake, snake, snake!

Jack bawled, 'Jesus!' The reptile was thick as a tree trunk, brutally powerful, and utterly loathsome. The very sight of it turned his stomach. It stopped dead in the middle of his path, studying him with obvious appetite. 'Oh God!' He took an involuntary step back. The snake reacted by changing direction, coiling straight towards him. Tasting the air with flickering tongue, it kept its glassy eyes hypnotically fixed on what Jack intuitively knew it believed was a wounded animal, howling in pain, an easy meal.

He screamed again: 'Get the hell away from me!' At this, the snake paused. But only for a second. Jack hurled his flashlight. It bounced, went black, and skittered across the ground inches in front of the snake's head. As the flash rolled past, the snake touched it with its tongue.

METAL HARD COLD INEDIBLE

The python had encountered this sort of disappointment before – noisy machinery that squealed like prey but which was made of something other than meat. Trying to crush such things to digestible pulp was a waste of time.

THAT WHICH DOES NOT BLEED IS NOT FOOD

The python twisted – a long, lazy flex of predatory muscle – and returned to its original route. Shortly it disappeared from sight.

Jack had never been so shaken in his life. *Enough, enough, enough!*

Frozen seconds passed. He did not know how many as he stood motionless, all his senses stretched to their utmost, looking, listening, even sniffing for a hint of the ungodly animal.

The snake seemed to have moved on. He heard no more stealthy gliding sounds, hideously muscled strength coiling on a sandy trail, and saw no more seemingly endless length of scaled skin.

Christ Almighty! What was that thing?

Gone, it was gone. As he should go. He still had another half-mile of walking before he reached the end of the park, and the coastline closest to Malaysia.

It was not, however, a walk he intended to make without a flashlight. Not with snakes in the bushes and God only knew what else in the underbrush.

He'd thrown his light at the snake. It had gone out when it hit the ground. Jack sincerely hoped that the thing wasn't broken. He was not at all sure if he could handle being in this dark and dangerous place if it was.

His eye caught the glint of something on the ground – bright metal faintly illuminated by the sullen glow of city lights reflected off clouds. The flashlight had rolled to the base of a stubby, columnar tree. Jack paced five steps forward, then bent at the waist to pick it up.

Above him, just where his head had been a moment before, a two-foot section of tree trunk disappeared. One second it had been there, the next it was vaporized like something hit by a phaser blast on *Star Trek*. Nothing was left but a sawdust fog and an empty space in a tree – twenty-eight inches in diameter – that suddenly had begun to tumble.

There had been a noise too, brutally loud, an explosive blast of destruction making Jack's ears ring so loudly that he almost didn't hear Chan Gin's curse. 'Missed you, motherfucker!'

For the third time that night Jack Taft screamed – not with terror; he was well past that, and would never do it again. No, this scream was something else – it was the howl of a man shocked into towering fury.

– 9 –

Chan could not have asked for anything more: Taft standing still, forty metres distant, shadowed but silhouetted, as easy a target as a man might want.

He braced the Sugg-50's butt against the thick trunk of a mango tree to absorb the rifle's wrecking-ball recoil. Flicking on the switch that illuminated (but only faintly, the better to preserve his night vision) a reticle, he pressed his right eye to the telescopic sight. A moment later, his cross-hairs were level and steady on the back of his target's neck. Just then, Taft began walking forward, slowly picking his steps in the dark. No problem. Chan gently turned a knurl on the scope, lowering its elevation and adjusting the horizontal cross-hair for a point-of-aim closer than any at which he had ever fired the Sugg. He was eager to learn what sort of effect its mammoth slug would have on something hit at this particular range.

There was a faint breeze. Chan was too near his target for it to make a difference. He left the scope's windage alone. Taft was walking towards a tree, a tampine. A few decades earlier Singapore had been dense with them, but now they were endangered, almost logged out because of their hardness and durability.

Chan, knowing it wasn't necessary, but preferring a clean kill over something less tidy, laid a finger on the button that activated his laser sight. Taft stopped, straight and still at the foot of the tampine. *Now's the time.* Chan inhaled deeply, let half the breath sigh slowly out of his lungs, and tapped on the laser. It, like the cross-hairs of his telescopic sight, was now centred at a spot inches below Taft's neck, directly between Taft's shoulders. He let his finger tighten – easily, slowly, the way he'd curl it through a pretty woman's hair.

The Sugg roared, spitting a two-metre gout of flame, bucking like a big blue shark taking the hook. The mango against which it was braced groaned, and ripe fruit rained to the ground.

Forty metres away a tampine tumbled slowly backward. John Gregory Taft stood up screaming what was undoubtedly some arrogant taunt that Chan, ears momentarily deafened by the Sugg's percussion, could not quite make out.

Chan could not believe his eyes. Taft was, damn him, supernatural. *What sort of man is this?* he asked himself. *What sort of man can* feel *the tickle of cross-hairs on his back and sense the caress of a laser on his neck?*

Answer: the most dangerous kind of man, more dangerous than any he had ever met. The night seemed colder, and it came to Chan that he was afraid.

The American was in motion, sprinting down the trail, on to a boardwalk spanning a lengthy expanse of mangrove swamp. Chan could barely see Taft's shadow – no time to chamber another round in the Sugg – as the fugitive hoodlum vaulted over a railing, splashed four metres down into waist-high waters, and disappeared from sight.

Fear or no fear, Chan was running too, running harder than he had before, running as hard as he could. His marksman's peace – the trance-like unity of shooter, weapon, and target – was gone. He needed everything he had, all the air he could suck into his lungs and all the power he could force to his legs, every muscle straining in pursuit of an enemy whom he yearned to kill.

He pounded over the sandy trail, legs pumping, fingers fumbling another .50 calibre round from his jacket pocket. For the briefest of moments he thought about dropping the Sugg, going after Taft with a handgun, but he discarded the thought. Taft was far ahead. A pistol was imprecise at ranges greater than twenty-five metres. Accuracy was essential. The Sugg was his only hope.

His shoes hit the boardwalk, their rapid slap a tell-tale to Taft of where Chan was, and where, if the American bastard wanted it that way, he might be shot at. As he ran, Chan jerked open the Sugg's bolt, pressed home a round, slapped the breech closed. He kicked off his left shoe, then his right. One rolled to a stop on wooden planking. The other splashed into the slough. Bally loafers, made of glove leather, four hundred Singaporean dollars the pair. He didn't even think about the loss. All he thought about was leaping clear of the boardwalk railing, hitting the muddy water upright when he landed, and being ready to fire if he had a target.

Here it was, the spot where Taft had leapt into Sungei Buloh's most darkly overgrown morass, the very heart of its central mangrove jungle. And wouldn't you know it, the sonofabitch had instinctively run for the one place where the swamp sloughs branched.

Good, he's goddamned good, but is he better than me?

Chan did not vault the rail; not one hand on the wood, kick up, swing over, come down at an angle, hope for the best. Rather, he took it split-legged, sprinting scissored like an Olympic runner clearing a hurdle, and clearing it with easy grace.

Knees bent, Sugg held two-handed above his head, balls of his feet ready for the impact, he hit the water and the sucking mud beneath it. The jolt of his drop forced him deep enough that water lapped his neck. Tepid and cloying brown stuff splashed his face, a liquid both salty and organic, the taste and temperature of fresh blood.

He forced himself erect, hip-high in the channel. The faintest of currents tugged at his pants' legs, the pressure of a gently rising tide.

He was very still now. Completely motionless. Listening. Only listening.

Taft was sure to be moving slowly, the better to be silent. But if the gods smiled, he would not be as perfect in his silence as he seemed to be at other things. Instead he would slip in the mud, stumble on a sunken log, come to some place where the waters were too deep to be forded and had to be – *splash, splash* – swum.

A faint breeze stirred the trees. Mangrove leaves rustled overhead. The quickening tide whispered with a feathery voice. Out in the straits, a boat horn hooted, its note soft and distant, muffled by the rank foliage of the nature preserve. Some small animal coughed, and Chan heard the scrabble of tiny claws as it scampered up a tree. Frogs were still booming their croaks, all disproportionate to their size, and the park's nocturnal birds continued to go about their noisy business, uninterrupted by the arrival of two creatures, slow bipeds, unlikely to threaten their nests. Chan, immobile, listened.

And heard.

Up the left channel, to the northeast, there was a faint sound of mass moving through water slowly, but not quite slowly enough to go unheard. Soft, secretive, rhythmic – it was the sound of someone swimming as silently as he could. It was Taft, of course, still trying to reach his rendezvous at the observation tower.

I BULL MALE AND HUNGRY MOVE MY TAIL WITH LAZY GRACE PUSHING FOR OPEN WATER THERE IS NO PREY HERE IT IS A DIS-APPOINTING PLACE

Taft wouldn't swim fast; the risk of being heard was too great. That gave Chan an advantage. He'd known this park all his life, played in it while it was another wild place on an island largely given over to wilderness. And so he knew how to move through these waters more swiftly than Taft, but more secretly.

It took him a moment to find a suitable log – a length not quite as long as he, nor overly thick. Tide-borne, it drifted up the channel. Chan pressed his weight on it. *Just right.* If he tried to straddle it, it would sink. But with his body half on, half off, it would float well. Best of all, it was mostly trunk, only one shattered branch, and that meant it was sufficiently streamlined for his purposes. He rested the Sugg horizontally across the trunk, holding it in both hands, pulling it back hard against the stumpy branch. Then he bent at the waist, resting his torso over the log, but leaving his legs free in the water.

He kicked into the mud. The force propelled him faster than an average man could swim. And with no sound at all. After a few seconds, the tree trunk began to slow. Chan kicked down again, pressing forward, speeding up. And again. Four kicks. Seven kicks. Nine kicks. He found the rhythm of the thing, had it down pat.

Ahead, up the tidal channel and against the incoming current, he still heard soft water sounds, closer now, much closer.

FEATHERED CREATURES ARE FINE FINNY ONES TOO BUT BEST OF ALL WARM BLOODED THINGS SWIM LOW EYES ONLY ABOVE THE SURFACE AND FOOD FINDS ITSELF TO YOU THERE IS NO NEED FOR HASTE

Chan was overtaking Taft. Kick by kick, metre by metre, he was gaining. As long as Taft kept swimming slowly, silent running. Chan could keep closing the gap. No doubt Taft was holding his own ears open, listening for the giveaway splash of a man in pursuit. But Taft would hear nothing. Nor would he know the skills that a young Chinese boy learned decades earlier, compliments of equally young Malay friends experienced in finding marsh birds' nests, there to thieve eggs that would be, in that era of poverty and internecine war, welcome dinner for the night.

The channel curved. A tiny islet, a tangle of mangrove roots and mud, lay twenty metres ahead. The incoming tide coursed on both sides of it. Which side would Taft have taken? Chan listened. The swimmer, now much nearer, had gone to the right. Chan kicked into the mud, steering his improvised float in that direction, and stirring wavelets in his wake.

THERE IS ANOTHER IN THESE WATERS AND IT IS BEHIND SO SILENT IT MUST BE ANOTHER OF MY SCALY KIND

Sometimes this ploy of using a log, pushing silently through sloughs and estuaries, had produced even more profitable results for Chan and his friends. Birds' eggs were tasty enough. But tastier still were birds themselves, and if you knew how to use a loop of handwoven twine in the proper way, you'd return home that evening a hero bearing the makings of a most majestic feast. In those days – Singapore a troubled third world backwater – meat was scarce. Such shortages were, of course, of no issue to Chan Gin, the son of prosperous parents. But among his friends, among the Malay families who lived on this coast and fished its shores, newly caught Siberian plover, all plumply resting here in their migrations, were a prize beyond price. Then too, there were crab to be found, but only if you knew where to look and were agile with a digging stick. Young Chan most certainly was agile, proudly contributing to the cookpots of the parents of his friends.

Those days were poorer days – but they were somehow better. There was an edge to things. Life's uncertainties were sharper. People made their own decisions, thought about alternatives, and sometimes took daring risks. But today? *Ha!* Today, most Singaporeans were timid creatures, too well cared for and too well protected, hiding behind the voluminous skirts of an all-embracing government. It was . . .

There he was! Chan saw him! Not thirty metres away!

THE OTHER COMES CLOSER WHO DARES CONTEST THIS TERRITORY THAT IS MINE

Taft was only the faintest of shadows, a dark smudge on darker waters. But, no question, that smudge was swimming almost-but-not-quite silently up the channel, was nearly at the end of the mangrove islet, headed directly for the route to the observation tower. Chan bent his knees, pushed his feet into sucking mud, and kicked harder.

Another minute. That's all it would take. Ten or twelve metres behind Taft, and he'd swing the Sugg's muzzle around, brace its butt on his shoulder (brace himself for a brutal kick that could fracture his collar bone), aim, squeeze, and end the night's festivities with, pun intended, a bang.

At a distance of ten metres, the Sugg's bullet carried the force of a runaway freight train. It would blow the goddamned drug dealer apart. They'd be looking for his pieces for a week. And they'd find them scattered over an acre of wetlands.

He could hardly wait.

Closer now. Fewer than eighteen metres away. The punk still hadn't heard him, still didn't know how closely death pursued.

Fourteen metres. Now Chan could make out the full length of his enemy's body, dark and more floating than swimming on the surface of the slough. Just another few seconds . . .

NO RIVAL BY ITS SCENT BUT PREY, FRESH PREY AND LARGE AND FLESHY GOOD MEAT THIS BREED SOFT AND RICH WITH BLOOD

The log bumped into something. A shoal of mud. It was stuck, wouldn't go forward, not another inch.

If I'm going to take him, it's gotta be now!

THE PREY STANDS IF I AM TO TAKE IT IT MUST BE NOW

Chan rose, began swinging the Sugg to his shoulder. He knew he could ignore the niceties of telescopic sight and laser. At this distance all he had to do was aim down the barrel, squeeze the trigger, take the punishing recoil, and hope that such piece-parts of the late scumbag John Gregory Taft as splattered his way were not the truly nauseating ones.

HERE HUNGER TURNS TO SATIATION

The rifle was rising, halfway home, and Chan felt his smile begin to form. Something pressed into his back. Behind him a voice whispered, 'Hands up, Chan. Drop the gun.'

AND FOOD TO FEAST

Two thoughts passed through Chan Gin's mind. The first was: *My God! What have I been chasing for the past five minutes?* The second was: *Shit, no!* The latter thought giving recognition of the fact that, shocked by Taft's ambush, he had reflexively tightened his finger on the Sugg's trigger.

AS I STRIKE

Twelve thousand foot-pounds of energy spewed from the rifle's muzzle. Hurled back by the velocity of its monstrous recoil, it leapt out of Chan's hands, the butt slamming into Chan's ribs with the force of an elephant's kick . . .

. . . fierce white pain . . .

IN WATER LIGHTNING

. . . a long curtain of blackness descending . . .

THUNDER

Chan Gin was no longer to be counted among the ranks of the conscious.

MORE KILLING THAN I

An estuarine crocodile, fourteen feet from tip to tail, reeled at the cataclysmic force of a .50 calibre round exploding mere yards from its snout. Shocked and stunned, it dived, racing for the safety of the straits.

– 10 –

Chan was awake, although not yet ready to open his eyes. There was some pain, a knife edge sawing at his right side, but it was distant, oddly blunt, deadened by low-level shock.

He tightened his stomach muscles. The contraction sent a jolt up his torso. *Broken ribs,* he thought. *They'll have to be taped.* He wasn't going to move very fast until they were. He probably wouldn't move very fast afterwards either.

In the unlikely event there was an afterwards.

Intuitively he knew he hadn't been knocked out long. A few minutes at the most, just enough time for that prick Taft to pat him down and strip him of the familiar weight of his weapons.

And, Chan noticed, to pilfer the spare handcuffs he kept clipped to his belt, using them to chain his left wrist to a nice, solid mangrove root.

Well, I'm fucked. He wasn't particularly frightened. After all, the American hoodlum was a professional. It would be over fast enough.

He opened his eyes. Taft was there, near but not near enough to reach. Not that Chan could go for him, not with his ribs caved in.

Afterwards he'll dump me in the estuary and a croc will come along and . . . Oh Jesus! Suddenly Chan knew himself to be frightened after all.

Taft spoke as soon as he saw that Chan was awake. His tone was curiously conversational. 'You sure do carry a lot of guns,' he said. One of them, a lightweight Ruger, dangled casually from Taft's hand, pointing only vaguely in Chan's direction.

It looked like the lousy puke was going to taunt him before pulling the trigger. *No way. You can kill me, asshole, but laughing at me you do not get to do.* 'Better safe than sorry.'

'And this thing,' Taft pointed at the Sugg resting across his knees. 'What is it, some sort of rocket launcher or something?'

Taft was trying to look cool, but Chan could see the heat bubbling beneath his surface. The goddamned dirtbag wanted to pulp his face with a pistol butt, wanted it bad. Chan couldn't blame him; had their positions been reversed, that was *precisely* what Chan would be doing at this very moment. 'Don't try to pull my chain, Taft. It's just a rifle.'

'*Just?* Hell, man, it blew a tree in half.'

'Yeah, anti-tank guns'll do that,' leaving to the cocksucker's imagination what it would have done to him.

Taft swallowed hard. 'Who needs an anti-tank gun?'

'Me.'

'Christ, what for?'

'Things I want bad.'

'For instance?'

Like you, motherfucker, Chan thought, but did not say. The police psychologists – *not that those assholes' opinions are worth a shit* – said that when a bad guy wanted to talk, it was a positive sign. Chan decided to keep the conversation going: 'For instance six, maybe seven years ago, I was in hot pursuit of a stolen semi. A cop named Kumar was driving my car. I was in the back seat with the Sugg. We're on the Bukit Timah Expressway. High-speed chase. Semi's doing about a hundred and fifty klicks. So I tell Kumar to pass the guy, get in front of him. Which he does. Then I break the rear window out, point the Sugg at the semi's front grille, and pull the trigger. Bullet splits the engine block, splits it right in two. Hey, Taft, you ever seen what happens to a high-balling semi when its engine blows up? Very nice. Very gratifying.'

Taft's eyes goggled. 'Christ, that's sick.'

'I kill criminals, Taft. It's my job. I do it very well.'

'You're insane.'

'Wrong. All I do is enforce the law in ways that get noticed. Send the bad guys a message. But crazy, no. The only crazy man around here is you.'

Taft grinned. It was the first time Chan had ever seen him smile. He didn't like the way it looked. 'If I'm crazy, then how come you're the one chained to the tree?'

'Fuck you, Taft.'

'And the very same to you, my friend.'

The two sat silently. Seconds stretched into minutes, and all Chan could think was why Taft didn't get it the fuck over. *What are you waiting for? What are you up to? Come on Taft, you dildo, cut to the chase* . . . Finally, the American spoke. 'Your ribs are pretty messed up. I could tell when I was collecting your guns.'

The words were a surprise. Likewise their sympathetic tone. Again Chan wondered what the bastard's game was. Whatever it was, the only way to handle it was to sneer in his face. 'I can tell too.'

'And there's a hole in your back from the branch.'

'*Branch?*' Chan already knew what Taft meant. The oldest trick in the book – the fact that he'd fallen for it made him want to howl with shame. *This* was the humiliating revelation the evil sonofabitch had been waiting to make. 'You stuck me up with a fucking branch?'

'Yeah. Remember, I hate guns.'

'Shit!'

'Anyway, its not a bad hole. Not deep, I mean. I put a handkerchief over it because it was bleeding.'

'Up your ass, Florence Nightingale.'

Taft shook his head in annoyance. 'You know, Chan, you're a real pain in the butt.'

'I try.'

'Tell me something. When you and your buddies came crashing into my hotel room, why weren't you wearing your badges? If you'd had 'em on, I would have surrendered.'

'I don't need no stinking badge.'

'*The Treasure of the Sierra Madre*, 1947, Houston directing Bogart, Holt, and his own father. Actually the line is, "I don't have to show you any stinking badges."' Chan's eyes widened. Taft clearly was a man of culture and taste even if he was a goddamned gangster. Taft continued, 'So why don't you need no stinking badge?'

'Hell, man,' Chan growled, 'I had my warrant card in my hand.'

'Your what?'

The question brought Chan up short. Did this shitheel really not know what a warrant card was? *No, not possible* . . . But he was an American. He expected plainclothes cops to have their tin clipped to their jackets. He wouldn't know that in Singapore . . .

'Taft, you fuckfaced liar, you know damned well what a warrant card is.'

'Nope.'

'Police IC, man!'

'IC?'

'Identity card. Authority to kick doors, kick ass, bust scum like you. I had it in my hand when you opened the door. It was right under your fucking nose.'

'So how was I supposed to know what it was?'

'Don't give me this shit, Taft! I don't want to hear it!'

Taft frowned. Standing, half speaking to himself, he muttered, 'Dumb damn cops don't even wear badges. Jesus, why am I not surprised?'

As Taft rose, Chan could see two other pistols, both his prized property, stuffed beneath the man's belt. 'I thought you said you didn't like guns.'

'I don't. But you know, they sort of grow on you.' Taft was smiling again; Chan was liking it even less. 'Anyway, because I'm a nice guy, here's what I'm going to do. I sort of hate to leave you here with your ribs broken, but there's no other way. But once I'm over in Malaysia, I'm going to call—'

Chan shuddered – mortal terror and instant, uncontrollable fear. His voice quivered as he interrupted. 'You're leaving me for the crocs, right?'

Taft's own voice was suddenly higher, risen by more than a single panicked octave. '*Crocs?* You mean like *crocodiles*.?!'

'Don't do it, Taft. Just put a bullet through my head. Or if you want to hear me scream, give me a couple of gut-shots. But for God's sake, let me die like a man instead of fucking meat!'

'You people have crocodiles out here? *Crocodiles!*' Very suddenly Taft sat back down. 'Oh Jesus!'

There was something going on in Taft's mind. What it was, Chan did not know. But it was important that he find out. He shook his head, trying to clear it of pain, shock, and bone-chilled horror at the thought of being chained to a tree, weaponless, and watching the waddling approach of a hungry maneater.

Taft's voice had dropped to a whisper. 'There was this thing in the water. It swam right past me. I'd just jumped up on this island. Then you came by. I figured the thing in the water was a, I-don't-know, manatee or something.'

'Croc. In the dark, I thought it was you. Mostly the bastards come across the straits and—'

'*The straits?*' Taft was shouting again. 'I'm planning to go for a midnight swim and there are crocodiles in the pool!'

Chan was unable to help himself. He barked a laugh. It hurt like hell. 'Swim? What about your boat?'

'What boat?'

Something was wrong here. Chan hurt too much to know what.

Taft was speaking quickly now, an exasperated man on the border of losing his temper. 'Look, all I want to do is get to someplace safe. Is that too much to ask? I mean, if I can find somebody who will just sit down and listen to me instead of trying to shoot me every time I cross his path, then I can explain things. But no, there's no one in this lousy country who wants to do that. All you get in Singapore is a nutball named Chan with enough guns to rearm Iraq plus other guys with more guns plus you people want to hang me and I haven't done a goddamned thing. *Jesus H. Christ!*' Taft windmilled his arms and looked up at the sky as if searching for God. He was ranting out of control. 'Then there was this snake! Big as a bulldozer! Jesus! I really needed that! Worse than this it does not get! That's what I figured! But noooo! There's more to come! Because then we get ocean-going crocodiles! The only way off this goddamned island has crocodiles! Aw man, that does it! I've had it!' Panting, Taft let his head drop between his knees.

Chan thought it was an impressive act – a befuddled civilian quite thoroughly innocent of wilful wrongdoing – for a moment there, he'd almost believed it. But of course it was only a master impersonator performing his role, and there was no way in hell it was true.

Taft looked up at him with bitter resignation. 'Okay,' he babbled. 'Okay! I'm not going into the water! Right? Yeah, right! Jack versus the crocodiles is not an even match! We're talking Notre Dame versus the Little Sisters of the Poor!' Chan had never heard the metaphor before. It took him a second to appreciate it. Taft fumed on. 'So what am I supposed to do? I can get out of this lousy swamp for one thing, right? While you were knocked out, I climbed through all the mud and grunge on this crummy little island, and the boardwalk is just on the other side! So I can go over there and walk out, right? I mean I can do this! No problem, except that you get munched by the local residents!'

'You could shoot me.'

Taft screamed: 'What? Is this a multiple choice test?. Pick one of the following! Leave you to get eaten! Shoot you! Or none of the above!'

Chan's instincts kicked in. Taft was bobbing and weaving like a man on the brink of delirium. *Vulnerable*, Chan thought. *I can nudge him and maybe he'll . . .* 'Taft, stop your damned pussy whining.'

Taft's head snapped up. 'Say what?'

'You're burbling like a fucking baby.'

The American spat through clenched teeth, 'Don't you call me a baby.'

Interesting. Taft's reaction was out of all proportion to what Chan had said. He knew he'd struck a nerve, couldn't resist needling it again. 'What, Taft, you don't like being told you're a crybaby?'

'Screw you!' Face red, eyes wide. Chan was gratified. 'Hey, whimper and wail all you want, buddy. But do me a favour and do it somewhere else. Namby-pamby sissies get on my nerves.'

Taft's nostrils flared, 'I. Am. Not. Namby. Pamby.'

'Shit, son, I'm the one with the broken ribs. But you don't hear me bitch, bitch, bitching. Real men don't snivel, Taft. Real men take their medicine. You wanna know what I think your problem is, Taft, I think—'

'SHUT UP!' The sheer heat of Taft's shouted command took Chan aback. 'I do NOT want to hear your stupid opinion. Just who the hell do you think you are anyway to talk to me like that?'

'Good question, Taft. Just who the hell do you *think* I am?'

Taft's jaw hardened and he simply glared. *Gotchya, you sonofabitch*, Chan thought. *Damn but the headshrinkers are right: it is better to keep 'em talking.*

– 11 –

Five minutes had passed. Maybe more. Taft had stalked off into the bush. Chan knew he hadn't gone far. He could hear the American's voice, low and angry, but couldn't quite make out the words. *Talking to himself. A head case. It figures.*

Then he was back, perched on a log, drumming his fingers on his knees, and breathing hard like a man who'd sprinted a long race. Wondering what twisted scheme the evil bastard had come up with, Chan snarled, 'So?'

Taft answered with a growl of his own, 'So, can you walk?'

'With these ribs? Not far.'

'Why am I not surprised? Okay, then, I'll have to carry you out of here.'

'Can't do that either. You try to drag me across this mangrove island, lift me four or five metres up to the boardwalk, one of my ribs is going to puncture a lung.'

'Chan, has anyone ever told you what a pain you are?'

'Yeah, you. By the way, the other thing is this: even if you did manage to carry me out of here, Poh Kay Siong and his boys are waiting at the exit. First they'd shoot you. Which I'd like a lot. But then they'd shoot me, and put the gun in your hand. That part, I like a little less.'

Taft was shouting again. '*Poh Kay Siong? Who the hell is Poh Kay Siong?*'

Chan told him.

Chan had never seen a man concentrate so hard. You could almost hear the devious dickhead's mind at work. The intensity with which he thought seemed to create an aura, a near-visible shimmer of raw intellect at work. It was as if he was using psychic fingers to pick up puzzle pieces, mentally ordering them, finding the pattern into which they fitted, and assembling them into a seamless solution. It was, in some sense, exhilarating to watch him think; in another sense, it was exhausting.

As Taft silently prowled the inner reaches of his brain, Chan did some hard thinking of his own. Was it possible that Taft was as innocent as he claimed to be? You could argue that. You could argue that someone who didn't know what a warrant card was would go on the run if a bunch of armed police crashed into his room. You could argue he'd dump his stolen guns at the first opportunity. You could even argue that given the chance to feed his tormentor to the crocodiles, he'd try to save him instead.

You *could* argue that.

In which case, you were dead meat. Because if Taft was nothing more than a blameless corporate hack come down to Singapore to do a little business, then the fate of the in-your-face cop who tried to kill him would be a hell of a lot nastier than being eaten by crocodiles. Crocs worked fast, but the government would stretch things out across whole goddamned decades.

Guilty. You're guilty as charged, Taft. Innocent men don't resist arrest, don't steal police weapons, don't kidnap stewardesses and don't shoot up cabs. You, you miserable fucker, are guilty, guilty, guilty and I am going to make you dead, dead, dead.

Taft, his meditation apparently over, shook himself back into the physical world. He stood up, glanced around, and nodded. 'Okay, Chan, I've figured this out.'

'I'm pleased for you.' *You rotten fuck, you've humiliated me three times in a row!*

'Here's how it works. I leave. You stay. Before I go, I give you a gun. And one single bullet.'

'I'm liking this already.' *People who humiliate me once die ugly!*

'But I don't unlock your handcuffs. Which means you don't shoot me.'

'That's a serious leap of faith.' *So just imagine what I'm going to do to your ass!*

'Not at all. If you shoot me, you'll stay cuffed to that tree because the key is in my pocket, and my body will be too far away for you to reach. Then you'll stay right where you are until someone finds you. Or something.'

'That sucks.' *I'm going to piss on your grave, buddy.*

'Doesn't it though? Hey, I heard your voice when you started begging me to kill you rather than leave you to get eaten. That's why I know you're going to let me walk. You're going to want to keep that one bullet in case a crocodile comes strolling by.'

'Thanks loads.' *Presuming I can put you there.*

'My pleasure. Less pleasure, once I get out of this damned swamp, first thing I do is send for help. I figure you're going to spend an hour or so in the dark—'

'Unless you take the shortcut,' Chan said, hating himself for doing so, hating the idea of being chained for an hour more. 'Let me tell you about the shortcut.' *Poh – he's the answer. He and his gang are still waiting in the parking lot. And – don't I wish I knew why – they've got a real hard-on for you, Taft.*

'Ah,' replied Taft, 'at long last you're beginning to act reasonable. So tell me about this shortcut, Chan. And while you're at it, tell me how to use this damned bazooka of yours.'

Chan, thinking of crocodiles, swallowed hard. 'Yeah. Sure. And there's a couple of other things I should tell you too. In fact, I'm even going to tell you a gimmick that might get you past Poh Kay Siong.' *Then, if you're as good as I think you are, asshole, you'll live long enough for me to find you. If you're not, tough shit for us both.*

– 12 –

Trembling on the floor of Superintendent Chan's Range-Rover, surrounded by men who would murder her without a second thought, Zaitun cowered in the cloak of her misery

She was nothing but a flight attendant, someone her employer referred to as a 'Singapore Girl', no different from any of the others the airline advertised for: 'Single, below 26 years old, at least 1.58 metres in height, slim and attractive with a good complexion and a nice warm smile.'

The smile would do her no good if one of the men prowling the Sungei Buloh parking lot glanced into Chan's Rover. Slender attractiveness would merely ensure they amused themselves before killing her. And they'd delight in the bruises her good complexion showed before they finished their fun.

They were, all of them, that kind of man.

She'd known who they were as soon as Chan ordered them out of their cars. Some were Singaporean, others from nearby lands. They were the loan-sharks who flung acid in the faces of borrowers who did not pay, the arsonists who worked the protection racket, the drug dealers who flouted Singapore's death penalty.

They were hatchetmen, and they killed.

Being this near to them made her flesh crawl. She knew exactly what they'd do if they discovered, crouched below eye level in Superintendent Chan's Range-Rover, a pretty young girl who, for the past half-hour or so, had been eavesdropping on every word they said.

'Chances like this don't come along very often.' The speaker was a short man, pudgy, and dressed in a suit of tasteless green silk. His name was Samuel Lin, and people said he had once burned a man to death with a Toshiba laundry iron.

'It is a matter demanding grave reflection, and not a step to be taken hastily.' That was Poh Kay Siong, *Tsung li*, the most senior of Singapore's crime lords.

'A week ago that bastard shut down three opium dens. And killed two men, both of them mine. I'm out ten thousand dollars a day on the opium and fifty thousand each to the dead men's families.'

'One owes an obligation to the heirs of one's associates.'

'One owes Chan Gin a bullet behind the ear.'

'Now is not the time.'

'There'll never be a better. He's going to be coming down that path any minute. If I put a couple of holes in him, then leave the gun in Taft's hand—'

'I think not. The sound of the Superintendent's rifle – unmistakable in its thunder – tells us he has performed the service required of him. There is no honour in repaying him with violence.'

'With all due respect, "honour" is not in Chan's vocabulary. If he thought he could get away with it, he'd kill us all. He's crazy enough that one of these days he'll try.'

'Reflect, my friend, and you shall conclude that the superintendent will not trouble us much longer. Chan is a man of times gone by, and his methods are not the methods of our modern days. I do not think it long before those who rule lose all patience with him. Then steps will be taken, as they always are in such matters, and we will be relieved of a bothersome impediment without having to resort to the measures you propose. Better not to risk a deed that might provoke our easily provoked government.'

A third voice joined the conversation; Zaitun had not heard it before. 'Speaking of Chan, shouldn't he be back by now?' Nervously curious, Zaitun peeked into the darkness. Thin and thinly moustached, the speaker was unmistakably Teng Kwoengmi, notorious for his unsuccessful battle to bring Singapore's fiercely independent prostitution industry under mob control. The three – sadly handsome Poh, fat Lin, skinny Teng –

stood together some small distance from a black BMW coupé. Teng cupped a cigarette in his hand. Lin, hands in pockets, hunched his shoulders while frowning at the ground. Poh, a few paces away from the other two, glanced over his shoulder, looking at the path from which, Zaitun prayed, Chan Gin would appear.

Ready to drop out of sight if anyone turned towards her, Zaitun quickly surveyed the parking lot. At its distant end four men sat on the ground playing cards by the light of a Hum-Vee's headlamps. One man had disassembled a pistol on the bonnet of a BMW, and seemed to be cleaning it. Another man – clearly Poh Kay Siong's chauffeur – had a soft buffing rag in his hand, and was slowly, carefully, lovingly polishing the midnight blue surface of his master's Cadillac Seville. A crack of lightning split the night. The Cadillac leapt a metre into the air. Lin and Teng dropped to the ground. Poh whirled. The Cadillac's hood flew open; sparks spewed from the engine compartment as if a madman was arc-welding steel inside it. Poh's chauffeur, tumbling head over heels well above the ground, seemed a ragdoll hurled by an angry child. Three men were running low, pistols in their hands, searching out targets. The Cadillac jolted back to earth, and within it something snapped, metal shearing in two. Fat little Lin, belly-crawling like a pudgy snake, yelled, 'It's Chan! I warned you he'd try something!' An ordinary man, so ordinary you'd think he was an accountant, or perhaps a shopkeeper, had a stubby black thing in his hand. Zaitun thought it looked like a mechanic's grease gun, but yellow flames stuttered from its front and each flame snapped like a fire-cracker and she could hear the bullets whipping through marsh grass and reeds, and quite oddly she was worried about the little birds who might be nesting there. The night turned white. Zaitun had not been looking towards it when it happened. If she had been, the explosion would have blinded her. As it was, she turned her head in time to see the fireball rise from the place where Poh's Cadillac had been, spread itself into a bright red dome, and fade into streamers of oily smoke. A rainfall began, not water, but hot twisted metal. Someone was screaming. More than one person. Poh Kay Siong was on his back, the front of his shirt ablaze. Teng hurled himself towards Poh, began beating the flames with his hands. A gangster, one of the mainland thugs, pushed himself to his knees with one hand; with the other he emptied an automatic pistol randomly into the undergrowth. Another lightning bolt clapped thunder. A sand-brown Hum-Vee, the one furthest from Zaitun, suddenly rocked as a hammock taken by a gust of wind. Liquid splashed from a tank gouged open, torn loose, almost ripped from the truck's body. Several men began to swear, different words but similar meaning. A heavy piece of rubber, once the wheel of a Cadillac Seville bounced down on to the parking lot's gravelled surface. The wheel was flaming, looking like some sort of fantastic religious symbol, an icon to be found painted on the wall of a Hindu temple but never, not ever, seen in the real world of everyday experience. A man, Zaitun recognized him as one of Lin's, scrambled towards the wheel. It rolled faster than he could move, and quite shortly intersected the stream of gasoline pouring from the wounded Hum-Vee. Zaitun squeezed her eyelids closed. The heat and light of the explosion etched upon her vision images of her veins, around which danced multicoloured phosphors. Eyes open again, she could not see clearly; nor did she wish to see clearly what had happened to that man, Lin's man, who had tried to stop the burning rubber tyre. One of the BMWs was on fire, its surface covered with gasoline, a man inside shrieking and futilely trying to shoulder open its burning door. The sound of gunfire had stopped, but not the curses. They were louder, more ardent, and more profane. She caught a glimpse of movement through the front windshield. She turned her head. Someone was there, black with mud, the only white his smiling teeth. He bent out of sight. A moment later he stood, and standing next to him was the killer from China, the man the gangsters had handcuffed to the Range-Rover's front bumper. But now the handcuffs were off. The killer started to speak. The black man, a nightmare shadow outlined against flames, pressed something against the killer's knee and pulled the trigger and the killer fell screaming. Zaitun swivelled on the floor. The door of the Range-Rover opened. The man slid behind the wheel. He looked down at her. His teeth were white, so white, and his smile was so broad. He reached towards her, wound his hand in her hair, pulled her head up. His face came lower, she knew who it was. He drew her hard, pressed down with equal hardness, forcing his lips against hers, all full of urgency, but no brutality whatsoever. He smelled. Swamp smell and mud. The odour of gunsmoke and sweat. Oil and the tang of vegetation crushed beneath his feet. And more than anything else, the overpowering aroma of a male animal at its most dangerous. He kissed her, he devoured her, he smothered her and swept away her will. Passion and masculinity flowed from him, she did not so much as think about pushing him away and in any event it would not have been possible. Then he tilted his head back, still smiling and showing his teeth, and said, 'It's all right. You're safe now. I'm here.' Without knowing why, she believed him.

– 13 –

Jack kept pushing buttons and turning dials until someone, a woman, answered Chan's radiophone. 'Central dispatch. This is Constable Song.'

There was an intersection ahead. Slowing for a right turn, he downshifted. 'Police emergency. Patch me through to Officer Leung.'

The woman paused. He heard her fingers click on a keyboard. 'There are eight Leungs on the force. If you could . . .'

Twenty years as a businessman had schooled Taft in the art of remembering names and titles. He thought back to hearing Leung radio Chan in Zaitun's apartment. Chan had called him – *what?* – Hal. 'Hal Leung. Corporal Leung.'

'Corporal Harold Leung, CID. I'll connect you.' The radiophone clicked. Spinning the wheel right, Jack accelerated. In the distance he could hear the rising scream of sirens. The explosions at Sungei Buloh had been heard, the fireballs had been seen, emergency vehicles were on the way.

He glanced down at the woman. Still cowering on the Range-Rover's floor, she watched him with an uninterpretable expression on her face. He wished she'd sit properly and fasten her seatbelt. That would be safer. 'Get into the seat. Buckle up. I'm from New York and I'm a lousy driver.' She didn't move, merely kept studying him with dark, meditative eyes. He shrugged, and turned his attention back to the road.

The radiophone buzzed. Jack guessed it was ringing Leung's line. After the second buzz, a man answered crisply. 'Leung here. Is that you, sir?'

'No. This is John Taft . . .' He liked the sound of it. '. . . John Gregory Taft.'

'Oh hell.'

'Pay attention. I'm only saying this once. Your big-mouth boss is chained to a tree in Sungei Buloh. You know where Sungei Buloh is?'

'I know, goddamn you, and—'

'Shut up! Just listen. His ribs are smashed and there's blood. Not much, but some. He needs a doctor ASAP.'

'You're going to hang—'

The neighbourhood was dark, a zone of one-storey warehouses and light industry factories. The sirens – fire engine and ambulances – were to his left, and coming closer. He didn't want the Range-Rover to be seen, least of all by people with mobile radios. He had to find an alley, a wall, somewhere without lights, a place to hide.

'Would you please be quiet? I'm trying to help here. God knows why, but that's what I'm doing. Have you got that?'

'Got it. Same as I'll get you.'

Taft could almost taste the loathing in Leung's voice. Once upon a time, very recently in fact, being the object of such hatred would have bothered him. But it didn't bother him now. He thought it would never bother him again. 'Fine. I know where you're coming from. Now, as I was saying, there are fire engines headed out to Sungei Buloh—'

'*Fire trucks?*'

'Yeah. Bunch of cars belonging to a guy named Poh Kay Siong and his flunkies were in my way. Now they aren't.'

'Jesus, Taft—'

'Those people are going to need medics too. Or body bags, depending. So what you should do, Leung, is get on the radio pronto. Call the Fire Department. Tell them to rún a stretcher team out to where Chan is and order a med-evac helicopter to the parking lot. Another thing, Chan said to tell you he's in the part of the park they call "the mangrove arboretum", northwest corner, not far from the prawn pond.'

There was another intersection. No red light, only a stop sign. Jack slowed, but didn't stop. He swung right, away from the sound of approaching fire engines.

'Taft, if you've hurt the superintendent—'

'He did it to himself, although I doubt if he'll admit it. In fact, knowing the jerk as I do, I'm sure he won't. Now I've got one other thing to say to you, Leung. Pay close attention. I am *not* a drug smuggler. What you people found in my briefcase was a plant. Believe me or not, that's the truth. Believe me or not, I can prove it. Do you understand me, Leung? I can *prove* it.'

The radiophone hissed as if there was static on the line. But it was not static. It was the sound of Harold Leung inhaling sharply. Jack allowed himself a nasty grin.

'Prove it how, Mr Taft?'

'Later, Corporal, we'll talk about that later. Meanwhile, you get some medics out to where your boss is, and hope they find him before the crocodiles do . . . hang on . . .'

Up ahead Jack spotted what appeared to be a major feeder road. A green sign, large and well lit, announced, 'Kranji Expressway'. He couldn't go that way, there'd be too much traffic on the freeways, and, no doubt, plenty of police cars too. He braked, readying to make a U-turn.

'Leung, you still there?'

'Yes.'

'Well then get off your lazy butt and call the medics! Much as I hate your boss, I'd hate it even more if he got eaten. Know why? Why is because if that happens, then I won't get to see the bozo *really* suffer!'

Pure bravado. Nothing but a bluff. There was no evidence to exonerate him. There couldn't be. Not in Singapore, at least. But that hadn't stopped him from lying. The lie had come easy, surprisingly so. As, for that matter, had all that had preceded it.

Sitting slumped and drained, Chan handcuffed to a tree, it had come to him that he was as good as dead. The police wanted him.

A mobster named Poh Kay Siong wanted him. Sooner or later one or the other would get him. They'd shoot him or they'd hang him, it made no difference really, because the end result was the same. He had no friends here, no place to hide, and no route off what was a very small, well-patrolled island. Therefore, all the logic and reason available to him told him that he was going to die. And that was that.

Then, numb and exhausted, a thought came to him – less a thought than a small faint voice whispering within the inner reaches of his mind. It was barely audible and quite hesitant in its words. What it shyly said was: *If logic and reason tell you that you're doomed to die, then why not say, 'To hell with logic and reason?'*

Well, that made sense.

As did what followed. Even kissing Zaitun had made sense, when you thought about it, which he hadn't. After all, the odds against his ever being able to kiss a beautiful woman again were infinitely long. Besides, he'd never stolen a kiss before, and didn't want to die without knowing what it felt like.

Pretty damned good, that's what it felt like.

Same as everything else.

John Taft speaking. John Gregory Taft.

2
New York

– 1 –

Gabrielle glanced at her watch. Almost time to go. Olivia had called twice, confirming their rendezvous in front of LBTech's Fifty-Seventh Street headquarters. 'Six-thirty, pet. Remember, punctuality is the politeness of princes.'

Gabrielle was a woman for whom punctuality was coinage of a floating currency. The sweetly implied criticism in Olivia's quote (*What clown said that punctuality is a virtue, oh yeah, Oscar Wilde*) was meant to communicate in no uncertain terms that

Olivia Thatcher was bound and determined to burgle the offices of Jack's company.

With Gabrielle as her unindicted co-conspirator. Or indicted, as the case may be.

There was an enormous bronze plaque hung in *EPS*'s reception lobby. At Jonathan Harley Sutton's command, it had been engraved with a quote from Mark Twain: 'The heaven-born mission of journalism is to disseminate truth; to eradicate error; to educate, refine, and elevate the tone of public morals and manners, and make all men more gentle, more virtuous, more charitable, and in all ways, better, and holier, and happier.'

Some suspected Twain of satiric intent, although Jonathan Harley Sutton claimed not to be among the ranks of the doubters.

Trenchcoat on, armed with briefcase and umbrella, Gabrielle strode into the lobby. Simon Burton was there, his cock-of-the-walk smirk aimed at Jonathan's plaque.

He turned. Legs straddled. Arms folded. Frowning. First at her, then at his watch, then back at her. Speaking in the plum-coloured tones favoured by the Royal Shakespeare Company, he drew her name into three long syllables – 'Ga-bri-elle.' It had been more than a decade since she'd heard him use that particular tone of voice. It rankled as much as ever. 'What *are* you doing here?'

Trying to push past him wouldn't work. Simon was the sort of man who would seize her by the upper arm, keep her from leaving. Then there would be an incident. She knew she'd be better off talking her way around him. 'I'm going for the night.'

'But you are supposed to be on an airplane to California. Hot on the trail of your customs fraud story.'

'I'm postponing it.'

Simon arched his eyebrows. It was something he did too well. Gabrielle suspected he practised the gesture each morning in the bathroom mirror. 'My dear, have I miscommunicated the urgency of that particular article?'

She answered as levelly as she could. 'Something's come up. The story will have to wait. I'm late, Simon . . .' She tried to edge around him. He took a step closer.

'The woman says "wait!" Do my ears deceive me? Gabrielle, you are *committed* to doing that story. The pages are allocated. The graphics department has begun preparing cartoons to explain to our readers precisely how various customs fiddles work. I've woken our San Francisco bureau chief from his long and lingering slumber, and had him dispatch a freelance photographer to follow in your footsteps click-click-clicking snapshots whilst you conduct your interviews. And now you tell me that the story will have to wait? Dear lord, Gabrielle, surely you've not forgotten the meaning of the word "deadline"?'

'Simon, I said something's come up—'

'Oh, I can imagine.' Simon was sneering as only Simon could. She was willing to bet he practised that too. 'Your little shipping clerk. The one who had the temerity to smuggle illicit drugs in the briefcase you gave him.'

'Damnit, Simon, I'm going to be late for an appointment. Let me by.'

He shook his head. The gesture was meant to exhibit a weary sadness. But his voice was full of smug triumph. 'A word of advice. It would be much better if you were to accept it now; steel yourself, as it were. The man's a thorough villain. Of this I am assured by sources who are rather the best sources one can have. So too do they assure me that the Singaporeans plan to make an example of him.' Simon paused, sidled closer, and painted the semblance of sincere concern on his face. 'Gabrielle, you are not the first woman who has been misled by a rogue. I know that thought is cold comfort, but I offer it in friendship and in sympathy. And, in friendship and in sympathy, I tell you this: the very best thing you can do now is put him out of your mind. Pretend he was a bad dream. And distract yourself, Gabrielle. Distract yourself from thinking about him any more.'

'What do you have in mind?' As if she didn't know.

'First, I have in mind that you *must* go to California. That is imperative. I can assure you that the story you are working on is of sufficient urgency that if you do not report it, your career will be in jeopardy. More important, it will give you something upon which to concentrate, the better to distance yourself from bad memories.' Smiling his falsest smile, Simon paused, then added: 'Another recommendation. It would not be a bad thing if – in the interests of putting your Mr Taft out of your mind – you were to expand, as it were, your social horizons by dating other—'

'Simon, you are despicable.' As she pushed past him, he reached, as she knew he would, for her arm. 'Touch me, Simon, and I'll have you up on harassment charges!'

Simon pursed his lips as if tasting something sour. 'I mean no harm, Gabrielle. I've only your best interests at heart.'

'Simon, get the fuck out of my way and get the fuck out of my life.'

'You are a foolish woman.' He took a step backward. Gabrielle strode past him, and into an open elevator. As the doors hissed shut, Simon's genteel English accent disappeared, abrasive Australian brass replacing it: 'Foolish, bloody foolish; if I weren't so smitten by you, I wouldn't bother . . .'

– 2 –

Miraculously a cab was letting a passenger off right outside *EPS Magazine*'s front door. A damp-looking man, no umbrella to protect him from the rain, had been preparing to climb in. Gabrielle shouldered him aside, snapped LBTech's address to the driver, and, as the taxi edged out into traffic, pulled a file folder of printouts from her briefcase. 'Switch on the light, will you?'

'S'cuse me, lady?'

'The light. I need to read back here.' The driver complied. Gabrielle began flipping through the latest batch of documents her librarians had retrieved.

They were useless. Not a single line contained the least hint that anything was amiss at LBTech. The company's financial reports were immaculate. The accountants gave it a clean bill of health. Eight different stock analysts graded it 'Accumulate Aggressively'. Standard & Poors granted LBTech's bonds a rating implying that the company was as sound as the US Treasury. The only pending litigation were the usual class-action suits filed by fee-hungry California lawyers in the hope that, same as every other company in America, LBTech would rather settle out of court than subject itself to the expensive distraction of a trial. Nobody from the Federal Government was investigating LBTech. No angry debtor had placed any liens on its assets. No dubious compen-sation programmes were in place to reward . . .

Gabrielle suddenly stopped turning pages. Something had caught her eye. It was nothing more than a hint, a faint odour in the evening air, an ambiguous whiff of something in, of all things, a credit report. *Now what the hell . . .*

'Dis da place, lady?'

She glanced up. The cab was at the kerb outside LBTech's building. Olivia Thatcher, protecting her mouthwatering sable coat with an enormous cobalt umbrella, stood to the left of the revolving doors. Gabrielle passed the driver a five-dollar bill, telling him to keep the change.

At six-thirty in the evening, LBTech was an empty shell, the business district's equivalent of a ghost town. Nonetheless, the distinctive smells of corporate life still hung in the air – scents of partially eaten sandwiches hastily consumed at desks then tossed into wastepaper baskets, the acetone tang of magic markers, a barely perceptible hint of ozone mixed with photocopier toner, the bouquet of inexpensive cosmetics applied by underpaid secretaries before departing for the day, and most of all, the acrid aroma of overstressed white-collar workers, their deodorants faded by evening into the not-quite-rancid fragrance of middle-management insecurity.

Olivia and Gabrielle stood in the thirty-fourth floor's grubby reception area. Olivia motioned Gabrielle towards a worn sofa covered with tacky imitation leather. Gabrielle sat down. Olivia remained standing. 'The executive suite is one floor up. We'll keep ourselves busy down here for an hour before going there.'

'Doing what?'

'Pilfering files to our hearts' content. This is where the logistics worker-bees live, dear. Haven't you ever been here?'

Gabrielle shook her head. While she knew that before he was promoted Jack's old office had been on this floor, she'd never visited it. Jack claimed he was embarrassed by its size, although she suspected he was more embarrassed by the fact that his old girlfriend was housed on the same floor. Deferring to his wishes, she made a point of never meeting him at LBTech.

One arm extended, Olivia turned a pirouette. 'This place reminds me of nothing so much as a maze for laboratory rats. Hallways leading off in all directions. Cramped cubicles and minuscule rooms. The walls all the same depressing shade of old ivory. Imagine being one of the poor little creatures who work here, snuffling after your food pellets, always afraid you'll receive an electric shock instead. In *our* company, my husband insists on a minimum one hundred and fifty square feet per office worker. He says anything *less* turns them into soulless drudges.'

Gabrielle frowned. 'We're not here to discuss office amenities, are we, Livy?'

Looking slightly chagrined, Olivia answered, 'No. I suppose not. There are some things I need to tell you, my dear. I suppose I was trying to postpone the inevitable.'

Leaping to the wrong conclusion, Gabrielle whispered, 'Oh God, is Jack really involved in—'

'Of course not,' Olivia snapped. 'What I have to say has *nothing* to do with that.' She took a breath, bracing herself for what she had to say. 'Although I do have equally grim news. It seems your young man can expect no help from the government. I have spoken at some length to those snivellers in Washington. As has my husband, Scott. We take no comfort in what we were told. It seems that official State Department policy is non-intervention. Moreover, the current administration has no desire to be accused of being "soft on drugs", and from what I've heard goes on in the White House I can imagine why.'

'Won't they even look into Jack's situation?'

'I'm afraid not. Although tomorrow Scott will fly down to Washington and try to twist a few senatorial arms. Meanwhile . . .' Olivia withdrew a folded piece of paper from her purse and passed it to Gabrielle. '. . . I was sent this via facsimile. It is, I am told, the *official* US policy statement regarding citizens who fall foul of Singaporean law.'

Gabrielle squinted at the page:

Visitors should be aware of Singapore's strict laws and penalties for a variety of offenses that might be considered minor in the United States, including jaywalking, littering and spitting, as well as the importation and sale of chewing gum. Singapore imposes a mandatory caning sentence on males for vandalism offenses. Caning may also be imposed for immigration violations and other offenses. Penalties for possession, use, or trafficking in illegal drugs are strict, and convicted offenders can expect jail sentences and fines. Singapore has a mandatory death penalty for many narcotics offenses. Commercial disputes that may be handled as civil suits in the US can escalate to criminal cases in Singapore and result in heavy fines and prison sentences. There are no jury trials in Singapore. Judges hear cases and decide sentencing. The Singapore government does not provide legal assistance except in capital cases.

'Oh my God!'

'Quite frankly, it *is* rather worse than I expected.' Heaving a sigh, Olivia set her jaw. 'Now there's something else I have to tell you. It is very much a secret, pet, and I must have your promise that you won't breathe a word. Yes? Very well then. Joel Greenberg is proposing to sell off this company. The buyers have offered a most attractive price, *and* an even more attractive personal deal for Joel. I would not tell you about it except that something out of the ordinary happened at yesterday's board meeting just before Joel unveiled his little scheme. At the time, it struck me as an unnecessary violation of protocol; now, however, I wonder if there wasn't more to it than met the eye. You see, even though Jack was out of town, Joel positively insisted on having the Logistics Department's results presented to the Board – although there was really no need to do that, none whatsoever. It could have waited until Jack was back in town.'

'I don't get it.'

'It's not so much *what* Joel did, as *how*. I'd almost say he was acting as if Jack *was not* the departmental vice-president – as if the question of who should run Logistics had not been voted upon, decided, and closed. You see, there were two candidates for that position, and the manager Joel assigned to do the presentation was his personal candidate for the job, someone whom the Board rejected. That struck me as untowards behaviour – a slap in the face to the Board, and even more of a slap to Jack. Not, of course, that I have any problem with young Denise, but . . .' Olivia stopped herself, giving Gabrielle a questioning look. 'And tell me, dear, what does your *very* peculiar expression mean?'

'Denise Donald. She and Jack were . . . uh, well, they had a thing together once. Jack doesn't like to talk about it, but when they split, he says it was pretty bad. She sent him letters, made threats, tried to sabotage him in the office, and—'

'*That* might explain a very great deal. While Denise makes a favourable first impression – forthright, self-controlled, de-sexed enough not to trouble the boys . . . why *ever* are you looking like you want to choke?'

'De-sexed?' Gabrielle's voice rose. 'That isn't the way I heard it!'

Olivia looked momentarily irate. 'Do give me credit for recognizing a performance when I see one. After forty . . . well, after several *decades* in the business world, I am intimately acquainted with all the ploys a woman must use to get ahead. Indeed, I believe I invented many of them!'

'Sorry.'

'As I *was* saying,' Olivia sniffed, 'the truth is Denise can be rather *intense* at times. If Jack broke up with her, I can picture her being . . . well, shall we say, vengeful. Indeed, it takes very little effort to imagine her playing the part of the office Lady Macbeth, and *relishing* it.' In a softer voice, pensively, she added, 'Her face is as a book where men may read strange matters—'

'Meaning what?'

'Meaning that I, as the Board's token woman, was delegated to tell her that Jack had won the promotion. She was livid at the news – although she did her level best not to show it. I suppose she might have been angry enough to strike back. Perhaps doubly so if Jack used to be her sweetheart, if *that* is the proper word. Then too, she made quite a to-do when Jack designed a new logistics strategy. Asian operations were the centrepiece of his plan, and he proposed some rather dramatic changes. But of course Denise manages Asia – it's her little fiefdom, you know. She was positively speechless when she learned what he intended to do.'

'She tried to stop him?'

'Of course not, dear. This *is* corporate America. People who can't sense which way the wind is blowing don't last very long. She did what anyone would do: promptly put herself forward as the plan's most ardent supporter.' Olivia sighed. 'Corporate politics are *so* predictable.'

'You think she's behind what happened to Jack?'

Olivia smiled. 'It would do my heart good to learn so. See here, pet, although he doesn't know it yet, I am out to stop Joel Greenberg from stealing this company. If it happens that something wicked is going on at LBTech, then it is quite possible the buyers will back away from their offer. If the person behind the wickedness turns out to be someone Joel sponsored for a vice-presidency . . . well, so much the better. Few business transactions can survive that sort of embarrassment.'

'And few chief executives.'

'The thought *has* crossed my mind.' Olivia's expression suggested it was a pleasant thought indeed.

'What about what Jack said to me. The lead he gave me. I still think he's worried about some sort of customs fraud at LBTech.'

'All the more reason to burglarize . . . oh my, that's not the word I mean at all . . . the Logistics Department's files. It *is* the organization responsible for moving things across national frontiers, you know.' Smiling grimly, Olivia consulted her watch. 'Now, I believe it's time for us to get to work. We have some felonies to commit.'

– 3 –

Walking behind Olivia, Gabrielle eyed anonymous office doors. A few – metal, painted matt white with a hint of blue – were closed. Most were open. All had little black plastic signs on them, engraved white letters picking out each occupant's name. The signs were in metal brackets, as easily replaceable as the employees whom they identified.

So many offices. So many names. She knew none of them. Not here. Nor in all the other office buildings she'd visited as a journalist. Executives kept reporters away from corporate cattle pens like this one – tiny cells ten feet wide and eight feet long, furnished with ugly metal desks cramped against windowless walls, and cheap vinyl-covered chairs. Middle-aged middle-management accessories were, she thought, the mark of Cain, calculated to demean, an ever-present reminder of the fundamental axiom of corporate life: once you reach the age of forty, you don't have to worry where you're going because you're already there.

A nameplate made her stop, stop dead. 'L.B. Tischmann'. She knew him, had interviewed him more than a dozen years earlier. He'd been in his sixties then, bright of eye and bawdy of speech. In those days, LBTech had still been L.B. Tischmann Technology, named after the feisty entrepreneur who had started it with nothing but five hundred dollars in capital and an unshakable belief in his own abilities.

Gabrielle turned the doorknob, pushed, looked into a dim room. It was a tiny office, as barren as all the others. She shivered. L.B. had built a multi-billion-dollar company only to be forced out of its executive suite by his own son-in-law. Now, a man who created forty-five thousand jobs around the globe, and who was a figure respected by most employees more than their fathers, had for a monument a wretched little cubicle, and even his proud name had been erased from the identity of the enterprise he'd founded.

'Gabrielle?' Olivia had placed her hand on Gabrielle's shoulder.

'Sorry. I was thinking about . . . well . . . thinking.'

'About L.B. and his son-in-law? Well, Joel Greenberg is due for his comeuppance on that matter too.'

The two had started walking down the hall again. Gabrielle was preparing to ask her friend what might be in store for LBTech's president when, as they passed an open door, she heard the sizzle of a catty voice, '. . . and you know the reason why women fake orgasms, don't you? It's because they *think* men care . . . oh, hold the line for a second . . . Olivia? Is that you?'

Stopping just beyond the doorway, Olivia clenched her teeth and whispered, 'Drat!' Then, smiling as false a smile as Gabrielle had ever seen, she peered through the door. 'Good evening, my dear. Whatever are you doing in the office at this hour?'

'Getting caught up. Come on in. Bring your, uh, friend in too.'

Gabrielle glanced at the name tag by the door. She cursed silently. Of course it would be *that* woman!

Taking in furniture and occupant at a single glance, Gabrielle stepped into the office of Jack's former lover. Denise Donald was making her apologies to whomever was on the phone. She was not exactly what Gabrielle had expected – but then Jack always had been a bit elusive when she questioned him, grilled him really, about Denise's appearance. Attractive? she'd ask. Yeah, he'd mumble. Built? Oh definitely. (She didn't like the swift certainty of that reply.) Big boobs, huh? Well, yes. Perky ass, I'll bet. I suppose you could say that. And she's a natural blonde. I guess, but I'm a guy, you know, and I can be fooled.

Like hell.

Denise was more than merely beautiful. She was, *goddammit*, perfect. An inch taller than Gabrielle, a cup-size larger, tiny waist, *real* California-golden-girl hair, big blue eyes, peaches 'n' cream complexion, and, worst of all, she looked younger than her years, which, *sonofabitch*, numbered three fewer than Gabrielle's.

Declining an offered seat, Olivia said, 'Denise, this is my friend Gaby.'

Gabrielle thrust her hand out. 'Pleased to meet you.'

'Denise Donald. Nice to meet you.' Denise's expression had not changed. She didn't recognize the name or connect it with either Jack Taft or *EPS Magazine*. All she did was take a single, lethally judgmental look at Gabrielle's apparel – the comfy travel clothes she'd been wearing all day. Gabrielle could almost hear the other woman's unspoken question – *And what elementary school do you teach at, Gaby?*

Gabrielle stopped short of grinding her teeth. No surprise, Denise was expensively and faultlessly attired, albeit in the most insipidly goodie-two-shoes style imaginable – a vivid blue Chanel suit, pink silk blouse, obligatory (and carefully coordinated)

Hermes scarf; two-tone *forgodssake!* Ferregamo footwear, a string of cultured pearls, two scintillating rings that positively screamed she had a rich boyfriend, and the kind of lacquered manicure that members of the working press had neither the time to sit still for nor the salary to afford.

And underneath it all, I'll bet she's wearing something hot and slinky from Perla. Damn you, Taft, I know she is!

As she knew it was all a disguise. Same as her office – bland earth tones, tasteful museum prints, everything tidy, and not a single touch of individuality – Denise's clothing was intended to conceal its wearer's character, not reveal it.

'Olivia,' Denise asked, 'what brings you up here after hours?'

Olivia lied beautifully: 'Nothing important. Gaby and I are having dinner at Le Chantilly. Since I was in the neighbourhood, I thought I'd stop by and pick up a couple of documents I need for the next directors' meeting.'

'I thought the directors' offices were upstairs.' Denise's right eyebrow twitched, a gesture that Gabrielle suspected signalled snide amusement at the idea of elegant Olivia dining with such a casually dressed companion at one of the city's most WASPish watering holes.

'They are. I was showing Gaby around. Because LBTech has so much notoriety I thought she'd—'

'Taft.' Denise's voice changed hardly at all, just a little colder. 'Hard to believe, isn't it? A man like him, I mean. Not that I knew him well, but I never would have guessed that he'd be involved in anything as sordid as drug smuggling.'

Gabrielle heard a low humming coming from somewhere in the room – the sound of some piece of idling office equipment. There was nothing in sight. She wondered what it was. The fact that Denise was lying through her teeth about not knowing Jack didn't make her wonder at all.

Olivia answered, 'I'm sure he's innocent. The whole thing is some sort of dreadful mistake.'

'Well, I hope so.' She sounded sincere; Gabrielle knew she was not. 'Even though it would mean I'd have to move back down here again.'

'Back here again?'

Gabrielle let her eyes flick right and left, searching for whatever it was that was making the noise. It seemed to be coming from behind Denise's desk, just below eye level.

'You haven't heard? Joel's asked me to move upstairs. You know, to take over Jack's job. At least temporarily. I guess you and the rest of the Board will have to approve it, if it's more than temporarily.'

Curious, Gabrielle inched forward. Another foot or two and she'd be able to peer over Denise's desk, see what was softly whispering out of sight.

'We will. However, LBTech can't get along without a Head of Logistics, and you know how highly I regard your qualifications. I'm sure you'll do a fine job until Jack comes back.'

'If he comes back.' *Bad move, lady*, Gabrielle thought. *You said that a little too eagerly.* 'Which I hope he does.' *Nice save.*

The humming machine behind Denise's desk was off-white, boxy, three feet high. There was a small tray pulled out of its side; a pile of documents was stacked on the tray. Beneath the thing there was a wastepaper basket filled to the brim with sixteenth-inch-wide strips of paper. It was a paper shredder. From the fullness of the trash basket, it looked to Gabrielle as if Denise had been running it overtime.

Denise caught Gabrielle's eye, glanced down at the shredder, then, in a voice only slightly higher than it should have been, said, 'Old reports. I was cleaning out my desk before moving upstairs.' Olivia stepped forward, saw the same thing Gabrielle saw, and asked, 'What with lawyers and discovery procedures and all of that legal tomfoolery, I thought corporate policy was never to throw out anything. Or has policy changed?'

'No. But . . . well . . .'

'And *whatever* kind of documents could you have, my dear, that are so sensitive they have to be turned into confetti?'

Denise shrugged. She stopped looking at Gabrielle and Olivia, instead staring over their shoulders. Only then the expression in her eyes changed; it said, *I could use some help now.*

Some hours later, reflecting on the unpleasantness that followed,

Gabrielle would think to herself how accomplished Denise's performance had been. She'd been perfectly controlled, completely composed, had not given the slightest hint that all the while she and Olivia had been talking, a man had been standing in the doorway behind, eavesdropping.

'Denise, I don't think you need to answer that.' To which words Joel Greenberg added, 'And do me a favour, pick up the phone and call building security. I want a guard up here. Immediately.'

– 4 –

Olivia had her hands on her hips, temper barely in control. 'This young woman is with me, Joel.'

'Escorted or not, I won't have strangers prowling around our offices after hours.' Joel had folded his arms. He was a tall, handsome man who clearly worked hard at keeping himself a little too fit. Gabrielle distrusted him on sight.

She heard something tapping behind her. Denise had lifted the phone and was using her exquisite manicure to key in a number.

'I am here on board business. My friend is keeping me company.'

'We have policies on these things, Olivia.' Raising a hand to display a wedding band less costly than his tie, Joel looked less like a hard-working corporate president than a Hollywood caricature – Michael Douglas in *Wall Street*, Gordon Gekko, moussed-back hair and wearing what was easily ten thousand dollars' worth of executive *haute couture* on his back – not counting accessories.

Olivia's voice turned stiletto sharp. 'Joel, I won't have you . . .' She stopped, reddening as she heard Denise speak into the telephone. 'Security? Yes, this is Ms Donald on the thirty-fourth floor. I'm with Mr Greenberg. We've found a reporter trespassing on the premises. No, no authorization. Her name is Dunn, Gabrielle Dunn. Thanks, we'll be waiting.'

Click.

Smiling like a tiger, Denise purred, 'She's with *EPS Magazine*, Joel. She's Jack's girlfriend.'

Gabrielle's cheeks burned. Denise's Little Mary Sunshine routine had been an act; all the while the bitch had known precisely who Olivia's informally dressed companion was.

Joel gave Olivia a sharp look. 'I'll want an explanation, Olivia.' He shot his cuffs, threw out his chest, stood in a posture reminding Gabrielle of nothing so much as an alpha male primate asserting his territorial rights.

'I've given you my explanation.' There was iron in Olivia's voice.

'Not good enough,' he snapped. 'See here, Olivia, I've been having as damned difficult a day as I can remember. First thing this morning, I learned that the man whom my Board of Directors made Vice President of Logistics against my wishes is a drug smuggler. Next I had to explain to the journalists and analysts that, no, it is not the case that every cargo container of electronic components LBTech ships has a few kilos of narcotics secreted inside. No sooner was I finished with that chore than my secretary alerted me that Drug Enforcement Administration agents were in the lobby, brandishing a search warrant and demanding access to Jack Taft's office. And no sooner had that happened, than I received a very disturbed telephone call from . . . well, from the people we discussed at the last board meeting.

He shot a wary glare at Gabrielle. She in turn blinked innocently, as if not having a clue as to what 'people' he was talking about.

'Those people are concerned, Olivia. They'll be even more concerned if they learn a member of my Board is tiptoeing around the premises at night with a reporter in tow.'

Gabrielle put her hand on her hips. 'We're here to try to help Jack. I'm not interested in any of your secrets.'

Denise curled her lip. 'Corporate secrets aren't what worries Joel and me. What worries us is that a journalist with a dope-dealer boyfriend is looking for evidence she can cover up. Right, Joel?'

'Denise warned me to expect something like this from you, Ms Dunn.'

Gabrielle, seeing red, shouted, 'Now look, Greenberg—'

'No, you look. Look on your desk tomorrow morning. You'll find a press release announcing that this corporation has terminated Jack Taft's employment contract, pledged full cooperation with the Singaporean authorities, and turned over to Federal agents the full and complete contents not only of Jack's office, but also his personnel file, and every other scrap of information we have pertaining to the man.'

'You bastard.'

'Hardly. I am simply a chief executive with a fiduciary duty to his shareholders and a legal duty to duly constituted authority. As a board member, Olivia will assure you that, were I to do other than I have, LBTech would be at risk. That said, you should be aware that every document that might incriminate Taft, or for that matter exculpate him, is now in the hands of the authorities. Accordingly, if you are here to look for evidence to destroy you're wasting your time.'

Olivia rested her hand on Joel's wrist. 'Joel, calm down. I know you're upset, but you're misreading the situation.'

'How?'

'If Jack isn't guilty—'

'It makes no difference. I won't have him in this company. He's history.'

'The Board put him in his job, not you Joel.'

'He's fired, Olivia, fired for cause. As Chief Exec, I get to do that. It's all spelled out in his employment contract. And in mine.'

'Joel, I think the word "cause" is open to question—'

'Not if he's swinging at the end of a rope in Singapore.'

Olivia set her jaw. 'Very well, Joel. Let's focus on *that* issue. Suppose that he's not guilty. Suppose LBTech has information that would prove him innocent. How would you feel if he were condemned because you refused to let Gabrielle look for it.'

'Mighty damned fine.'

'*Joel!*'

Greenberg pursed his lips. He'd said the wrong thing to a director, and he knew it. 'Sorry. I didn't mean that. I'm upset . . . the publicity, the effect on our stock, you know we have . . . an important negotiation going on. And this drug scandal is making them mighty damned skittish. If our . . . arrangement . . . with these people falls apart, it will be Taft's fault.'

'My theory is that it may be someone else's. If we can find evidence—'

'As I said, all of his records are in the hands of the authorities.'

'Joel, I am asking not as Jack's friend; I'm asking as a board member.'

'The answer is still no. The company is involved in sensitive discussions. I can't have a reporter pawing through things. Besides, Ms Dunn is far from a disinterested party. We'd be legally liable if she concealed evidence. I will not have her looking in our files. Not on the record, not off the record, not under any circumstances whatsoever.'

'What if we're looking for something that wouldn't be in Jack's files, something in someone else's?'

'Beg pardon?' Greenberg narrowed his eyes, glanced at Denise, who was still smiling behind her desk, and licked his lips. 'What's that supposed to mean?'

A grey-uniformed security guard – peaked hat, rent-a-cop badge, wooden truncheon and flashlight hooked to his belt – materialized at the door. 'You the people who called for security? Oh hiya, Mr Greenberg, I didn't recognize ya wit' yer back turned.' Joel nodded a patrician's acknowledgement. 'Yes, Len, we did call security. I'd like you to escort this woman . . .' he pointed at Gabrielle '. . . to the front entrance. And do me a favour, leave a note at the guard desk describing her in case she tries to come back in after your shift ends.'

Olivia spoke in tones of ice. 'Very well, Joel. But before I go, I have one question for you. Where was Denise Friday? Where was she the afternoon before Jack left?'

Joel's facial colour brightened, and his voice rose. 'You're out of line, Olivia! Not even a directorship gives you the right to make accusations like that!'

Denise's smile broadened. Reaching out, she rested her hand on Greenberg's wrist. 'I don't have a problem answering Olivia's question, Joel. None at all. That afternoon I was with Joel.' She paused just long enough to maximize the impact of the words which followed: 'Wasn't I, darling?'

3
Singapore

Back there at Sungei Buloh, Jack kept himself above things – not way up high or disengaged, just a bit remote, almost as much a watcher as a participant.

Sure, he'd done all the things Chan told him to do, crazy as they were – bracing the rifle, levelling the scope, caressing the trigger, running like hell. But he'd done them coolly. Or nearly so.

Nonetheless, he'd felt an animal stir in his belly, a big cat stretching to unsheathe its claws. No denying that. Also no denying he'd kept it down, forced it back, refused to let it growl into the light of day.

And so, he'd handled himself well, not lost his self-control, done the right and reasonable thing. Hadn't he?

Of course he had.

But if I did, then why . . . Jack licked his lips . . . *then why am I feeling like* . . . He rubbed his chin . . . *it would have been better if I'd* . . . And chewed the inside of his cheek . . . *just said screw it, and* really *let myself go?*

In an odd frame of mind – sated but not quite satisfied – he wheeled his stolen police Range-Rover through a prosperous neighbourhood, rows of semi-detached houses, Mercedes-Benz and BMW sedans kerbside before every home. But for bright streetlights, the finishes of the cars gleaming beneath them, all was dark and not a soul was to be seen.

He drove slowly, trying to emulate the stalker's pace of a prowl car on patrol. He'd never had a strong sense of direction, but thought – although he could not explain the intuition – that he was well south of Sungei Buloh, five miles at least, and maybe more. Although what that implied, he could not say. He simply steered at random, letting instinct rather than thought choose his direction.

He glanced at his dashboard clock. The green LED winked from

4:57 to 4:58. He wondered how long to sunrise. Two hours, he supposed. Then people would be up and about, walking their dogs, jogging, readying themselves for the day ahead, and wondering what a police Range-Rover was doing inching up and down their streets.

On the other hand, some of those people would have their radios or televisions on. They wouldn't be asking themselves about the Range-Rover; the morning news would have filled them in. Then they'd be reaching for their phones.

He glanced at Zaitun. She was still on the floor, still looking at him with an expression that he could not read. He tried to smile at her, thought he did a credible job of it. 'You OK?' he asked. She didn't say anything. Nor did the look on her face change by even a millimetre. 'I can let you out here,' Jack continued, 'or we can drive a bit further. Whatever works for you.' She remained silent. 'I've got some cash in my pocket. In case you need the subway fare or something.' No answer. 'You should get out, you know. Someone's bound to spot me sooner or later. Then the cops will come. You don't want to be in this car when that happens. Heck, you want to be miles away.' She stared at him neutrally. 'Looks like there's a major intersection a couple of blocks ahead. I bet one of the bus lines runs on that road. Why don't I drop you there? You can catch a bus, or, I suppose, find a phone booth. Yeah, that would probably be best. Find a phone and call the police. That way they won't think you're with me – you know, helping me or something.' Zaitun made no reply.

Jack slowed at the corner of two residential streets. He looked left and right. Low on the horizon he could see an astonishingly bright star. It reminded him of the one thing he disliked about city life: you didn't get to see the stars. It wasn't even worth trying.

'How can you prove you're innocent?' Jack was startled by the sound of her voice.

'In Singapore? I can't.'

A sullen accusation: 'You were lying.'

'Not really. I've got a pretty good idea who put the drugs in my briefcase.' *Only it's not a good idea because I don't know how. All*

I know is that it couldn't be anybody else, because nobody else had the motive.

'Then you can prove it?'

I sure as hell hope so. 'Probably. There'll be evidence. A dab of spilled heroin. Threads snipped out of my briefcase's lining. That kind of thing. The police could find it. All it would take is a good forensic scientist or a drug-sniffing dog or something. If I could get back to New York and explain things to the cops, they'd get a search warrant. Then when they go through her things . . .'

'Her? A woman?' Zaitun was now sitting straight. She'd unwrapped her arms from around her knees, and was resting them on the Range-Rover's seat.

'Yeah.' Jack smiled bitterly. 'Oh yeah.' *Who else could it be? Nobody. There was no logical alternative. It had to be Denise. But how? Method, motive, and opportunity. That's what investigators looked for. He had method and motive, two out of three. If he couldn't reason through the other one, he was as good as hanged.*

Zaitun pulled herself off the floor, and began to tug a seatbelt over her lap. Jack shook his head. 'Intersection's coming up. I really think you ought to hop out.'

'I want to talk to you for a minute.' *I want to talk to you too. I want to talk to anybody sane in this damned country.*

He tapped the brake, slowing the Range-Rover, glancing over his shoulder before pulling to the kerb. 'Since we're on speaking terms again, what's that thing in the back, the big thing where this car's rear seat should be?' He'd noticed it when he first climbed in the Range-Rover, but hadn't given it any thought – a three-foot-high, four and a half-foot-long black cylinder.

'Propane.'

'Propane?' Jack gulped. 'Like liquid propane gas?'

'Yes. Lots of government vehicles are propane-powered.'

Jack leaned his head against the steering wheel. He whispered, 'Oh God! Aw, hell.' Not looking at Zaitun, he continued, 'Christ, I'm sorry! Back there in the parking lot, with me blowing the living daylights out of everything, and you're sitting in a car that's a bomb on wheels!' He bounced his forehead twice on the steering wheel, groaning, 'Dumb, dumb, dumb.'

'You didn't know.'

'Yeah. But then I don't know a lot of things, a whole lot. Hell, I could have gotten you killed. All those explosions . . . I should have—'

'I didn't think about it. I was too frightened to think.'

Jack wanted to hide his face with shame. 'Look, why don't you get out of the car? I'm a wanted man, and people could start shooting at me any minute. Besides, I almost got you blown up. Plus, I know I got you arrested and charged with being an accessory to—'

'Superintendent Chan told you that?'

'Uh huh. The whole story. My fault, of course. For what it's worth, I'm sorry about that too. And I'm sorry for forcing you to take me to your apartment, and I'm sorry for tying you up, and I'm sorry for dragging you into all this trouble. So, look . . .' Jack fumbled Peter Quint's wallet from his pocket, emptying its contents in Zaitun's lap. '. . . I won't be needing this. They'll be coming for me pretty soon, Chan's people or Poh's, so take this and catch a cab or something.'

She took the bills, folded them, and put them on Jack's side of the dashboard. 'Why did you say that back in the parking lot?'

'Say what?'

'That everything was all right, that I was safe because you were there?'

'Oh, that.' Jack blushed slightly. 'Uh, well, I was worried about you. I mean, Chan told me that you were in his car, and there were all these thugs around, and you were hiding. And I thought, well, I was the guy who got you into this mess, so I had to be the guy who got you out. I mean, you're a nice girl, or you seem like a nice girl, and I was worried what those guys would do if they found you in Chan's car, and it was all my fault, anyway . . .' Jack's voice slowly tapered to silence.

'You really aren't guilty, are you?'

Jack met her gaze. It was forthright, inquisitive, and, he thought, not unsympathetic. There was something on her mind, something he didn't understand but wished to. 'I really am not.'

'A woman really did put those drugs in your briefcase?'

'Definitely. No question.' *Liar. There are still questions. Plenty of them . . .*

'And you can prove it?'

'That's my plan.' *Good old Jack Taft would choose to avoid the whole bitter business, cover it over, pretend it never happened. But John Taft . . . John Taft wanted revenge.*

Zaitun gave him a look of frank curiosity. Her eyes really were astonishingly lovely. In fact, her face was lovely. No question, she was a gorgeous woman, and desirable. Jack Taft wouldn't have made that particular observation – the part about desirability. But it came easily enough to John.

She clicked her seatbelt closed. 'Drive up to the intersection and turn right.'

'I think you should get out.' *I don't meant that.*

'Just do it. I'm going to show you where to hide.'

Jack obeyed. Five minutes and two miles later, Zaitun calling out directions, Jack found himself on a dirt road, driving slowly beneath shadowing trees. Apart from instructions as to where to turn and what signs to watch out for, Zaitun had spent the trip in thoughtful silence, keeping her eyes averted from him. But as the Range-Rover rolled to a stop in a small, wooded glade she turned towards him again. 'I have one more question,' she said.

'Yes?'

'When you climbed in the car, why . . .' She stopped, pressed a finger against her lip, then continued, '. . . why did you kiss me like that?'

'Ah.' John (not Jack) Taft smiled. 'I suppose I should explain about that.'

FIVE: A TIME TO KILL

> You will forget your name
> You will forget your face
> No one will know the day you die
> With no name and no face.
> You have been blotted out,
> The state can do that.
> Iris Murdoch – *The One Alone*

THRASYMACHUS: And the different forms of government make laws democratical, aristocratical, tyrannical, with a view to their several interests; and these laws, which are made by them for their own interests, are the justice which they deliver to their subjects, and him who transgresses them they punish as a breaker of the law, and unjust.

Plato – *The Republic I*

1
Singapore

There are hot hatreds, and there are cold, no clement climates in between. Chan's was the burning kind, bright crimson, and aflame. His blood surged at the disgrace of what Taft had done to him. Chest tight, heart suddenly too large for its cage and pounding to escape, a yellow curtain of fury descended before his eyes, and he unknowingly clenched and unclenched his fists, fingers seeking his enemy's throat. There is a clarity to such madness, a pinpoint focus on the subject of one's murderous intent; vision narrows for sharper acuity; uncommon hormones flood the system; deeper breaths heighten the blood's oxygen content; stored-up sugars flow to muscles; and all lust, craving and desire distil into a single overpowering imperative: revenge.

He'd do it. He'd track Taft down. Corner him. Alone, just the two of them. Face-to-face, one-on-one, man-to-man. There'd be requital then, the redressing of wrongs, the settling of scores, and the payment of a very sizable debt.

And in Corinth Medea cried, 'Vengeance is a bottomless cup! I will pour and pour!'

It was eleven in the morning when Chan, ignoring doctor's orders, limped into Singapore's Central Police Station. The CPS was an old building, no central air-conditioning, only individual cooling units in its office windows. Nor was it as attractive as the fancy new high-rises occupied by more prestigious government bureaux like the Port Authority, the Housing Development Board, and, flashiest of all, the Tourist Board. Nonetheless, Chan was fond of the old station. He liked its damp open breezeways, he liked its washed-out blue walls, and he liked the way it smelled of brass polish and sweat and leather and well-oiled firearms. Those were cop smells, and that's what he liked most of all.

He trudged slowly down a half-enclosed walkway to the private office to which he'd been entitled since being promoted to the rank of full superintendent. Deputy superintendents lived two to a room – two desks, four chairs, a single highboy to stow their personal gear. It got old, sharing an office with another man. You began to notice his cologne, and after a while, you came to detest it. Or maybe it was the way he cleared his throat before picking up the phone, or how his stomach started grumbling forty-five minutes before lunchtime. Or maybe you just didn't think he was a very good cop because every time you came into the office he was there, and that meant he wasn't spending as much time on the street as a good cop should.

Or whatever. Chan preferred privacy, and that was that.

As he walked deeper into the building, he encountered the usual guys – and the usual joking solicitude that is, after all, an injured policeman's due. But two officers looked at him in a funny way. One, a big burly Sikh, smirked. That particular Sikh was known to want a private office of his own.

Something was wrong. Chan could taste it in the air.

He closed his office door behind him, eased his aching frame into his chair, and called Hal Leung. Somebody else answered; said Hal had asked the guard at the Pearl Hill gate to let him know as soon as Chan showed up; said Hal was already on his way to Chan's office.

Wrong. Badly wrong.

Leung burst through the door without knocking. His complexion was pasty. He hadn't grabbed any sleep. It showed around his eyes.

'Street dope,' the young corporal blurted, laying a file folder flat on the shiny surface of Chan's always shiny desk. 'Junkie-grade street dope. More baby formula than anything else. Some of the packets have been stepped on a dozen times.'

Chan closed his eyes. His rubs hurt. His head hurt worse. 'The lab reports,' he whispered. In a moment of weakness he thought of adding, *the ones you didn't get around to reading yesterday.*

'Taft's dope is a dozen different blends from a dozen different sources.' Leung slumped into a chair in front of Chan's desk. He put his hands on his chin, looked Chan in the eyes, and said, 'We are fucked.'

'No question,' Chan sighed.

'And I haven't even told you about the fingerprints yet.'

So Taft had been innocent all along. Chan knew it as soon as Leung opened his mouth. Nobody in his right mind would smuggle ordinary street dope into Singapore. It wasn't worth it. Heroin peddled by your friendly neighbourhood pusher has been diluted so many times that it's almost valueless – fifteen dollars a hit in Singapore, depending on supply, demand, and how busy Chan Gin had been the night before. If the stash found in Taft's briefcase had been high grade, it would have been worth a hundred thousand dollars. But it had been thinned down to a lousy sixty straws of bargain-basement junk, nine hundred bucks at the going price.

Anyone risking bootlegging a load of dope into Singapore would smuggle drugs of a high enough quality to make it pay. Not the penny-ante crap that was sewn into Taft's bag.

Add to this that the strength of Taft's heroin varied from packet to packet, that it had been processed with different chemicals and stepped on with everything from powdered milk to baby formula to tapioca pudding, and you were left with the unpleasant certainty that the stuff came from multiple sources, and had been purchased from multiple dealers.

Street dealers. At full retail.

Given that fact, and that fact alone, the only reasonable conclusion was that some incompetent amateur had gone trooping around his or her city buying nickel and dime bags of low-level dope to plant on a nobody named Taft. Damn it all to hell, Taft lived in New York – a half-hour stroll around Washington Square and his enemy could have picked up enough scag to fill a dozen briefcases.

Insult to injury, there were fingerprints all over the place. Every sachet had them on it. Full sets and partials. None of which matched the ones Taft had so nicely left in his hotel room.

Innocent. The lousy sonofabitch was innocent. And – much, much worse – Chan should have known it all along.

Leung rubbed his eyes. 'Now what happens?'

Chan gingerly edged a hand into his jacket, fumbling for a toothpick. He grimaced. Stretching his ribs hurt like hell. 'Somebody talks. The lab. Fingerprint guys. Whoever. "Heh, heh, heh. Looks like old Devil Cop screwed the pooch this time."'

'Screwed the pooch?'

'Messed up, Hal. It means messed up bad.' Chan blew through his lips. 'Then somebody else tells his pal, and his pal tells a pal, and pretty soon everybody on the force knows.'

Leung groaned, 'Including the commissioner.'

'Especially the commissioner. Who will not be a happy man. Same as always, first thing, he starts thinking about the political implications. He's going to remember how much the Americans like to beat up on Singapore. Hanging. Flogging. Censorship. Silencing of dissidents. All that stuff. It makes the Americans bitch. And when the Americans bitch, the big boys get upset. So how many outraged letters of protest will the Americans fire off when they hear that one of their own has been wrongly charged with a hanging offence? Lots. Then the American newspapers will start in. You know what those guys think about this country. We're their favourite whipping boy. And after that, we'll get the human rights nuts on our case. Hell, Hal, compliments of Mr Taft, we'll have protesters marching outside the Singapore embassy in Washington.'

'Or, worse, the Tourist Board.'

Chan winced. 'You know, the government's spent the past twenty years sucking up to the Americans, trying to persuade them that we're the vital heart of Southeast Asia, free-market friend to one and all. Jesus, this year we spent six hundred million dollars on tourist development alone! Then – *bang!* – the cops ruin the country's image by chasing a guiltless businessman all to hell and gone, trying to send him to the gallows. You know how the Senior Minister is going to react to the news? Do you have any idea?'

'He's going to get grumpy again.'

With painfully closed eyes, Chan whispered, 'Grumpy? Oh yeah, definitely. Grumpy like that guy in *Bring Me the Head of Alfredo Garcia* was grumpy. Grumpy like a man who just approved four-point-three billion in economic incentives to attract American business to Singapore. Which will be real goddamned grumpy, Hal, I guarantee it. The commissioner is going to be shaking in his boots. He's going to have the chief of staff in his office and the heads of the Inspectorate and Public Affairs departments too. And he's going to be whining, so how do we get out of this mess? Somebody's going to answer: cover-up. Somebody else is going to say: won't work. Another guy will say: let's tell the truth. Then, after they kick that asshole out of the room, they'll all sit around scratching their butts until one of them thinks of the obvious.'

'A sacrificial offering.'

Chan shot out a finger. 'Got it in one. First off, they'll issue an apology. Second, you and me get indicted. Third, after our sentence is up, we'll be lucky if we can find jobs gutting fish on Pulu Ubin Island.'

'We can leave. Emigrate.'

'The government doesn't let anyone leave without a certificate of good behaviour. Which we won't have. Ditto no passports. Ditto no money. They'll seize everything, bankrupt us right to the bottom of the social ladder, same as they always do. You know how it works.'

Leung nodded. He knew. Every citizen knew. Life in Singapore was good so long as you didn't cross the line; but go OB – Out of Bounds – and they crushed you like a bug. Case in point: during the last election an opposition candidate named Tang went OB, criticizing the ruling powers in a campaign speech. The government sued for defamation, and shortly thereafter the courts ordered Tang to pay seven million dollars in damages.

'We could pre-empt them, sir. Go public. Say we made an honest mistake.'

'Might work for you. Won't work for me. The guys upstairs have been waiting a long time for me to screw up. Now that I have, they won't pass up the chance to get me. But you, Hal, yeah, you could . . .'

Leung squared his jaw. 'No way, sir. I'm with you.'

Chan twitched an eyebrow in acknowledgement. 'Thanks.'

The corporal nodded. He was merely doing for Chan what Chan would do for him. No thanks were needed. 'So now what do we do?'

'Find Taft.' Chan bit down hard enough to snap his toothpick. 'Bust his ass and bust it hard. Which I'm going to enjoy. I've got that fuckface on weapons charges, auto theft, kidnapping . . .' Chan stopped. He glared at the younger officer, who was refusing to meet his eyes. 'What? What now, Hal?'

'Ah . . . well . . . you'd better look at this, sir.'

Leung slid two documents across Chan's desk, One, sealed in a zip-lock plastic bag, was Rajiv Sethanar's note to Taft. The other was a lab report on the drug residue the police laboratory had found on the note. Chan read the note, his face becoming darker with every line. 'Under the influence of Rohypnol,' he whispered. 'Total inhibitory loss. Amnesia. Not accountable for his actions. No criminal liability. Well, that's just ducky. Oh yes. That is the frosting on the cake.' Suddenly his voice rose to a bellow: 'SONOFABITCH! I'M GONNA KILL THE FUCKER, AND TO HELL WITH IT!'

– 2 –

Sometimes Chan thought about it this way: one day the devil, who looks like Robert Preston in *The Music Man*, pops up. He's got a contract in one hand and a pen in the other. He smiles, and winks, and sidles up, saying, 'Have I got a deal for you. Listen up, friend – and you are my friend – bargains like this come along but once in a lifetime, and sometimes less than that. I have a sale going, prices slashed to the bone, everything must go. Now here's what I've got to offer. First: peace and prosperity, and I mean one hundred per cent of each. Add to that universal employment, high wages, and a mighty fine social security programme. Extra special, I'm throwing in subsidized air-conditioned housing, the best public transportation system in the world, beautiful parks to relax the eye and comfort the soul, blooming flowers to tickle the nose, good schools – none better – pretty near no violent crime, and streets clean enough to eat off. Why, believe it or not, my friend, you even get sparkling clean public toilets. Plus the water you drink will be purer than a pristine mountain stream, the air likewise, and vexing disease-bearing insects will be as rare as an honest lawyer. Moreover, I'm going to bankroll your kids' college educations. Yes sireebob! If your sons and daughters want to study at Harvard, Heidelberg or the Sorbonne, I'll happily pick up the tab. Add to this irresistible proposition the fact that I'm going to give you reasonable laws, laws you can live with, laws that any right-thinking human would obey automatically. Low taxes? You want it, you got it. Great medical care? It's all part of the package. No ethnic or religious or political strife? Why, it's my pleasure to deliver it. It's all there, and it's all yours for the taking.'

So you look at the devil and you ask, 'What's the catch?' And the devil says, 'No catch, my friend, none at all. But, you know there is a price, correct? Howsoever, it's almost zero, an unbeliev-able bargain, cheaper than this it does not get, and people the world over would line up for miles to buy one-tenth of what I've got to sell.'

'How much does it cost?'

'Virtually nothing. I'm telling you it's a steal. All you have to do – just like it says here at the bottom of this absolutely binding, utterly unbreakable social contract – is give up one insignificant little thing, a mere bagatelle, hardly worth discussing.'

'What?'

'Swear you'll never, and I do mean never, ever tick off the ruling powers. This is insignificant, correct? It's not like I'm asking you to sell your soul. All I'm saying is that you keep your head down, your lip zipped, and follow orders. That's it, and that's all. Now think of everything you get in return. Is it worth it? Hey, you'd have to be nuts to turn down all the goodies I'm offering here. So that's the deal – clean and sweet and simple, and no catches, hidden clauses, or fine print. Now here's the contract, and here's the pen. Come on, friend, sign on the dotted line, and be prepared to live happily ever after.'

Chan would lie on his sofa, fingers knitted behind his head, and think: every damned tame little mouse in Singapore had signed on the dotted line. If they hadn't, they pretty much weren't around any more.

And, the hell of it was, the devil *had* delivered. He'd done exactly what he promised. The deal *was* a great deal. Everyone who had signed the contract was happy that they had.

Then Chan would say to himself: *I haven't signed your fucking contract.*

And a small voice would leer: *the hell you haven't.*

And he'd pick up something heavy and throw it hard at the wall.

In the end no one would stand beside him. He'd broken the social contract, broken it big time, and it wasn't Robert Preston who would come to collect the bill.

Not that the government gave a good goddamn about Taft's innocence. All they cared about was the scandal: Taft giving interviews to the *Wall Street Journal, Forbes, Business Week,* and God help us all, Larry King.

Businessmen reacted to such things. Executives had qualms about a country that flogged petty criminals and hanged a few dozen serious felons every year. Yeah, sure, they loved the safety of the streets, and the squeaky clean environment, and all of that. But, no, they weren't entirely easy about the methods and techniques that kept things that way.

Once Taft started shooting his mouth off about the methods and techniques to which he'd almost fallen victim – well, slightly more than almost – there would be hell to pay. Hell, in the present instance, being governed not by its accustomed deity, but rather by Senior Minister Lee Kuan Yew.

Nor could anyone other than Chan himself be blamed for the fiasco. Responsibility was his and his alone. He should have known Taft was innocent, should have known it back in the Samsudin girl's apartment if not earlier. A drug dealer, a real one, would have blown Chan away on the spot. And wouldn't have dithered about his innocence. Wouldn't have left his one and only gun behind. Wouldn't, wouldn't, wouldn't . . .

But Chan had been humbled by the lousy lowlife sonofabitch. Twice. First time the scumbag got the drop on him in the hotel.

Second time in that girl's apartment. *Now, fuck me, it's three times!* And Chan hadn't thought about the evidence, not for a moment. All he thought about was vengeance. Jesus, but he'd wanted to see Taft dead!

Still did, if the truth be known.

Damn, but he hated the bastard, and although his hatred burned bright he could not warm himself at its flames. Defeat is bad. Disgrace is worse. A man may be forgiven many sins, may even forgive himself. But no penance redeems the sin of failure. Fail secretly, and you will punish yourself down all your years. Fail publicly, and society will do it for you.

What is worse than the mockery of inferiors, snickering behind your back?

Chan peered into the future, searched for his fate, and shivered at what he saw. There was no price he would not pay, no sacrifice he would not make, to avoid the destiny Taft's innocence foretold.

Leaning back in his chair, steepling his fingers beneath his chin, he began to think. And did so for a very long time.

Ruination might be avoided – *might* – and all of his problems solved, if Taft kept his mouth shut. Were the sonofabitch persuaded not to talk, there'd be no embarrassment in high places. No embarrassment meant no rain of destruction on the head of Chan Gin. Just a polite nudge aside, off to some quiet corner, and a subtle hint that his career was finally, if not officially, at an end.

Charlie, we want you to run the United Way campaign this year.

Of course, there'd have to be a cover-up too. But given the choice between losing face in front of the world business community or kicking dirt over a most unpleasant pile of shit, every government in the world, most of all Singapore's, would opt for a cover-up.

But only if Taft kept silent.

Or was silenced.

Now there's a thought.

– 3 –

After a sleep delightfully untroubled by nightmares, Jack awoke. Whatever doubts he had had about Gabrielle (which he knew were truly doubts about himself) seemed to have fled. Being male, and therefore being somewhat dense on such matters, he didn't quite understand why.

Beside him, a glowingly naked Zaitun sighed in her sleep.

He stretched, smiled, opened his eyes. A rain shower, now gently ending, pattered on the Range-Rover's roof. A single drop splashed through the slightly open window and on to his lip. He licked it, and found it honeyed. He angled his head, studying Zaitun as she dozed on the seat. She'd curled into a little ball like a sleeping child, and looked as innocent. A light sheen of sweat made her amber forehead glow where it peeked from the chocolate tangle of her hair.

He wondered how old she was. In her early twenties, he supposed, young enough to be his daughter if he had married early. Slightly embarrassing, that – sweet and pleasant and tender, but nonetheless a bit improper.

He felt a little guilty. He felt a little happy. The emotions went well together. He knew his conscience would bother him later – cheating on the woman he loved, taking advantage of a lovely young girl, behaving like some sort of sex-crazed animal . . . Oh, yes, he'd have regrets.

But not right now.

Jack leaned closer, inhaling deeply of her perfume. Her moist, slightly parted lips looked so unspeakably desirable. Ye gods, but he'd glutted himself on them last night. The shackles of self-restraint had slipped off; he didn't even notice they were gone. He'd sought only to take from this lovely girl all that he wanted, yet mysteriously sensed that both gave, both took, and that was the greater pleasure for them both.

With Zaitun, he'd become another man, someone whom he'd always feared. Once, painfully, Denise had trained him for her demon lover, a role for which he was unfit. He abominated it, and in the end abominated himself. *No more of this*, he vowed, applying to his next lover, Gabrielle, all the studious caution and selfless gentleness he could muster.

But all at once . . . just this last night . . . devil take the hindmost, he'd run up the black flag of piracy, and . . .

He blinked. A vision, a fantasy, a dream came to him. He had never held dreams in much regard; they were disturbing things, a predictable source of unhappiness. They made you want what you couldn't have, and worse, inspired you to desires that, if you dared fulfil, left you drained, disappointed, full of regrets. Still, this dream, the one tantalizingly before his eyes, might be different. Truly, it might.

Jack, who took no action without consideration, and pondered every choice long and hard, remembered a line from *Faust*, the tortured scholar begging of Mephistopheles that he might discover something so perfect and wonderful that he would *say to the fleeting moment, stop thou art so fair.*

Jack had found his moment; it had as its single imperative one thing and one thing only: that he, a man who never lived for the moment, seize it. *Carpe diem*, lowering his face to Zaitun's, he did.

Zaitun was out of sight, behind some bushes. Jack, a model of discretion, had strolled to the opposite end of the clearing.

The air was damp and sweet with rot, but not unpleasant. Jack, an uncertain city dweller, stood warily eyeing the surrounding rainforest with mistrust. It was green, too green, a riot and a revel of green, every shade and hue – avocado, absinthe, apple, Kelley, Lincoln, cucumber – greens beyond number, more than he could name, and he had never known that this single colour, this simple word 'green' spanned so varied a spectrum or embodied such an improbable diversity of green, green, greens. The foliage too was unexpected, slightly sinister. Huge leafy things with drooping fronds bordered the small glade, and brown ropy vines snaked around trees that did not seem entirely natural. Their barks were scaled and shingled, lizard-looking; he could not say whether they were coniferous, deciduous, or not real trees at all.

Barely seen through leafy vegetation, a patch of blue water flashed distant highlights. Jack stood on his tiptoes trying to get a clearer view. Down from the hill upon which he was parked, parklands rolled away, green tinging to blue tinging to purple. And at the farthest distance, wide lakes, all turquoise in the afternoon sun, beautiful and still.

Zaitun came up beside him. She slipped her arm beneath his,

standing for a quiet moment watching what he watched, before saying, 'Bukit Timah. Tin Hill. There isn't any tin, though. Only an old rock quarry.'

He, not yet ready to speak, nodded. She continued, 'After the Malaysians and Thais and Indonesians log their countries out, this will still be here, the last rainforest in Asia.'

'I find that hard to believe.'

'I fly over those countries, John. I see what's happening . . .' Taft suddenly tilted his head up. '. . . What? What's the matter?'

'Nothing.' He studied the jungle canopy. It shrouded the clearing like an umbrella. Chan's Range-Rover would be invisible from the skies.

'Planes and helicopters can't see us. Even if they did, they wouldn't think about it. Superintendent Chan's car is the same model as the park rangers use.'

Jack nodded. He believed her. There was no one else he could believe.

His stomach rumbled.

'Hungry?' Zaitun asked.

'Yes.' He thought about it. 'No. I mean not really.' That was peculiar. But for a single orange, he had eaten nothing for more than two days. He should have been ravenous. Instead, the idea of food was not especially interesting. Another odd thing: his slacks. Singapore's relentless humidity seemed to have made them stretch. Even though the belt was notched in its last hole, they kept slipping. He slid his thumbs through the rear belt loops, tugging them back.

'I'll get us something to eat.'

Suddenly wary, Jack gave her a sideways stare. If she asked for the keys to Chan's Range-Rover . . .

Before he could speak, Zaitun had disappeared into the forest.

The freshly picked mangoes were delicious. Reddish orange, dripping juicy, so soft that they had to be eaten with a spoon. There was only one spoon in the glove compartment of Chan's Range-Rover. Sitting beneath a fragrant gulaxia tree, Taft and Zaitun shared the spoon, he feeding her, she feeding him. He thought that he should feel silly – a middle-aged man gambolling in a *Green Mansions* fantasy, Zaitun in the role of Rima the jungle girl. But he didn't feel silly, not in the least. Quite the contrary, he felt agreeably content.

The irony was not lost on him. He'd spent most of his childhood, all of his adult life, a careful, comfortable conformist. Non-confrontational and nondescript – that was even-tempered Jack, the man who made no waves.

But now he was John, not Jack, Taft. In the course of two days, everything good old Jack stood for, every principle that had guided his life was overthrown. He'd hurled caution to the wind, let slip the reins of self-control, needs must when the devil drives, and, contrary to every expectation, he'd had the time of his life! Surprise, surprise – fighting back was . . .

Fun!

The frustration on Chan Gin's face. Outfoxing and outfighting hoodlums. The anarchy that followed. The exhilarating narcotic of successful escape. God, it had been great!

The real kick was learning that he was as good as any of them. Better even. Better than a bunch of professional thugs. Better than a gun-crazed cop. Better than them all!

What was the sweetest of all was that Chan *knew* Jack was better. Back in Sungei Buloh Jack had rubbed the swaggering bastard's face in it. God, but he hated that lout, so typical of his breed. A tough guy. A loudmouth. A steal-your-lunch-money steal-your-girl kick-sand-in-your-face bully, a C-grade-point-average jock sneering at anyone who got an A, a big beer-bellied foreman who gave 'prissy college boys' all the scut work, a windbag sales executive who vetoed a young logistics analyst's suggestions because he was too dumb to understand them, a purple-faced guy on the street who bumps into you when your back is turned because he has a chip on his shoulder and everyone is his enemy and you're . . .

'What are you frowning about, John?' Zaitun leaned forward. There was a smear of mango juice above her lip. 'Nothing,' he said, sullenly ignoring the urge to lick it off.

'Tell me about it.'

'I said it was nothing,' he snapped. *Whoops, no need to be surly.*

'I meant about . . . well, last night you said you knew who put the narcotics in your briefcase. The woman who framed you. I think you should tell me about that.'

Jack nodded thoughtfully. He *did* need to speak to someone about what had happened, or what he believed had happened. The logic he'd puzzled over was not entirely satisfactory. There were holes in his reasoning, questions that he couldn't answer, mysteries unsolved. Talking it through might help break the logjam.

He stared down at the ground, rich black soil, still wet with recent rain, and began spelling it out for Zaitun.

– 4 –

The briefcase was brand new in a shopping bag from the store at which it had been purchased. He'd carried it back to his office, transferred the contents of his old briefcase into it, locked it, and slid it beneath his desk. There it stayed until he left for the day. After that it was with him every second, straight through the weekend and straight on to the plane. It had never been out of his sight.

Except once.

That Friday afternoon, the afternoon upon which Gabrielle had given him the thing, he'd spent two hours in a conference room. He was one place, the briefcase another. Therefore it followed with inexorable logic that the bag had been tampered with during those two hours.

The meeting ended at five. Just as it was breaking up, Denise came in and apologized for missing it. She said she'd been . . . she'd been what?

He closed his eyes, remembering, painting the scene as he had always been able to do, sharp and vivid and detailed. Somebody was at the back of the meeting room, erasing the whiteboard. Paul. It was Paul back there. He was an obsessive scribbler on whiteboards. Two other people were chatting in the corridor outside. Tilly and Marianne. Everybody else had left. Jack himself was getting ready to leave. Denise walked in. Her hair was a little wind-teased on this, a windy day. She had her impractically fashionable attaché case in her right hand, an oxblood Coach leather purse over her left shoulder. Bright green suit, jacket buttoned at the waist, canary-yellow scarf around her neck. Her colour was high, a flush on her cheeks. She *looked* like she'd been outdoors, walking quickly as New Yorkers always walk, click-clicking heels perfectly paced to make sure you made the next stoplight, were across the street before it changed, already hurrying towards the next intersection, eyeing the pattern of the traffic lights, timing your steps so that you never lost a second, were always on the hustle and on the move . . .

'Sorry, Jack. I tried to make it back sooner. But you know how demanding he can be.'

He? Had she told him the name of the customer she was visiting? He didn't remember.

'Did I miss anything important?' She was a little out of breath, her words came in small sharp puffs.

'No, not really.'

'I'll talk to Paul Monday morning. Make sure I get caught up.'

'Sure. Fine. Do that.'

And that was it. Thirty seconds at the most. Then she was gone.

So how did she get at a locked briefcase in his office? For that matter, how did she know he had a new briefcase?

Braintwisters. Unsolvable riddles. He had no answers.

'John,' Zaitun asked, 'you said no one knew you were going to Singapore.'

'Yup. Nobody but my boss, Joel Greenberg. But Joel wasn't in the office that afternoon. I tried to call him twice. His secretary said he wouldn't be back until late. Besides, Joel wouldn't resort to a trick like this to get rid of me. If a chief exec wants you out of the way, he's got a million easier ways to do it.'

'Then how did this Denise woman find out about your trip?'

'Beats me. Maybe I let something slip.'

'She must hate you very much.'

'You don't know the half of it. When I broke off with her, she was like nothing I've ever seen. Furious. She made my life hell. Every dirty office politics trick you can think of.'

'Why didn't you stop her? Face her down?'

Jack shook his head. 'Not my style. I don't do confrontation. I figured she'd just give up and leave me alone. And I was right. Or at least I thought I was.'

'But if she's the one who did it—'

'There's *nobody* else it could be,' he said a little too quickly, knowing (but wanting to deny) that somebody else knew about the trip.

But it could not be Gabrielle. Nothing was less probable than that. It simply wasn't worth thinking about it.

He thought about it.

And suddenly saw what he'd overlooked.

Poh Kay Siong? he'd shouted at Chan. *Who the hell is Poh Kay Siong?*

Last of Singapore's gangland chiefs, Chan, cuffed to a tree, answered. *Drugs, gambling, the protection racket, arms-running up to Cambodia, you name it, he's got his fingers in it. And he wants to kill your ass even more than I do.*

What for? I've never even heard of him!

Oh, Christ, Taft, spare me your fucking lies! Poh's the guy who sent those hatchetmen to ice you at Raffles.

Raffles? Hatchetmen? Oh . . . I'd almost forgotten. You mean the man you shot while I was on the floor?

There were two. Another was in the hall outside your room. Another thing – the thugs who tried to kill you outside of the Samsudin woman's apartment – they were his too.

You're saying those were crooks not cops!

Of course they fucking were! Come on, Taft, don't play games with me.

Both the police and *the mob are trying to kill me!*

Some guys are just born lucky.

What for? Jesus, what for?

You tell me. If I knew why that bastard hates you—

Honest to God, I don't know him. I can't even begin to imagine—

Horseshit! Why don't you just quit this goddamned charade and confess?

To what. For God's sake, man, I haven't done anything!

Well fuck, have it your way. But listen to me, asshole, Poh's got his hands on a restricted multiband radio scanner and is eavesdropping on police communications. He knows everything that's going on—

Restricted?

Yeah, and if I could catch him with it, I'd be able to bust the bastard at last. In this country the cops and the military take communications security seriously. Radio Shack doesn't do a hell of a lot of business in Singapore. But what the fuck do you care about that? Listen up, dickhead, the thing you should care about is this: there's only one way out of Sungei Buloh, and Poh's got a fucking army waiting for you there. Plus the Samsudin girl is in my car and I don't want her hurt, so here's what I'd do if I were in your shoes . . .

Obvious. The whole thing was obvious. Once you knew about Poh, you knew about Denise. And once you knew about Denise, you knew – method, motive, and opportunity – that there had been a flaw in your logic, that all your careful reasoning was based on a faulty premise. Which meant you had to change the premise. Which meant . . .

He wasn't sitting in a rainforest with a beautiful woman. He was elsewhere, drifting peacefully in a place where puzzles and predicaments reduced themselves to their most elemental components. Here, the light was strong and clear and pure, and you could see how those elements, so perplexing in the empirical world, were designed by destiny to dovetail in one and only one way, each piece fitting into its mates so perfectly that you were astonished you'd not noticed before this perfect mosaic, to transcendentally reasonable, impeccable, exquisite, crystalline.

Rapt in astonishment, he at last saw what he'd been too blind to see. It was so simple, so straightforward, so elegant. The puzzle pieces were who, how, when, and why? He'd been expending all his energy thinking about the 'how'. But that wasn't what solved the puzzle. No, not at all. The key, the single puzzle piece that unlocked all the others was *when*. Answer that one question, and the whole thing fell into place.

He knew the answer. He knew – not a flash of insight but merely the gears of logic grinding out a correct conclusion – betrayal.

He went cold, arctic ice, translucent blue and rimed with frigid fury.

Zaitun shook him. Her hand was on his shoulder and she shook him hard. 'John?' she asked, genuinely concerned. 'John are you all right.'

'Quiet! I'm thinking!'

– 5 –

With her chin resting on knees, arms wrapped around her legs, Zaitun had been watching him for more than an hour. His eyes were distant, and he barely moved but for occasionally stroking his chin – although, from time to time, his mouth twisted slightly into almost frightening frowns.

He did not frighten her, although she knew he could if he wanted. Any man who set his mind to it could frighten any woman. But John was not a man to try. He was a better man than that.

She was glad she'd chosen him. Not the first man she'd embraced, he had something the others lacked: true passion, the genuine thing, nothing held back, nothing at all. The ferocity of his hunger – more honest than any she'd known – heightened hers; he was completely there, all of him; his commitment was total, totally hers for that time. She'd never felt the like, nor imagined it possible.

The others – oh they – when she thought of them she thought not of their kisses, but only of the useless things they'd offered. Two had been rich businessmen smug at the beauty they'd seduced, both asking her if she wanted pocket money, shiny baubles, unimportant things like that.

The third, the last, ardent in his faith, proposed marriage.

Marriage? In Singapore? Call it by its true name; say what it really is: prison. A predetermined number of pregnancies as set by statutory law, a Housing Development Board flat, and, at the end of the road, comfortable retirement compliments of the Central Provident Fund's generous social security plan. True, she might prosper, might reap the promise of the Singapore dream. But what was that dream? *Kiatsu* was the dream. Winning was the dream. We're Singaporeans, they said, fast on our feet, hungry for success, and we never lose. Hustling, hardworking, sharp as tacks, we lions of the Orient want our 'Five Cs', and we want 'em now.

The Five Cs – you heard it everywhere – cash, credit card, condominium, career, car. That's all Singaporeans yearned for.

There was more to life than that.

Even as a child, she'd wanted to escape the narrow bounds of her confining island, thirsted for a place where things were less predictable, where risk was not merely permissible but expected, and where tomorrow did not look like today.

Although, now that she thought on it, this particular day looked like none other she'd lived. After all these years of acquiescent conformity, she'd gone OB, far OB, and there was no question about that.

Out of Bounds. The thing a Singaporean fears most. There was a fence in the nation that outsiders never saw. Inside was peace, comfort, wealth if you wanted to work for it, a safety net if you didn't. But outside was disgrace and loneliness. If you stepped over the line, went OB, you were shunned. Friends no longer came to visit. Neighbours left you alone. Even relatives made sure they were not seen with you, or at least not in public.

Outcaste. Pariah. Out of Bounds.

What Muslim woman takes an unbeliever lover? What good Singaporean consorts with a wanted man? What upright citizen sits beneath a gulaxia tree when she should be running for the nearest Neighbourhood Police Post?

A woman who knew her own mind. One who would do what was right regardless of the state. She was Out of Bounds, an enemy of the people, and she'd never been happier in her life.

*

John shook himself out of his reverie. His frown was gone, replaced with a gloriously wicked smile.

He stretched, slowly drawing his arms back and rolling his shoulders. 'I know what I have to do.' He grinned.

'Yes, John?'

'For a while, I thought it was the port – I mean the Port of Singapore – I thought that was the only way I could get out of this country. You know, sneak on board a ship, stow away down in the bilges, stay hidden until it docks in another country. I think I could pull it off because I know a lot about shipping and a lot about what goes on in a port like Singapore.'

'It's very well guarded.'

'I know. I've read their literature. Even so, I think I could get past them.'

'Then I'll take you there. After dark, we'll drive—'

'Uh uh. It's too risky. One mistake and a security guy or longshoreman would notice me. Even if I got on a freighter, some seaman could spot me. Then the captain claps me in irons, throws me in the brig, and turns me over for extradition at his next port of call. At sea for a couple of weeks, there's too much that could go wrong. What I need is something that's fast and simple. And that means the American Embassy.'

Zaitun's heart leapt in her throat. 'No! John, they have police there! All around it! I heard them talk about it while I was in the station. That's where they're expecting you to go. They'll kill you.'

John shook his head. 'Look, once I'm inside the embassy – well, hell, it's American territory and no one can touch me. I can tell my story to someone who'll listen. They'll let me get in touch with people in the States – my lawyer, my friends – and maybe I can even persuade the New York cops to have a heart-to-heart chat with a certain redhead.'

Zaitun blinked. She thought earlier, she wasn't sure when, John had said the woman who put drugs in his briefcase was blonde. She must have misheard him, and the point wasn't important anyway. 'John, please don't. Don't even think about going there.'

'You know, last night that big jackass Chan taught me something. Oh yeah, him and his "Hey Taft, you ever seen what happens to a high-balling semi when its engine blows up?" And then telling me how to use his artillery. I think that bozo is going to regret teaching me that stuff.'

'You can't go to the embassy. They'll see you as soon as you are within a block of it.'

John was smiling like a wolf, eyes narrow and teeth showing. He looked so confident, the most confident man she'd ever met. 'Yeah, they probably will. But when they do, will they notice me? That's another question entirely.'

'What are you smiling about, John?'

'I've got some fun in mind.'

'What?'

'Take off your clothes.'

Zaitun blushed. 'Oh, that.'

'Yeah.' John laughed as if he'd just heard the funniest joke. 'Oh yeah, now that you mention it, that too.'

2
New York

– 1 –

Jack, a cozy-comfy teddybear, has his arm around her waist as he speaks Yeats's lines: Take, if you must, this little bag of dreams; unloose the cord, and they will wrap you round. She answers, are you truly looped in the loops of my hair? He replies that he will walk with her among long dappled grasses and pluck till time and times are done the silver apples of the moon, the golden apples of the sun. O love is the crooked thing, she says, there is nobody wise enough to find out all that is in it. To which he responds, Time to get up, Gabrielle. It's almost nine.

What!?

'We've got to get to work. Come, dear, rise and shine.'

Not Jack. Who? Oh God! Olivia.

'Coffee,' less a word than a groan.

'On the nightstand. It's my husband's special blend. He has it flown in from San Francisco, you know.'

Gabrielle knew. Just as she now knew where she was: in the guest room of Olivia and Scott Thatcher's Sutton Place *pied à terre*. She'd been there all night.

Olivia's driver had been waiting in the no-parking zone in front of LBTech. Holding an umbrella, he whisked them both into the back of his limousine, then swung an arrogant U-turn in the middle of Fifty-seventh Street, taking them straight east to the Thatchers' city residence.

With a talent that made Gabrielle green with envy, Olivia had whipped something together in the kitchen – a magical lemon pasta and a green salad of sufficient freshness to tell her that coffee was not the only foodstuff the fabulously wealthy Thatchers had flown in daily. Then, eating in the kitchen, the two women tried to make sense out of what Denise had said, and out of how Joel Greenberg had behaved.

Somewhere along the line Olivia opened a bottle of wine, a St Francis Merlot, '94 vintage. A small Sonoma winery, Olivia said, twenty thousand cases a year. Not available in the east. She and Scott, guess what, had it flown in.

Later, in the living room, surrounded by the files and printouts and reports that Gabrielle had pulled from her briefcase, Olivia had opened a second bottle. By the time Scott Thatcher returned from a late business dinner, the two had moved to Olivia's office, were using Olivia's computer and board-level password to study LBTech's internal databases. By that point, a third bottle had been opened. Or at least Gabrielle hoped it was only the third . . .

She needed the wine. It calmed her increasingly terrible fears for Jack, made her forget the expression of catty triumph on Denise Donald's face, and how very, very much Gabrielle wanted to bloody that bitch's nose.

It was three or four in the morning when Olivia had tucked her in. And now it was . . . what? . . . *Jesus!* Nine o'clock!

Gabrielle sat bolt upright.

Bad move. A massive bell tolled in her brain, Gothic cathedral chimes pealing contrition for wrong-doers. Overindulgence, too, is a sin; so the nuns had tutored her in her classroom; so she now knew. Her skin felt clammy. Sweat beaded over her upper lip. She clasped a steaming mug of coffee between trembling hands. She sipped. She shuddered. She felt not one whit better.

'Try some orange juice, dear.'

Gabrielle obeyed. She turned her eyes up to Olivia's hovering face. Olivia, no less wine and no less sleep than she, was radiant. *I hate you . . .*

'Here are some aspirin. Wash them down. Now a nice vitamin pill. That's good. Oh dear! The bathroom's to your left . . .'

Feeling well enough to regret how she felt, Gabrielle slumped next to Olivia in the living room. She held a document between her unsteady fingers, one of the countless reports *EPS*'s librarians had downloaded from computer systems the day before.

Far from remarkable, the document was an ordinary, everyday corporate credit report, little different from the credit reports that TRW and Equifax maintain on every citizen in America. It was, in point of fact, the same report that had tickled her subconscious while cabbing it to LBTech the night before. Now she knew why.

Individual citizens are required to pay their bills promptly. If they do not, interest payments and other penalties are exacted. Withhold payment too long, and the bill collector repossesses your car. In contrast, corporations are held to more forgiving standards, nor do repro men stake out the parking lots of *Fortune* 500 companies. Thirty, sixty, ninety days or longer can elapse between the receipt of a fair and valid invoice and the issuance of a cheque. After all, if a multi-billion-dollar company is your customer, you know it's going to pay what's owing.

Some day.

But until it does, you, the hapless supplier of goods and services, are out of pocket a hefty sum of money. Accordingly, before accepting an order, you study your customer's payment history, accessing databases that record such histories in excruciating detail.

Gabrielle examined LBTech's payment history. As expected, the report showed that, as an international wholesaler, LBTech ordered massive quantities of electronic components from every manufacturer in America. They were all listed in the report, alphabetically: AMD through Zilog. Neatly arrayed in columns next to each supplier's name were figures showing how much LBTech owed, and how long the debt had been outstanding.

Respectable corporation that it was, LBTech paid promptly. Most of its bills were settled in fewer than forty-five days, none longer than sixty. Nothing wrong there. What was wrong – *what might be wrong*, Gabrielle thought – was that a handful of bills had been paid at once. *As in immediately. As in the day they are received. Like clockwork.*

Which was weird. Nobody pays their bills that fast.

Olivia peered over Gabrielle's shoulder and looked at the company named on the printout. 'Kitsunē? I know them. Scott and I have had trouble with them in the past.'

'If I understand what this credit report says, Jack's having trouble with them now.' Olivia shot her a questioning look. 'Kitsunē's a big Japanese conglomerate – finished goods: cars and watches and radios and personal computers and all that stuff. They don't make components. They buy them from distributors like LBTech. But if they buy from LBTech, why are they sending it bills? LBTech should be billing them.'

'Which means what, my dear?'

'Off the top of my head, I'd say it means kickbacks.'

Olivia's lips paled. '*That* is a word no member of a board of directors wishes to hear.'

'Kitsunē is an Asian company, right? And Denise is Director of Asian Operations. Livy, we need to get back on your computer. I think I know what's going on.'

– 2 –

Gabrielle never could watch her friend at a keyboard without being slightly nonplussed. No one expected a woman of Olivia's wealth and status to be a computer whiz – until they remembered that her husband was the entrepreneur behind one of the world's largest data-processing companies, and recalled that his wife had been his partner and collaborator from the very day, thirty years earlier, he'd created the thing.

Nor did Olivia Thatcher deign to use an ordinary personal computer. No 'Intel Inside' for her. On the contrary, Olivia's computational weapon of choice was a Silicon Graphics OCTANE2, a desktop device bearing the same relationship to a Pentium-powered PC as a Ferrari does to a cement truck.

Asking for her user ID, the SGI's screen announced that she was logging-on something called 'UNIX(r) System V Release 4.0'. Olivia entered her own name, then, in response to a request for password, keyed her mother's name, SOPHIACARTER, all caps, no spaces.

Disdaining menus and canned reports, she invoked the database's dialect of IBM's Standard Query Language, SQL, quickly typing a cryptic (to Gabrielle's eyes) string of parentheses and abbreviations. Moments later her high-speed laser printer whined. Thirty-seven pages of reports – twelve pages per minute – spit into its bin.

Olivia and Gabrielle had what they wanted.

They had nothing at all.

The reports listed no payments to Kitsunē. None. Gabrielle felt her stomach sink. Olivia turned back to her keyboard, and typed another command. In response, LBTech's remote database displayed a single line on the screen: LAST PAYABLES MASTER UPDATE/PURGE 19:18 HRS OCT 26.

Olivia, who never swore, swore.

'What's the matter, Livy?'

'Somebody's tampered with this database! Minutes after you and I were *escorted* off LBTech's premises, compliments of Joel and his inamorata, person or persons unknown – *I don't think* – logged into LBTech's mainframe, accessed this database, and purged a few records from it. I believe we can guess which line items were erased.'

Gabrielle's voice was tremulous with despair. 'Then there's no evidence to help Jack.'

Olivia answered, iron in every word. 'Quite the contrary.' Swinging back to the keyboard, she hissed, 'One of corporate

America's dirty little secrets is its excess of superfluous databases. Really, it's quite like a profligate child with too many toys. The marketing people have their own databases, as does the Finance Department, as does Human Resources, the factories, the Shipping department, and everyone else. My dear, I can name one well-known company where every transaction must be processed through sixty-four separate and wholly unsynchronized database programs. The waste is unspeakable. The chaos is all consuming. How they make money, I shall never know.'

'LBTech?'

'No better and no worse than most. Twelve major databases, and I do believe this is the one we want.' Olivia tapped her fingernail on the screen: LBTECH HR PAYROLL BENEFITS AND COMPENSATION.

'The personnel system? Good God, why that?'

'LBTech pays its salespeople bonuses, pet. Those bonuses are calculated as a per cent of booked sales. For that reason, not only does every sale have to be pecked into our order, inventory, and control system, it also has to be entered into this database – together with the identity of the salesperson. And so . . .' Olivia's fingers danced across the keys, '. . . not to anyone's surprise, or at least not to *mine*, we discover that the salesman assigned to Kitsunē is no salesman at all, but rather a director from the Logistics Department, one Denise Donald by name.'

'I'll be damned.'

'*Somebody* will,' Olivia promised, no small triumph in her voice. 'Now let's look at these orders. Dear me, how curious, this fiddle seems to have been going on for only three months. Not a coincidence, I believe. After all, it was at the last board meeting we voted Jack as Vice President, and that meeting was three months ago. I imagine the Lady Macbeth of LBTech started getting revenge for losing the promotion as soon as I gave her the bad news.'

The computer displayed three order forms in overlapping windows. Olivia clicked through them one by one. 'What's your guess here, pet? Do you see a pattern?'

'I think so. Each order is about double the size of the one before it. First, fifty thousand dollars, then a hundred, and the last one for two hundred. It's almost as if—'

'As if Denise's customer didn't quite trust her to deliver the goods. They're slowly working their way up, making sure she can do what she says she can, increasing the dollars every month. And look, every order is different. First it's mostly multi-alkali photo-cathode image intensifiers, whatever they may be, and ablative ceramic heat shields. Then it's passive interferometer equipment and hardened differential analysers and, my goodness, oxygen rebreathers – that's scuba gear is it not? And . . . Gabrielle, whatever do you think a milspec frequency agile multiband radio scanner is?'

'I don't have a clue.'

'Well we needn't concern ourselves with what odd and usual electronics Denise's customers are ordering. All we need do is understand the math. And the math, my dear, is this: Denise is booking orders for somewhat more than they are worth – by about twenty per cent I should say – and billing these Kitsunē people accordingly. They pay promptly. Equally promptly, on the first of every month, Kitsunē quote-discovers-unquote the overbilling and requests a refund.' Olivia pointed to the credit reports Gabrielle's librarians had retrieved. 'Then Denise taps a command into her computer to remit that refund, and a cheque is automatically cut. No one has the time to audit each and every bill issued by a company the size of ours. There must be millions. Besides, billing errors happen all the time, and no one would give these few discrepancies a second glance. Besides, it's all done by computer, and so it *must* be right.' Olivia sniffed at the thought.

'I don't get it, Livy. I mean, what's the point.'

'The point, my dear, is a mathematical one. We pay our salespeople a seven and a half per cent commission. Denise is collecting that commission on overstated sales. True, she hasn't embezzled very much so far – only about ten thousand dollars – but if those Kitsunē orders were to continue to double for another three months, the sum would be closer to fifty thousand.'

'Big bucks.'

'Very big. And, now I believe we understand what lies behind

your young man's troubles. Denise is working some fiddle with . . .'
Olivia clicked her mouse, typed a few more characters, and read
from the screen, '. . . something called Poh Kay Siong Enterprises,
Ltd, licensed agent, Kitsunē Trading, Singapore. No doubt Jack,
clever boy that he is, would have uncovered it as soon as he set foot
in LBTech's Singapore office. Accordingly, Denise took steps to see
that he *never* reached that office.'

'We've got her! Hot damn, Livy!' Gabrielle flung her arms
around Olivia, and gave her a kiss.

– 3 –

Olivia made eight phone calls. Seven were to arrange a conference
call among her fellow LBTech directors, all but for its chairman,
Joel Greenberg. The eighth was the conference itself. 'All in favour
of a special audit, please say "aye". Thank you, the ayes have it,
and the motion is passed. All in favour of appointing Olivia
Thatcher head of the audit committee, please say "aye". Yes,
Charlie?' Olivia listened, eyes upturned at the ceiling as if
searching for heavenly inspiration. Very patiently she continued,
'That's right, Charlie, you heard me correctly. I am afraid Joel is
carrying on an affair of the heart with Miss Donald. I know it is,
Charlie. Thank you, Charlie. The motion is passed unanimously.
Is there any further business? No. Very well, then. I believe we
have agreed to meet face-to-face this evening. Yes, Charlie, I know
you have a dinner engagement. No, Charlie, I don't think it would
be a good idea for you to miss this meeting. Fine, Charlie, we will
begin without you. Thank you very much everyone. I shall see you
at seven, and imagine I will have much to report. Goodbye.'

Turning to Gabrielle, Olivia rolled her eyes. 'Poor Charlie is
simply at sixes and sevens over this. Well, *of course* we all know
crime *is* rare in the corporate world; still, when it happens, one
would think that a grown adult – good gracious! the retired
chairman of a *very* large bank – would do more than dither, dither,
dither!' Olivia smiled and touched her chest. 'Dear me, but I find
this all *quite* exciting. It makes me feel like one of those
intimidatingly capable detective-story women. You may call me

Cordelia or VJ or something like that. Now I shall call our accountants. One look at this situation and they'll notify the police. I imagine Denise will be in handcuffs by mid-afternoon.'

Gabrielle, pacing the length of a priceless bokhara, shot her a glare. 'I say we go beat the truth out of her with a rubber truncheon.'

'Hardly,' Olivia sniffed. 'I've a young district attorney friend. His ambitions are *much* greater than his campaign chest. He and I talked while you were in the loo, and I expect he'll have little trouble finding evidence to exonerate Jack in Denise's apartment.'

'What if she's destroyed the evidence, Livy?'

'Then he will offer her a plea bargain – confess to framing Jack, and the charges will be reduced. But I doubt if things will reach that pass. My *very* ambitious young district attorney will be publicizing this story to the hilt. He's promised to assert for the cameras that Denise is being investigated not only for embezzlement, but also on suspicion of being behind the narcotics charges against Jack. Once CNN airs *that* news, the Singapore Government will back down very quickly. And, given our company's grotesquely inflated PAC fund contributions to those useless people in Washington, Scott will see to it that more than one senatorial letter of outrage is faxed to Singapore. Before this day is out, Denise will be in jail, and the Singaporeans will put Jack on the next plane home.'

'What about that weasel Joel? He's up to his neck in her swindle.'

'I doubt that *very* much. True, Denise must have used his executive-level computer access to tamper with that database. But there's no evidence Joel himself *gave* her that access. Quite the contrary, I imagine she filched his password. Understand, my dear, Joel Greenberg has much bigger fish to fry than what is, in the final analysis, a rather minor fraud. His compensation – base, bonus, and options – is well into the seven figures. Moreover, the profits he would enjoy from selling off LBTech dwarf any amount Denise might plunder. It wouldn't be worth his time. So, no, Joel is not involved – if he was, he would have erased *both* the payables *and* the human resources databases.'

'That's it? Sorry, Joel, your girlfriend is an embezzler. See you in the office Monday?'

'Oh *no*, my dear. Last night I promised that Joel would get his comeuppance, and he will. Word will get out that he was carrying on an affair with a thief, of that I am certain. As I am certain that whoever breaks this front page-news will reveal that Joel's misbehaviour scared away a very attractive acquisition offer.'

'Oh,' said Gabrielle weakly. 'You mean me.'

'You *are* a reporter, dear. This *is* news. And once you print it, Joel *will* resign. The Board will see to it that he has no choice. Then – afterwards – well, I imagine Joel Greenberg will never hold another executive job as long as he lives. However, that's by the by. Right now, I must call our accountants and get the ball rolling. The sooner this business becomes public, the sooner the Singaporeans will send Jack home.'

Gabrielle's voice dropped to a whisper. 'They have to catch him first.'

Olivia burst into laughter. No lady-like titters for her, she had a deep booming laugh that filled the living room. 'Well, there is that, isn't there. He really has been *astoundingly* foxy, hasn't he. "They seek him here, they seek him there . . ." the Scarlet Pimpernel of Singapore. I'm utterly *delighted* to find he has such resourcefulness in him. Although, I suppose, it *may* just be luck.'

Gabrielle's throat caught. 'Luck,' she whispered. 'Dumb luck and nothing but. I know him, Livy, and I know that's all it is. Jack's got a lot of good stuff in him. But none of it has anything to do with heroism.'

'He may surprise you.'

'I'd like that, Livy. I'd like it very much.'

Olivia turned to lift the phone. All in all, it had been a gratifying morning. Joel was soon to be disgraced. The resulting scandal meant LBTech almost certainly would not be sold off to the highest bidder. Young Jack Taft would come home safe and sound. And best of all, quite really the nicest thing, it seemed that Gabrielle at last had admitted to herself how she felt about the boy.

Only one thing troubled Olivia, a small nagging itch of a problem, annoying only in that it seemed to be a loose thread – young Jack had told Gabrielle she should look into 'customs scams' – the implication being that he thought one was afoot at LBTech. But while Denise's deceit might be called any number of things, it could *not* be called a customs scam. It was a simple sales commission swindle, not excise avoidance, diversion, grey market goods, or any other import–export fraud. And that was peculiar because Jack was a *very* precise boy who always used the correct terminology.

Well, perhaps he misspoke. Or perhaps Gabrielle misheard. In any event, it's quite unimportant. So thinking, she picked up the phone and dialled LBTech's auditors.

– 4 –

Note: Special Definition. For purposes of this subparagraph, second and third generation image intensifier tubes are defined as having: A peak response within the 0.4 to 1.05 micron wavelength range and incorporating a microchannel plate for electron image amplification having a hole pitch (center-to-center spacing) of less than 25 microns . . .

Denise closed her eyes. She'd been reading this awful stuff all afternoon. It was giving her a headache. And she was only fifty-three pages into it – eighty more to go. The Federal Register. Rules of the Bureau of Politico-Military Affairs. Revisions to ITAR, the International Traffic in Arms Regulations.

Borrrrr-ing.

Still, she had to work her way through the tedious thing, didn't she? It listed all the technology that Poh was so eager to get his hands on. Besides, the sneaky little Chinaman had already tried to slide an order by her without paying a special premium – oh no, his dopey e-mail message whined, these components aren't on the restricted list, not at all, they're merely standard parts and I shouldn't have to . . .

Bullshit. They were too on the list, although it had taken for ever to find them.

After she'd given him a piece of her mind, Poh promised he'd never try to fool her again.

And if you believe that one, little girl . . .

And so she worked through the regulations, line by dreary line, a yellow highlighter in her hand.

A lot of it was irrelevant – hi-tech materials, chemicals with too-long names, bullets and bombs, surface-to-air missiles, the list went on for ever. She waded onward, looking for the good stuff, the arcane electronics parts and assemblies that the Department of Defense did its very damnedest to keep out of North Korea, China, Pakistan . . . the stuff that Poh Kay Siong wanted most.

And would continue to get if, but only if, he took care of Taft *tout* fucking *suite!*

Damned little Chinaman! She'd warned him about Jack's impending trip to Singapore only hours after Joel, post-coitally talkative and eager for Denise to strut her stuff in front of the Board, had spilled the beans. Poh had ample time to prepare. There was no excuse for his fucking up so simple a job, no excuse in the world. *Jesus, Taft is a wimp and a wuss and how the hell has he managed* . . .

The intercom's buzzer sounded. Denise liked the sound of it. Logistics directors didn't get intercoms on the desks of their shabby little offices. Logistics vice-presidents did.

Of course, Taft's office was in need of serious work – better furniture, new carpet, get those insipid pictures of ocean-going freighters and loading cranes off the wall, replace the brass lamps with nice ceramics, then . . .

The buzzer sounded again.

Irritated, she tapped the 'on' switch. 'What is it? I thought I said I wasn't to be disturbed.'

'Sorry, Ms Donald, but some men are here to see you.' Josephine. Taft's loyal little secretary. Denise had already called human resources, instructing them to find a replacement. 'Tell them I'm busy. Tell them to schedule an appointment if they want to talk to me.'

'Ms Donald, these men . . . well, I don't think they're the kind who need to make appointments.'

3
Singapore

– 1 –

Nightfall found Zaitun napping in his arms. The sunset chittering of birds did not disturb their sleep, nor, after full dark, the awakening cries of nocturnal creatures.

She was first to come from sleep. Kneading his shoulders until his eyes opened, she thought, as a woman will, that he was a sweet man and sufficiently wise not to take these past several hours more seriously than he should.

He awoke. They kissed, just affection, passion spent.

Then another meal of fruit, hushed conversation, the careful rehearsing of strategies, and much impolite laughter at the outrage they planned to cause.

Then it was time, and Zaitun was both sad and happy, and very soon now she could never go back to being the person she had been.

At 10 p.m., John turned the ignition switch in Chan's Range-Rover.

Smiling innocent as a Botticelli angel, Zaitun sat next to him. She was ready, perhaps even anxious, for the plan to begin. A Malay proverb came to her mind: *Kuman di seberang laut mata nampak, gajah di depan, mata tak nampak.* You can see insects across the sea, but you can't see the elephant in front of your own eyes.

That was Singapore. Critical and disdainful of the faults of every nation in the world, but utterly unable to admit its own.

Unless and until someone had the temerity to rub the nation's nose in what it really was.

Can I do this, she asked herself.

She knew she could. It would be risky and it would be improper and it would be wholly out of character for a good Singaporean girl. Even more so for a good Muslim woman.

So much the better. Ho sei liao – *It's settled.* I will *do it! I will!*

When it was over and done, she would have flouted every rule and broken every commandment. Every shackle she'd ever worn would be shattered. The landscape of her life would be forever changed, and she would have no regrets about that.

Who could ask for anything more?

She was going to poke her fingers straight into the eyes of not merely the authorities, but also every bigoted zealot who'd ever berated her. Among the ranks of the devout her name would become a synonym for unchaste brazenness. Scandal and trespass. Impious, infamous, shocking behaviour. An affront to both Church and state. Shame and disgrace and denunciation.

She was beside herself with joyful anticipation.

– 2 –

Ten-forty-three in the evening.

The big white clock on Chan's wall was his enemy now. With every three hundred and sixty-degree sweep of its second hand another minute disappeared. One less minute to find Taft. One minute closer to what promised to be his last day in the station house.

The Chief of Staff's secretary had already called. The conference (the word she used was 'meeting', but what she meant was 'hearing') was scheduled for 8 a.m. The usual flack-catchers from public affairs would be there together with a couple of senior officers from the Staff Inspectorate Department. And a deputy commissioner. A *deputy*. Make a note of that. Chan was such a hot potato that the Commissioner was sending a flunky rather than coming himself.

Bad karma.

More bad karma. A reporter had rung him up – one of the Aussies from a Sydney newspaper. The fact that the call came from a foreign journalist rather than a native one meant that the local press had been warned off. There would be an *official* story on the Taft affair. When there was an *official* story, no other version was allowed. Foreign papers contradicting the *official* story had their import quotas reduced. Outfits used to selling ten thousand copies in Singapore suddenly discovered they were only licensed for fifty. *Not that we censor the press in Singapore, naw, not us, this is strictly an import–export issue . . .*

The Aussie smelled a story big enough to risk government retaliation. That meant one big goddamned story. The kind that produces international headlines. The kind that the government *really* hated.

Word was getting out. Hell, word *was* out. An hour earlier he'd strolled downhill to grab a bite at the CID cafeteria. In the dingy dining room on Eu Tong Sen Street, he found that the Singapore Police Force had suddenly come to consist of three kinds of cops: one, a very small minority who came up to him, quickly whispered that they'd try to help if they could, then equally quickly scuttled off; two, a somewhat larger minority who smirked at him, then snickered something inaudible in their partners' ears; and three – the vast majority – fellow officers who refused to meet his eye, backed away when it seemed he might approach them, looked worried and nervous that he as in the same room as they.

Superintendent Chan Gin was going down. Nobody wanted to come along for the ride.

Ten-forty-eight. Damn, the clock was slow tonight.

He figured he had until midnight – maybe a little later – to find Taft. After that the news crews would be off duty, at home asleep, and wouldn't get to the scene fast enough. But if his plan was going to work, he had to have cameramen there. *One o'clock at the latest.*

It was a good plan, solid, well thought-through, and most assuredly noisy and messy and right smack dab in the public eye. There'd be no way it could be covered up. The government would have to grit its teeth and say, 'Well done, Superintendent Chan.' Oh sure, they'd know the story was fishy. But they'd go along with it. If Taft, the embarrassing bastard, wasn't around to mouth-off to the press, they really wouldn't care about the rest. Saving face was the only thing that counted.

Then Superintendent Chan Gin would be able to retire with dignity and (he admitted it now) depart from a nation which no longer had a place for people like him.

But only if someone spotted that evil sonofabitch Taft. Goddammit to hell, every uniform in Singapore was looking for the *orang putah* fucker, but no one had a clue as to where he was hiding. The stoolies and squeals were hunting for him too. True, three-quarters of them would call Poh Kay Siong ten seconds after they called Chan. That was only to be expected. But none of them, not a single one, would call Poh first. They'd been warned what Chan would do to them if they dared.

One call, Chan prayed. *Only one. Just tell me where he is. Let someone see him and pick up the phone. Come on, God, make it happen.*

As soon as he knew where his prey was, he'd be in action where he belonged. Everything was ready to go. Hal Leung had looted central stores of all the equipment they needed. The cars were in place, the weapons were loaded, and Chan himself was costumed for the event.

He was now wearing STAR BDUs – the midnight-blue battle dress uniform of Singapore's paramilitary Special Tactics and Rescue Squad. Over his blouse, he'd strapped a bulletproof Kelvar chest shield, and atop that a black leather assault vest. The vest's pockets bulged – two grenades and plenty of extra ammunition. The sheaths in his lightweight jungle boots held CIA-issue knives – polycarb fibre, nine-inch blades rimmed with surgical steel. For backup, he'd tucked into his right pocket a tilt-barrel .32 calibre Beretta Tomcat. Seven rounds, fifteen ounces, effective enough at close range, and tonight would be close-range work.

Close range . . . that's why the holster beneath his left arm held not his prized FBI-model Smith & Wesson Sigma, but rather a D-Max Sidewinder, a mammoth handgun, five pounds in weight, a foot and a quarter in length, all burnished steel but for its bulky Hogue Monogrips. No ordinary six-shooter, the D-Max revolver would fire either fat .45 calibre rounds or .410 scattershot. This latter load transformed the weapon into an astonishingly accurate handheld shotgun: twenty-one lead pellets out of twenty-two in the centre ring each and every time. Of course at any real distance, those pellets wouldn't kill an enemy, but, no question, they'd sure as shit spoil his day. Equally important, the big heavy thing boomed like a cannon, belched flame like a dragon, was simply the scariest handgun you could shoot. In Chan's experience, all he had to do was pull the trigger once, and the bad guys started begging to be thrown in a nice safe jail.

The door opened. It was Leung. He too was dressed in STAR blue, and carried his own munitions dump of equipment. Leung raised his eyebrow in an unspoken question. Chan shook his head. Leung slumped into the seat in front of Chan's desk. He had two cans of soda, a Coke and a Sprite. He offered Chan the Sprite. Chan, needing caffeine, took the Coca-Cola.

'How are your ribs, sir?'

'Not bad. I put on an orthopaedic corset this afternoon. Real tight. That and this . . .' Chan gestured at his martial clothing, '. . . keeps everything where it's supposed to be.'

'You'll take it easy though, won't you, sir?'

'Hell, no!'

Leung laughed. 'Why am I not surprised?'

Chan stood. 'Mind the phone for me, would you, Hal? I've got to hit the head.'

Leung looked perplexed. 'The head, sir?'

'I'm going to the bathroom, Hal. Be back in a minute.'

Two Land Forces officers were standing by the sink, chatting and washing their hands. One was a certain big smug Sikh. The other was a short, plump Malay. Mutt and Jeff. They turned quiet when Chan came in, stayed quiet until he reached the urinals. Then the big one, Mutt, smirked.

Chan glowered. 'You got something to say to me?'

The Sikh thought about it. On one hand, a half-dozen wise-cracks came to mind. On the other hand, Chan Gin – disgraced, dishonoured, and destined for a bad end – was still Chan Gin. 'Only to wish you luck, Superintendent. Only that.'

As Chan re-entered his office, Hal set the phone back in its cradle. He turned and beamed at the superintendent. 'What's up, Hal?'

'We don't have to worry about finding Taft any more.'

'Huh? Why?'

'He's just blown up the American Embassy.'

Chan looked at the clock. 10:57. 'Damn, I'm glad to hear that.'

– 3 –

10:53

A woman screamed in the night.

Her terror and despair rose above the wail of fire engines weeping through the streets. She was near, and the sound of her fear was coming closer.

Gurkha sergeant Prithvi Bahadur craned his head through the third-storey window, peering over High Street's bustling traffic, down the tree-shadowed length of Loke Yew Street. The woman's anguished cry came from that direction, somewhere around the corner, up Armenian Street before it intersected with Loke Yew.

A young constable turned to Bahadur. 'Sarge . . .?'

Bahadur waved him to silence. He put his binoculars to his eyes – good binoculars, Zeiss Night Owls. But the Loke Yew block was too dark. He could see little, could only catch the barest hint of motion, men moving in abandoned buildings along Armenian Street. Those men, like STAR sergeant Bahadur, were hiding in wait, rifles ready, in gutted buildings behind the American Embassy. Bahadur slipped the binoculars back into their case.

A shadow flitted down Armenian Street, and the shadow keened.

Bahadur threw his Austrian-made bolt-action 7.62 mm Steyr-Daimler SSG to his shoulder. The rifle stretched a hundred and fourteen centimetres, most of it barrel, the longest barrel you could get on a factory rifle, a length promising the exquisite accuracy which a police sniper requires of his tools. Gripping the stock and nestling the polymer butt against his shoulder, he peered through his Foxbat nightscope. Suddenly, everything was clear, sharp, no longer shadowed. The scope amplified light thirty thousand times, rendering the pitch-black street a baleful green, brighter than the brightest day.

The woman was half naked. More than half. Her legs were bare, no slacks, only panties which, illuminated by the nightscope, seemed to burn as molten steel. A loose cotton shirt – a man's shirt – hung from her torso. The shirt was torn, its buttons gone, and Bahadur could see her breasts, fine and young and firm, swaying as she fled.

She was at the corner of Loke Yew and Armenian, panting hard, sweat shining on her face. She hesitated, paused for less than a second, glanced behind her as if seeing some terrifying thing up Armenian Street. Bahadur's view was blocked by the buildings at the corner. The woman's was not. Whatever she saw made her scream again, this time louder and more terribly. She spun on to Loke Yew. Gleaming tears streaked her mud-stained cheeks. Her face was a mask of raw panic, blind fear at what pursued.

Bahadur hissed, 'It's the Samsudin girl, the one Taft kidnapped.' The constable looked through his own rifle scope. 'Jesus! She's beautiful!'

'That American bastard has molested her!'

She was running up Loke Yew now, straight towards Hill Street, straight into Bahadur's nightscope. The American Embassy was on her right. The Loke Yew block was short, and the girl was not far from bright lights and safety. She was, Bahadur allowed, breathtaking. Her legs were long, slender, stretching with the grace of a fleeing fawn's. He imagined the colour of her skin – corpse-glow green in the Foxbat's amplified light – it would be golden, as silken to the touch as the chocolate hair bouncing on the nape of her neck.

'Get down there!' Bahadur snapped. 'I'll cover you!'

'Yes, sir!'

The sergeant lifted his scope, drew a quick line across the empty buildings at the end of Loke Yew. Men were in motion. The other sniper teams stationed in those crumbling old row houses also were hurrying to the girl's aid. Bahadur turned to call the constable back. Too late. He'd already run down the stairs.

He looked at the woman again. She was past the embassy gate. A confused-looking American Marine guard took five steps out of his concrete-walled kiosk, stopped, and backpedalled, fumbling for the telephone.

She was coming into the halo of the streetlights now. Bahadur jerked his eye away from the nightscope. The amplified light was too bright, painful, nearly blinding.

He heard men calling. Leaning out of the window, he looked down. Not only was his own constable running to the Samsudin woman's assistance, but the backup sniper team, the one stationed on the second floor, was also on the streets. Bahadur cursed them for leaving their posts.

A fire engine raced north on Hill Street. Its lights coruscated across the American Embassy's monumentally ugly façade. The flashing colours – blue to red to white – washed over the running woman, who, suddenly out of the shadows and into the glare of one of Singapore's most heavily travelled arteries, did not slow her steps at all.

The two sniper teams stationed at the end of Loke Yew were sprinting up the centre of the empty, narrow street. Three more men, all like Bahadur in STAR midnight blue, were dashing towards them, towards the girl, from the Hill Street side. The woman herself ran shrieking into the rush of oncoming traffic.

A car, a dark green Toyota, slammed on its brakes. The taxicab behind it slammed into its rear bumper. Shattered glass glittered on the pavement. Another car swerved left to avoid the accident. A boy and a girl on a motor scooter tumbled over that car's hood, and slid bawling on to the street. A second fire engine barrelled up High Street, its driver weaving in and out of traffic, seeing too late the broken glass and stalled vehicles in front of him. The driver pulled left, pulled too hard; the cab jackknifed, the trailing ladder rig rolling on its side, sledding in a roostertail of sparks into, up, and over the central divider. Uniformed firemen somersaulted in the air, tumbling to the asphalt. And in the near distance the siren of a third fire engine rose.

Fire? Fires? Bahadur asked himself how many fire alarms had sounded in the past few minutes? Three or four. *Was something . . .?*

The Samsudin girl seemed oblivious to it all. She dodged and weaved among the squealing cars, quite as golden brown as he'd imagined, nearly naked, astonishingly lithe, and no longer screaming. Two of the three snipers from Bahadur's building were near her, near enough to be seen and near enough to be heard. She seemed not to notice them . . . no, say rather that she most definitely noticed them . . . and that she turned from them, turned to run in a different direction.

Sergeant Prithvi Bahadur swallowed hard. *Could it be . . .?*

He forced his eyes away from the anarchy of steaming, crumpled vehicles in front of the American Embassy, squinting hard down the narrow dark reaches of Loke Yew Street.

And there it was.

A dark blue Range-Rover Defender. White roof. Coloured flashers mounted across the top. A police vehicle. *The* police vehicle.

Taft.

The drug runner had left it squarely in front of the embassy's side entrance. No one had noticed. A splendidly near-nude woman, the ensuing chaos, the din of fire engines and percussion of collisions – all eyes had been turned elsewhere. With headlights dim, Taft had coasted down Armenian Street, turned on to Loke Yew, brazenly parked dead centre in what was, or was supposed to be, a perfectly laid sniper's trap.

Bahadur snapped his rifle up to his shoulder, peered hard through the nightscope. He pointed it first at the embassy's guard station. The guard was standing inside, shouting something out of the window. There was no hope of hearing it, not with a pandemonium of angry drivers, firemen and police officers in the centre of Hill Street.

The guard was facing away from Bahadur, looking down Loke Yew towards those soon-to-be-demolished buildings in which, only moments before, two STAR sniper teams had concealed themselves. The sergeant tilted the Steyr's barrel up and left. Then right. Then up and left again, weaving a marksman's web back and forth across the darkened street. Taft was there somewhere. Bahadur knew it.

And Bahadur was right.

He was at the very end of Loke Yew, his back flat against the crumbling brick buildings on Armenian Street. He stood clear and bright, all electric green in the nightscope's eerie luminosity.

Something fluttered to his feet, some sort of cloth, a piece of canvas. Taft had unwrapped the thing he had cradled in his arms.

Bahadur had seen that thing before, seen it on the police firing range, seen that madman Chan Gin demonstrate what a Sugg-50 was capable of doing.

Prithvi Bahadur thumbed his rifle safety to the off position.

Taft had the Sugg braced against the wall, pointed down the street. *At what? What's he aiming at?* Bahadur asked himself as he tugged back and slapped home the bolt of an impeccably engineered rifle, chambering a 7.62 mm NATO round. The target, no longer a man but merely a bullseye, was seventy metres away. The sergeant turned a knurl, raising the horizontal axis of the Foxbat's crosshairs by a single click, centring them steady and level on Taft's chest. He curled his finger around the trigger, simultaneously letting his half-breath whisper out. He began to squeeze, and as he did, he was still wondering what it was, what it could possibly be, that the American gangster was aiming at on a dark and deserted street.

The pain was horrible, instantaneous, beyond comprehension. It was as though a glowing needle had been punched into his skull. All at once Sergeant Prithvi Bahadur was blind. Light brighter than the sun at noon, brighter than the arc of a welding torch seen at eyelash length, brighter than any light Bahadur had ever seen seared into his right eye. Amplified thirty thousand times over by a Foxbat nightscope, what blinded Bahadur was not merely the volcanic glare of an exploding fireball, but the very heart and furnace of hell itself.

The sergeant screamed with shock, and was unconscious before smouldering metal began to fall from the sky.

– 4 –

Monroe Briggs had enjoyed his twenty years of wholly peaceful military service.

When he took the oath, he was twenty-two years of age, freshly graduated from ROTC. The Vietnam War had ended two years earlier. Briggs had missed it. So too did he miss the handful of brushfire wars (Panama, Grenada, those sorts of things) to which his impatient nation dispatched troops. By the time Iraq and Saddam Hussein came along, he was a full bird colonel, too close to retirement to be sent to the front – a career soldier who had never heard a shot fired in anger.

Like his father and his grandfather before him, Briggs had been a provost marshal, a military policeman dealing with the ordinary crimes of ordinary men, no less ordinary for being in uniform – drunken brawls for the most part, but also petty thievery, occasional rape, infrequent murder, drugs too often. The daily incident report at an MP station looks the same as the blotter in any police station in any city in the world. The only difference – military justice being close kin to the Singaporean kind – was the conviction rate.

Now supplementing his retirement pay – little more than $30,000 a year – with the more generous wages of an ambassadorial security chief, the former colonel enjoyed a pleasant succession of uneventful days. No different from any other State Department job, Briggs spent most of his time shuffling paper – forms to bail boozy merchant seamen out of the tank; forms to verify the identities of embarrassed tourists who'd lost their passports; forms to fund at taxpayer expense food, lodging, and tickets home for the clowns who made it as far as Singapore before their money ran out; and – more painfully – forms to secure medical and psychiatric treatment for such fools as, questing for elusive enlightenment, took up residence at hellhole ashrams and monasteries in India, Sri Lanka and Thailand, and who, six or eight months later, were evacuated riddled and raving with disease. The women were the saddest cases; mountebank monks and charlatan gurus used them up, hollowed them out, left them bewildered, wounded, deranged.

But for the infrequent arrangement of security (female bodyguards preferred) on behalf of boondoggling congressmen, Briggs had little opportunity to use his police experience. After all, his duty station was Singapore, a country whose docile citizens would never dare mass before the American Embassy to picket, protest, or riot. No one, not even outside terrorists, loved death so much as to try. There was *never* any trouble in Singapore.

Until now.

Driving down to the central city from his suburban townhouse, Briggs used his cellular telephone – speaking to the police, the press, and one very frightened Marine Corps guard – to piece together the story. The man who broke into the embassy was John Gregory Taft. No question about that. The police were supposed to be on the lookout for him, had snipers stationed in the gutted buildings on Armenian Street behind the embassy and across the road on Hill. They should have got their man before he was within fifty yards of the embassy. Situation normal, all fucked up: they hadn't.

Apparently a young woman had suddenly materialized naked and running for her life. The snipers had abandoned their watch to give aid. No one noticed Taft suddenly appearing at the embassy gate.

Filthy and unshaven, the drug smuggler had demanded entrance. The Marine guard, safe behind a high fence and a secure gate, had replied – as he was expected to do to obstreperous nighttime visitors – that the embassy's hours were eight-thirty to five-fifteen, weekdays only. 'This is an emergency,' Taft had said. 'It always is,' the Marine had jeered.

'I'm an American citizen.'

'That's what they all say, buddy.'

'I have to see the ambassador.'

'In your dreams.'

'Jesus, do I look like the Islamic Jihad or something?'

'Nah, you just look like another over-the-hill hippy who's run out of money.'

Taft had spun on his heel and walked to the rear of the Range-Rover he'd parked on Loke Yew Street. The Marine shouted after him: 'Move the car, Mac. You're blocking the gate.'

'Not for long.'

Briggs did not know precisely what weapon it was that Taft had secreted in the Range-Rover. However, he knew that the damned thing must have been God Almighty powerful. Whatever it was, Taft only had to shoot it once found. Right into the Range-Rover's propane fuel tank.

By all reports, it made a hell of a bang.

Moments later, Taft was inside the embassy.

Now there was a hostage situation.

Colonel Monroe Briggs (US Army-retired) was afraid that, after all these years, he was finally going to hear a shot fired in anger.

A military career does not foster a keenly developed appreciation of architectural aesthetics. Nonetheless, Briggs judged the American Embassy to be simply the most hideous building on earth. It appeared to be a four-storey copy of The Tombs, New York's notorious city jail. Grimly foreboding of aspect, not merely its windows but the very walls of the awful thing were barred. An ungainly array of antennas sprouted from the roof. The outer perimeter was guarded by a ten-foot-tall spiked-steel fence. Taken in total, the building's grotesquely penal appearance seemed designed to communicate unrelenting hostility, the xenophobic sentiments of an increasingly immigration-averse nation warning would-be visitors of the fate in store for them should they have the grave misfortune to have their visa applications approved.

No huddled masses yearning to be free need apply.

Not that any huddled masses would be applying for a while. Taft's explosion had seen to that. The place was a wreck – the gate blown away, the fence mowed down, glass shattered out of the windows, guard shack topsy-turvy, and a sizable chunk of concrete wall on the north side crumbled to dust, leaving nothing but exposed beams and bent re-bar behind.

Briggs sighed. *And I always thought nothing could make the damn place look worse.*

The Singapore police escorted him through the rubble. Not far away a news crew aimed lights and camera at the security chief. Briggs squared his jaw, looked resolute, strode forward decisively. The footage would air in the US; he wanted his masters at the State Department to be comforted when they watched it. Lean and martial, Monroe Briggs looked precisely the right man for the job.

Which, in point of fact, he was.

The interior of the embassy was surprisingly unscathed – and, as ever, an embarrassment to behold. Its blue walls were scuffed and dirty, its matching blue carpet faded with age, its moulded blue plastic chairs caked with the grime of decades. Worse, all around, on every battered metal desk sat the sort of computer terminals that American business had junked back in the days when Briggs was still a buck lieutenant. Those antiquities predated the personal computer revolution, harked back to the era when word processors came not with hard disks, not with floppy disks, but with magnetic tape cartridges. Their tiny screens were dimly lit with amber characters, their cracked plastic cases ivory with age. *Were things*, Briggs always asked himself, *so bad, was America so impoverished, that the only computers its diplomatic corps could afford were built before the oldest Spice Girl was born, and manufactured by companies that had been bankrupt since the Carter administration?* Apparently the answer was yes. In architecture, furniture, and technology, the ambassadorial face America put to the world was one that would shame even so impoverished a Third World nation as Bangladesh.

Briggs marched briskly down a hall, wheeled right, and stopped outside the deputy consul's office. He took a deep breath, forced an expression of relieved concern on to his face, and stepped in.

Taft was sitting there, behind the deputy's desk. He had a diet Pepsi in one hand and a black automatic in the other. *Glock Model 27*, Briggs thought. *Nine in the magazine, one in the chamber, enough to go around.*

The Marine Corps guard was sitting glumly on the floor, the telephone he used to call Briggs by his side. He did not meet Briggs's disapproving stare. Next to the guard a signals clerk and three relaxed-looking FAA inspectors played poker. Singapore headquartered the Federal Aviation Administration's South Asian operations; its twenty-four-hour-a-day staff was responsible for making sure such dubious airlines as operated in the region did not depart for the US without meeting minimal safety standards. The FAA inspectors did not seem frightened by Taft – but then after the things they had seen in the sky, it would take more than an armed maniac to scare them.

Taft, as might be expected, looked even more at ease than his hostages. Of course, given what the man was, cold-blooded calm was only to be expected. Briggs smiled widely. 'Mr Taft.' He beamed. 'Thank God you've made it here safely!'

Taft looked confused. It was precisely the reaction Briggs had hoped for. Superintendent Chan Gin of the Singaporean police had filled him in on Taft's lame alibi. Now he intended to play it for all its worth. 'I'm Monroe Briggs from the State Department. But everyone calls me Joe.' Bullshit. Everyone called him *sir*. 'I can't say how happy I am to see you here.'

Blinking as though he didn't quite understand Briggs's *bonhomie*, Taft wiped a grubby hand across a filthy cheek. Briggs noticed for the first time what a foul-looking piece of work the fugitive was. Flecks of dirt and vegetation clotted his hair. His clothes were tatters, held together more by dried mud than anything else.

'Mr Taft, I want you to know that the US Government isn't going to take this lying down. The Secretary of State himself is drafting a letter of protest about how you've been treated. It will be worded in the strongest imaginable terms.'

Taft's eyes flicked left and right. 'Uh . . .' he grunted.

'Pisspot Oriental quote-democracies-unquote simply don't get to arrest American citizens on trumped-up charges. The case against you is full of holes. It wouldn't hold water in the United States, and we intend to see to it that it doesn't hold water here.'

Somewhere beneath grimy and unshaven cheeks, white teeth showed. Taft seemed to be smiling, although uncertainly.

'Well, you're safe now, Mr Taft. This is the American Embassy, US territory. They can't get you here. If they tried, it would be an act of war.'

Taft finally managed to get a coherent sentence out. 'The guy who's after me, the cop, he's a crazy man.'

Briggs nodded enthusiastically. 'Oh yes, we know about Superintendent Chan, Mr Taft. All about him. He should be kept in a cage. But don't worry, as I said, you're safe now. You're under the sovereign protection of the United States of America. The stars and stripes still mean something. Especially to flyspeck countries like this one.'

Taft's shoulders slumped as if a great burden had been lifted from his back. Briggs was almost beside himself with delight. It was working! Just like they'd taught him in the terrorist negotiation courses he'd taken, Taft was actually buying his act. Briggs gave the drug smuggler another nudge. 'The ambassador will be here shortly. He's bringing his personal attorney to see to the situation. Oh, and there's a reporter from the *New York Times* on the way. He's very anxious to interview you.'

'The *Times*?'

'You're a *cause célèbre*, Mr Taft. Quite frankly, the New York papers have been waiting for an opportunity to nail the Singapore Government. Now you've given it to them. Of course, we can postpone the interview if you're too tired to talk. But I think it is in your best interest not to. The more public pressure we put on these fascist thugs, the better it will be for all of us.'

Taft's dumbass smile broadened. The ignorant idiot actually believed Briggs's professionally scripted line of crap. 'You're saying I don't need this any more?' Taft held up his pistol. *Oh please, God*, Briggs thought, *please, please, please.*

'Keep it if it makes you feel safer.'

'Uh . . . Mr Briggs . . . er, Joe . . . I don't know much about these things.'

'Of course you don't.'

'I might hurt somebody . . .'

Christ, what an actor! The man sounded exactly like you'd expect an innocent victim to sound. 'Just push that thumb switch there on the side, it's the safety . . .'

Taft pushed the wrong button. The pistol ejected its magazine into his lap. 'Oops,' Taft muttered, looking mighty chagrined. Briggs thought it the finest performance he'd ever witnessed. 'Mr Taft, from what I've heard, you've had a pretty rough time. There's a shower in the ambassador's office. Probably a razor too. And maybe we can rustle you up a change of clothing. Would you like that?'

For a moment Briggs worried that he'd gone a little too fast, pushed a little too hard. But Taft sighed, 'Yeah,' and Briggs knew he had his man.

He turned to the guard. 'You, soldier, run down to the locker room and find a shirt and slacks that will fit Mr Taft.' The guard wore an expression of dismayed disbelief. 'Something about your size. If it fits you, it will fit Mr Taft. If you've got some civvies downstairs, just bring them up. Don't worry, we'll reimburse you.'

Standing, the guard shook his head in amazement. Briggs held his breath. Taft did nothing, barely even looked at the Marine. *Dear God, I don't believe it! This is actually working!* All those training programmes were paying off.

'Hey, John.' One of the FAA men spoke up. Taft turned to him. 'Okay if we leave now?'

'Oh sure. Sorry for keeping you guys.'

'No problem. And hey, man, good luck.'

'Thanks. Same to you.'

All at once, the hostages were gone. Monroe Briggs, Colonel US Army-retired, was alone with John Gregory Taft. He was beside himself with delight.

Shaved, showered, wearing faded blue jeans and a rugby shirt, Taft appeared to be a different person: just a normal, clean-cut American businessman – although a very, very tired one. For a moment Briggs felt a little sorry for him. But not much.

After Taft had tidied himself up, Briggs had steered him down to a windowless room on the embassy's first floor. Taft, keeping up his innocent act, hadn't even commented when the security officer pocketed his pilfered Glock 27.

Now Briggs and his unwitting victim were seated in matching blue plastic chairs across from one another, a cheap laminated desk separating them. Taft had his back to the wall. The fact that there was no escape didn't seem to bother him. 'This', he asked, 'is the ahh . . . interview room?' To his credit, Taft seemed perturbed by the utter shabbiness of his nation's embassy. 'I mean you actually let foreigners see this . . . ah . . . it looks like you furnished it out of the Goodwill Industries store.'

''Fraid so, John.' They were on a first-name basis now.

Taft pursed his lips. 'That stinks.'

Briggs nodded. He didn't like agreeing with a drug dealer, but the man was right.

'Anyway, Joe, you said you had some questions for me.'

Briggs consulted his watch. Eleven-fifty-eight. Everything had been in place since eleven-forty-five. There was no need to continue the charade. 'Actually,' Briggs smiled, 'actually there's something I want to tell you first.' Taft leaned forward, eager to listen. 'What I want to tell you is this. There's a myth that almost all Americans believe. None of us in the State Department knows how it started. And we do our level best to tell people the truth. But somehow the message never gets through. Everyone who comes into this embassy – everyone who comes into every American Embassy in the world – keeps on believing it, even though it's one hundred per cent dead wrong.'

Taft furrowed his brows.

'The myth, John, is this: the myth is that American embassies are American territory. That's total bullshit. Neither our embassies nor anyone else's are sovereign territory. Hell, man, we rent this building, same as we rent 'em most everywhere else. This particular one belongs to the government of Singapore. If they wanted to come in here without knocking, they'd have every right in the world. It might cause a diplomatic incident if they did, but nonetheless it would be their right.'

Taft looked bewildered. Briggs pressed on, eager to finish his fun before Taft tried something: 'But if they knock, or if we give them permission, then there's no trouble at all. And, of course, as diplomats, we try to go out of our way to cooperate with the host country.' Briggs swivelled in his chair, reaching out and seizing the doorknob. He turned it, pulled, and said, 'You can come in now, Superintendent.'

Chan Gin's muscular frame filled the doorway. Briggs, in his own day a low-key sort of policeman, didn't care much for the unequivocal blood-lust on the superintendent's face. Nonetheless, he felt happy, as all good soldiers feel happy, when they've made it through another day without hearing a shot fired in anger.

– 5 –

You're a hopeless case, son. No I'm not. Just look at you; everything you've done has only made your situation worse. I haven't done anything a real man wouldn't do. You think you're a real man? No, I only think I'm me. What's that wisenheimer crack supposed to mean? It means I'm not you. So what? So I've made something of my life. Sure you have; you've made yourself gallows bait.

'Excuse me, Superintendent. Shouldn't you cuff the prisoner?'

'Uh uh, Mr Briggs. There are cameras outside. We want the world to see we're treating Mr Taft gentle as a baby.'

'What if he tries something?'

'Take a guess.'

Okay, Dad, here's my guess; my guess is that you're afraid of things, afraid of everything; you've spent your whole life afraid of the world and trying to keep out of its way. The world's a dangerous place, Son, and there's plenty to be afraid of; better safe than sorry is the most important lesson there is.

'Good thing your country's new embassy is nearly finished.'

'It's even uglier than this one, Superintendent.'

'That sucks.'

'Tell me about it.'

I'll tell you about it, Dad, I'll tell you. You were born with a part missing, but I wasn't. When you saw that, you hated it. Oh Dad, you had the smarts. Maybe you even had the hunger. But what you didn't have was the will. You had talent, but you never did anything with it. You sat there gnawing on your guts, sick with envy at everybody who made something of himself. When I came along, you saw I was somebody who could make something of himself, have a position and responsibility, and the respect you never got because you never tried to earn it. You couldn't stand that, could you, Dad? Could you?

'Christ almighty, Superintendent! How many men have you got out there?'

'About fifty uniforms. Two dozen plainclothes men.'

'You really don't want this one to get away, do you?'

'It'll be Bosnia on a bad day if he even tries.'

Try? Try? Whenever I tried to use what I had, you stopped me. You said I didn't have what it takes, wasn't strong enough, smart enough, good enough. You said all I'd do is call attention to myself, make people think I was a show-off, make them want to take me down a peg. Remember when that kid beat me up and took away my lunch money? You said it was my fault for letting him know I had cash in my pocket. Jesus, Dad. Jesus!

'Are those television crews, Superintendent? They shouldn't be on embassy grounds.'

'They're here with my permission. Piece of advice, Mr Briggs: tug down your jacket from behind. Yeah, like that. It makes your shoulders look broader on camera.'

'Thanks.'

'The other trick is to twist the prisoner's arm up like this. See, it makes him put his head down, while you keep yours up.'

Keep your head down. No one likes a smarty pants. You're not better than anyone else. But the thing is, I am better than a whole heck of a lot of people. I've got some good stuff in me. I am a guy who can handle himself. I do have what it takes. I know that now, I know it after all these years. You're nothing, Jack, nothing – like father like son. As the twig is bent, so the tree inclines, what's bred to the bone . . .

'Okay, I'll handle it from here. And you, Taft, don't even think about smiling at the cameras.'

'Superintendent, on behalf of my government, I'd like to thank you for taking this man into custody. I certainly hope he gets what's coming to him.'

'Oh, he will. And sooner than he thinks.'

Blinding lights. The rising murmur of onlookers. Shouted questions from the press.

Shut up, Dad, just shut up. I will be with you always. The hell you will.

– 6 –

Zaitun wore loose fisherman's trousers, a floppy smock, and cheap sandals. She'd stuffed cotton balls in her cheeks, and tucked a small foam pillow under her waistband. Squinting, she walked with a distracted waddle, trying to look as much like a myopically pregnant Muslim matron as possible. Under the streetlights her hair, swept back and wet, shone greasy. To give the illusion of a skin condition, she had stippled her chin a half-dozen times with an eyebrow pencil.

She'd thought of the disguise herself, and was proud of it. It worked – the policemen holding back the crowds across from the American Embassy never even looked at her.

She'd bought the costume piecemeal in the Indian quarter, only a single subway stop from City Hall. As she left the quiet neighbourhood, she ignited two trash-can fires and set off four fire alarms. The streets in that part of town were narrow, and the fire department was not having an easy time.

Timing herself strictly to the clockwork agenda she and John had agreed on, she'd taken the MRT to Marina Centre, dropped burning matchbooks in litter cans located on the third and fourth floors of the indoor shopping mall, paused on her dash back to the subway to set off another fire alarm, and boarded – right on schedule – Singapore's indomitably punctual subway. She exited at City Hall station, where she ignited one more fire, and tripped one more alarm. Then she was ready to tear her clothes off.

She checked her watch. Perfect – she'd timed it to the very minute. If Allah smiled on Mr Taft, and Zaitun prayed He would, then a chain of minor fires and false alarms stretching from Bukit Timah to the central city would have so disrupted traffic that he could travel with impunity the back-street route she'd mapped out for him. The clamour of engines, the flashing of sirens, police rescue squads dispatched from stations all over the island . . . for a few brief minutes, everyone would be distracted and no one would be looking for a stolen police Range-Rover. John could drive the half-dozen or so kilometres to the American Embassy in complete safety.

But safety would end as he approached the place. Another distraction was needed.

Zaitun Binte Samsudin – daughter of Samsudin – stood in Fort Canning Park, up the hill behind the American Embassy. It was dark; the shadows beneath whispering fishtail palms were deep. As she slipped off her denims, the night air caressed her legs. She seized the tails of her white cotton shirt, jerking as hard as she could. Buttons popped, the shirt flew open. She shrugged it off, quickly unfastening her bra. She shivered – not with cold, for it was a clement tropical night, and her trembling was not fear or nervousness or conscience. Undressed but for panties, Zaitun shook with unanticipated pleasure, the thrill of the forbidden making her quiver with borderline erotic delight. Good Muslim girls, good and law-abiding Singaporeans, do not strip bare in the warm night air of public parks. But there is rapture in the illicit, and broken taboos are pleasurable things.

She bent at the waist, placed her long fingers around her ankles, slowly stroked up her leg, higher, belly and breasts, neck and hair. It was wonderful to touch herself, to know she was not seen but could be seen, and most wonderful of all to know that for just this merest moment she was free.

Zaitun had lived twenty-three years of unquestioning obedience to the laws of a strict society, a stricter religion. Nothing she had ever done brought her greater joy than preparing to violate every code of the society that made her who she was.

Nudity and shameless delight were not John's idea. He had merely suggested she smudge her shirt, undo a few buttons, and start screaming. She hadn't told him her real intentions. She didn't think he'd approve.

Nor would he approve of her later changing into the disguise she'd secreted at a construction site not far from the American Embassy. He had told her – ordered her in a stern tone of voice – to let the police take her, and to cry and wail that she was a helpless victim. She smiled, the Eastern woman's eternal deference to male command, and said of course she would.

But she wouldn't.

Now she waddled slowly back and forth, an anonymous member of the crowd milling on the sidewalk across from the embassy. She had her hands clasped over her belly, and kept puffing between her lips as if with an excess of unaccustomed exertion. '*Alamack!*' she exclaimed in a fine *ah huay*'s bumpkin's accent. 'Something's happened at the Americans', lah?' A well-dressed woman glanced at her. Zaitun could almost hear her think: *This one's missed the*

bus back to Lim Chu Kang – the boondocks. The woman
answered, 'It's that narcotics dealer, the one in the newspapers.
He's run amok.' She turned away, peering across at the brightly lit,
slightly smoking embassy façade. Zaitun harumphed, 'Well,
they've got him now, lah?'

'Oh look! Isn't that Chan Gin?' It was a squeal worthy of a
teenager spotting a rock star.

Zaitun focused on where the woman was pointing. A man in
midnight blue, shining leather, many straps and more weapons,
was climbing out of an unmarked Mitsubishi Lancer GLX – unmarked Singaporean police cars were a bit of a joke; not only were
they all Lancers, but they also all bore licence plates beginning with
the letters 'QX'.

Chan stood, turned away from the embassy, flashed a grin
towards the crowd, and flipped a toothpick between his lips. 'Some
man, lah?' said Zaitun. The woman sighed, 'Single, too.'

At the sight of Chan a handful of people, those who had pushed
their way to the front of the police line, tried to surge into the
street. With locked batons a row of helmeted officers pushed them
back. Men began to shout – cheers for Chan, curses for drug
traffickers, suggestions that Changi Prison be open to the public on
the day of Taft's execution.

Chan merely smiled and waved, then turned his back and began
walking slowly – a well-practised cowboy gait – through the
paramilitary STAR officers massed around the embassy.

Worried sweat beaded on Zaitun's forehead. They should not be
allowing Chan to enter the embassy. It was American territory,
wasn't it? Police weren't permitted inside. But if that was so, then
why was the legendary superintendent strutting his bullyboy way
through the front door?

It was not supposed to happen this way. John was supposed to
be safe in his own country's embassy. The diplomats there were
supposed to listen to his story, put him in touch with his friends
and his attorney in the US, keep him out of Chan Gin's hands until
the American police could find proof that would clear him.

'This one, they should give him the cane before they hang him.
And after they cut him down, lah?' The woman's eyes were hot;

she patronized Zaitun by appending a low-class 'lah' to her question. Zaitun wanted to slap her.

A bank of aluminium floodlights snapped on. The embassy's ruined façade turned stark white, bright as day. Two television news photographers, heavy Sony video cameras resting on their shoulders, climbed to the top of a van. Another cameraman, this one with a woman commentator in tow, took up position – the woman standing so that the smouldering embassy entrance could be seen behind her, the cameraman slightly crouched so that his lens was level with her eyes. Newspaper photographers too were circling the embassy entrance, drawing closer, periodically test-firing their flashguns to make sure batteries were fully charged.

They were getting ready to take front-page photos.

Of what?

It was wrong. The press people were *inside* the police lines, not outside. The Singapore police never permitted that. Yet Zaitun could see that young officer, the corporal, the one who the night before had seemed to be Chan Gin's assistant, waving the reporters closer, ordering STAR commandos to step aside so that the cameramen had a clear field of view.

Zaitun was suddenly afraid. When a criminal was brought to justice, reporters were forced to stand a discreet distance from the arrest, behind police barriers, were refused permission to come close in, push microphones in the accused's face, shout questions, snap photographs. It simply wasn't done. Foreign journalists who tried lost their accreditation; Singaporean reporters lost their jobs.

But the television women, the newspapermen, were dead in the centre of things, milling like a herd of cattle ready to stampede, and this was very far from the proper order of things in decorous, well-behaved Singapore.

Chan Gin was planning something horrible. She knew it.

The young corporal, Chan's man, suddenly pushed his way through the STAR men and shouted a command to the officers supervising the police line. Those police, the ones keeping order on Hill Street and restraining the crowd from pressing close to the embassy, immediately stepped back. For a moment no one seemed to know what to do. Then the mob surged forward. Zaitun, shoved from behind, stumbled into the street.

Chan was going to kill him. That was the only explanation. He was creating a scene, allowing a riot. Mob violence, a beast not run loose in Singapore for twenty years, was what the government feared most, the one and only permissible reason for police to use their truncheons, their tear gas, their guns. In the chaos and confusion, it would look like John was escaping. Chan would have the excuse he needed.

The crowd flowed into the middle of Hill Street. Ordinary men and women, submissive Singaporeans, shrieked and ran and shouldered their neighbours aside. Some screamed for the pure pleasure of screaming, others swore and cried for hanging. The STAR officers, eyes invisible behind visored helmets, stood aside.

Just as Chan wanted, the news team would record it on videotape, and the tape would show a crowd of onlookers raging out of control, a riot in the making, anarchy in the streets. And a prisoner who might be trying to flee. And Chan Chin stopping him with a single shot.

There was nothing Zaitun could do to prevent it.

The pillow came loose from beneath her waistband. She pulled her trousers' drawstring tight. No longer moving of her own volition, she could turn neither left nor right, but was borne along by the press of raging citizens, scenting blood and hoping to be close to the kill.

These things had happened in the old days, or so they said. Just as they said Chan Gin was usually at the heart of them. He had a way with the press; when he was bringing down a wrongdoer, he liked to have them near.

Traffic had been cleared from the street. Officers stood both north where Stamford Road crossed Hill, and south at the Coleman Street intersection. The lights atop two dozen police vehicles – cars and vans and trucks – strobed from white to red to blue. Another bank of camera lights flashed on. Zaitun was at the kerb, directly outside the American Embassy, somehow pushed by the crowd to its very front.

Three forms appeared in the shadowed embassy door. Floodlights spun in their mounts, electric white focused on Chan Gin, John Taft, and a tall square-jawed Westerner whom Zaitun had never seen before. The crowd howled at the sight of them. Chan was showing his carnivore's teeth. John was blinking, blinded in the light.

A handful of men, one in a suit, the others dressed more casually, were running ahead of the rest of the mob. Their voices were shrill, their words incoherent. Chan and John were five, now six, steps away from the embassy. The tall Westerner fell behind them. The running men tore into the mass of journalists surrounding the embassy, collided with them, tried to push by. An expensive Nikon camera shattered on the ground, and a stand of camera lights glowing with heat tumbled forward. The hot glass exploded, stinging the legs of those within its range. A woman – Zaitun knew her face from the evening news – lashed out with her microphone, clipping a man above the ear. The man thrust his arm out like a football player, driving it between her breasts and sending her backward. A red soft-drink can arced through the air, caramel-coloured soda splashing as it turned. It missed John's head, then bounced off the embassy wall.

The young corporal began yelling orders. All at once the STAR troopers began to move. Their batons were above their heads, their shields were locked before them, and they moved into the onrushing mob with ruthless precision.

The times that everyone tried to forget, the history they *wanted* you to forget, returned to the streets of Singapore. Blood and screams and the rapture of unthinking violence and all of it came back as if it had never been gone, but was always there, hidden from sight beneath the skin, repressed but not extinguished because even the most brutal urges are, for all their bestiality, no less a human emotion than any other.

Chan pushed John towards the unmarked Lancer in which he'd arrived. Zaitun could see the hungry expression on the super-intendent's face, knew that he was ready to do what he'd planned. She screamed. Her voice was drowned by the roaring of the mob, the mechanical tread of marching STAR commandos.

A dozen men, mad with the madness of crowds and exalted by

the delirium of riot rocked a news van forward, once, twice, three times and over on its side. Two cameramen jumped from the top, came down on the shields of marching STAR officers.

Curses of hate. Cries of pain. The howls of a hunting pack hungry to devour. Any second now guns would be drawn and Chan would have what he wanted.

John was bent low, the Lancer's door was right in front of him. Chan stumbled back. It was false, false. Zaitun saw it clearly. Nothing touched him. John had not so much as moved his arms, not even gestured at the superintendent.

Chan pretended to trip, reel from a blow, spin away from John. John was sliding forward, off balance, an uncertain expression on his face. The gun in Chan's hand was bright, large, steady. John's back was turned, his head was halfway into the Lancer. Chan brought the gun down, his left eye was closed, his right was sighting along the barrel. Two STAR men wheeled out of the line, dropped their shields, pumped their legs, racing towards John, Chan, the Lancer.

Not human, only animal, the swirling crowd wailed with a single voice, and this too was freedom.

It was all so slow, even Zaitun's mounting screams seemed stretched beyond the limits of experiential time into some realm where the clock was clogged with mud, and each tick of the second hand took an hour to complete its minuscule movement.

John was nearly in the Lancer, hands on the steering wheel and pulling himself into the driver's seat. Something showed on his face, hope perhaps, but it was a lying hope, and Chan's thumb moved the hammer back and the pistol was firm in his grip. Zaitun was five metres away from him, too far, she could not reach him, and he pulled the trigger.

But his feet were out from under him, had slipped without her seeing it, and he was falling backward to the ground. His bullet went higher and higher into the night.

John was turning the ignition key, throwing all his weight on the accelerator pedal, a sour smoke of burning rubber spewing from the Lancer's rear wheels. The car fishtailed, rear end thudding into one of the STAR policemen. He somersaulted back. The other tried to draw aim on the car. The mob flowed around it, blocked his sight. One rioter aimed a hard punch at the windscreen; his blow shattered the glass and with it his bones, and he squalled so loud that not even the roar of a hungry mob could drown him out. And John was gone into the night.

– 7 –

'Did it work, sir?' Hal Leung whispered, glancing over his shoulder to make sure no one was close enough to hear.

Chan grimaced as he tightened his corset. The force of his carefully feigned fall had jarred the thing loose. And his ribs hurt like hell. 'Yeah, Hal, it worked.'

'Now what?'

'Now I climb in my car and you climb in yours. I turn on the transponder and Mr Taft becomes a phosphor blip on my tracking screen.'

'He won't knock the tracer off, will he?'

'Uh uh. It'd take a chisel to get it off his shoe heel.'

'He didn't notice?'

'Naw. I planted it while I was patting him down.'

Leung nodded warily. 'Then I'd better get to my car.'

'Yeah. But give me a couple of minutes once we're rolling. As soon as I'm sure I know where that bastard is running for, I'll start calling out coordinates to you on the radio.'

'You're certain Poh Kay Siong will be monitoring the broadcasts?'

'No question in my mind. No question what he'll do about Taft either.'

Zaitun studied the subway map. She counted two stops south on the blue line from City Hall – the W2 station, Outram Park. It was the closest station to the port.

That afternoon she and John had spoken at length about how he might escape from Singapore. There were only two choices: the embassy and the port.

The embassy had failed him. The Port of Singapore was his only hope. That had to be where he was headed.

She heard a train pulling into the platform. The port. Outram Park station.

Zaitun spat two cotton balls out of her mouth, and sprinted for the turnstiles.

Jack drove. He knew where he was going. The port. A ship. Escape from Singapore.

Then a long voyage home.

He'd make it. Back to New York. Back to Gabrielle.

Definitely back to Gabrielle.

There was something he wanted to discuss with her.

Six: A Rough Shoot

There are two modes of acquiring knowledge, namely by reasoning and experience. Reasoning draws a conclusion and makes us grant the conclusion, but does not make the conclusion certain, nor does it remove doubt so that the mind may rest on the intuition of truth, unless the mind discovers it by the path of experience.

Roger Bacon – *Opus Majus*

SOCRATES: Here, then, is a discovery of new evils, I said, against which the guardians will have to watch or they will creep into the city unobserved.
ADEIMANTUS: What evils?
SOCRATES: Wealth, I said, and poverty; the one is the parent of luxury and indolence, and the other of meanness and viciousness, and both of discontent . . . indeed, any city, however small, is in fact divided into two, one the city of the poor, the other of the rich; these are at war with one another . . .

Plato – The *Republic IV*

1
Singapore

– 1 –

He's not running scared. He'll never run scared again. True, there's a brightness to his cheeks and a big black ball in his stomach. But it's not fear. It's brute anger.

That sadistic bastard Chan set him up. No handcuffs. Keys in the ignition. The murderous sonofabitch pushing him into the front of the car, not its back. No question, Chan was planning on making it look like he was trying to escape. And Jack was certain what the madman had intended to do after that.

He'd choked, almost frozen, when he felt Chan reel away in a feigned stumble. For a moment, there was no hope, none at all. Then, miraculously, Chan slipped, giving Jack the opportunity to do what he had to do, the only reasonable and logical thing he *could* do: dive into the driver's seat, and get to hell out of Dodge.

Chan . . . *Jesus!* It wasn't like Jack hadn't saved his useless life out there in the swamp. Hell, he'd even gone so far as to summon medical help. But did Chan appreciate it? Of course not. The goddamned gun-crazed thug was still trying to kill him.

No good deed goes unpunished.

The treacherous swine had even planted a pistol on the front seat of the car. *Yes, your honour, the fugitive was armed. Sure, your honour, I was concerned that bystanders might be harmed. It's true, your honour, I had no choice . . .*

God *damn* him! If Jack ever saw that toothpick-chewing thug again – and he almost hoped he would – the gun would get put to good use. He'd blow that evil Nazi's heart out.

Steering the stolen Lancer with one hand, Jack hefted the pistol. It was one of the small ones, the same model as he'd left behind in the embassy, and it felt good in his hand. He curled his finger around the trigger. That felt even better. *Chan, you nincompoop, how could you be so dumb as to leave me a gun? Do you think I don't have the guts to use it? Boy, are you wrong. I'll use it all right, and I'll . . .*

Suddenly suspicious, he gave the pistol a questioning look. *If I were Chan, what would I do?*

Easy answer: I'd give me an unloaded gun.

He fumbled for the eject button, pressed it, and let the magazine pop into his lap.

Far from empty, it was full of shiny brass cartridges. Jack pursed his lips. *Now what the hell is that jerk up to . . .* There was something odd about the bullets. He looked again, feeling his face go crimson as he saw . . . *Bullets? No, not real bullets.* The cartridges were stubby, no bright slugs peeked out of the casings, they were tipped with red wax, the damn things were blanks.

Jack howled with rage.

Chan glanced down at the tracking monitor's screen. There was Taft, clear and crisp, a green phosphor blip speeding towards the East Coast Parkway's Dunearn on-ramp.

That Singapore was a small country made things easy for the law. You could load a map of the entire island on to a CD-ROM – not only the highways, streets and alleys, but everything, every building, and every shack, all of it, and it was all there on Chan's dashboard. Link the US Government's Global Positioning System to a few ground-based antennas, and you had a technology that could pinpoint a man's location to the nearest metre. Hell, if your quarry was in a high-rise, you could even get his altitude, figure out the floor he was on.

Chan looked forward to the time – it couldn't be too far – when every Singaporean would be required by law to wear a transponder like the one he'd planted on Taft. When that day came, and it couldn't come too soon, people like Poh Kay Siong were going to go out of business.

But then Poh was going out of business anyway. In fact, it would happen tonight.

Chan laughed out loud. Things were finally going his way.

*

Jack slammed on his brakes. Forgetting that the bloody Singaporeans drove on the left side of the road, he'd headed up the off-ramp.

Throwing the Lancer into reverse, he wobbled back to street level. The on-ramp was a hundred yards behind him. He tugged the steering wheel, ignoring the fact that he was heading the wrong way down a one-way street. A pick-up van flashed its lights, blew its horn, veered out of Jack's way. Jack extended his middle finger at the driver. He was in that sort of mood.

He pulled a tight turn at the ramp, cutting off a mid-range Nissan four-door. Braking hard, the Nissan fishtailed its rear end over a kerb and into a metal safety rail. *Bozo*, Jack sneered, *you should've bought the ABS option.*

The parkway was nearly empty – nothing but a few distant tail-lights disappearing in the misty dark. It was the graveyard shift, and all good citizens were home in bed. Jack pressed his foot hard against the accelerator. The Lancer responded nicely. *A hundred and forty kilometres per hour?* Jack asked himself. *That's how much? Eighty some miles an hour.* He floored it. One hundred and seventy kilometres per hour. *Much better!*

He smiled with grim pleasure. Chan had missed something – let an important piece of data slip by that pea-sized organ that passed for his inadequate brain. Sure, the big jackass had frisked Jack, patted his pockets, his legs and even, thorough man that he was, Jack's shoes and socks. But what Chan hadn't done was check the contents of Jack's pockets. He'd heard the rattling of coins and the crinkle of paper – Jack's small hoard of cash – and ignored it. The dumb jerk had forgotten what had happened the night before, hadn't thought about the fact that Jack had given him a gun loaded with a single bullet, and was too meat-headed to ask himself what Jack had done with the other cartridges that had been in that particular pistol's magazine.

Should have asked that question, buddy-boy.

Because if Chan had been smart enough to wonder what had happened to the ammunition, then he might have been clever enough to figure out the answer: Jack had dumped the bullets – nine of them – in his change pocket. Where they remained all day.

Where Jack, not really thinking about it, had pulled them out before showering at the embassy, and, together with his cash, casually put them into the blue jeans he'd been lent by a humiliated Marine Corps guard.

Now they were in Jack's lap. Very shortly the useless pistol Chan had planted on him would be useless no more.

Giving Taft a gun loaded with blanks and then sending him face-to-face with Poh and his hatchetmen was, Chan acknowledged, a pretty rotten trick. He was proud of it.

Chan snickered at the idea of Taft standing there, blazing away fruitlessly with blanks. The lousy bastard would distract Poh's boys long enough for him and Hal – Devil Cop and son – to get around behind the mob, get the drop on them. *Hands up, you're under arrest. The charges? Sure, Poh, I'll tell you the charges: armed assault; firearms possession; attempted homicide. With me and Hal as witnesses. Plus our friend and ally, Mr Taft. Try beating that rap, shithead.*

Heh! It couldn't fail.

Although Taft might get killed in the process.

Oh darn.

But probably not. Word on the street was that Poh promised a big reward to whoever took Taft – with an absolutely *enormous* bonus if the American was delivered alive. Chan figured that the warlord had lost so much face in Sungei Buloh that it would take more than Taft's death to restore his honour. Poh probably wanted to cart him off to a godown somewhere, have some quality time with the sonofabitch, make him scream for a few hours or days or weeks before slitting his throat. That was the kind of guy Poh was.

So no, Taft might be emptying his useless pistol at the mob, but the mob would not be emptying its more useful ones at him.

Maybe.

Or maybe something would go wrong. Poh's boys might get a little antsy when Taft started pulling the trigger. One or two of them might even be annoyed enough to shoot back. In which case . . .

Tough darts.

Whether Taft was dead or alive, Chan's ingenious cover-up scheme would work. In fact, it might work better if Taft wasn't around any more. Then Chan wouldn't have to threaten the cocksucker with weapons and kidnapping charges, wouldn't have to worry him about reneging on the deal as soon as he learned there was no way in hell those charges could be made to stick.

Plus he'd have Poh on a murder rap. Which was better than armed assault any day of the week.

Chan shrugged. Taft's fate was in the hands of the gods. As long as Poh went down and Taft didn't contradict Chan's well-rehearsed story, he just didn't give a fuck whether the miserable bastard lived or died.

Did he?

Shit, no. Hey, Taft, life is hard and then you die. Welcome to my world.

He glanced at the monitor. Taft was headed west on the parkway. That made no sense. To the west there was no escape from Singapore, nothing out there except a bunch of tourist parks, the open-air studio where the Hong Kongese made their silly action movies, and the end-of-the-road, no admittance, warning: high-voltage electrified fence, beware of patrol dogs, intruders will be shot, Singapore's national military reserve.

You couldn't get off this island if you ran to the west. East was the way to go. There were marinas out there, and little sampan ferries to Pulu Ubin and the outer islands. You could steal a boat, make it across the straits to Malaysia or down south to one of the islands off Sumatra. That's what a smart criminal would do. However, Taft, damn his eyes, wasn't a smart criminal. He wasn't a criminal at all. He was only an innocent civilian.

Chan's throat tightened, and a bitter look crossed his face.

Only an innocent civilian . . .

There it was. A high mesh fence. An endless expanse of docks receding into darkness. Ships, their lights a cloudy nebula behind a lowering fog. And cargo containers large as railroad boxcars, stacked one on the other, marching as far as the eye could see.

The Port of Singapore.

And, yes, just as Jack expected, the highway curved round it, arching up above street level, and higher than the fence line.

He could do it. He could do *anything*. He'd never doubt himself again.

Lower Delta Road
Sentosa Island
Cable Car Station

Jack braked hard at the exit, slewing across three lanes. He almost overshot the off-ramp, made it with smoking, squealing tyres. There were no other cars on the road, no one screeched and swerved to avoid the New York school of driving at its finest. Pity, he'd rather hoped someone would have noticed.

The Lancer swung around a curve and down to street level. Now all he had to do was ditch the damn car, sprint back to the highway, jog a few hundred yards and jump.

How far down? Fifteen feet? No, more like twenty. It wasn't going to feel good when he landed. There'd be some pain. He could live with that.

It was a good night, he thought, an *ideal* night for a fugitive on the run. The air was dense, denser with each passing moment; a low grey fog descended to a height of seven storeys, soon five storeys, then three. Another quarter of an hour and all would be obscure, cloaked in dirty cotton, and he, fleeing through shadows, would be all but invisible.

No one can see. No one can hear. He *would* make it. He *would* escape.

And then . . .

Then he'd find his way home, and settle up his bills. Settle them Chan Gin style.

He *would* do that too.

Zaitun leapt off the subway at the Outram Park MRT stop. A computer voice cautioned the handful of people in the station that the last train of the evening was departing; five minutes later the turnstiles would lock and the automatic entrance gates would close.

She dashed up the escalator and on to the streets of a familiar neighbourhood, the shops and stalls around Singapore's central train station. She'd ridden that train north across her narrow island, over the causeway, up into Malaysia. She had relatives there, close cousins who lived twenty kilometres east of Kuala Lumpur.

Maybe, she thought, *maybe there's some way I can take John there. We could stow away on a train, escape to my cousins' farm . . .*

Not likely. Security was tight. Border guards checked every car and every compartment. She and John would be arrested. And besides, there were no trains at this hour in the morning.

A ship was John's only hope. Zaitun intended to see that he made it on board one.

Turning south, the soles of her sneakers squeaking on slick pavement, she began to run. A heavy mist was sinking over the city, coating everything with a slippery veneer. If there were any cars on the parkway, they'd be going slow. That was good, she'd have time to crouch down, curl herself into a ball, avoid notice by making herself look like a bundle of illicit litter marring Singapore's otherwise spotless highways.

Breath coming easily, Zaitun raced with practised speed. She loved running, jogged mornings, her hair braided into a thick rope bouncing behind her; blue shorts, white T-shirt, training bra, legs stretching and muscles stretched, moving fast and faster, more running towards than running away, and always by herself and for herself, no duty to society implied. Exhilarated in her solitude, she ran alone.

In the distance, muffled by night and fog, she heard the squeal of automobile brakes, the sound of a car gunning its way around an off-ramp. Was it John exiting at Delta Road?

She picked up her pace.

The only lights – fuzzy in the moist distance – were over the port. That place was a twenty-four-hour-a-day operation. There would be workmen and vehicles and guard patrols.

John was going to need help getting past them.

Zaitun already knew how to create the necessary diversion.

Chan tapped the brakes, slowing and steering into the exit lane. The surveillance beacon showed Taft off the expressway, moving slow enough to be on foot. In this part of town, there were only two places he could be headed: the train station or the port. From the direction the bastard was taking, it looked like the port was his target. That made sense – the last train north had departed long ago. Besides, Taft's dossier said he was a logistics expert; he'd know everything there was to know about ships and shipping.

The port.

Chan's jaw tightened. Taft's shipping knowledge would give him an edge in the port.

He reached for his radio handset to tell Leung . . . to tell Poh Kay Siong.

His hand froze. Was he going to do this? Was he capable of putting an innocent man in harm's way?

Did he have a choice?

He wrapped his fingers around the handset. It was plastic, warm to the touch, not cold like a pistol aimed coldly at a moving target. A radio was a weakling's weapon, no honour in using it. But it was all he had, and could prove as lethal as any gun he'd ever fired.

Damnit all! I almost don't want to do this. What the fuck is the matter with me?

He snapped it out of its cradle. A red LED winked. Chan pressed the 'send' button.

And said nothing.

There's no other way. Poh comes after Taft. I grease Poh. A whole bunch of punks go to jail. I give Taft the credit. Hey, if he gets killed along the way, they'll erect a statue in his memory. Big brass plaque: 'Fallen Friend To Singapore Law Enforcement'. Then the birds crap on his head for a hundred years and I'll be a happy man.

'Hal, this is Chan Gin.'

The radio crackled. 'Yes, sir.' Chan could hear deep reluctance in his corporal's voice. Leung knew as well as he what the *real* outcome of Chan's plan would be. Sure, they could lie to each other – and to themselves – that Taft might make it through the night alive. But both knew the odds were against it. Poh's gunsels wouldn't know Taft was armed with an impotent weapon, firing blanks. As soon as he pulled the trigger, they'd shoot him dead. Pretending that they wouldn't was only a convenient fiction, salve you smeared on your conscience to make it sting a little less. And, yeah, what you'd done kept the government from frying your ass, and it took down a lot of bad guys whose bills were way overdue. But one of the guys who went down wasn't a bad guy. Which was why you lied to yourself same as you planned to lie to everyone else. *A brave man died today, a man who volunteered to disguise himself as a drug trafficker in order to help us bring to justice the* Tsung li *of our nation's last surviving* chiu chow *brotherhood. I, like every law-enforcement officer in Singapore, now honour the memory of* . . .

. . . *the memory of* . . .

. . . *an absolutely innocent schmuck who just happened to piss me off!*

Twenty car lengths back, Corporal Leung could only faintly make out Chan's brake lights through the fog. 'Sir? Are you there?'

The superintendent did not answer. The radio hissed, silent at the sender's end.

'Sir?'

Chan's tail-lights disappeared. The superintendent had exited at Lower Delta Road. Hal Leung, a law-abiding cop, flicked on his indicator.

'Sir, please answer.'

Not a sound. Chewing his lip with worry, Leung accelerated, taking the exit hard. He felt his rear wheels slip as he spun into the curve. Instinctively he steered into the slide. His car righted itself, rolled down the ramp to the street.

'Sir, this is Corporal Leung. Are you all right, sir?'

He heard the sound of a deep slow sigh, then, 'Yeah, Hal, I'm fine, just fine.'

He took a deep breath. He didn't like doing this, didn't like it at all. But orders were orders, junior cops don't challenge senior cops, and nobody in Singapore questions authority. Tasting ashes, he spoke the words he had rehearsed with the superintendent hours before: 'Sir, are you tracking the accused fugitive John Gregory Taft?'

There was a long, long pause before Chan answered, 'Yes, I am. I am tracking the fugitive John Gregory Taft on a surveillance monitor.'

'Sir, can you tell me the accused's map coordinates or present location?' The words were spoiled meat badly cooked, the flavour of rot and corruption. 'And could you speak loudly and slowly, sir? There's a problem with my radio.'

Leung waited for Chan's answer. And waited. A bad fog was coming. Visibility was down to tens of metres. He recognized the signs. Another fifteen or twenty minutes and you didn't measure visibility in tens of metres. You'd be lucky if you measured it at all.

'Sir, I repeat, can you tell me the accused's coordinates or present location?'

There was Chan's car, parked by the kerb. The brake lights were still on. But the door was open, and the interior light shown dully through the rear window. Leung braked to a halt. The superintendent was still sitting in the car, Leung could see him.

'Sir, do you copy?'

'Yeah, Hal, I copy.'

'The accused's coordinates or present location, sir? What are they?'

'Twenty-two-point-eight vertical, one-ninety-four-point-zero horizontal.' Hal Leung's stomach turned at what the superintendent had done.

Poh Kay Siong's *Jade Lady* sliced Singapore's south coastal waters off the Marina Bay Country Club. Here, close into shore, the yacht could race at its thirty-seven-knot top speed, kicking up white waves at its bows, churning black seas bottle green at its stern. Further offshore, full-throttle speed was impossible. Singapore serviced a hundred thousand transoceanic ships a year, one arriving or departing every three minutes, eight hundred at anchorage or in a berth at any given moment of the day. Only a fool hot-rodded a sports yacht in crowded Singaporean waters.

Standing on the dim-lit bridge, Poh studied the night. 'It seems,' he said softly to Teng Kwoengmi, 'the years weigh heavily on Superintendent Chan Gin. He is no longer the man he was.'

Teng, rail thin, wolf hungry, worried the bandages swaddling his left cheek. 'What makes you say that?'

'Reflect, my friend, upon the superintendent's pathetic little charade outside the American Embassy: the redoubtable Chan Gin allowing a felon to flee in an auto conveniently equipped with a key in the ignition. Then he follows in a slow and desultory pursuit – two cars only, and only two men. Is his design not shamelessly self-evident?'

'Not to me.'

'You have heard him, heard his pitiable pretence, the ever-so-stilted dialogue between Chan and his underling.' Poh's gentle voice sharpened with the slightest hint of scorn. "Oh, sir, please tell me in a loud slow voice the accused fugitive's map co-ordinates." Pah! Can you doubt that this childish make-believe was meant to do other than give us a man whom Chan himself trembles to take?'

'Yeah,' Teng grunted. 'Chan knows we have a scanner. He knows we're listening.'

Poh sighed deeply. He glanced through the forward window. A freighter, anchored in the roads just outside the harbour, loomed through the fog. Poh's steersman tapped the wheel, guiding the ship slightly starboard. 'Tonight I mourn the shadow of a man who was our redoubtable foe. At long last age blunts the razor edge of Chan Gin's thought; no longer does his fox's mind course ahead of his enemies. Do you not think this sad?'

'Not particularly.'

'But it is. Imagining himself a tiger-trapper of days gone by, mighty Chan stakes out a Judas goat, John Taft by name, that its bleating will attract his prey. Such a transparent strategy could well succeed were we tigers less cunning, and he, the hunter, more merciless. But – behold! – mercy is in him. The hunter has a conscience. Faint of heart, he shrinks at sacrificing his goat, thus reading us map coordinates that lie at a considerable remove from where the bait is staked out. Now is the superintendent unmanned. Compassion, that most fatal of vices, clouds his thought and leads him into error.' Gesturing at equipment secured from Miss Donald but far too useful to resell to customers in China, North Korea, or Cambodia, he continued, 'My friend, do you not think that were Chan the man he once was, then of certainty he would have foreseen that if we of the brotherhood had the craft to obtain a police radio, so too have we the art to secure a device capable of intercepting the police tracing system?'

Running his fingers through the silver hair at his temples, Poh glanced at a bright green blip named Jack Taft. 'Steersman,' he ordered, 'set your course for the port. The Tanjong Pagar Docks, I think, down by the Roro Ramp.'

Chan slumped in the driver's seat, one leg dangling out of the open door. Leung had taken the passenger's side, closing his door for no particular reason. Chan pulled two toothpicks out of one of his assault vest's pockets. He slipped one between his lips, offering the other to the corporal.

Leung shook his head. Chan dropped it in the ashtray.

The toothpick bobbed in Chan's mouth. He sucked its point between his two front teeth, teased it with his tongue, and began to chew at its tip. Finally he slid it into the corner of his mouth, saying, 'Well, this sucks.'

'Sir?'

Chan sighed. 'I couldn't do it, Hal. Just couldn't. Twenty-seven years on the force, more dead men than I can count, and I simply could not do it. That useless sonofabitch is innocent, and I can't risk him getting shot. Not to save my own butt. Not even to take Poh down. Shit! It's like I've got a fucking code of honour or something. Can you believe that?'

'Yes, sir, I can.'

'I've floated them out on the tide, Hal. I've deep-sixed them in swamps, in landfills, and there's a couple beneath the runways at Changi. For every one that's stood trial, there's another that didn't. But whether I busted 'em or blew 'em away, they all had one thing in common – they fucking deserved it. I never did the other stuff, Hal, never. I don't do dissidents, and I don't do innocent men. And if you ask me if that makes me cleaner than the guys that did, the answer is you bet your ass it does.'

'I know that, sir.'

'Jesus fuck, but I hate letting Poh get away. Christ, I could taste the bastard's blood. I had him this time, Hal. After all these goddamned years, I had him! Send Taft to the chop, and – *bang!* – no more Poh. It would have been justice and it would have solved my problems and it would have made Singapore a cleaner place. But it would have made me one of them – one of *them*, Hal! I'd be no different from the rest of those smirking assholes. Well, fuck you, Charlie, I *am* different, and I *am not* one of you, and I *have not* signed your fucking social contract . . .' Chan, whose voice had risen to a shout, fell silent. He was breathing hard, and worrying his toothpick with his tongue.

'The bitch is,' he whispered, 'that I should have known. A pro – a real one – would have wasted me on the spot. There in the hotel, in the girl's apartment, out in the swamp . . . Shit, Taft could have popped the cap any time he wanted. But he didn't. Instead he tries to convince me he's innocent. Stuffs his gun behind a sofa cushion. Bandages the hole in my back. Gives me a weapon in case I bump into a croc. Is that what bad guys do? No it is fucking not. So did I know he wasn't a bad guy? Yeah, somewhere deep down inside, I probably did.' Now Chan's tone changed, bleak bitterness filling his voice. 'The thing is I hated him, Hal, hated him so goddamned bad I couldn't think about anything other than getting even . . . dropping the hammer on him . . . watching him bleed. And now . . . oh hell . . . I still want to kill the cocksucker. I mean, getting my ass whipped by a genuine hardcase is something I can live with. But shit! Taft's an amateur and, fuck me, Poh's right and the government's right and they ought to put me down like a damn diseased dog!'

Chan paused, waiting for Leung to contradict him. The corporal did not. Instead he moodily stared out the window, quietly asking, 'So what are we going to do, sir?'

Chan answered with defeated resignation. 'Pick up Taft. Once he's in custody – protective custody – I'll drop you off somewhere. Then I'll go to the stationhouse and face the music. I'll try to cover for you, Hal. But, you know . . .'

Leung nodded gloomily. He knew.

'Okay. Let's get this farce over with. I don't want Taft getting close to the Port Authority gates. They've got cameras to look at the top of the trucks and at the undercarriages. Bastard tries to hitch a ride in, and he's—'

Leung cast a nervous glance at the tracking monitor. 'Sir, he's almost at the gate now. I mean, he's only a few hundred metres . . . uh . . . sir . . . I think we've got a problem.'

Glowering at the screen, Chan snapped, 'Now what?'

'He's up on the four-lane, sir, not down on the street.'

'Nah,' Chan growled. 'He's walking under the parkway, crossing to—'

'Look at the altitude register, sir. It says he's way above ground level.'

Chan frowned. He reached out and slapped the side of the monitor. The altitude register didn't change. It's bright red LED read-out said Taft was six point three metres into the sky. 'Impossible!'

'No, sir. He's on the parkway! He's running away from the gate!'

'What the hell . . . This damned computer must be busted. You can't trust electronics. I've told you a million times—'

Leung shouted: 'The fence, sir! The port's fence line runs along the parkway! Right there! Right at that curve!'

Spitting out his toothpick, Chan slammed his door closed. He turned the car's ignition key. 'I'm not believing this. Goddammit, I knew I should have let him get killed!'

'Oh God!'

'Now what?'

'He's back at ground level, sir! And this time, he's on the other side of the fence!'

It was some old Errol Flynn movie. Jack had seen it on television as a boy. The film was about paratroopers, and the drill sergeant –

was it Ward Bond who'd played the part? – had lectured Flynn and the other trainees on how you were supposed to land from a parachute drop. Jack didn't remember the dialogue. All he remembered was the sergeant telling his men to keep their knees bent, and to roll when they hit the dirt.

There also was some nonsense about falling backward, but Jack wasn't about to jump backwards off a twenty-foot drop.

The jolt punched the wind out of his lungs, made him feel like he'd jarred fillings loose from his teeth. Unlike Errol Flynn's stunt double, Jack did not curl athletically into a tumbler's tuck and roll, coming up crouching like a cat, all ready to sweep up his silk parachute, fold it in a ball, and stash it beneath bushes hidden from the sight of patrolling stormtroopers. Rather he came down hard, and with an audible crack. Folding over, feet flying out from under him, he tumbled bruisingly on his left side. The momentum of the fall propelled his legs over his shoulders, forcing him into a bone-crunching somersault, dropping him prone and dazed face first on wet asphalt.

A woman's voice, young and sweet and tender: 'John, are you all right?'

Jack shook his head in confusion. Reality had shattered into many fragments. True, those fragments were coming together again, but slowly.

'Are you hurt?'

He turned over. An improbably beautiful face – amber skin, wide contemplative eyes, full lips, exotic cheekbones, utterly adorable – materialized before him. Jack closed his eyes, then looked again. She was still there.

'John, say something.'

'What the hell are you doing here?'

Her lovely lips opened; no words came out.

'Christ, now I've got you to worry about along with everything else.'

Her eyes were slits. Her nose flared. She inhaled through clenched teeth. Tossing her hair, Zaitun began to rise. She hissed, 'How dare you!'

'This is no place for a girl.'

'I am *not* a girl!'

'It's too dangerous.'

'I want dangerous.'

'Beat it, woman, just hit the bricks.'

'You need me. You need my help.'

'I don't need anybody's help. Never have. Never will.'

Zaitun turned, striding into the night. Every purposeful step shouted that Jack Taft would never see her again.

Good, he thought. *Good. I did the right thing. I made her go away. Now there's no risk of her getting hurt. Good.*

Less good was the way he had done it. Less good was where the words had come from. Less good was that the anger he'd always kept bottled inside was bubbling and only inches from boiling out of control.

Jade Lady slowed, her steersman backing water as the yacht coasted towards a high concrete pier on her port side. Barrel-sized black polycarbonate bumpers lined the wharfside, each bumper two metres long, a metre and a half wide, hollow and chained to the concrete. The steersman knew that it would not do to bounce the *Jade Lady* against those bumpers. Such might nick her skin or mar her paint. Poh Kay Siong had sent men thirty metres to the bottom of the harbour for less.

Poh himself was standing on the deck, chatting quietly with Samuel Lin and Teng Kwoengmi. Short plump Lin had lost both his eyebrows and most of his hair – all seared away by the previous night's explosions. It gave him the aspect of a happy little Buddha, although he was not, never had been, a merry man. 'What about Chan?' Lin asked, punctuating his question by jacking back the slide on a .45 calibre Model 1911A automatic.

'We who survive him will honour his memory.'

'That lunatic won't be easy to take down.' Teng, scratching the bandages on his vulpine face, spat his words.

Poh waved his hand, brushing away Teng's concerns. 'Our informers advise me that the superintendent injured himself last night. His ribs are taped, and he is moving slowly. He will be easily dispatched.'

Lin drew an imaginary bead on an invisible target. 'I've been waiting for him a long time.'

Poh eyed Lin's automatic with mild distaste. He had grown up in the era of the silvered kris and silken cord, intimate devices demanding a certain delicacy of art. He considered firearms crudely impersonal, and would have preferred not to use them. 'Let us be sure,' he said, 'that whatever weapon is employed against the superintendent's person is left behind, and that Mr Taft's fingerprints are impressed upon it. Teng, would you be so kind as to instruct the workers in this necessity.' Poh pointed to the twelve men clustered along *Jade Lady*'s rail. One of those men was sufficiently boorish to be smoking on his ship. Poh made note of his name for future discipline.

Teng replied, 'Sure. But what about the rest of the guys?'

'They have been radioed and are *en route*. However, I imagine this evening's sport will be brief. What is to be done will be done before they arrive. Ah, now I see we are at our destination. Go give our workmen their instructions.' Poh paused, reflecting on the dishonour that Mr Taft's behaviour had brought upon his name. At first dispatching the man had been meant only as a favour to a business colleague. Now it had become a personal affair. That Taft had eluded Poh's hirelings three times would cause others among Asia's *Tsung li*s to question Poh's leadership. That Taft had single-handedly destroyed Poh's fleet – and his personal vehicle – would make them laugh. Much can be borne, but never mockery. Such a stain must be erased. Mr Taft was obliged to pay this debt, and to do so in a manner both protracted and elaborate. 'One final instruction. Be so kind as to advise the workers that Poh Kay Siong is of a beneficent frame of mind regarding the question of remuneration. The reward for Mr Taft alive and whole is doubled; the prize for his corpse, however, is reduced by half.'

Chan rolled to a stop at the Brani Terminal gate. A guard in a green jumpsuit stepped from his shack. Chan already had his warrant card out of the window. 'Police business.'

'Yes, sir. You're Superintendent Chan, aren't you, sir?'

Chan switched off the ignition, sat silently for a moment

listening for the sound of a radio playing in the guard shack. There was none. The guard was a good little Singaporean, a perfectly disciplined white mouse who would not distract himself from his duties by listening to music or, Chan's present concern, news broadcasts. That meant he could not know what had happened fifteen minutes earlier at the American Embassy, and therefore could not guess why Chan was at the port.

'Yeah. Open the gate.'

The guard nodded. 'Is there a problem, sir? Should I alert the Port Authority Police?'

'Yes,' said Hal Leung.

'No,' shot Chan, who, under the very best of circumstances, disapproved of policemen employed by independent agencies.

The guard blinked. Chan gave Leung an ugly look. Leung started to say something but thought better of it.

'I shouldn't call for backup, sir?' The guard wondered why Chan and his partner wore full battle dress.

'No. This is routine, nothing I and Corporal Leung here can't handle on our own.'

'Yes, sir.' The guard saluted, thinking that Chan's reputation being what it was, he dressed that way all the time. He disappeared into his shack. The red and white striped crossbar blocking the entrance began to rise. The guard put his head through the door. 'One thing, sir. Please remember the speed limit in the harbour yard is forty kilometres per hour. There are velocity sensors and alarms . . .'

Tyres squealed as the superintendent's tail-lights disappeared.

Jack, edging his way south through a maze of boxcar-sized cargo containers, sought calmness in statistics. The Port of Singapore was huge, nine hundred land acres all told, the first source of the nation's ever-growing wealth. Every year the place processed eight hundred million tons of cargo, thirteen million containers, a hundred and twenty thousand ships, enormous volumes of goods pouring through the seventy-five berths of the largest and most efficient operation of its kind in the world.

Efficient. That was the key word. Singapore was relentlessly efficient. In the early seventies when Jack earned his college tuition by working a longshoreman's night shift, it took a dozen sweating men and a baulky tango crane twelve hours to wrestle all the containers off a big freighter. But these days – at least in Singapore – three guys did the job, and finished it in fewer than eight hours.

Automation, it was all automation.

Automation meant fewer people.

Singapore ran the whole show with seven thousand five hundred employees. Jack did the math. A big chunk of workforce would be computer types, administrators, support staff, the folks serving chow in the port canteen. Another percentage were always on the water – guys driving water witches to keep the harbour squeaky clean, other guys out in the bunkering area inspecting ships for gas leaks, pumping water on board, loading up provisions. Divide, divide, multiply – adjust the result for three shifts a day. Yeah, all things being equal, there'd be twelve hundred workers out and about on the nighttime docks of Singapore. That worked out to little more than a single man per acre, and most of them would be on docked ships or up in the operations cabins of big post-panamax cranes. Besides, an acre is a lot of land; in the night, in the fog, the odds of anyone noticing a lone Westerner slinking in shadows were mercifully low.

He flattened himself against a metal wall. All around, painted rows of green and red and blue containers – twenty feet long, some longer – were stacked one on top of the other, five high. The old familiar names, the premier names of international shipping, comforted him: Mitsui, OCL, Matson, Hanjin, American President Lines, Crouos, Hyundai, Maersk. This was his world. He knew it better than anyone.

My turf, he sneered. *Come on, Chan, try to get me on my turf*.

His temper was still hot, but he was slowly bringing it under control. He'd cool off eventually, he knew that. All he had to do was keep his mind off that murderous oaf Chan Gin, and he'd calm down.

He forced himself to inhale deeply. Once, twice, three times. The air was damp, cooling to the lungs. *First things first*, he thought.

Forget about Chan. Don't think about Gabrielle. The only thing that counts is getting to a ship.

The fog was closing in, a grey blanket thirty feet above ground. Singapore boasted that 96 per cent of its sea-going customers were serviced within a half-hour of asking for it. Nights like this one – visibility soon to be measured in feet not yards – accounted for the other 4 per cent. Things were slowing down. No one wanted to risk the kind of accidents that happened when a pilot couldn't see his berth.

Jack peeked around the corner of the last container in its row. He was at the edge of a lane, wide driving spaces separating the enormous cargo boxes. Not far, out in plain view, two dozen bright yellow forklifts had been parked for the evening. Past the forklifts, a three-storey building was nearly invisible in the mist.

The reefer yard? Jack asked himself. He glanced left and right, then sprinted in a quick dash across the street, past three forklifts, down low, stopping crouched in the shadow of a fourth. He was closer to the building now, could hear the humming of its power plant, could see steam venting from its roof. No question, it was the reefer yard. The inside of that particular building was a cold chest, storage for refrigerated containers packed to the brim with produce.

No escape that way. Hide yourself in a cooler full of chilled rambutans, and you'd arrive at your destination frozen stiff.

Nor did any of the big cargo containers afford a way off the island. Singapore was a duty-free storage port. That meant small freighters brought in cargo from all over South Asia, depositing it in Singapore's zero-theft yards until bigger, ocean-going vessels called for it. Even if Jack could break into a cargo container (and they all were securely locked), there was no way he could know where the freight was going, or when it would get there.

His only hope was a ship.

Zaitun watched from the shadows. John was hiding beside a yellow forklift. He seemed to be all right, was making steady progress towards the water.

Of course she wouldn't abandon him. True, he'd screamed

insults at her, but she'd forgiven him for that. After all, he had ordered her to turn herself in to the police. She was Muslim, a woman indoctrinated from birth in subservience. She should have obeyed his command.

Like hell.

Now, she'd see him to safety, stay behind him and out of sight, he'd never know she was there unless he needed her. But if he did . . .

Something whispered wetly over nearby asphalt. The sound was to her right, whatever made it was hidden by a long high row of maroon cargo containers. It sounded like some sort of vehicle . . . a truck . . . a car . . .

'This is totally fucking unacceptable, Hal.' Zaitun shuddered at the sound of his voice.

Chan threw his Lancer into reverse. He'd steered down another damned blind alley, no exit, only cargo containers stacked in an impenetrable steel wall.

'There's not much we can do about it, sir.'

'Every damned street and dwelling in Singapore is supposed to be in that computer. So why the hell is the goddamned port nothing but blank space on my screen?'

'I think it's because there really aren't many fixed structures here, sir. I mean, they keep moving all this stuff around, stacking it up wherever there's room. It wouldn't make sense for the programmers to put it on the disk, sir, because as soon as they did, the port people would move things and the disk would be all wrong.'

Chan glowered. 'Damn! He's moving again! Son. Of. A. Bitch. If that shithead gets to a ship—'

'We could call an emergency, have every ship put on hold.'

'Forget it! This port dumps two billion dollars a year into the treasury. The government would sooner let Taft escape than piss off the shipping trade. Now, how the hell do I get out of this maze?'

'Left, sir. Right between those two stacks. I think . . .'

Chan slammed the transmission into first, gunned the engine, and double-clutched up to third gear. Hal Leung put his hands on the dashboard.

*

Headlights cut through the fog. The car's interior light was on, and Jack could make out the driver's face.

He became a statue in the night.

Stillness not motion is the hunter's art. Wolves watch. Lions wait. Nothing is more perfected in its patience than the tiger.

Antique voices whispered: do not in danger seek solace in reason; seek rather your ancestral predator. Logic's civilized stuff, what you learn in school and all of society's urbane conventions are but a straitjacket for the carnivore within.

His nostrils flared. He touched the pistol in his pocket, wrapped his hand round the comforting rake of its grip, probed a finger for the curve of its trigger. In the heart of a most personal darkness, he was a shadow frozen in shadows, eyes narrow the better to focus on that one single thing of interest: the quarry, the target, the enemy, the prey.

Old stuff, ancient skills, bred to the bone three million years ago. He'd never felt this, *never*!

Pure concentration. The full muster of every resource. Mind and body wholly unified in singularity of purpose. Pursuer not pursued. Hunter not hunted. Killer not victim. Already good, it could only get better.

He brought the pistol into shimmering night. Now it had come to this now; he had not sought it; indeed, he'd tried to escape it; but here it was, and he was man enough to do what had to be done.

The gun is not the weapon. The anger is the weapon. Use it, control it, aim it, channel it, it will *solve your problems.* In a perfect state of fury, Jack Taft smiled.

A voice crackled on the radio. Somebody from CPS dispatch was calling for Superintendent Chan. Leung reached for the microphone. Chan stopped him. The caller was babbling something about Taft and news from the United States. Chan snarled, 'There was a firearms accident. Your weapon accidentally discharged, right, Hal?'

'Whoops,' said the corporal as the radio turned to splinters.

*

Last night Chan had told him how to use a rifle. It hadn't been hard to learn. All you did was brace it, look through the telescope thing on top, and centre the crosshairs on your target. Worked like a charm.

This pistol business was another matter. The thing was short and lightweight, and all it had for sights was a notched metal plate at the back and thin metal blade at the front. Jack put his arm out straight, trying to fit the blade into the notch, and fit both over Chan's brightly illuminated face.

It didn't work. No matter how steady he held his hand, the damned thing wobbled all over the place. The slightest twitch, the very beating of his pulse, put the pistol out of plumb.

Gripping the gun in both hands and squatting on his hams, he laid his arms across the business end of a forklift truck, bracing the butt of the pistol flat on level steel. Big improvement. Everything was nice and steady. Chan's car was coasting nicely towards him, and the blade was in the notch and the both of them lined up handsomely with Chan Gin's head.

Jack curled his index finger around the trigger. Chan had said when shooting you were supposed to exhale slowly through the nose. Well, Chan was the expert, and Jack always welcomed the advice of men who knew their jobs. He inhaled. He let his breath out in a long, slow stream.

You've been trying to kill me ever since I set foot on this lousy island, you big bag of shit. Now it's my turn.

He squeezed the trigger.

The gun barked and jumped, the barrel leaping upward by at least an inch. Jack watched fragments of Chan's grille explode into aluminium shrapnel. *Nuts*, he thought. *Missed him*. He was already drawing a bead, ready for his second try.

Poh Kay Siong turned quickly. He looked into the dark, searching for the source of the fog-muffled shot. 'Gentlemen,' he whispered, 'I imagine that was Superintendent Chan announcing his presence in an all-too-predictable way. I should say he is near the reefer yard. If so, then Mr Taft cannot be far way. Make haste, but remember your orders – this night the superintendent is to greet his ancestors; Mr Taft is to greet me.'

'Fuck!' cursed Chan, now prone on wet pavement. 'Live ammo! Jesus, I needed that!'

A .40 calibre round pulverized the asphalt inches from his face. Chan tugged his own gun free of its holster.

There had to be a trick to pistol shooting that he hadn't mastered. He'd fired three shots now, missed three times. Annoyingly, each time he had the sights perfectly aligned with Chan's head. The first miss had hit the grille of Chan's car; the second gouged a crater in the hood; the third burrowed into the pavement.

Jack ground his teeth – three bullets gone, and he'd only had nine to begin with.

The goddamned gun was unreliable, that's what it was. You could put the wretched thing in a vice, lock it in rock solid and utterly unshakable, and still the blasted thing would spray bullets all over the place. Infuriating!

'Mr Taft, please throw your weapon down.' Chan, who had seen fit to roll beneath his car, was calling to him.

In your dreams, asshole!

'We have to talk. Look, I know you're innocent. This whole thing has been a mistake.'

You and that Briggs guy have the same scriptwriter, Chan?

'Taft, you want me to say it? Okay, I'll say it. I screwed up. I admit it. I apologize. Now would you please not shoot at me.'

The problem with a pistol is that you've got to be close to your target. Otherwise the thing is useless. No accuracy at all. Damn!

'Come on, Taft. There are cops all over the place. The Port Authority has its own private police force. Three hundred and eighty officers. They're going to get here fast, and they're not going to appreciate that what's happening here is merely a misunderstanding.'

On the other hand, if I hold the thing really steady, and get it just right, maybe I can tag the bastard. Hell, one more shot, and maybe I'll get lucky.

'Taft, be reasonable. If I didn't know you were innocent, would

I come after you with only one other cop?'

Last night, pal, you came all by your lonesome.

'Speak to me, Taft. Say something.'

Let's see, he's maybe thirty-five yards away and I'm shooting low. Aw hell! I know what the problem is – it's gravity! At this distance, the bullet's falling. All I gotta do is aim higher.

'We have to talk, Taft. I can explain this mess. Please, Taft, answer me.'

'Hey, Chan!'

'Yes.' There was relief in Chan's voice. But not for long.

'Tell me something.'

'Sure.' The pathetic bastard was trying to sound friendly.

'What's the worst insult in the Chinese language?'

Chan didn't even have to think about it: '*Ko-pao, jih ta tsu-tsu.*'

'Translation?'

'Roughly speaking it means. "I bugger the corpses of your deceased ancestors."'

Jack screamed, 'Okay, buddy-boy, then this one's for your granny!'

Poh, ear cocked towards the faint crackle of distant gunfire, signalled his men to a halt. The fog was thickening with alarming speed. Now it deadened sound as much as it cloaked sight. The grinding of heavy machinery and the curses of working men had become all but inaudible. Had Poh not been listening, and listening hard, he would not have heard the dull report of a pistol fired in the night.

Teng Kwoengmi was flushed and breathless from the short run up the wharf. The man smoked too much, Poh thought. Americans and American cigarettes: a curse carried on the shoulders of all Asia. 'Boss?' Teng panted. 'What's wrong?'

Poh put up his hand, silencing him. He kept still, listening for the sound of another shot. There was none. Nor could he hear oaths or cries of exultation, although in this muffling mist, he could not expect a human voice to travel very far. All in all, the fog was a blessing. It cast a shroud of silence and invisibility over things, and that was to be desired.

'Boss . . .?'

'Yes, my friend, something is wrong. We hear gunfire, four shots now. Yet the shots are not all at once, a pistol emptying its magazine, then another pistol raised. Rather they are spaced far apart, as if fired by a marksman taking careful aim, pausing with each pull of the trigger.'

Teng looked confused. Lin understood at once. The pudgy little axeman blurted, 'It's not Chan.'

'Correct,' Poh sighed. 'The superintendent's signature style is missing, don't you think? Chan is nothing if not predictable, a man for firing as many rounds as rapidly as he can, the steps of Laigong the thunder god striding through the clouds. Had it been he whom we heard, there would have been fifteen or thirty bang, bang, bangs all in a row, would there not?'

'Who is it then?'

'I fear we must assume it is Mr Taft. I should not have thought that he would have laid hands on a weapon in the few minutes since his feigned escape, but it appears that he has. This adds an unwelcome layer of difficulty to our task tonight. Pass the word to the workers – let them spread out and advance with prudence.'

Chan purred, 'We're going to have to shoot him, Hal,' and there was rapture in his voice.

The superintendent was sprawled under the vehicle, the soles of his shoes directly beneath the rear axle. Leung, crouched behind the car, leaned low to answer. 'Looks that way, sir.'

'I don't see any choice. The bastard's gone amok. Nearly got me that time.'

'Yes, sir. I understand, sir. Given the range and shooting conditions, he really is quite an astonishingly accurate marksman.'

Speaking slowly, and through tightly clenched teeth, Chan growled, 'I taught the shithead everything he knows.'

'Should I aim for his legs, sir?'

Chan thought about it before answering grudgingly, 'Let me do it. I've got a Sidewinder, buckshot in the chambers. If I can get a few metres closer to the sonofabitch, I can pepper his legs. That'll make him drop his gun, I guarantee it.'

'Any ideas on how to get closer to him, sir?'

'Not at the moment. I think we've got to wait for him to make a move, then you—'

'Sir!' Leung was no longer whispering.

Chan swore and began scrabbling backward. In the reefer yard engines were turning over and headlights were coming on. Those headlights were moving straight at Chan's car.

The control configuration of a Hyster Challenger-model forklift had changed little since Jack's days on the New Jersey docks. The ones Singapore used were H155s, extra-large counterbalanced brutes with seven and a half-ton lift capacities. As a working student Jack had never driven anything half as powerful. The principles were the same, though. Ditto the safety mechanisms. Ditto the tricks that experienced longshoremen taught shavetail apprentices on how to override them.

Scuttling across wet asphalt, Jack fumbled for another ignition switch, and sent a fifth forklift into motion.

The cloud cover had sunk to five metres, a churning slate roof over the dockyards. Probing fog tendrils coiled down, wrapped themselves momentarily around pillars, pylons, lampposts as if tasting and savouring the goods of the earth. Then, uncoiled and searching, they moved on.

The forklifts cut streamers through the mist. Behind blinding headlights, the machines looked to Chan like a browsing herd of grazing beasts, slow-moving and ponderous, dull dumb dinosaurs who would unthinkingly tread flat anything so foolish as to stand in their way. They rolled forward at a lazy walking pace, lift arms like mandibles testing the air for the scent of fodder. Their pneumatic tyres made a soft squelching sound, and their engines purred a faintly curious grunt.

Hal Leung was back inside the Lancer, fumbling for the ignition. Chan yelled at him to be quick. The corporal swore in response.

'Hal, come on!' Big heavy things, the forklifts were capable of hoisting seven thousand kilos to a two-storey height. They had mass, they had weight, they had momentum. There would be no stopping them.

'The keys, sir? Where are the keys?'

The machines carried engines strong enough to punch their lift blades through cinderblock walls. Oversized tractor wheels made them capable of climbing stairs, or, any second now, rolling up and over the hood of a low-slung car, crushing it like a soda can left on a busy street.

'Fuck the keys!'

The headlamps were beacons, arc lights reflecting off wet black asphalt, casting moving shadows across the painted metal sides of cargo containers, and illuminating the half-turned profile of a young police corporal who was too brave for his own good.

'I've got time, sir.'

Chan slapped his hand to his right pants' pocket. Nothing. The left? Empty. That was wrong. He always carried his change and his keys and . . .

Shiny circular metal glittered on the ground. Coins, a trail of them leading to beneath the car. They'd fallen out when he rolled . . .

'Get away, Hal!'

'Give me the keys, sir!'

'Do . . .' Chan was in motion, all energy thrown to his legs, '. . . it . . .' Hal was half in the car, his rump on the seat, both legs dangling out of the driver's side door, '. . . now!' But his torso was bent towards the ignition, and his waist was too far to reach, and both his arms were beyond Chan's grasp as the blade of the first forklift scored a gouge in the car's fender, pushing it left and directly into the path of a second forklift. That one's lift arms were high, up to their maximum height, not pausing but recycling and coming down, and its front wheel crawled up on the bumper of Chan's car, pushed it down, rolled over the hood, crumpling it like a wadded paper cup pitched into a waste bin.

Chan hurled himself at the ground, arms outstretched like the lift blades of a forklift truck, wrapping them around Leung's legs, twisting his torso and levering away, rolling, rolling, rolling out of the path of another orange-yellow Hyster and another, and one of them brushed his leg but he was already away, and his ribs screamed with the most excruciating pain, and Hal was going, 'Oh my God, I am heartily sorry for having offended Thee . . .' as a pale yellow Mitsubishi Lancer GLX, an unmarked police car with a QX licence plate came to scrap metal.

Short, pockmarked, and indistinguished but for his enthusiasm for knifework, Homi Bhave might have spent his entire criminal career as an ordinary *goondah*, cheap muscle on the streets of Bombay. However, Homi once saved the life of an important man, and when, several months later, the law finally decided to bring Homi to heel – the charge being assault with intent to kill – that important man made arrangements with other important men to take Homi out of harm's way. He was pensioned off to Singapore, given odd jobs that fitted his talents by Samuel Lin.

Tonight Homi Bhave was a part-timer in the employ of the *chiu chow* brotherhood. The work paid well, and there was a chance of a rich reward.

The prize for capturing this Taft fellow doubtless would be larger than the one for snuffing out Superintendent Chan Gin. Indeed, the very honourable Poh Kay Siong had not mentioned a specific price for the superintendent's life. Nonetheless, Homi was confident that it would be ample. And, as Taft was nowhere to be seen, but Chan was lying flat and grunting with pain almost at Homi's feet, there seemed to him an element of predestination about affairs, as if it was his karma to collect the superintendent's head. He could almost hear the clink of new coins in his pocket and the crinkle of folded bills overflowing the capacity of his wallet.

Homi much preferred his knife, favouring the curve-bladed Malaysian parong, a machete-like mainstay of South Asia since the days of the China Seas pirates. However, in the interests of conformity, this night he had armed himself from Poh's weapons locker with an Israeli-made Golan double-action 9 mm automatic. Homi was left-handed, and the pistol's ambidextrous magazine catch and decocking levers were a boon to him. As he thumbed back the hammer, Chan Gin drew and fired his chromed Sidewinder, pulling the trigger six times, emptying all six chambers with immediate thunder and proximate lightning, shredding to red confetti the belly and groin, chest and face, of the late Homi Bhave, whose karma came as a surprise only to him.

*

Smiling faintly but with great satisfaction Poh Kay Siong softly said, 'Now indeed I believe I do hear the superintendent's music. Samuel, my friend, let us march to the sound of Chan Gin's drums.'

Homi Bhave's pistol, unfired and with ten rounds in its magazine, one in its chamber, skidded across slick asphalt, disappearing between two stacks of cargo containers. A lithe female form danced from the shadows, scooped it off the ground, and faded unseen into the dark.

Well begun is half done. Chan recognized the pile of leaking hamburger from the night before. He was – it had been – one of Poh's pet snakes. There'd be others around, maybe all of them, and Poh Kay Siong for sure.

Which meant Poh had tracked Taft to the docks. That was a gift from the heavens, the god of gamblers smiling on the high sheriff of hell. Chan had another chance to save himself from disgrace – or rather the same chance. All he had to do was outfox Poh, rescue Taft, and blow away, oh, say, maybe a dozen or so hatchetmen, then call a press conference.

His adrenaline was up; his pain was down; Chan fingered a speedloader out of his pocket. Six more rounds, and unless he missed his bet, plenty of targets.

Let the good times roll.

Jack stopped, flattening himself against a wheeled metal pylon. The flare of gunfire, matchstrikes in the mist, was in front of him, not behind. He'd fled in a circle, was back near the reefer yard. The damned containers, stacked so high, were a rat maze. Night had betrayed his always faulty sense of direction.

But not his hearing. Jack heard the clatter of feet on pavement, the anxious whispering of eager men. There were seven or eight of them spread out down an alley separating two cargo container rows. They bore objects in their hands, black mostly but some shining chrome, and they clutched them in a fashion that had become all too familiar.

Jack looked left, right, back, forward. He was in the open, no place to run, no place to hide, no hope of defeating eight hoodlums with his five remaining bullets. There was only this single pylon, too narrow for concealment, and its twin a dozen yards away. Poh's gunmen would spot him any moment now, and the pylon would be no protection at all.

He looked down. His feet were on steel tracks, railroad tracks.

He looked up.

Salvation presented itself.

Shoes in pockets, Jack eased himself softly, secretly up a flight of fourteen grilled metal steps. The better to be silent, he forced himself to take short shallow breaths. He crawled low across a steel platform dimpled with anti-skid treads, and raised his hand to the door latch.

It moved. It was unlocked.

The door whispered open. Jack crept in.

The pylon against which he had been crouching was no pylon at all. It was the girdered limb of a bridge crane. Shaped like an inverted 'U', towering seven storeys into the sky, the crane was one of two dozen in this part of the port, the Tanjong Pagar Terminal. Singapore used state-of-the-art post-panamax cranes quayside at each berth to haul freight off ships, stacking it at the wharves' borders. Mitsubishi-manufactured bridge cranes took over from there, hoisting cargo containers left by the post-panamaxes, moving them forty tons at a time from water's edge to the port's central storage areas. On busy days the things were constantly in motion, rolling on four-foot-high steel wheels at a stately three miles an hour, walking speed, across a network of railroad tracks, lofting containers to and fro in preparation for their forwarding to distant lands.

Bridge crane number TT171 was painted vivid yellow, big black letters PSA – short for Port of Singapore Authority – emblazoned on its side.

Jack saw a single control panel on the wall, and it told him where he was: the monkey rack, the crane's elevator. The rack could take him up a hundred and thirty feet into the air to the top stage, up to the gantry and the giant engine that did the bridge crane's business. He didn't want that. Being seven storeys in the air, nowhere to run, was the very last thing he wanted.

He wanted the OA, the operations cabin where the crane's controls were located.

Crouching low, Jack glided out the door and on to a catwalk. If the equipment hadn't changed since he was a working student, there'd be two OAs on the crane, one up atop the gantry and one at ground level. All he had to do was get inside.

He edged along the metalled walkway. It was damp with fog, soaked his socks, made his feet tingle with the wet. Someone near by whispered, 'Slow down.' Jack froze. The voice was only feet away. 'That fucker Chan's just on the other side of this thing.'

Two men. They were hiding in the shadows directly below Jack. 'I'll take him,' said a short Buddha-bald man. His partner – tall, lean, wolfish, bandaged – replied sternly, 'No, he's mine. I owe him.'

Jack held his breath. Other hunters stalked the veld, seeking the same quarry as he. Fine then, let them have the prey. The enemy of my enemy is my friend. Fight or flight is not always a coward's choice.

Carefully, gently, silently placing his foot on dimpled metal, Jack took a single step forward, paused, then took another.

'He cost me a hundred thousand last week. I say I do him.'

'Sam, I am the senior man.'

The OA was not far, another few yards. Jack's heart was hammering, and he wanted to gulp breaths in great huge draughts. He forced himself to inhale slowly. The air seemed blast-furnace hot. He was sweating again, too. A bead dripped down his temple, fell stinging into his left eye. Unwilling to risk hand motion, not daring to wipe it away, Jack blinked. And took another step.

'Teng, I want him. I'm not letting you get the glory.'

'We'll share. You have a knife?'

'Always.'

'I shoot. Then you cut. Whatever souvenir you want, whatever you think will impress the honourable Poh the most.'

'Then gut-shoot him. I want him alive when I put the blade between his legs.'

'Excellent suggestion.'

Another three yards, another yard and a half, Jack was there. He flicked the door latch open, slipped to the cabin floor, and drew one long, cooling breath of relief.

Teng Kwoengmi stretched flat on the ground, belly-crawling behind the cover of the bridge crane's front wheel. His fine tropical worsted slacks were covered in grease, ruined. It was not too high a price.

He let his head peek out from his cover, and licked his lips. There was Chan, just like a target in a shooting gallery, no more than a dozen metres away. The fool was sitting on the ground, his legs halfbent at the knees, fumbling a speedloader out of his pocket and preparing to recharge one of those preposterously over-powered handguns that he so favoured. Another man, a junior cop from his looks, was standing behind Chan, making solicitous noises about the superintendent's ribs. Teng wondered if he should take the kid out first. Bad idea. Chan was too dangerous.

He snaked forward, bending his body around the crane's wheel. He could feel the earth vibrate beneath him, the slow thunder of enormous machines trundling on their tracks. In the fog-shrouded distance horns tooted and a yard siren sounded, warning workers that yet another piece of heavy equipment was preparing to heave into ponderous motion.

Revolvers had always been Teng's preferred handweapon. Automatics had too many moving parts to be reliable; they put the shooter at risk of a round jammed between magazine and chamber – clumsy to clear, fatal if an enemy was near. But revolvers? They were simple things, and could be trusted.

This night Teng Kwoengmi put his trust in a long-barrelled .357 magnum Ruger Blackhawk. The smuggler from whom he'd purchased it sold it to him chromed with smooth walnut grips. Teng had the pistol blued, black rubber used to replace the wood.

He rolled half on his side, snugly seating his hip against the cold metal of the bridge crane's four-foot-high wheel. Extending his right arm before him, his cheek against his biceps, he settled the Ruger's butt on the asphalt. The paving was flat. The target was near. His aim was steady, although he winced slightly at the sound of yet another nearby warning siren. Whispered softly enough for Sam Lin, but not Chan Gin, to hear, Teng's last living words were, 'Okay, motherfucker, suck on this.'

The human heart is an organ of singular power. If, as is not uncommon in Eastern lands, a condemned prisoner is beheaded, the victim's still forcefully pulsing coronary muscles will propel from his suddenly depressurized arteries a fountain of blood that can geyser fifteen feet or more – a crimson streamer rippling across sandy jailyards, leaving a faint contrail of steam in even the most humid air.

The bridge crane sent into motion by Jack, unknowing that Teng Kwoengmi straddled its track, was rated for a burden of forty tons, a ponderous mass sufficient to crush to pulp anything that lay in its path – metal, stone, or flesh, it mattered not. The immense force of a seven-storey steel structure applied against and atop Teng's midriff caused the hoodlum's body to burst like a balloon. The gout of blood that fountained from his severed torso was the very least of it.

Something hot and reeking slapped into Samuel Lin's face with the impact of a well-aimed punch. His mouth was open, jaw slack, breath sharply inhaled over tongue and teeth. The object sprayed a rank mist of intestines and their fresh contents down his throat. Lin, eyes closed with burning blood, waved his hands in futile horror, nausea welling up from his stomach, acid vomit bubbling through his nostrils. Not far away, small comfort, he could hear the gags and chokes and spattered puke of other men sickened beyond mere disgust at the damnation of what once was Teng, was now a thing of many skittering parts.

Lin reeled forward blindly, feet skidding on an organ of unknown identity. A paste the consistency of warm oatmeal, strong-smelling remnants of a rich dinner, matted his shirt. Still retching, he fumbled at his buttons to tear off the abhorrent fabric.

'Sam Lin.' The voice was frigid, hollow as an ice cave, remorseless as a judge proclaiming capital sentence. 'Put down that fucking gun.'

Lin drew a sleeve across his face, forced open his eyes. There was Chan, an ebony shadow in the fog, lit from behind, arms akimbo, and holding burnished steel in his hand. There was also steel in Sam Lin's hand, and he brought his automatic up to shoulder level, hammer cocked with his thumb, elbow locked, finger already going tight.

'I said put it down,' a coal-black monotone, void of mortal passion.

The automatic bucked in Lin's hand, its sharp crack making his ears ring. Lin started to smile, stopped, Chan was standing there, same as before, not moving a muscle, not moving an inch. The other cop, the young one, was crouching down, hand under his armpit, sinking into a combat marksman's stance.

Chan Gin purred, 'Cool it. This meat is mine.' Lin took aim and shot again.

The devil was untouched. Sam Lin wrapped both hands around the butt, pointed slow and steady, fired. Chan grunted, not hit, merely laughing.

'Sam, you asshole, is that a surplus US Army .45?'

A fourth shot. A fat slow slug percussed into a slate-grey Mitsui-OSK cargo container. Some sort of liquid, brown and volatile, bubbled out.

'You know, Sam, that's the dumbest gun a man can use. Good marksman, me, for example, counts himself lucky to get one out of five in the centre ring with one of those. Most people are happy if they hit the target at all.'

Blinking sweat from his eyes, Lin snapped off three fast ones, each the sound of a sledgehammer smashed on concrete.

'Got a barrel that's too thin, badly seated against the block, vibrates like a dildo.' Chan was pacing forward, walking death, vengeance incarnate, and agent of retribution for Sam Lin's life of sin. 'Fuck you, Chan,' pulling the trigger again, knowing it was useless, knowing that they'd named Nemesis a devil for the very best of reasons.

'Hal, get out of here. Find those Port Authority clowns and tell 'em to evacuate the civilians.' Leung stood, started to speak. Lin turned the gun towards him and missed.

'Sir . . .'

'There are more of them over in the shadows. Get me some backup, too. Do it now. And, oh yeah, don't forget to call the TV stations.'

How could he stand there talking so calmly? Sam Lin had the gun. Sam Lin was the shooter. Chan simply dismissed him, it was almost as if the man didn't care, and there was no dishonour greater than that. Lin shot again.

'Last chance, Sam.'

Eight metres, Chan was only eight metres away. There was no way Sam could miss, he knew it and he fired. Twenty-one out of twenty-two .410 pellets ripped into Samuel Lin's plump round face, none in his left eye, two in his right. His world went poppy scarlet, red as a cheap woman's lips. Sharper than needles, twenty-one more spikes punctured his chest, thrust him backward howling as yet another piercing cascade tore his shoulder with leaded claws. A fourth volley killed him clean, and the last two were wasted but that they cleared Chan's pistol, making room for a fresh load.

Body parts and blood and the smell of fresh death and three hoodlums down and ordinary men didn't know how good it made you feel.

Chan Gin's chest expanded, full of joy and air. Pain? What pain? Broken ribs were irrelevant, not even inconvenient, and if anything the fire of them was the spur that goaded him on.

Here were targets for his anger, men he loathed, and they fucking-well deserved to die.

He was born to this, as were his enemies. The outcome could never be in doubt. *Chenghuang*, high sheriff of hell, had come again to the garden of his labours.

The bridge crane's controls were wholly new, utterly unfamiliar, Jack had never seen anything like them. Nineteen, twenty, twenty-one years old, he'd driven one of the things. Back then it had been all levers and rods and a great big wheel with a handle on its rim. Now it was nothing but electronics.

The OA cabin was built of sheeted steel, rugged as a tank's cockpit, indicator lights all over the place, a single fluorescent light on the ceiling. A black radio phone hung on the wall. Instead of a central control console, there was only a grey-screened personal computer displaying a Microsoft DOS menu. Jack eyed the keyboard, warily tapped a random key.

The beast growled. The crane began to roll.

He glanced through the rear window: gun-wielding shadows everywhere. Moving away from them was good. Moving faster would be better.

He listened for a voice. Unloving and remote, it should have whispered some fatuous proverb, something like: *He who turns and runs away* . . . But there was no voice. Jack was alone in his mind. At last.

He eyed the computer menu. All the choices were abbreviations. 'FRWD – F1'. That must have been the key he tapped. 'RVRS – F2'. Reverse? As in go backward? Yeah, probably. 'GRPL↑ – F3'. Who the hell knew what that meant. Ditto 'GRPL↓ – F5'. What was a 'GRPL' anyway?

Oh yeah, he thought. *Grapple. Sure.* And LCKL, the F6 key, was lock left. F7, LCKR, was lock right. Likewise unlock. Actually the computer system looked pretty easy. Even logical. Although Jack was not in a logical mood.

Curious, Jack pressed the F5 key. A motor hummed. Craning his head, he looked through the cabin's left window. The hoist engine was turning somewhere out of sight, the cargo claws – the hooks that latched on to multi-ton containers – were descending through fog glow, and the window starred with frost as a bullet ricocheted into the night.

Jack dropped to the floor. Another slug cannoned off the glass.

Bullet-proof glass? Jack asked himself. *Of course.* Always and everywhere in a deep-water port. Things fell, accidents happened, you designed your control cabin to protect the occupant from harm.

A small sign at floor level caught his eye. It was embossed metal, painted bright yellow, black letters:

SPEED GOVERNOR OVERRIDE
Do **NOT** engage without supervisory approval
14 kph maximum with this equipment

A recessed toggle switch was positioned beneath the sign. Jack threw it. The bridge crane jolted, accelerating to a faster speed. Lifting his head, he peered out of the window. The crane was moving at a good clip, eight miles an hour or thereabouts, a quick jogging pace. There were still men out there, and they still had guns in their hands, but they weren't using them. *Can't run and aim at the same time, can you, you jerks?*

'Thanks, Taft. I owe you one.' A voice called in the dark, and Jack knew who it belonged to.

What fresh hell is this?

He looked to his right. Chan Gin was ten or twelve yards away, hanging on the bridge crane's other leg, clinging to the broad yellow-orange steel girder. His body was visible to Jack but out of sight from the armed men running furiously after him.

'You saved my butt back there, Taft. Don't think I don't appreciate it.'

I did what!?

'That bastard Teng had me cold. You made a cool move running this sucker over him. Obi-wan has trained you well . . .'

I saved your useless life? Damn!

A shot pinged off the cabin's exterior. Jack felt his face heat red with rage. He slid the window wide, roaring, 'Chan, you shithead!'

'Don't worry, I'll get you out of this.'

Jack shrieked with unbridled fury, '*You!* You'll get me out of this! If it wasn't for you, you asshole, I'd be—'

'Taft, kindly shut the fuck up and listen. Like I've been trying to tell you, I know you're innocent. So just lie down on the floor where it's safe, and . . . oh, come on, Taft, don't point that thing at me.'

The swaggerer, the blusterer, the strutting alpha male. He's strong, virile, sexy, and although you'd think that would be enough to make him happy, it's not. He needs something more. He can't be proud unless you're humbled. He can't feel good unless you feel bad. He can't be high unless you're low. Whatever you have, he wants. Whatever he wants, he takes. And if a woman prefers you to him . . .

Jack had got back to La Guardia early, called Gabrielle in the office. A secretary said she'd just telephoned, leaving word that she was taking the rest of the day off, and could be reached at home if needed.

He decided to surprise her. *Taxi! Take me to the corner of Seventieth and Broadway.*

As he paid the driver, he saw her climbing out of her own cab. With Simon. She was a little wobbly, and Simon had his hand hard and firm on her ass. She didn't seem to mind one little bit. The two swept giggling by the doorman and into her apartment building.

He waited. Walked a narrow orbit up and down the street outside. Finally the doorman, who knew Jack by sight, left his post. Jack was a generous tipper, and usually had a pleasantry for the man. His name was Lew, and he said, 'For what it's worth, Mr Taft, I ain't never seen him before. I ain't never seen no one with her before but you. And you know, I think he got her pretty plastered, 'cause she's a nice dame and she doesn't . . . well, you know.'

Jack knew. Jack flagged down a cab. Jack never said a word about it. Nonconfrontational Jack never would.

But he sometimes shot a questioning look at Lew when entering Gabrielle's building. Lew would return a solemn stare and shake his head, mouthing, *Uh uh, he ain't been back.* And once, to Jack's unstated question he whispered, 'You got nuttin' to worry about, Mr Taft. That day, she threw the bum out. Swearin' like a soldier, she was. I think it was a mistake, Mr Taft, you know, same as everyone makes mistakes.'

And in that restaurant, the Friday Gabrielle gave him the brief-case, Simon had bullied up to their table, and Jack could see it in his eyes, in his gloating eyes, and the triumphant smirk that one man gives another and that every man knows – *Hey, loser, I've fucked your woman, and I can fuck her again any time I want, so I guess we both know who's the better man.*

He'd wanted to kill him. But he didn't even clench his fists. Instead, same as always, he'd swallowed what he felt, and he'd smiled. But still, he wanted to kill him, and even now he wanted to kill him, and if he had the chance he'd do it without a second thought . . .

However, Simon Burton was far away. On the other hand, Chan Gin, Burton's brother under the skin, was near by. Same voice, same puffed chest, same bully-boy leer, same fuck-you insults, same . . . same . . . same . . .

The only difference between Simon and Chan was that Chan was in his gunsights, and Simon was not.

Target of opportunity.

Jack braced his pistol on the windowsill, the muzzle out of the cabin's window, aimed straight at nearby Chan. Up a notch for gravity. Left a skosh for the breeze. He had it now, had it pat, knew how it was done, and was looking forward to it. All he wanted, his sole desire and consuming passion, was to murder the sonofabitch, do it now, see him scream and fall and bleed and die . . .

'You don't get it, do you, Taft? Poh wants you a hell of a lot more than he wants me.' A contradictory bullet sparked steel above Chan's head. He seemed not to care. 'Think about it, Taft. You're the one with a price on his head. I'm the only way you make it out of here alive.'

'Wrong!' Jack swung his pistol in an arc, plucked a target out of the night, sent his victim skidding face down.

'Very nicely done,' barked Chan – John Travolta, *Broken Arrow* – 'Almost as good as me. Now there are only eight of them left. And you've got how many bullets left?'

'All I need is one!' steadying the gun.

'Plus I bet there's another car-load or two of thugs on the way.'

Another lie, the goddamned bully, blowhard, punchout artist, and if the ugly fuck had bothered to listen to him none of this would have happened; but oh no, that wasn't the way his sort handled things, they never listened, they just walked right over you, and he'd never put up with that shit again. Least of all from this prick!

'So let's try something different here, let's try to cooperate with the law. If you'd done that in the first place—'

'I'd have a noose around my neck!'

'There is that.'

Jack's sights were on Chan's chest again, little more than ten yards away, an easy shot. His hand was steady. No more trembling. Now he knew the art of it. Let the rage go. Forget the fury. Serenity replaces wrath. Centre yourself in the heart of the marksman's perfect peace. Meditate. Seek clarity. Become one with the target as the target is one with you. Justice is in you, and retribution is owing . . .

'Have we got a deal, Taft?'

But greater retribution was due and payable in New York. Shoot Chan and he would not collect it. And the guilty would escape, and he would die. *Goddamn it all!*

'Taft?'

Old age told on Poh. It lived in his knees, leached the air from his lungs, rode weighty on his back. Such burdens, the price of maturity and thus wisdom, made him feeble when he needed to be strong. He could run no more.

Shouting encouragement at those who raced after fleeing Chan, escaping Taft, but unable to keep pace with his young workmen, he slackened his gait to walking speed.

Such infirmities were his despair. Too soon now, he would have to retire, take up residence in some pleasant resort on the Gulf of Thailand. Infrequent visitors would call to honour him. He would be ancient Poh Kay Siong, alone but for visiting grandchildren, and they only during the lunar New Year holiday.

How sad, sad as the fall of blossoms in northern lands, sadder than springtime for a man grown weary in his years.

He removed a snow-white handkerchief from his breast pocket, using it to blot, but not to wipe, his brow. Well then, he reflected, let this night be the capstone of his career. His dream could still be preserved: his brotherhood not merely surviving, but strong in a federation not bounded by Singapore's paltry borders, a nation unto itself, and greater by far than the tiny republic created by a boyhood rival.

Only Chan and Taft stood in the way, and they were easily brushed aside. It would be soon now, soon. Their runaway crane was rolling straight and true for the southernmost end of the port – the Roro Ramp where Poh had docked his beautiful *Jade Lady*. The crane could not be more than a hundred metres away from a place where the two men had no choice but to stop. Beyond lay only water, fifteen kilometres of rolling sea separating the shores of Singapore from the fetid outer islands of Sumatra. Taft and Chan were trapped. The end was near.

Honour demanded he be in at the kill. Best not be late. Poh quickened his painful steps.

On the East Coast Expressway, a crowded Hyundai passenger van began to slow, easing into the left lane, preparing to exit at the Port Authority. A television truck well above the speed limit, its driver wide-eyed, swerved into the exit. Another was right behind.

Rising and falling sirens cut the night. The Hyundai's driver glanced out his window. Down below, emergency lights blinked white to red to blue as they streamed through the Brani gate.

Shrugging a silent question, the driver looked at his superior for guidance. That man shook his head.

'What's up?' asked one of the hatchetmen in the van's back.

Peering down at the pell-mell of policemen at the port's main gate, the man in charge answered bleakly, 'On the day after tomorrow, the brotherhood will elect a new *Tsung li*.'

'What about tomorrow?'

'Tomorrow we collect contributions for Poh Kay Siong's defence fund. Or his memorial, as the case may be.'

Chan shouted, 'Trouble, Taft!'

'What now?'

Chan had hooked a leg around a safety bar. His back was flat against the heavy girder bracing the crane's left limb. 'Guy just jumped up on your side. He's behind the monkey cage. I can't see him.'

Jack stared into the night. He could make out nothing on his side of the crane. But somebody moved on Chan's side, down at the very rear. It was only a shadow, bent low, duckwalking with something held in a grip between both hands. Jack tried to draw a bead. The man was too fast, scuttled out of sight behind the rear wheel carriage. Aflame with anger, he screamed, 'You've got one on your side too.'

'Hell, we got a problem here. I think the sucker behind you has got an Ingram.'

'What's that?'

'Bad karma. Special Forces surplus from Vietnam. Cyclic firing rate one thousand and forty-five rounds per minute.'

'This is like a machine-gun?'

'Very like.'

A sound like a buzzsaw in sheet metal. A hard hail pocking the control cabin's wall. Shattering glass clinking on a steel floor. The whistle of wind through a hollowed-out rear window, once bullet-proof glass, now fragments because no glass, no matter how rigidly forged, can withstand the impact of multiple high-velocity rounds poured on to its ruggedized surface.

'Like that,' Chan added.

Jack saw the world through a yellow curtain; he felt swollen with power, in complete command of his rage, able to make of it a weapon in the world. There was nothing else now, no reason or logic, only the ardour of war, which is the most meditative of human activities.

He jutted his torso out of the cabin's open side window. His arms were locked straight, the pistol level with his eye. He could not see the man behind him, the man who had just emptied a thirty-round magazine in his direction, but he could see the man lurking behind Chan. That man was standing, aiming, motion-less, a very fine target indeed. Jack made him dead with a single bullet.

A second shot, simultaneous with Jack's, cracked near by. Chan was leaning coolly against his girder, one knee propped on a ladder rung, elbows braced on its tip, thick smoke gouting from his enormous revolver. At the other end of the crane, two men fell in the speeding machine's wake, rolling limp, sprawling lifeless on the pavement.

Chan boasted, 'Mine hit the ground first.'

Jack, exalted, roared back, 'Mine was taller!'

In the distance Poh Kay Siong heard the bravado of shouting foes. To his dismay, he felt his face redden, a warning of approaching passions most unsuited for situations such as the one at hand.

He fought to bring himself under control. Still, it was insufferable – those men, the superintendent and Taft – they were ridiculing fellows of the brotherhood.

There would be laughter all across Asia for this night. His peers would deride the name of Poh Kay Siong, incompetent doddering old fool from Singapore, the warlord who could not make war, the *Tsung li* whose entire army was brought low by a single policeman aided by, of all the preposterous things, a plump Western businessman. Who among us wishes to do business with a buffoon such as Poh? Who wishes to make alliance with such an unreliable man? Who will risk the penalties involved in trading restricted electronics if Poh cannot maintain calm in his own homeland and territory?

No one.

They would shun him. All dreams and plans turned to dust, he would be the last of Singapore's *Tsung li*s, the one who presided over the end of once-great brotherhoods, and the memory of his name would be worse than a disgrace.

It would be a joke.

Poh burned with shame. Only blood – blood and more blood – could save him now.

Chan fired another round – no longer buckshot in the pistol but fat, heavy .45 ammo and it worked just fine. The Sidewinder spit a flaming yellow plume, bellowed like a cannon, recoiled high and hard, came back level, hungry for another target.

The dead man spun like a dancing dervish, arms akimbo, his gun spiralling away into the night. He tumbled at the feet of another runner, and that runner leapt over the corpse of his fallen companion. Chan took him at the apogee of his hurdle, jerked him in midair, sending him down with a hurtful look of surprise on his face.

God, but he loved this! It was the good old ways of the good old days. *Who's the best? Who's number one?* And he killed another.

Yeah, he'd been off his feed for a while, out of his groove and making mistakes. But, uh uh, not any more. *Chenghuang* was back, and he'd pull this off same as he always had. Poh's crowd slaughtered, Taft rescued, he himself exonerated. He could do it, oh yes, and you there, die motherfucker, die! The pistol leapt. The target tumbled.

And all he had to do when it was over was persuade Taft to play ball. That wouldn't be hard. The sonofabitch was showing promise, looking good – he was a kindred spirit, Taft was, a brother beneath the skin. Yeah, definitely, once the garbage out here on the docks had been disposed of, Taft would listen to reason.

And speaking of Taft . . . he was standing straight and tall and howling, 'Well this is intense!' Chan grinned widely, but briefly. He was looking forward in the direction the crane ran. He didn't like what he saw.

'Taft!'

Jack's heart was pounding. He felt good! It was as though some Technicolor narcotic coursed through his veins. He was twenty years younger, thirty times stronger, elevated into an ecstatic realm of amplified sense and unbridled power. He had transcended the pale boundaries of ordinary madness, had become more than an inferno raging out of control, was turned omnipotent, supernatural, the almighty wrath and rage of God Himself. He was werewolf beneath a hunting moon, tiger taut at quarry, predatory perfection, master of mind and body, more fully concentrated and alert than . . .

'Pay attention, Taft! We've got a serious issue here!'

Teeth clenched, lip curled, foam flecking the corner of his mouth, Jack peered out of his window. Men were still chasing the crane. The nearest was a half-dozen yards behind it. He looked to be a promising target. Fine, quite fine. Jack could handle that . . .

'Not that way. Up front!'

Jack turned, stared, frowned. He didn't see the problem. There was nothing in front of the crane, nothing at all.

Which was precisely the problem.

Poh tallied corpses as he trotted in Chan's bloody wake. Here was the ruination of dreams. Good men, and loyal. A friend of thirty years sprawled face down. Beside him, lazy in death, lay the son of a man he himself had reluctantly dispatched, and to whom, in apology, he promised a stepfather's role. And there, Ling, stupid but ever-reliable Ling, come to cadaver's clay.

Poh, who was a man of few emotions, felt moisture on his cheeks.

Jack stared blankly at the control computer's screen. The menu offered him many options. None of them appeared to be 'stop'.

He darted a look out of the front windshield. The fog cover had come lower, was down now to the height of his cabin's ceiling. It was as if he were in a passenger jet, gliding beneath a cloud, momentarily to soar up into its wispy embrace. Directly ahead, not twenty yards away, the bridge crane's rails stopped. A small wooden barrier, red and white candystripes, marked their point of termination. Beyond that there was an expanse of concrete, an unpleasantly abrupt-looking edge, and what unquestionably was one hell of a lot of water.

'Taft, you doing anything over there?'

'I'm working on it!'

Jack raced a slippery finger over the keyboard's function keys, F1 through F15. Motors hummed, and a bank of lights came on. The crane, however, did not so much as pause; it rolled inexorably forward, eight miles an hour, eighteen yards from the end of the track and maybe less.

Sweat beaded on Jack's forehead, dripped down his cheeks.

Where the hell were the brakes?

Metal clashed on metal. Jack darted his eyes towards the left window. He'd pushed enough buttons to send the grapples lower. The crane was racing over a stack of cargo containers, colour-coded ivory, the letters 'OOCC' painted on their sides. The things were piled two high in most places, sometimes three. Dangling grapples clawed at those, the topmost containers.

'Come on, Taft. I'm getting nervous.'

Me too. But he had an idea, something to buy a few seconds . . . Fifteen yards . . .

Jack paused for a second, timing himself to the conjunction of enormous lift hooks with enormous containers, and simultaneously tapped the F6 and F7 keys – 'LCKL' and 'LCKR' on the computer menu – lock the left and right grapples. Four pincers, each the size of a bulldozer's shovel, snapped shut. Two, as Jack had hoped, seized the top of an OOCC container. Two did not. Jack cursed as he'd never cursed before.

The container was of standard size, twenty feet long, one of many trans-shipments originating in Thailand, destined for Yokohama. Nissan, Toyota, and Mitsubishi had moved an astonishingly large portion of their light truck production to Thailand. Labour was cheaper, taxes were low, and the country itself had emerged as the world's largest market for pick-ups. For this reason, the OOCC container that Jack had partially, but not entirely, taken hold of was full of truck parts. It weighed just shy of fifteen tons.

The container, meant to be moved level, steady, slowly, and most definitely by four rather than only two corners, groaned as it swung off its stack, wobbling shakily in the air. Seven storeys above the ground, up on the bridge crane's gantry, a lift engine not designed to swing off-balance fifteen-ton objects began to smoke. Steel shank mountings groaned as they rent out of plumb, shredded scrap ripping from their footings. A control cable shorted out, lighting the fog with electric fire. A half-ton Mitsubishi motor tore lose, launching into a fiery plummet.

As Jack had hoped, the crane's forward momentum slowed. As he did not hope, the crane began to rock violently on its tracks . . .

　　. . . eleven yards . . .

　　. . . as he smashed the 'reverse' key down.

The container, hanging at an angle not intended by the crane's designers, shrieked loose of its grappling claws, rotating slowly in its fall, coming down from a three-storey height hard and sharp on one of its corners. Jack, utterly petrified, watched fifteen tons of gyrating metal pirouette a crater into asphalt, groan sickeningly towards the crane leg upon which an equally petrified Chan Gin stood, and then tumble backwards with a hellish grinding, shattered paving exploding all around, the men in its path not even having time to scream.

Shuddering like a commuter plane in a bad storm, the bridge crane bucked a wheel off its rail. The monstrous momentum of an oscillating container and sudden high-speed reversal of its engine had wounded it, unbalanced its centre of gravity, sent it rocking uncontrollably towards . . .

　　. . . seven yards . . .

A flaming motor crashed in the crane's wake, hot oil a small inferno spreading on the ground, burning droplets igniting the shirts and hair of men, once stalking killers, now screaming victims.

Jack looked towards Chan. The laughing madman was standing splay-legged on the crane's wheel carriage, grinning like the very devil. He had two black balls in his hand, brought them to his mouth one by one, spat the pins out, tossed the grenades in high slow arcs towards where the survivors of Poh's small army milled in confusion. 'Crowd control!' he howled as the crane reached the end of its tracks, reduced a small wooden barrier to dust, and juddered on to the centre of the southernmost and last pier in the Port of Singapore.

The *Jade Lady*'s steersman, who in his heart regretted his complicity in Poh Kay Siong's many crimes, thought it a sight of terrible beauty. Who could have believed that an object so enormous – a tower of weighty steel – might actually leap into the air? To the steersman's eyes, the machine seemed alive, a dancing cat on hindpaws, waving its claws in the air. A pursuit of butterflies, perhaps. Why, it even growled like a cat, albeit one much larger than his wife's, a frightful majesty of appetite. Great blocks of concrete gouged out of the very fabric of the wharf bounced about the behemoth fluttering feet. So colossal was the crane, they seemed the merest pebbles. The tower brushed fog aside, parting curtains of ephemeral cloth, smoky silk draperies, opening to reveal a stage upon which apocalypse was performed. Fire flowers, two bright explosions, bloomed one behind the other. For petals they wore the silhouettes of burning men, lifted into the sky, flying acrobats in a circus of flame. Another daredevil dived and tumbled, and he wore the face of *Chenghuang* the devil, whose icon the steersman knew, and thus understood that life's requital was imminent, restitution and atonement for deeds he should have repented sooner. The drunken crane, tottering but keeping upright as a tipsy man will do, staggered onward with twitching steps, one leg up, then the other, reeling with a wonderfully careless gait, unalloyed carnage everywhere, the limping foot searching for stable ground, not finding what it sought but instead tripping slowly off the brink of a shattered quay, faintly perplexed to find air not ground beneath its step, leaning forward with muddled intoxication, and tilting, tilting, tilting woozily forward, all the mass and weight of the thing embraced by gravity and pulled by a magnetic attraction quite irresistibly towards the *Jade Lady*'s bridge.

Where it crushed her down. Where shivered wood and metal and fibreglass came to splinters. Where the steersman died in black water, and in awe.

– 2 –

Chan stood at the water's edge, shaking his head, forcing himself down, regulating his breath, concentrating on his heartbeat. You had to do that after a killing fight. It was a junkie's rush, pure euphoria, and it kicked like a mule. Didn't last, though. And detox was a bitch. Even Chan, who knew how to control the after-effects, felt a tremble in his fingers and a weakness in his knees. The agony of fractured ribs – fled before an adrenaline wave – was creeping back. Chan bit his lip against the pain.

He heard limping footsteps behind him, Taft's voice mumbling with amazement, 'Shit, fuck, shit.' Chan felt a small glow of approbation. He'd not heard Taft swear in a manly way before this night, and was pleased to know the American had it in him. Still facing the water, speaking quietly in a reverent tone, he said, 'You know, Taft, I've done some damage in my time. Major stuff. But nothing, man, nothing like this. I've got to confess I *am* impressed.' He smiled and felt good about it. Taft wasn't so bad after all. The guy had handled himself like a man. Feeling a slightly grudging respect for the no-good bastard, Chan began to wonder how to explain things to him. *Okay, Taft, I've got a small favour to ask.* No, that wasn't right. Begging struck the wrong note. *Listen, Taft, I can still bust you on so many charges* . . . Yeah, intimidation was *always* the way to handle it. *But if you'll play ball with me, we can clear this mess up.* Dismissing the fact that thus far intimidation seemed to roll off the lousy prick's back, he began to work out the details of his proposition.

As he plotted his script, Taft reached the ruined edge of the pier, stared blankly at floating fragments of his handiwork, and, after a few moments of silence, whispered in a curiously prayerful tone of voice, 'Hey, Chan, you got a spare gun?'

Chan turned. Taft was, he allowed, a real mess. The American's face was blackened, his shirt was in shreds, and his right pants leg was ripped from hip to cuff. He had a long nasty abrasion down his thigh, and a bleeding cut on his cheek. Chan bet he'd be coming down from his high soon, and, being a civilian, probably would collapse green puking sick with regret. Sympathy demanded Chan humour him. 'Sure. Always have, always will.'

'Can I borrow it for a second?'

Chan shrugged. The sonofabitch looked like he was in a weird state. But then what the hell, he himself was feeling pretty hyper too. 'Don't see why not.' The Sidewinder was gone, lost somewhere when he jumped off the crane. He still had his Beretta Tomcat in his pocket. He handed it to Taft. 'What do you want it for, anyway?'

Taft's lips curled. His pupils were red pinpricks, and the lustre of madness glowed within. Chan wished he'd noticed those eyes, thought about their lunatic glitter, realized that Taft was still drunk with the frenzy of what had gone before. 'To kill you with, you prick.' And the gun was pointed directly at the bridge of Chan's nose.

In a much louder voice Poh Kay Siong ordered, 'Drop the pistol, Mr Taft.'

Chan let his eyes slide away from Taft's face. Poh was standing up the wharf, a half-dozen metres away. It appeared that he'd found the Sidewinder. Bad news, Chan was pretty sure there were still two rounds in it: .45 calibre, not shellshot.

Taft's hand shook. He was crazed with the delirium of battle, lunacy rippling across his face. The damned fool was going to try to spin around and outgun Poh. 'Do it, Taft. He's aiming straight at your head, and he's too close to miss.' The whites of Taft's eyes showed. He was gone, far gone. Chan had seen it before, and knew to fear it. 'You'll be dead, Taft. Do what he says.' Taft wasn't listening; he'd gone to that place where you hear nothing but the voices inside you. The muscles around his neck tightened, and Chan knew the stupid fool was going to try something. And Poh's muscles were tightening too.

Chan spat. The gob of saliva splashed on Taft's right cheek. Taft jerked. For a moment, Chan feared he'd empty the gun into his face. 'What . . .?' Taft whispered, his words coming from a long way away. 'Drop the damned gun, asshole, drop it now!' A barely audible 'Oh' and the Beretta clanked to the ground at Chan's feet.

Taft, face blank, turned. Poh eased off, but only slightly. Chan took a deep breath. 'Poh,' he said in as agreeable a voice as he could muster, 'half the cops in Singapore are going to be here any minute. The only thing you get if you pull that trigger is no mercy from the judge.'

Poh shook his head. Like Chan's, his voice was calm and polite, a man holding a friendly discussion with his neighbour. He might have been enquiring after the weather, or casually chatting about the progress of his rose garden. 'Not so, Superintendent. I gain one other thing. You of all people should know it is a prize beyond price.'

'What?' Chan shot a glance at Taft. The American was a statue, frozen stone.

'A dish tasted too often by you, too infrequently by me: revenge.'

'It's not worth it, Poh.' Taft was shivering. Chan could almost hear his knees knock. What he'd done this night had hit him, and he didn't like the taste of it. *How does it feel to be a killer, Taft? Especially when you know you're good at it.*

'Perhaps. But all else is gone, Superintendent. Vengeance is all that is left to me.'

Chan shrugged in answer. Taft found his voice. He whispered hoarsely, 'Jesus, do something!'

Chan hissed back, 'There's nothing to worry about. I'm wearing a bulletproof vest.'

Taft squeaked, 'What about me?'

'You're screwed,' Chan answered, no longer liking Taft, not liking him at all. 'Hey, Poh,' Chan continued, 'before you pull the trigger, you mind telling me why you've been trying to grease this schmuck?'

Poh, no more familiar with Chan's Americanized slang than Hal Leung, responded with a puzzled look. Chan politely gestured at Jack. 'I mean kill fuckhead here.'

'Drugs, of course. As I said last night.'

'Bullshit. The stuff in Taft's briefcase was street dope. Worthless.'

Taft muttered, 'That figures.' In his mind another piece of the puzzle clicked into place.

Poh sighed with genuine regret, 'Ah, how slovenly. But then she is such a careless woman, isn't she?'

Jack blinked. 'She?' It was the last puzzle piece. 'You mean Denise Donald, don't you?'

'Quite correct, Mr Taft. I compliment you on your quickness of mind. You are as dangerously clever as Miss Donald warned. Perhaps more so, now that I reflect upon it.' Poh steadied his sights on Jack, thinking him the greater threat, and thus the one to be dispatched first.

'What have you two been up to?' asked Jack.

'A commercial affair. Nothing but business.'

'Electronics on the export restriction list? Smuggled in routine shipments to a legitimate customer? Then intercepted and re-routed to the Chinese or the Iraqis or whoever?'

Poh nodded. 'There are always buyers willing to pay premium prices to those who can supply what they desire.'

'Big bucks?'

'Money is not important. Friendship is. It had been my hope that powerful foreign friends might be my legacy to my heirs. Instead, I leave only ashes. I blame you for this.' Poh thumbed back the Sidewinder's hammer. 'Miss Donald is a foolish woman. Had she, distrusting my capabilities, not placed drugs in your briefcase and summoned the superintendent, my workers would have dispatched you in your hotel room. Then none of us would have been brought to this unpleasant pass. Do you know, I almost wish I had her beneath my gun rather than you.'

'She didn't do it.'

As Poh, taken aback, snapped: 'Then who did?' frozen lightning exploded behind him. Chan shouted, 'He did it himself!' Poh, outlined in incandescence, began to turn. Jack shrieked, 'What did you say?' Poh spun back to face his two perfectly illuminated targets. Chan laughed. 'He's been with me all the time. It was a set-up, Poh. You fell for it.'

'You lying . . .'

'Shut up, Taft!'

A pistol shot rang out, not the cannon boom of Chan's Side-winder, but the flat crack of a long-barrelled revolver. Poh turned again, this time fully, and saw the Samsudin woman, a black silhouette framed by arc lights, ten paces before a television camera crew, thirty paces from where he stood, and she shot again. Chan grunted as a misaimed round ricocheted from concrete and punched into his right calf. Hurt like hell. Clipped the bone. His knee buckled. Taft was already on the ground. A third shot whistled wild into the fog. Poh, genteel mask fallen, raged, 'Women!' and Taft was back up with the Beretta in his fist.

'Give me that, Taft!'

'Get bent!'

'Live from the Port of Singapore. This is TCS Channel Five, Alexandria Wu reporting. Behind me, crimelord Poh Kay Siong . . .'

Poh pointed his gun at Zaitun, remembered the contents of his weapon's chambers, two bullets and two bullets only, and whirled, searching for Jack and Chan.

'You've been had, Poh! You fell right into a trap . . .' Chan wanted to add 'asshole' just to make Poh angrier. However, he was on camera now, and had to watch his mouth. '. . . you ignoramus . . .' a good word, and literate too '. . . just like Taft and I planned.'

Taft howled some curse, but it was unintelligible. He was low, running crouched, both arms out, pistol in a two-hand grip, dashing straight into the muzzle of Poh's weapon. It was the bravest thing Chan had ever seen, and he hated Taft more than ever. Why didn't the idiot shoot, goddamn it, shoot? And it came to Chan that he was trying, but didn't know where the safety was, and was mere feet away from the Sidewinder's mouth. Poh fired, a belch of flame high into the night, he tumbling and turning because the Samsudin woman had managed at last to hit her mark, and Chan was more in love with her than he had ever been with any woman. Poh slumped to one knee, pushed himself erect, and staggered forward, and Taft, that moron, still hadn't figured out where the goddamned safety was. Oh yes he had, and Poh reeled, the last bullet from his weapon exploding into the ground, fragments flung wide enough to burn Chan's cheeks.

'Who?' whispered Poh, doubled over in gut-shot agony. 'Chan lies. You did not do it. Tell me who.'

'Quiet, Taft!'

The camera crew was dashing forward. Live footage beamed to satellite. Everyone in the world would see it. Poh sank to hands and knees, crawled forward, collapsed.

'Who?'

'Taft, keep your mouth shut.'

His mind on final things, and not really caring, but merely curious here at the last, Poh asked again, 'Who?' And in a voice Chan prayed was too low to be picked up by the approaching microphones, Taft answered, 'Nobody you know. Just a guy who's been screwing my girlfriend.'

'This is poetry. You would not be alive had not two people wanted you killed.'

'Three,' Jack whispered to the dead man, thinking of Chan and how to settle things with him. But Chan was already there, holding his bleeding leg with one hand, and with the other pressing a knife point into Jack's back. 'Here come the reporters,' he hissed, 'and you're not going to say a single goddamned word except that you're going to agree with everything I say. Got it?' Jack, now drained and uncaring, shrugged. 'Sure, why not?' Then he fell to his knees, vomiting, but it did not matter because the cameras were already focused tight close-up on Chan's face, and he, one arm on his fellow hero's shoulder, began to lie as fluently as he had ever done.

As he spoke, it came to Chan that this night he'd been as near to witnessing childbirth as he ever would. For this puke-stained American shuddering at his feet was, in no small sense of the word, newborn, and no longer the man he once had been. Would that man be a better man or a worse one? Chan did not care. All he cared about was keeping the useless bastard quiet long enough to get him on an airplane, get him far away from Singapore, send him home, and never, ever, have to see the pain-in-the-ass sonofabitch again.

Seven: Thing to Love

Four Months Later

> Don't plume yourself he fights for you;
> It is not courage, love, or hate,
> But let us do the things we do;
> It's pride that makes the heart be great.
> Robert Graves – *To Lucasta on Going*
> *to the War – for the Fourth Time*

SOCRATES: See too, I said, the forgiving spirit of democracy, and the 'don't care' about trifles . . . These and other kindred characteristics are proper to democracy, which is a charming form of government, full of variety and disorder, and dispensing a sort of equality to equals and unequals alike.

Plato – *The Republic VIII*

Olivia Thatcher dabbed her eyes with a handkerchief. Weddings made her cry. She believed herself to be a big softie at heart, and, in a certain sense, she was.

The bride was glowing, glorious in white, white roses in her arms. The groom was a model of masculinity in his tuxedo. Olivia particularly approved of the fact that he looked much less hunted than most men did at such ceremonies. Best of all, the church was a proper church, and the minister a proper man of God, and all the solemnities had been respected. It was, Olivia thought, much the most perfect wedding she'd ever attended.

But for a slight impropriety on Jack Taft's part.

He had kissed the bride more ardently than he should have. Longer too. Olivia could tell that it made Chan Gin angry. She saw his fingers twitch, as if he wanted to put them around Jack's neck. And, now that Olivia thought on it, Gabrielle had been glowering too.

Jack had just smirked. Really, he'd become a different man. He had even gone to the rather preposterous extreme of insisting that people call him 'John'. Well, Olivia would *see* about that.

Although, oddly, the new name seemed to fit. He was thinner now, one might almost call him lean. He cut a dashing figure, best man in a best man's tux, ribbon and medal of civic merit – the twin of the one worn by Chan – across his chest.

Olivia hoped her pictures would turn out well. The day before, the day upon which Senior Minister Lee Kuan Yew had awarded both Jack and Chan their honours, she'd snapped and snapped and snapped. Then later, after the speeches outside Singapore's seat of government, she'd tried to get the two to pose together shaking hands. But for some reason or another both had hurried off in opposite directions.

Well, she'd have other opportunities to photograph the two handsome lads together. After Chan and his lovely wife returned from their honeymoon, the recently retired superintendent would be coming to New York as his country's cultural attaché to the United Nations. It was an odd position for a former policeman, but, she'd been told, the government had pressed the appointment on Chan Gin in the *most* insistent way.

Olivia peered through the crowd at the wedding reception. She caught Chan's eye, nodded at him. He smiled back. Zaitun unlinked her arm from Chan's and waved her fingers.

They would, she thought, do well in New York. With looks like theirs, how could they not? She jotted a mental note: a small dinner party at the Thatcher's Sutton Place *pied à terre*, carefully selected guests, an early introduction for Mr and Mrs Chan to the *right* social circles. It was the least she could do for two such lovely children.

She looked around for Jack – well, John – and Gabrielle. The best man should be at the groom's shoulder. Or so Olivia had always been taught. But no, there was Jack and there was Gabrielle, and the both of them were at the very opposite end of the room from the newlyweds. My, didn't they make a pair: him a proud possessive lion, she his dutiful lioness.

Olivia weighed Jack. He was a changed man, no question, and all for the better. He had more starch in him for one thing, was proving himself an uncommonly strong executive at LBTech – and that suggested possibilities. What with the scandal and Joel's resignation, the company was operating under a black cloud, and without a CEO. It could do worse than promote someone of Jack's talents.

Joel, she thought, *how deserved his comeuppance had been.* And how swift. No sooner did the news of his affair with Denise break, than his wife had filed for a ten-figure divorce settlement. Shortly after *EPS* ran Gabrielle's exposé, LBTech's shareholders had come after him with a class action suit of their own. The man would be in court for the rest of his life – which was both less and more than could be said of Simon Burton.

What a spectacle *that* had been! Olivia thought she would never get over the sight of Jack, bruised, scabbed, rumpled, and straight off his airplane, storming into Gabrielle's apartment, growling in a voice she'd not known he possessed: 'Just one thing, Gabrielle, just one. Did that jerk Burton know I was going to Singapore?' And Gabrielle had grasped it all at once, and blurted something unladylike. Then Jack was gone. She and Gabrielle had raced after him. But he'd caught a cab, and was well away. Of course, they knew where he was going. However, they did not know how . . . well . . . *extreme* Jack was going to be: glass shattered all around the front door of Simon's brownstone; Simon's apartment door kicked off its hinges; Jack pushing the badly bloodied Australian out of the window. Persuading him to stop had been quite a chore.

Nor was Simon especially grateful for the gesture. But then what did one expect from a man like that – a man who conceived the most appalling hatred for his former girlfriend's beau, trying to frame him for a capital crime in the deluded belief (as *all* men are deluded in *one* way or another) that if Jack was out of the way, Gabrielle would return to his arms?

Poor Gabrielle, Olivia thought. She was *simply* furious with herself for not seeing that Simon was behind the whole wretched business. She cursed herself for overlooking the fact that Simon, who should not have known Jack's travel plans, had asked her out on a date because her 'glorified shipping clerk' had gone to Singapore. Add to that the fact that he'd casually admitted knowing she'd given Jack a briefcase and Gabrielle should have realized at once that he'd pawed through her office, finding both the briefcase and her note wishing Jack a good trip to Singapore and points east.

However, not until Jack burst into her apartment and barked his question did the pieces fall into place – although it was only later when Jack spelled out his logic, impeccable as ever, that the whole dismal scheme became clear. First premise: a crimelord of Poh Kay Siong's importance would not send men to kill him at Raffles without a money motive. Second premise: the only money Jack was involved with belonged to LBTech. Conclusion: the only person at LBTech in a position to represent meaningful money to Poh was the company's director of Asian distribution, a woman who hated Jack to begin with, and who, therefore, had to be behind Poh's attack.

Third premise: if Denise had indeed sent Poh to kill him, then she would not have wasted her time planting drugs in his briefcase; with Poh as an ally, there was no need. Fourth premise: she'd never had a chance to touch his bag. Conclusion: no one at LBTech had the opportunity to frame him.

Fifth premise: the only *method* by which the drugs could have got into the briefcase was before Gabrielle had given it to him. Sixth premise: only someone with access to Gabrielle's office had the *opportunity* to tamper with the bag. Conclusion: somebody at *EPS Magazine* had a *motive* to want Jack Taft out of the way.

Now who could that be? And why?

The why of it was something Jack never articulated – although, unless Olivia missed her bet, he had discussed it privately with a much abashed Gabrielle. And at length. Given Gabrielle's subsequent hangdog behaviour, Olivia suspected the truth of the matter was that she'd had some, well, shall we say, involvement with Simon rather more recently than she'd admitted. And that, Olivia did not doubt, had been Simon's motive for wanting to eliminate Jack.

Not that any of them could do much about Simon's guilt. A cover up of some scale was under way. Gentlemen from the State Department, Yale graduates each and every one, had materialized with considerable speed, and forbidden Olivia, Gabrielle, Jack, and Simon himself to breathe a word about what had *really* happened. They'd used the conventional phrases: 'the national interest', 'authorized at the highest level', 'our best friend in Southeast Asia', and similar balderdash. And one other phrase, spoken once Simon had been spirited off to the hospital. That phrase, in which Jack seemed to take uncommon delight, was: 'Leave Mr Burton to us.'

It was unclear what they had in mind until Simon, quite hastily, decided to return home to Australia. A *most* unfortunate decision as it turned out. His plane developed engine troubles over the Pacific, and was diverted to Singapore, where a young man by the name of Sergeant Harold Leung discovered that Simon, foolish Simon, had secreted a bottle of one hundred and fifty ecstasy pills in his luggage. The newspapers said he'd be eligible for parole in fifteen years . . .

Olivia permitted herself a private smile. *All's well that end's well*, she thought, lifting a champagne flute to her lips and whispering a small blessing on the heads of those recently wed and those whom she hoped soon would be.

After chatting briefly with the State Department handlers who'd insisted on chaperoning Jack to Singapore, she left the room, searching for her missing husband. He would, she expected, be somewhere outside, stalking through Raffles Hotel's beautiful gardens, furiously puffing a cigar and raining imprecations on each and every member of the Singapore Government for banning indoor smoking.

As always, he would need the consolation of a loving wife.

Gabrielle hissed through clenched teeth, 'You didn't have to kiss her like that.'

'I was just doing it to annoy Chan,' lied Taft. Lately lying was coming easier to him.

'Well, it annoyed me too.'

Good. He thought the word but did not speak it. Instead, he mentally ticked off yet another harmless falsehood believed. Getting away with them was downright addictive. He'd have to do something about that. 'Okay, sorry. But don't expect me to apologize to the sonofabitch.'

'Oh, John! You and he should make up. Be friends. Put all the things you told me about him behind you. Besides, he's not a policeman any more. He can't hurt you.'

'Yeah? Well, did you see what his buddies on the force gave him as a combo wedding present and retirement gift?'

'No.'

'Lifetime memberships in the National Rifle Association. His and hers.'

Gabrielle snorted. Champagne bubbles whisked up her nose, tickled, brought tiny tears to her eyes.

Taft asked, 'You OK?'

'Fine.'

'Looks like you're crying. Do weddings make you emotional?'

'No. Yes. Sometimes.'

Taft clasped his hands behind his back, rocked slightly forward on his toes. 'Well, on the subject of weddings, Gabrielle, there's something I've been planning to ask you.'

Gabrielle smiled. 'John, you're not going to try to propose marriage to me, are you?'

He didn't miss a beat. 'Of course not.'

'*What!*' Gabrielle spat. 'What the hell do you mean, you're not?'

John Taft dodged left, barely avoiding the splash of champagne she flung at his face. *Whoops*, he thought, *wrong answer*.

ACKNOWLEDGEMENTS

SOCRATES: Then the first thing will be to establish a censorship of the writers of fiction.

Plato – *The Republic II*

I owe much to the Government of Singapore for its exceptionally courteous cooperation while I researched this book. Special thanks is due to the Singapore Tourist Board, Parks Department, Housing Development Board, Police Force, and Port Authority for their assistance. Likewise the staff of Raffles Hotel and the American Embassy as well as several journalists, local businesspeople, and friends went out of their way to be helpful.

And went out of their way to ask that I not name them.

When they spoke to me of their nation's shortcomings and political oddities, to a man and to a woman, they dropped their voices, looked warily for eavesdroppers, and begged that I not mention their identities. Apparently Singapore's ruling powers do not take criticism kindly, no matter how well intentioned such criticism may be.

However, it is not my part to complain. Even less is it my part to try to urge Westernized values on an Eastern land. We Americans have tried our hand at that before, and the results were not pretty to look at.

**SIMON &
SCHUSTER**

FOUNTAIN SOCIETY

Wes Craven

From blockbuster director and screenwriter famous for
SCREAM, SCREAM 2, and NIGHTMARE ON ELM
STREET, comes the first cloning thriller, combining
cutting-edge medical technology and a terrifying
government conspiracy.

A top-secret government operation is launched to
confer immortality on a select, elite group of
government scientists - a sinister plot of such cold
brutality and evil that it has to be kept secret from
everybody, even those who may one
day benefit from it.

Wes Craven's FOUNTAIN SOCIETY is a book that
chills, thrills and satisfies like his own movies,
building to a climax of unspeakable tension and shock.

PRICE £16.99

ISBN 0 684 84660 8

**SIMON &
SCHUSTER**

THE SIMPLE TRUTH

David Baldacci

A heart-stopping story of an evil conspiracy at the core
of the American legal system . . .

As a young soldier, Rufus Harms was jailed for the
brutal killing of a schoolgirl. Yet, after twenty-five
hard years of incarceration, a letter from the US Army
reveals new facts about the night of the murder – and
the evil secret shared by some of Washington's most
powerful men. Rufus turns to the only man who can
help ex-cop turned criminal attorney, John Fiske.

But for both men time is already running out. Their
enemy is buried deep within the system and is
completely ruthless in protecting the truth …

PRICE £16.99

ISBN 0 684 85830 4

POCKET
B O O K S

GOLDFINDER

Keith Jessop

The incredible true story of one man's discovery of the ocean's richest secrets.

'Outstanding, inspiring, and beautifully told, no true tale of the sea makes better reading' CLIVE CUSSLER

Keith Jessop is the most successful treasure hunter and salvage diver in history, a man who has made - and lost - millions rescuing treasures from the deep. The son of a penniless Yorkshire mill-girl, he left school without a single qualification and started salvaging scrap metal from shallow water wrecks off the coast of Scotland using the inner tube of a tractor tyre covered in wire mesh as a vessel. GOLDFINDER is the story of Keith's progress from aquatic Steptoe and Son to salvaging the richest prize of all - over five tons of Russian gold - from the bottom of the Arctic Ocean.

Price   £6.99

ISBN 0 671 01048 4

POCKET
B O O K S

CHINOOK!

The Special Forces on War and Peace

David McMullon
with Robin Eggar

'The most exciting book about Special Forces
helicopter flying I've ever read'
John Nichol

'Flying in a Chinook is like wrestling with a force of
nature. You have to treat it with constant respect. Or
one day it will catch you unawares and tear you apart.
It has never suffered fools gladly'

David McMullon served for eight years with the
Special Forces Flight Chinook squadron, the helicopter
equivalent of the SAS. This is the true story of his elite
flying career.

Price £6.99

ISBN 0 671 01599 0

**SIMON &
SCHUSTER**

This book and other **Simon & Schuster** titles are available from your book shop or can be ordered direct from the publisher.

Please send cheque or postal order for the value of the book, and add the following for postage and packing: UK inc. BFPO 75p per book; OVERSEAS Inc. EIRE £1 per book.
OR: Please debit this amount from my:

VISA/ACCESS/MASTERCARD ....

CARD NO ....

EXPIRY DATE ....

AMOUNT £ ....

NAME ....

ADDRESS ....

....

SIGNATURE ....

Send orders to:
Simon & Schuster Cash Sales,
PO Box 29, Douglas, Isle of Man, IM99 1BQ
Tel: 01624 675137, Fax 01624 670923
http://www.bookpost.co.uk or
e-mail: bookshop@enterprise.net for details
Please allow 28 days for delivery.
Prices and availability subject to change without notice.